LOW COUNTRY

LAMENTATIONS

By Frank Malmsteen

Featuring excerpts from Lowcountry Lamentations,
by Erica Edwards

An Entertainment

Also by Frank Malmsteen

Recondite Oblivion

LOW COUNTRY
LAMENTATIONS

Featuring excerpts from Lowcountry Lamentations,
by Erica Edwards

An Entertainment

**BROAD
RIVER
BOOKS**

LOW COUNTRY LAMENTATIONS

Copyright ©2023 by Frank Malmsteen

All rights reserved.

Published by Broad River Books, an imprint of Muddy Ford Press, LLC, Chapin, SC

Library of Congress Control Number: 2023935285

ISBN: 978-1-942081-35-7

Cover art by Franco Accornero

Author photo by Christian Guerrero

**BROAD
RIVER
BOOKS**

Acknowledgments

Borges stated in an interview that in the end all poems become elegies; this is no less true for any art form. I raise this because when I began working on this project Anne Rivers Siddons, Pat Conroy, Dorothea Benton Frank, and Virginia Mixson Geraty were all alive, but here today, in April of 2022, all of them have gone on to their reward.

The main character of this book (Erica, who becomes Savannah) quotes generously from these writers. If you read a section that you like in the ensuing pages, particularly if the words come from her mouth, then you can rest assured that it was not written by me, but by one of these fine authors.

I would like to thank Katherine Macedon, who performed every kind of editing that one can perform on this novel. She was an instrumental force in honing the prose into something readable and enjoyable.

I would like to thank my dear friend Dave Johnson for his encouragement, insight, and relentless sense of humor.

Finally, I would like to thank Cindi Boiter, my editor and publisher. She is a tireless promoter of others and a selfless supporter of all. Even though she does not have to, she takes her light and shines it outward, and the world is a brighter place because of it.

To DoraAnn

SOMETIME AROUND THE END OF
THE TWENTIETH CENTURY

ONE

In a certain city in South Carolina, whose name I do not wish to mention, there lived a young lady named Erica Edwards who read so many Southern novels that something inside her brain popped loose. It happened one day while she sat in her bedroom reading *Low Country* by Anne Rivers Siddons, beach music playing lightly in the background, a faint voice tempting her with the pleasures that one can only find underneath boardwalks amongst dead cigarettes and ancient dirt. There was no audible report given, and one could not tell that the change had occurred simply by looking at her, but the string that holds sanity, located just south of the cerebellum, had unquestionably been severed.

The results were disastrous. Once an upstanding young woman from a well-respected family, she now lived under the delusion that the world set forth by her Southern authors was her world, and she an active participant in the drama.

The first symptom was that she began to hate her father. The second one was that she began to have strong sexual feelings toward her mother. Other signs of the malady began to appear—and the reader will soon see them in effect—until she was Erica Edwards no more, but Savannah D'Bergeolet.

To begin where we need to begin, Savannah found herself sitting at the law school library at the University of South Carolina, just as Pig, Mark, and Will had done in Pat Conroy's *The Lords of Disci-*

pline. She had somehow come to believe that a super-secret group of madmen called the Ten had decided to drive a black man out of the Citadel, a military college located in Charleston, South Carolina. She saw this university as an evil force of Southern white male oppression, although blacks and women had joined the ranks some time ago, causing the Southern white male oppression to lower in direct proportion to the amount of melanin and estrogen in the barracks. But all of that is neither here nor there, the main thing being that she thought this, and given that, one can hardly blame her for plotting to capture a former member of the Ten and force him to reveal the identity of its current roster. She eyed her prey as he pored over his law books, wondering how a man could walk the earth with such little care when the deeds that curled in his wake would damn even a Christian to hell.

The only problem was that the man had not graduated from the Citadel. In fact, the only place that he could claim to have graduated from was his middle school, although that would be untrue as well because it did not have formal graduation ceremonies. His only connections to the formerly all-male military college were that his shoes bore the school colors and he currently resided in the same state as his non-alma mater. But to Savannah, these facts were not so. The rotting Band-Aid that covered a wound on his finger from a dog bite seemed to her a large golden ring imprinted with the school insignia, his long, unwashed hair appeared fashioned in military style, and his clothes, dirty and wrinkled, starched to Citadel perfection. She imagined that he had married a woman who had once participated in the Miss South Carolina pageant and now kept house, but as said, none of her imaginings were even remotely correct. The truth to this part was that he had not suffered physical affection in over five years and had no house for anyone to keep, only a poorly maintained apartment. As to the examination she imagined him studying for, there was none, because he was not a law student. His reason for being there was to work up a groundless complaint against the city police for kicking him off of a park bench during the summer solstice. In sum, she was, to put it mildly, way off base.

2

The plan was this: she would somehow get him in the trunk of her car, tie him up, then take him to some train tracks located in or near the Congaree Swamp. There were train tracks that the trains actually used, and there were train tracks that they no longer did. Savannah would tie him to the non-used variety—although he would not know this—and extract a confession from him as he felt his fate come a'rolling. The major obstacle would be getting him in her trunk, and once she got him in her trunk, tying him up. The book had simply cut from spying on the guy at the law school to him lying in the trunk, so it could be said that it was lacking in this respect, although not by Savannah, who would consider such a statement akin to blasphemy. Given that Pig, Mark, and Will were physical men—boys, really, they were in the process of becoming men—Savannah reckoned that they had roughed him up somehow, probably with a blow to the head. She therefore readied herself for such a blow.

The readying did not have to be hurried. The gentleman spent hours looking over English common law in his search for his legal silver bullet. The replevins and liveries of seisin caused him great anger and frustration, and he took these feelings out on the miserable souls working behind the circulation desk, Savannah interpreting their looks of disgust as stemming from his Charlestonian snobbery, and not his lunacy and dire need of a bath. She could not imagine the three roommates sitting so long in static boredom, as everything seemed to happen so quickly in the books, but she accepted it as a Southern woman must accept such things and waited patiently, until they finally began clearing the place out and telling everyone to go home.

She watched him grab his three plastic supermarket bags, which she deemed expensive leather satchels, and proceed out of the library and into the main reception area. She was on his heels, working her fingers into a fist, thinking of the blow that she would have to land, thinking that, like in the books, it would have to be a hearty one that would render him unconscious.

As luck would have it, the man exited the law school through the doors located nearest to the parking lot, where her car awaited. It was dark outside, and the only sounds were their footsteps and the rustling plastic. Savannah studied him as he trudged along, not noticing his limp or the deep cough that he exchanged with the night.

When he set foot in the parking lot, she took several quick steps forward and gave him a sharp blow to the base of his skull. In response, he stood still for a moment, and in response to this, she struck him again. The man had often claimed that he had a steel plate in his head, for a period due to the Vietnam War, then on account of Operation Desert Storm, neither of which he had participated in, but the truth of the matter was that he was blessed with a skull thick on the outside and a brain thin on the inside. The sniffing of gasoline and spray paint fumes had damaged whatever was left from the fetal alcohol syndrome of his birth. He therefore registered that something had happened, that pressure had been applied to his skin and bones, but the normal effect of a concussive blow—that of the brain colliding with the skull and thus temporarily rendering it useless— did not occur, for the brain, so shrunken in size, had plenty of room to stretch out and relax, and no amount of shaking could ever cause it to reach one wall or the other.

The poor results deeply disappointed Savannah, and she quickly realized that the only way that the man was going to get into the trunk of her car would be by accepting an invitation, which she did not deem likely. Still, she continued to strike him, hitting his ears and throat as he turned around to face her, shouting at the top of her lungs, "Who are the Ten?!" to the rhythm of her fists. For, you see, a black man—a boy, really, he was in the process of becoming a man—was going to be tortured and maimed in order to keep the Citadel, which, as said, had integrated many years ago, racially pure. All of this rested on her shoulders: the evil of the generations before her, the fate of this one black promise, and although it was too much to bear, she had to, in fact, bear it.

4

When the gentleman finally realized that he was being attacked, the only thing that entered his mind was that this woman was trying to rob him of the precious cargo that he held in his bays of plastic. Who knows whether he determined her source of envy to be the digital watch that no longer worked, the collection of flashlight batteries, or the wool overcoat that he had not received in Operation Desert Storm? If it were any of these, it was sufficient grounds for him to employ brute force in his defense. As quickly as a brazen cat, he reached into one of his bags and produced a can of pepper spray, which he discharged into Savannah's tender face. The effect of the chemicals drew D'Bergeolet fists to D'Bergeolet eyes, and D'Bergeolet ass to concrete ground, where our heroine sat screaming in great pain.

The gentleman did not have much sense, but he did have enough to realize that for someone in his position, being seen standing over a crying girl in the dark of night was nothing but a recipe for jail, a dish forced upon the diner for a period of years. He therefore grabbed his bags, shouting "Livery of Seisin!" as a parting taunt, and fled, taking the mysteries of the Ten with him.

As she sat on the ground, her eyes swollen and burning, Savannah realized that her plan had gone to shambles. There would be no train tracks, and there would be no confession, but she did not leave empty-handed. The Livery of Seisin. Was it some warrior call of the Ten? The name of a European noble currently enrolled at the Citadel? Whatever it was, she would find out. The mysteries set forth at the beginning of her books were always delicately hidden, but with each chapter the riddle unraveled, until finally, at the end, everything was as clear as a summer morning in the low country. She knew that this would happen to her as well. Yes, there would be trouble in the journey, and probably the death of at least one or two beloved friends or family members, but at the conclusion there was never any stone left unturned.

It took an hour before she could see again, and when she finally arrived back home, the pain had subsided to a great degree. The ancestral manse was a handsome two-story house located in the Heathwood neighborhood, and the envy of many, but to her it was as dead as the stones used to construct it. For her, life lived in the low country—Charleston, the surrounding barrier islands—and that is what called her: life.

A cold compress assuaged her wounds and, after saying a rosary, or attempting to say a rosary on hippie beads she had bought at a pawn shop, she fell fast asleep.

TUESDAY

TWO

It had been a month since Creighton Starke had returned from his time in the wilderness. That was one of former president Nixon's favorite phrases, time in the wilderness, and although Creighton had never voted for Nixon and considered him a vile lizard of a man, he liked the phrase, too. Almost biblical sounding, this time in the wilderness. Only there had not been many trees in his wilderness or even open spaces. Like Nixon, for him it meant exile, licking the wounds caused by the knives of persecution, healing in his dark lair with plots to destroy his enemies and conquer the world. The hospital, and later the halfway house, were as far from feral as one could get, and yet he felt as though he had been backpacking in outer Mongolia, minus the suntan and gastrointestinal diseases.

They were kind to let him come back. They didn't have to, although according to the law they did, and it was a real show of support from the administration that they gave him the same office and lessened his course load to teaching one creative writing seminar. Because of this, he felt duty-bound to do a good job and put his mind behind his work. These kids would learn something this time around, and perhaps he would too, as life was about learning, whether in the wilderness or in society, which is one of the great things about it, the great things being few, the awful being many.

Speaking of which, he pushed his glasses to the tip of his nose and readied himself for something he dreaded. He held the beast in his

hands, weighing it, then opened it to the first page. There he began
to read as follows:

It was raining outside. The kind of rain that
one could only find here, banging and bashing,
spilling as though poured from a shrimp bucket,
carrying with it a wind that seemed to howl,
"Whipawee---whipawee," like the cries of the
fallen indians that had once inhabited the land.

She was scared to death. Scared to death in
the liberal sense of the phrase, with the feeling
that any moment might be her last. But this was
not simply becauuse of the storm. There was something else that was causing such fear. Something
she still to this day found unspeakable!

"You're gonna learn to like'em boy! I don't
give a d--n what you think they taste like!"

She sat in the darkness of the room that she
shared with Chicken John, trying to hold back the
tears that she shed for both him and herself. You
must not cry, she said to herself. A southerner
dos not cry.

Lightning streaked across the sky, followed
within seconds by a peal of thunder that seemed
to tear that house from its very foundations. She
jumped when she heard it!

"No, I'm not gonna let you put the g-d---n
sauce on it! And don't try and just swallow this
one like you did the last one! I wanna see you
chew it!"

It was too much for her to take. She could hear
Roy lauging with her father and she wanted to
tear his eyes out, to tear her father's eyes out,

9

to remove them both so that Chicen John would be okay. So that no one could hurt them. Where was everyone? Where was mother? Something had to be done so she picked herself up from the floor!

"Stop! Father please don't make him eat them oysters! He doesn't want to!"

He looked at her and smiled, the wicked drunken smile that she had seen so many times before.

"Shut your sass mouth and get out of here! Yahn!"

"Father, if he don't like them then he shouldn't be made to eat'em! Please leave him be!"

He let go of his arm and pushed him away so that he fell over a chair and into a table, knocking over the Pepsi Cola that Roy had been drinking. The drink spilled slowly onto the carpet, dragged down by the packets of sugar that Roy used to sweeten the drink. Roy laughed when he saw this, then returned his attention to the television set. Chicken John was crying.

"You gonna eat'em then?"

He glowered at her, the storm of anger within him as tempestuous as the one outside. She had to give him an answer. There must be an answer. But she did not want to eat them. She could not eat them. Her answer was no.

"Well if y'all ain't gonna eat them then you're gonna have to get the crab traps and get me some crabs!"

"Father we can't! Its raining outside! We'll be killed!"

"Do it!" he ordered.

There was no use in arguing. He was drunk and this drunkeness only added to the evil that grew inside of him like oysters on the pilons of a bridge. She walked over to where Chicken John lay, the sugar filled Pepsi making a stain on the carpet by his legs, and helped him up from the floor, saying,

"It'll be alright. I'm here. I'll protect you." Father y laughed.

They made their way out into the blinding rain, without a rain jacket on their backs and with only a tiny flashlight to guide their way. The land was covered in darkness and they held each other tightly in order to keep the wind from knocking them over."

"Savannah I'm scared."

"I know. I am too, but we must do what father says. We absolutely must!" she cried.

Somehow, someway, they made it down to the dock. The normal calm of the creek had been destroyed by the storm and the waves battered against the old wooden dock. They had to catch the crabs because that was what father had told them to do. How they ever would, she did not know.

As the wind knocked them to and fro, they desperately searched for the crab traps. They had to be somewhere. Chicken John was crying and so was she but the rain was falling down so hard that it was hard to tell that they were. At that moment, a bolt of lightning crashed down inches away from where they stood, sending them on their backs.

"No!!!!!" Chicken John cried. "I want to go back!"

But there was no going back. Not with Father back at the house. Finally after searching everywhere, she found a trap and she began to ready it, her brother by her side, finding refuge in her lap. And she was almost done when she realized that they needed bait. Where were the chicken necks? They had to go back and get the bait!

The slowly made their way back to the house, Chicken John still by her side crying. After a few minutes they could make out the lights of the house. There seemed to be a figure in front moving but she couldn't be sure. The crept closer, looking, searching, until they both knew who it was. It was father dancing in the rain, doing a two step while the thunder and lightning pounded the sky!

"Father! We don't have any chicken necks!"
"Where are my crabs?"
"Father we don't have any chicken necks!"
"Where are my crabs?"
"We don't have any chicken necks! Don't you see?! We can't catch any crabs unless we have chicken necks!"

Her voice trailed off as she fell to the wet ground of the lowcountry, Chicken John by her side, father still dancing and singing to the tune of a song on the radio,

"Where are my crabs? Where are my crabs?"

"Great God in Heaven," Creighton said with a sigh, throwing the manuscript on top of his desk and giving his thin lips a long suck. "Whipawee, indeed." He stood up from his chair and walked over to the only window in his office. "Yes, Creighton," he said out loud, although no one else was in the room, "this is what it has come to: not a New York penthouse or a visiting professorship at the Iowa Writers' Workshop, but this."

His view of the outside consisted of nothing but asphalt, and he thought to himself, as he had often thought to himself, how nice it would be to have a lawn there, a vaguely treeless lawn, where nineteen-year-old women would lay out half-naked and do nothing other than prematurely age their skin. But this is what it had come to. Not that.

She had approached him earlier in the day, after the first day of class, which is misleading in that it was not a day of instruction, but a mere chipping away at his teaching requirement. It had lasted no more than five minutes, just long enough for him to explain the semester's assignment to the students: two short stories that they would read aloud to the class. He told them that this would give them the opportunity to have their peers critique their work and force them to develop an ear, but in reality, it simply killed time. The moment he walked in the classroom he had cast aside his desire to actually teach. He did not fully realize this, but it was unquestionably the case.

Given the simplicity of the requirements and the dearth of any other topics discussed, he was confused as to why she wanted to speak to him.

"Mr. Starke?"

She was decent looking, not as cute as a lot of the coeds around, but for a man his age it was hard for an eighteen-year-old to look bad. In fact, the more he studied her, he began to think that underneath the shabby clothing, unkempt hair, reddened complexion, and bloodshot eyes a woman of decent conquest lay in wait.

"Yes, Miss…?"

"D'Bergeolet," she replied in a whispered shot, as though she was afraid someone else would hear it, "but please call me Savannah."

"Okay, Savannah, how can I help you?"

"I'm afraid I can't complete the assignment you've given us."

He furrowed his brow and motioned for her to come closer.

"Oh, really? Why not?"

With that, she produced from her backpack a stack of papers three quarters of an inch high. It was jacketed with a pink cover and apparently bound together by some local copy shop; the title read *Lowcountry Lamentations*. He took it and looked it over, checking its length with a thumb.

"Wow. I'm impressed. You wrote this?"

"Yes, sir. It's about my childhood in Charleston."

"Mm-hm." He placed it on the top of his desk, saying, "Well, I look forward to reading it. But tell me, why is it you can't complete the assignment? It looks like you already have the material."

"It's just too personal to read it in front of them," she said, her eyes darting back and forth. "And…and I'm afraid that word might get out and that my family would be ruined."

He glanced back down at the manuscript and scratched his beard.

"I understand," he said after giving a nod. "Well, maybe you could write something else that you could share with the class."

Her head shook in the negative. "No, I'm afraid that's impossible. Everything I write is too personal. I would prefer it if you would just read this and let that count as both my short stories and my class participation."

Two less short stories only meant two less episodes of gnawing pain. Without exception, the students could not write, and what they wrote about was as poor as their prose. Listening to countless tales of rape, murder, drug use, and football glory was enough to cause anyone to seek narcotic, if not suicidal, assistance. And if the stories weren't about those things, they were word-for-word plagiarized copies of short stories by Hawthorne or Kipling that these future purveyors of lore figured no one would have ever been insane enough to actually read. So, two less short stories. It was too good to turn down.

"Okay. I'll let you do that, but just don't let anyone else hear about our little arrangement. Deal?"

She nodded her head vehemently.

"Thank you, Mr. Starke."

"You're welcome. Now we'll see you on Thursday."

And as he sat and watched her scurry out of the room, he thought to himself that the young woman exiting was either a tortured genius or an absolute imbecile. Odds were on the latter. But an imbecile was just what he needed, a self-deluded imbecile, even better. Her receding backside appeared small but shapely in her ill-fitting dress and he tried to picture it, the sun from the Venetian blinds filtering through, touching the white squeezed between the flesh of his fingers...

He turned away from the sea of asphalt and looked over at his typewriter. It had now lay dormant for six years and each passing day of its unuse stood as a cruel reminder of the promise that he had once held as his banner. The framed clipping from *The Canton Chronicle Review of Books* sadly yellowed in the acid-rich matting, and he felt as though its adulteration mirrored the path of his soul. "Intriguing!" "Spellbinding!" "Mr. Starke takes the reader into the ordinary but leaves him captivated in the extraordinary!" "A must-read!" Yes, the book had been a masterpiece. It had taken him four years to write and two more to get published. Thus, a labor of love, with all of the romantic trappings of the stubborn genius fighting for his vision. The story itself was moving, the characters believable, the moral confusing, the language a battle wherein the author arose the victor. And then. Then. The agent. The martini lunches with his publisher. (There was actually only one lunch, during which no alcohol was served.) The book signings, meager though they were. The women at the book signings, unattractive though they were. The queries from the various English departments, pitiful though they were. The constant question as to when the next one would be coming out, painful as it was.

For the only problem was the next one. Like a baby turned sideways in the womb, it remained stuck, killing him in the process. He kept telling himself that he just needed to scratch something—anything—down and let it go at that, but he had both honor and principle. For him, a story needed to have some holy genesis, like one that came in a dream to the author as he lay in bed at night. A special present from the muse which he then took and shaped into an object even more beautiful than the gods had ever imagined.

He cursed to himself and punched the typewriter, making an fadskj on the paper that had been stuck in the machine so long that it resembled a forlorn burrito. The nonsensical letters fit in along with the rwqes, poius, xbvc,s and r1u209s that memorialized previous bouts of overwhelming frustration. How could he carve matter into a void? The white-hot eight-and-a-half-by-eleven supernova that burned up every idea that sprang into his head into a blackened crisp? At one point, roughly two weeks ago, he had even considered writing a novel about an author who was unable to write a novel, but even he could not sink that low. It would come. He knew it would. Only he feared that it wouldn't.

As he stood there, Savannah D'Bergeolet's manuscript eased into view, and with everything in his body telling him not to, he reached down, picked it up, and carried it out the door with him. It was his day to visit his son from four to six, and his former mother-in-law did not like it when he arrived late, early, or on time.

THREE

Roy Edwards preferred the day shift. Yes, nighttime contained more excitement—lonely girls, drunken couples, an occasional squabble—and yes, the daytime had its major drawbacks—boredom, dealing with sick people, dealing with old people, setting straight what had been left a mess from the night before—but he was willing to give up one and accept the other. You see, he needed his nights.

"Welcome to Blockbuster!" Sarah said when the door opened, and the bell rang. After five to ten seconds of silence, she lifted her gaze, found Roy, and tried to pin him to the Mystery rack with her disappointed stare.

Roy felt it and executed a slight pivot. "Welcome to Blockbuster," he muttered. He then turned back around and continued to pretend that he was lining up the tapes with the display boxes so that everything would be just so.

The customer wore a white shirt and suit pants, but no tie. Looked glum. Roy figured he was either sick or fired. Two movies—no, three movies—popcorn, and a two-liter bottle of Coke. Roy walked over to Foreign and pretended to line those up as well. Why even foreigners would want to watch foreign movies was a mystery to him, much less regular Americans. It was a rack that for all intents and purposes should not have existed.

Roy was not himself. Something was happening tonight, something that no other soul on the planet knew about except for his mother. Something that had been years in the making, that could very well affect the course of his remaining days. With all of that on the line, it was difficult to care about anything else, much less this job.

He watched a car drive up. The tapes slid down and clanged at the bottom of the drop-off box. A lady in her fifties, her hair in a bad perm, driving an old car, smoking a new cigarette. Were they late? The tapes? Roy did not care.

"Have you checked the drop-off box today?" Sarah asked.

Roy acted as though he had not heard her. The lady drove away.

"Roy, have you checked the drop-off box today?"

The tieless man stared at Roy, red-eyed and ashen.

"No," Roy said in a half groan.

"Will you?" Sarah asked.

"Yes," Roy said in a half groan.

He crossed the floor over to the bin. The glass wall led to an expanse of strip mall and telephone pole. *Raiders of the Lost Ark* played in unison across the store, approaching the part where the bald-headed German pummels Indiana Jones only to be pureed by the propeller.

Roy opened it and looked in. Tapes lay cold and lifeless at the dusky bottom. He gathered them together and trundled them over to the cashier's station where Sarah stood. Just last week, Sarah had been reprimanded by the manager for making personal calls on the company phone, so she was both chastened and resentful, and she gave the impression that she wanted to take it out on Roy. Roy knew Sarah from high school, and each of them was embarrassed to be working with the other, each for his and her own reasons.

"Better get those done before your mommy comes and picks you up," Sarah said.

Roy grunted at her, then began processing the tapes. A few minutes later he thought of something witty to say back to her, but at that point it was too late. Yes, even he knew that it was too late.

Einstein figured out the Theory of Relativity while working as a patent clerk. That's what his mother often reminded him. Some other people, she said, also had pretty meaningless jobs and ended up doing important stuff. His mother was nice. Pretty much everyone thought that.

The day carried on and he did what he had to do. When his mother came and picked him up, he slinked out the door with his head down, not even leaving Sarah with so much as a good-bye from Blockbuster.

FOUR

After a day of classes Savannah went home. It was unfathomable to her that they would have an unknown teach creative writing classes at the university, especially a Midwesterner, especially when the libraries were bursting with masterpieces from the South. The only way that she could make any sense of it was to reason that the university could not afford such geniuses and had to hire semi-respectable hacks willing to work for food and shelter. Still, he had promised to read her novel, and promised to keep silent about it. He at least had that in his favor. The pain would have to be revealed, there was no helping that, but first she needed to find Chicken John.

And there again it struck her: her life was melting away. Her marriage to Jonathan, to whom she was not married, was failing, as was obvious by the fact that she lived with her parents, and not him. Her children, who existed only in her mind, did not understand her sardonic wit and self-deprecating sarcasm, her defenses against her past and the horrific upbringing that she had suffered at the hands of the monsters she called mother and father. There were answers out there, and she knew where to find them: with Chicken John. Together, they would mine the past, reveal to each other stories that the other had forgotten, and make sense of childhoods that showed so much promise, only to be followed by such dismal adulthoods. After such a journey, and only after such a journey, could she reunite with Jonathan and be the mother to her children that she was supposed to be. But not before. Definitely not before.

At first, she had thought that Chicken John still lived in Waterford, South Carolina, where *The Prince of Tides* had taken place, but after consulting a map and not finding it on there, she remembered that the nuclear power plant was there now, and its top-secret status probably kept it from the cartographer's stylus. She therefore ransacked the mapped streets of Charleston and the surrounding rural roads, but no spot caused a light to flicker in her head, and she was left with the understanding that in order to find him she must venture forth.

With those thoughts in mind, she put down her Dorothea Benton Frank novel and went to see her father, as she would need an automobile for the fateful trek.

FIVE

Life was full of miseries. You could see them all around you, and even those you did not see seemed to enter your mind through telephone calls, television programs, the newspaper, or any other form of media that you were beaten with. Creighton Starke had a full share of his own and had always been cursed with more than your average fellow, but this latest appeared to be a pinnacle of sorts.

Yes, he had undergone an episode. Yes, they had had to sedate him several times and shoot electricity through his brain. Yes, he had attacked his uncle when he came to visit him. There were many yeses for the many questions that could be posed to the deponent as he sat in the dimly lit lawyer's office, wishing he had had the fortitude to kill himself when he had had the chance. But did that mean that he was an unfit parent? He wasn't drinking himself to sleep at night while his son lay his filthy body in his filthy bed, wishing that he had something to fill his filthy stomach. He didn't encourage him to skip school. He didn't use illicit drugs or partake of illicit sex in his presence. He had suffered a mental collapse, but what was that if not an organic failure? Would you keep a child away from a parent who had diabetes? Was that parent unfit to play unsupervised with the boy?

He sat in his brown Chevy Cavalier, the windows down, his eyes on the clock that electronically charted the minutes to his demise. It was hot outside and hot inside, and his armpits and groin felt uncomfortably damp. He had arrived twenty minutes early, and in most civilized societies this would have meant nothing as a parent should be rewarded for being early to visit his child, but a month or so ago when he had tried to force his way into his mother-in-law's house (ex-mother-in-law, he had to remind himself) she had thrust those stupid court documents in his face, telling him that four o'clock meant four o'clock, and the time after that she had had the bold audacity to call the police and attempt to have him arrested.

So now he waited until four o'clock. No, that is not the truth. Now he waited the slightest touch after four, so that she did not make him stand outside her door, her eyes focused on the watch dangling from her geriatric arm and count off the seconds until four o'clock had arrived. The indignities. The miseries. And he had twenty more minutes before he leapt into a whole new world of them.

Savannah's book was sitting in the passenger seat next to him. He looked at it, then thought of the copy of Barnes's *Flaubert's Parrot* that he had stuffed in the glove compartment, quickly deciding that at the moment he could not make the effort necessary to retrieve good old Julian. He therefore picked it up again, and began to read as follows:

```
I wear the shackles.
I wear the shackles and oftentimes think of
them on my wrists and around my ankles as I stum-
ble down the streets of the lowcountry, in search
of the childhood that I never had. It is these
shackles that shackle me. The losses that I have
undergone, of friends, of family, of innocence,
these are they, and they are them.
I cannot begin in the middle, and I cannot
begin in the end. No, I must begin where my
conscience tells me to, which is at the begin-
ning. For that is where it all started, at the
beginning, when life seemed so full of something
other than the horror that fills it now.
```

I was born a lowcountry girl in Charleston,
South Carolina on a night troubled with a hurricane. The story is this: my father was at this
time a shrimper and was out on the boat catch-
ing the largest catch of shrimp in the history of
the world. He had been drinking, as he was always
drinking, and did not pay attention to the fact
that he was caught in the middle of a typhoon in
the middle of the ocean in the middle of a very
small shrimp boat with two black men who were
educated in ways not taught at school and who
cared for my family as though it were their own.

"Don't you think we should be gwine back in
cap'n?" asked one of them as the wind lashed his
face.

"No." my father said.

"It sho seems awfull windy out here cap'n."
said one of them as rain pelted him.

"That's just the wind. The wind helps with
shrimp. It is a shrimping wind." said my father.

"It seems awful dangerous out here to me
cap'n." said one of them as water doused him.

"As it always is with the shrimping wind."
said my father.

My mohter was expecting my father at home at
any minute, as she was expecting me to come that
night. My brother Roy was watching television,
drinking a Pepsi Cola. My brother Chicken John
had yet to be born.

As we were staunch Catholics, my mother had
obtained a midwife from the church to help along
with the process and she was there, lighting the ceremonial incense and splashing around
holy water. Her name was Sister Joanna, and she

was an old black woman from the lowcountry who
had see the end of slavery through her own eyes
as a child. Ther were many black people in the
lowcountry at that time who had seen the end
of slavery and who were educated in ways not
taught at school, and who loved my family dearly,
although my father was someone to be watched with
a watchful eye.

"Lawd chile." said Sister Joanna. "You the
most beautiful woman I ever seed."

"Thank you." said my mother.

"You gwine have pretty children." said Sister
Joanna.

"I already have one." said my mother. "Look at
Roy over there." Mother nodded over at Roy who
was watching television.

Sister Joanna did not say anything in
response.

The hurricane hit just as the birth pangs hit
my mother. The roof was torn off of the house. The
foundations were ruined. Furniture flew this way
and that.

"You gwine have to push!" said Sister Joanna.

"I'm pushing." said my mother. "I'm pushing!"

"I seed it! I seed it!" said Sister Joanna.

"What is it that you see?" asked my mother.

"A chile!" said Sister Joanna.

That child was me, and if only the wind had
been a little stronger. If only the water had
risen a little higher, then I would not be here
to relate to you my tale of woe.

"Roy quickly! Get the cattle out of the barn!"
said my mother. "Roy. Do you hear me? Get the
cattle out of the barn!"

"I hears the cattle a'lowing." said Sister Joanna.

Roy was busy watching the television set that did not work.

"Is the child alright? We should get to the barn to check on the catttle!" said my mother.

"A girl chile." said Sister Joanna. The girl child of me.

"We should leave! Oh! What's this! What's happening?" said my mother.

"You got another chile comin!" said Sister Joanna.

The tension was palatable in the room. The hurricane was roaring. The furniture was flying. The cattle were drowning. I think that as I look back now that this tension was part of what made me so tense, and gave me the ability to be the poet that I am. Some say it is god given, but I believe it was given by that lowcountry hurricane so many years ago.

"Another child!" said my mother. "Roy! The cattle!"

"Yes'm! Another chile!"

And that child, a boy child, was my brother Chicken John.

We raced out to the barn to seek higher shelter as we were standing in three feet of water. Sister Joanna carried Roy and me and my grandfather carried my mother.

My grandfather pushed against the current and helped Sister Joanna and mother and me and Chicken John.

"Come! This way!' he shouted.

"We're coming!" shouted my mother and Sister Joanna.

When we entered the barn the cows who had not been milked were floating from their swollen utters. It was a magical moment of the lowcountry a place where things happen that happen no where else in the whole wild world.

"They haven't drowned!" said my grandfather. "They're floating!" he shouted.

The hurricane winds were whipping across the lowcountry.

We took the ladder up to the hay loft where we kept the hay and a noncombustible lantern. My grandfather lifted Chicken John and me and Sister Joanna lifted my mother up the stairs.

"Damn you Hardeeville D'Bergeolet!" screamed my grandfather with his shaking fist to the heavens. "You should be here but you're out shrimpin' in that shrimpin' boat! How am I supposed ot take care of your children! How! I'm an old man who has seen many winters and I'm too old to be takin care of these chil'ren a pregnant woman, and a nurse maid!"

"I ain't seen a hurricane like this since the summer of 1878! These winds are somethin' shore nuff!" shouted Sister Joanna.

"Watch out!" shouted my grandfather.

A beam from the roof fell and hit Sister Joanna on the head and killed her. She was dead from the impact.

"Roy help her!" shouted my mother.

Roy tried to do what he could for Sister Joanna but he could do nothing because she was dead from the beam that fell from the roof.

"Damn you Hardeeville D'Bergeolet!" shouted my grandfather as he held Sister Joana in his arms, crying like a baby.

The following morning my father returned with a boat full of shrimp and a stomach full of liquor. We all pretended like nothing had happened and acted like nothing had happened. I learned from this early age that this was how it was going to be in the D'Bergeolet household. We would pretend that nothing had happened when in fact a great deal had.

Creighton Starke set the book back down and wondered to himself if he was ever that bad. Or if he were that bad now. He had not written anything in so long that he did not know. The words might come like they did in years past, or they might appear on the page as something drafted by a child in crayon. He jammed a stick of gum in his mouth and looked at the clock; it was time. After a nose check in each armpit to gauge the gaminess of his shirt, he opened the door and took the first step toward the latest outrage.

SIX

Savannah entered the room where her father sat in his unwieldy leather chair, reading the paper. His sock-covered feet lay propped up on an ottoman, leading to the khaki pants, and a light blue cardigan sweater hung loosely on the thin frame of his shoulders. His lack of a chin spoke to successful inbreeding. A glass of red wine stood next to him on an end table, and every so often he lifted it to his lips and took a sip. He gave the certain appearance that he enjoyed being left alone.

But Savannah wasn't going to leave him alone. She came to a halt several feet away from him, waiting for him to pay attention to her, eyeing him with the hatred she had recently developed.

Even though he sat absorbed in the Beethoven piano sonata playing in the background and the article in front of his eyes, he could feel her presence. He did not want to acknowledge it, however. Between his daughter and his wife, he couldn't find a moment's rest in the house. Someone was constantly crying about something, whether it was the weather or the headaches that both seemed to receive daily.

"Father."

He cringed when he heard the word. From the moment of her birth, she had been taught to call him Daddy, but in the past weeks he had become Father, like some dour Anglican patriarch. He cast a tentative glance over at her as he turned down the newspaper and answered, "Yes, dear?"

"Father, we need to talk." She stepped forward, planting her feet firmly beneath her. Her red-streaked eyes seemed to blaze with madness, and the surrounding skin looked as though it had recently suffered sunburn.

"Okay," he said. "What would you like to talk about?"

"Why does it always have to be *me* who likes to talk about things?" she asked. "Why can't it ever be you?"

He folded up the paper then slowly put both it and his feet on the floor, his eyes never leaving her.

"I don't know what you're talking about, dear. Now please calm down. There's nothing to get upset about."

At this, Savannah cast her face toward the ceiling and stamped her feet.

"Nothing to get upset about?! Nothing to get upset about?! How… how dare you?!"

"I…I…" he stammered as he sunk deeper into the leather, hoping it would somehow suck him into it and take him away.

"How can you say that there's nothing to get upset about after the way you treated Chicken John?!"

"Who? Who's that bab…"

"So, you still act like he never existed?"

"Honey…"

"Don't honey me. Don't you honey me!" she shouted, her voice shooting up an octave. "Ever since we left Charleston you have forbidden the entire family from ever saying his name. But I'm saying it, Father! I'm saying it! Chicken John! Chicken John! Chicken John!" She stopped and glared at him. He was trying to think of how to respond when he heard the quick footsteps of his wife in the hall.

"What are you two yelling about?" she asked, entering the room, looking at him, then at Savannah. Savannah did not give a reply.

"Chicken John," he answered in a whisper.

"Chicken John? Who's Chicken John, Harry?"

"Ohhhhhhhh!" Savannah shouted. "You too? After all he's done to you, mother?"

"What has he done to me? What have you done to me, Harry?"

"Nothing," he said. "I swear to God. I don't know what she's talking about."

"Then why are you yelling?

"I wasn't yelling. I was just reading the paper."

"I can't believe the two of you," said Savannah. "Does everyone in this family suffer from amnesia? Huh? I mean, it's like everyone who lives here has gone crazy."

Mr. Edwards let out a stage cough.

"You can't treat people this way and not reap the consequences of therapy, suicide, impotence, and general malaise," said Savannah.

"How have we treated you?" her mother asked. "How have you treated her, Harry?"

"I don't know," he said. "She's talking about somebody named Chicken John whom she claims I've told her never to talk about ever since we left Charleston."

"When were you in Charleston?" Mrs. Edwards asked. "When did you take her there?"

"Never!" he exclaimed in his defense. "I've never taken her anywhere."

"Well then, maybe that's the problem right there. Sweetheart, come here. Daddy didn't mean to hurt your feelings, it's just that he can be cruel sometimes without even knowing it. Come here, precious."

Mrs. Edwards walked toward her; her arms opened for an embrace.

"No," said Savannah. "Get back. I'm going away and there's nothing you can do to stop me."

"Where?" asked Mrs. Edwards. "Where are you going?"

"I'm leaving and going back to Charleston to try and find Chicken John."

"Tonight?" Mrs. Edwards asked. "Honey, it'll soon be too dark for you to be driving and Daddy's got to have his car to go to work tomorrow and I've got bridge club."

"I don't care," said Savannah. "I'll take a bus if I have to."

"Sweetheart," said Mrs. Edwards. "Charleston's a few hours away. By the time you get there, it'll be time to come back."

"You don't get it, do you?" Savannah said. "Neither of you ever got it."

With that she turned and hurried away, her stamping feet echoing on the hardwood floor as she went.

"Erica, darling," Mrs. Edwards called, but Savannah was already making her way up the stairs.

"She doesn't want us to call her Erica anymore," said Mr. Edwards. His wife looked back over at him, her hands dug into the continental shelf of her hips.

"What? What are you talking about?"

"She told me the other day that she wants to be called Savannah like we used to call her."

"We've never called her Savannah."

"You know that, and I know that, but that's what she says." With a shrug, he reached down and picked up the paper.

"Lord, Lord," said Mrs. Edwards. "You've driven her crazy. You've driven us all crazy."

Her husband breathed a sigh of relief when she left, then took another sip of wine. This pinot was excellent, and it seemed to restore his sense of calm, a sense that he generally treasured. After contemplating shutting the door, he gave up the thought and resumed reading the article on sunflowers. He found the topic joyfully consuming, so it wasn't too difficult to ignore the sound of his wife calling, "Erica?…Savannah?… Honey?"

SEVEN

Once back in her room, Savannah began to pack in a fury. She threw a handful of paperbacks and a few dresses into her suitcase as her mother's voice called from downstairs, slowly trailing its way up to her room. Savannah's only response was to look for her sandals.

Within seconds there was a knock on her door and a voice saying, "Honey? Sweetheart?"

"Come in, Mother."

Mrs. Edwards entered the room wearing a piteous look.

"Now honey, you know Daddy didn't mean any of that stuff he said. He just lives in his own world." She took a seat on the bed next to the open suitcase that Savannah continued to fill. "He's just that way, and that's the way he's always been."

"Does *his way* keep him from remembering?" Savannah asked.

"Well sometimes, I guess," Mrs. Edwards said. "You certainly can't trust him to go to the grocery store by himself."

Savannah stared at her mother for a moment, then shook her head. She was so incredibly beautiful that she caused unhealthy feelings to overcome anyone who came near her.

"Mother, if you will excuse me, I must get going."

"But honey…"

Savannah hurried out of her room and made her way down the hall toward the bathroom where her brother Roy stood, his arms crossed.

"What's all the yelling about? I was talking to my friend Dave in Manitoba, and it was so loud I could hardly think."

"Up yours, zit face," said Savannah as she brushed past him.

"Mom," said Roy.

A heavy fog of stench blanketed the bathroom from Roy's most recent visit. With one hand holding her nose, Savannah began gathering her cosmetics and toiletries. Was it so bad living with Jonathan? Was it as bad as this? She could not remember him ever destroying a living space in such a way, nor could she have, for he did not exist. Chicken John. She must find Chicken John.

"Charleston? What's in Charleston?"

Savannah could hear her mother whisper something, to which Roy said, "Give me a break!"

He suddenly appeared in the bathroom, his face distorted with anger.

"What's this about you taking one of the cars? Huh? You know if Mom doesn't have a car tonight then Dad'll have to drop me off at Magik Merlin's, don't you? Huh?"

Savannah looked at him, her nose still pinched, and said, "That's your problem. You've made your bed; now you must lie in it." With her cosmetics bag underneath her arm, she strode past him again and headed back to her room.

"Mom!" Roy followed, right on her heels. "She can't take the car. It's not fair."

"Now Roy," said Mrs. Edwards, grabbing him by the arm in the hallway, "you know that you get to use the car sometimes when she doesn't."

"Yeah, but she's a girl," he said.

At this, Savannah stiffened. She ran back out of the room and into the hallway where her mother and brother stood. "I am not! I am a woman. A suffering soul who cannot find happiness until I return to Charleston and find Chicken John."

"Who's Chicken John?" Roy asked.

In response, Savannah turned and fled back to her room. After slamming her suitcase shut, she picked it up and headed out the door.

"Who's Chicken John?" Roy asked again.

"Your brother, you idiot!" said Savannah.

"I don't have a brother!" Roy said.

"Yes, you do," said Savannah. "Roy, don't you remember? The years we spent in the low country, when father worked as a shrimper and a Marine, and you and I went to school out on Yamacraw Island with all the little black children? We had the little house near the creek and Chicken John and I shared a bedroom. You used to drink Pepsi with sugar and Mother cooked Hoppin' John and clam grits every night. She was so pretty back then, weren't you Mother? And Father would come home from work drunk, and you wouldn't do anything about it. Don't you remember?"

"What are you talking about?" Roy asked. "You've lost your mind."

"Now Roy, don't say such things to your sister."

"But Mom, she's gone crazy and you're going to let her take the car so that Dad will have to drop me off at Magik Merlin's house."

"Ohhhhh!" Savannah screamed. "Walk to Magik Merlin, for all I care! His trailer can't be that far away!" She leapt down the stairs.

"Harry!" Mrs. Edwards shouted.

EIGHT

Visitation consisted of this: Creighton sat cross-legged on the shag carpet in his former mother-in-law's den, watching his son play with small male figurines outfitted with guns, flame throwers, and other implements of death and disfigurement, all while his former mother-in-law and her male companion, a former Navy man, who asked to be addressed as Captain Thurnbill, and whom he therefore called Skipper, drilled their eyes into his hunched back from their spot on the couch. He tried talking to the boy about his personal problems, about his novel, about the nice swimming pool at his apartment complex that he hoped he could come see one day, about the necessity of art, and in return received lectures on how lasers came out of certain plastic armaments and how Creighton was not very adept at playing war because dinosaurs did not have lasers.

This attempt at exchange had the cumulative effect of depressing Creighton to hallucinogenic depths.

The poor little bastard had no idea what was going on, or what had happened. He was growing up with the understanding that this was how fathers spent time with their children: in two-hour periods, sitting on the floor, as grandmother scowled from the couch and some strange man drank tea. The desire clawed at him to grab his heir and flee to the Cavalier, hope that it would start, then run off to the hills, but he pushed it aside and focused on the matter at hand.

The laser beam that had been shot at him was apparently a green one, and therefore he should not have played dead, as green lasers were healing lasers and did not kill dinosaurs. He tried to rectify his error by letting out a growl of rejuvenation, but Skipper's cautioning words made the rectifying irrectifiable.

"I am not scaring the boy," said Creighton. "You're scaring the boy with that fake eye you have in your head."

"Oh!" exclaimed his former mother-in-law.

"You listen here, psycho ward," said Skipper with a shaking finger. "That eye you're talkin' 'bout is'a cause'a cancer. You gonna sit there and make fun of a cancer survivor? Huh?"

"I didn't realize I was making fun of it just by pointing out the obvious. You were just talking about scaring people, and listen here, Skipper, you don't have to growl or shout or do anything out of the ordinary to scare anyone, much less a child. Just show them the evil eye."

"It ain't an evil eye. It's a cancer eye."

"Actually, it's not an eye at all. It's an abomination."

"Oh!" exclaimed his former mother-in-law.

"I'll tell you what an abomination is, nutcase: you. You're an abomination."

"Skipper, it's bad form to respond to someone's insult by repeating the same one they just used. Reach into that cancer-ridden brain of yours and try again."

"Phooey to you, fella," said Skipper. "At least I ain't had jumper cables hooked up to me."

"Well, fucky to you, asshole. Why don't you take that glass eye of yours and shove it up your ass? Or better yet, why don't I do it?"

"Oh!" exclaimed his former mother-in-law.

At this point, the boy began to cry and ran to the old crone, who took him in her arms and led him back to the kitchen.

"Nice job there, nutcase," said Skipper. "Cursing in front of your kid. Scarin'im. Nice job."

"Skipper, I will beat your ass if you say one more goddamned word. Just one more fucking word and I will kick your fucking ass."

"Jumper cables," said Skipper. "And unless I forgot how to count, nutcase, that'd be two, so I guess you got to beat my ass twice now."

NINE

It is difficult to describe exactly how her voice sounded to Harry Edwards, for it was not analogous to sound. It came as an image, a sensation. The accidental drop of the hammer onto the thumb, the nail being ripped from the finger. The moment he heard it, he cursed himself for not closing the door to the study and arose from his chair.

"I'm coming," he shouted back.

When he walked into the hallway, he saw that his daughter was already down the stairs, her suitcase in hand, his wife and son coming down after her.

"Dad," said Roy.

"What? What?" he asked. "What do all of you want?" The family seemed shocked by his anger—all of them except for Savannah, who beamed with a smile.

"You see," she said, "he's just like I told you."

Everyone stood in place.

"Jesus Christ," Mr. Edwards moaned. "Let's put an end to this. What is it, exactly, that you want?"

"Dad!" Roy said.

"Shut up, son!" his father shouted.

"Don't speak to him like that!" said Savannah. "He's only like this because of what you've done to him!"

"What have I done to him?"

Savannah dropped her suitcase to the floor and stretched to her full height, her eyes shining with defiance.

"You made him go out on the shrimping boat with you and watch you get drunk. You made him watch as you tortured me and Chicken John. You sucked every bit of emotion and decency out of him until he became what he is today: some ignoramus who sits in front of his computer all day talking to his fellow losers."

"Hey!"

"Shut up, son," Mr. Edwards said. "Erica—Savannah, whatever it is you want to be called—I am not, nor have I ever been a shrimper. Just the thought of shellfish makes me break out in hives. I'm an attorney and that's how I've always made a living. Now I don't know what's gotten into your head, young lady, but you need to stop this nonsense right now."

Savannah laughed at this. A forced hysterical laugh that made everyone stare at her with horror.

"Attorney, huh?" Conroy led her to the right words. "I wouldn't use your marrow to feed wild dogs or your wiry flesh to bait a crab pot!"

"What?" her father asked.

"You heard me. Now we all know that's a lie, because you've been a Marine fighter pilot and a shrimper, not an attorney, but if that's what you want to pretend to be, then so be it. Either way you are a scoundrel who sold our family land for the nuclear power plant, beat all of your children and your wife!"

"Erica! That's not true!" Mrs. Edwards cried.

"You are a drunkard who cannot show love for your family and you even betrayed Chicken John to the federal authorities! All for what, Father? Was it because you never knew love?"

Mr. Edwards really had no idea what to do, or how to respond. He watched as she continued to smile at him and the rest of the family stood dumbfounded.

"Young lady. . ."

"Stay away, Father. You can't hurt me now. I'm going to find Chicken John, who's a Green Beret, and your days on this earth are numbered once I do."

She picked up her suitcase and turned toward the door.

"Where are you going?" Mrs. Edwards asked.

"Charleston," Savannah said as she walked out of the house.

"Harry!"

"Let her go. She'll be back before the night's out."

"But what if she isn't?"

He ambled away without answering, thinking to himself that if she weren't, it wasn't his problem.

TEN

Skipper took off his shirt and Creighton Starke stretched out his shoulders and neck as the afternoon fell into shallow dusk around them. The old man then spat in his hands, wiped them together, and put up his dukes. Creighton noticed a faded tattoo on his right arm, signifying something years ago, nothing now.

"Come on, jumper cables. Show me what you got."

There was no way he could lose. The man was in his late seventies. Riddled with cancer. Creighton raised his fists and took a step forward.

"I'm gonna put that eye right up your ass, Skipper."

"Oh, shoot," said Skipper, raising a hand to touch it. "I forgot about that. Give me a second here."

"Of course," said Creighton.

As Skipper leaned his head back to take it out, Creighton ran forward and gave the old man a sharp kick on the shin followed by a punch that landed on the back of an ear. A wail erupted from Skipper's voice box and its sounding caused Creighton to be overcome with caveman bloodlust. He continued to rain kicks and punches on the elderly bones until he felt that each one would be the last, the *coup de gras* preceding the ceremonial placing of glassed eye into aged ass. But just as all was going well, his lopsided victory was arighted by an uppercut that Skipper landed in a stomach used to

43

holding only food and drink. The breath that moments earlier had frenzied out of Creighton's lungs vanished in a vacuum of pain. In response, in desperation, Creighton grabbed Skipper by the head and smashed his skull into his face. The resulting collision sent both men to the ground, Creighton on his back, Skipper to his side, both into howling.

When the smoke of mutual defeat finally settled, it was with weak knees and blurred vision that the author of *Finding It All in the Hole* staggered toward his Chevrolet Cavalier, imaginary sirens blaring off in the distance as the bearer of his unforgivable ex-wife speed-dialed 911. He wrenched open the door and set himself in the driver's seat, his hands shaking as they tried to place the key in the ignition.

He heard Skipper shout something from his hospital bed of grass, and this caused him to look over at the house through vision marred with blood and concussion. There, next to his mother-in-law, stood his son, his face blank from what Creighton could see, so blank that it did not even have a nose.

The engine started and Creighton raised his hand to wave good-bye.

ELEVEN

Savannah did not go straight to Charleston that night, although her intentions were such that she had not lied to her parents. She wanted to go to Charleston and had planned to be there within a day or so, but there were some things that needed to be taken care of first.

Although the characters in Conroy's novels were always loners, on the feminine side of the authorial fence the ladies always had companions. There was the crazy older lady, the wise black woman, and the friend about the protagonist's age who oftentimes seemed very simple but ended up teaching the main character a great deal about herself. This woman had to have a thirst for life, be slightly zany yet a little dense, and cause the protagonist to do things that she would not normally do, usually with humorous, yet worthwhile, results. Savannah knew of only one friend who fit the bill, and it was a good thing that she fit the bill, because Savannah had no other friends.

She arrived at Mitzi's apartment within a few minutes and sat in her mother's parked car, composing herself. When she was crying with enough vigor, she threw herself out of the vehicle and ran to the front door where she knocked loudly. Mitzi answered by the fourth pounding.

"Savannah!" she exclaimed when she saw her weeping friend. "What's wrong with you? What happened?"

"Chicken John!" Savannah wailed.

"Your brother that you've told me so much about?"

Savannah nodded her head.

"What? What's wrong? Did something happen to him?"

"I've found him," said Savannah with a mournful cry.

"Here. Come in. Jesus. Look at you. Come in."

Savannah did as she was told and entered Mitzi's apartment, running to the couch where she buried her face in one of the pillows.

"Savannah, why are you crying?" Mitzi asked. "This is great news."

Savannah did not respond.

"You've found your long-lost brother," said Mitzi. "This is something to be happy about. Now don't cry."

Mitzi had positioned herself next to Savannah on the sofa, gently stroking Savannah's blonde locks. After a few minutes, Savannah lifted her head, her tears gone.

"It's great news," said Mitzi.

"Mitzi, don't you understand what this means?"

Mitzi said that she didn't.

"This means that all of the lies that my family has been living for all of these years are about to come to light. The atom bomb that is Chicken John is about to explode right in the middle of the D'Bergeolet living room, and the fallout isn't going to be pretty."

Mitzi could be described by a person with a discerning eye as a young woman not very discerning to the eye. Her brown hair held no bounce or shine and any hopes for her eyes were dashed by the heavy weight of her thick glasses. Her breasts were minimum, her hips and thighs maximum, her complexion located somewhere in the middle of nowhere. In her, Savannah divined wit where there was none, and a zest for life when the truth of the matter was that a few centuries ago the young lady would have been sold off by her family to a convent where they wove shirts out of flax.

She looked at Savannah, silent, trying to figure out how her brother could possibly be an atom bomb.

"Well," she said, "then maybe you should just leave it alone. Chicken John has been living on his own for quite a while now, and maybe it's best for everyone to keep it that way."

"I can't do that!" said Savannah, taking a pillow and throwing it to the floor. "Good night, Mitzi. Things don't happen that way. Think about how boring the books would be if people just left it alone. They'd be terrible. No, what I must do is risk it all. I have to find him. Don't get me wrong: there's going to be a lot of pain and suffering before we're done. I'm sure someone's going to die. Suicide maybe. Cancer. Who knows? But in the end, Mitzi, you mark my words, in the end everything will be as right as rain, although we'll be left with the scars that allow us to think back on what all took place when everything's finally over."

"Okay," said Mitzi. "So what are you going to do?"

"What am *I* going to do? The question is, Mitzi, what are *we* going to do? You know I can't do this alone. You have to be there to give me your wit and wisdom, wit and wisdom that I won't understand at first, but that later I'll come to appreciate."

The thing that Mitzi liked most about Savannah, at least during the two weeks that they had known each other, was her profusion of compliments. These were oftentimes seasoned with coarse insults, but Mitzi was used to the latter and therefore could tolerate them as long as the former kept coming. (It should be noted that Mitzi did not understand which one *former* related to, nor did she grasp the concept of the *latter*.) However, she felt unsure about going on a quest with Savannah, especially during a school week.

"Can't we wait until fall break?" she asked.

"I wish we could," said Savannah. "If I had it my way, and events weren't pushing me toward it, I would wait until my parents were dead and my children grown. But it wasn't meant to be that way. We were meant to go now, and I don't see that we have any choice."

Mitzi thought about the classes she would miss; she pondered her grades. She was more than happy to help out a friend, but this seemed a bit much.

"I don't know, Savannah."

"I don't know either, Mitzi. The events that stand before us are going to be trying. Very trying. Excruciating. But what I promise you is immortality. When all of this is done, I plan on writing a book about the journey in order to cleanse myself of the experience, and this book will be a national bestseller that people will read for years to come. You'll be in it, Mitzi. You'll be there next to me when I finally find Chicken John. It won't be just something that you tell your grandchildren about, it will be something that your grandchildren read to their grandchildren."

"Jeez. When do we go?"

"Tomorrow," said Savannah. "Right now, I need to rest, although I know that I won't be able to sleep a wink tonight. I need to think, to prepare myself."

TWELVE

Did Creighton need to see a doctor? Are you out of your mind? Granted, he was bloody, swollen, and currently prescribed a great deal of psychotropic medication that he was not taking, yet a visit to the doctor would be the equivalent of showing all of your cool magic tricks to the residents of Salem, Massachusetts, during a rather unfortunate period in that fair town's history. No, dear reader, a doctor was absolutely not what he needed, while at the same time it absolutely was. The contradictions inherent in existence was a theme that he had explored meticulously in *Finding It All in the Hole* through the character of Osgood, the Filipino soldier of fortune who had once loved Belinda. "Damned if you do, damned if you don't," Osgood would often say to himself as he stared at the wallpaper in his boarding room for approximately seventy-five pages. Creighton had wanted this to be the cover art: the unreadable Asiatic face peering into the hole in the wallpaper (the hole that the reader would find represented so much) situated in a Kafkaesque room (how to make a room Kafkaesque was beyond Creighton, but these people were supposed to be professionals), but that, of course, was not what those idiots at Scribner's had done. No, apparently some complete imbecile who had never cracked a page of the book got mixed up after a night of cocaine and disco music and decided from the title that it was a work of science fiction. All signs pointed to the fact that this fool's brush was not influenced by Degas, Rubens, or even Pollock, but rather by movie posters from the Disney Corporation, for there, on the face of Creighton's baby, weeping like a cancerous polyp, floated a dead astronomical object with the words *Finding It All in the Ho-ooooooooo-le!!!!!* belching from out of its mouth. He had cried for two days straight when he saw it, threatened them with lawyers that he did not have, then attended a string of science-fiction conventions where the only books he sold were to a man in a Martian costume who had the audacity to say that he was buying them because he felt sorry for him.

So, the question was, where could he go? His office would clearly be an easy choice for them, so not there. Ditto with his apartment. His thoughts circled around the idea of holing up in a bar and drinking away the warrant for his arrest, but cigarette smoke bothered his eyes, and he didn't have any money. The authors of the past would have done something like that. Hemingway would have quaffed himself into a tizzy then walked away without paying a cent. But he was not Hemingway. Not only that, he felt sure that Hemingway would have hated him, and he Hemingway.

He circled the three points of his decisional triangle, finally landing on the apartment, but with a twist. Yes, he would go to his apartment building, but not his apartment itself. It was probably not a good idea, and in fact, it was almost certainly a bad one, but at the time, rocked with blunt-force trauma to the head, tired and hungry, and addled to begin with, that he even had ideas, regardless of their worth, caused him to feel great pride in his craftiness. It was time to be neighborly. To knock on the door of the constantly fornicating fellow who lived next door to him, who perhaps had even read *Finding It All in the Hole*, who perhaps had even enjoyed it.

THIRTEEN

The dot matrix printer had failed Roy in the end, blurring the final line of the directions to the edge of nowhere, and leaving him stranded near the border of it, so close that he could sense its proximity, but lost, nonetheless. In the dark of early evening, he pulled the van to a stop in front a house unfortunately located on a rural highway in Newberry County and walked toward the front door, drenched in terror on account of the dogs growling in the back, shrouded in doubt as to the sturdiness of the fence that separated them from his earthly shell.

A historic moment was about to take place. This was the evening that they had planned for over a year, the first meeting between Roy Edwards and a gentleman who called himself Magik Merlin. The internet brought people together, from as far away as Manitoba, but Magik Merlin did not live that far away, although he did live far away from Manitoba. Roy did not know what would take place or how he would find Magik Merlin to be in the physical realm, but he did know that with a man like Magik Merlin, one could only expect greatness.

Several knocks produced no apparent result, except to inflame the dogs who began hurling themselves against the fence, and he was about to run back to his father's car and lock himself in when a bearded man appeared, separated from Roy by a screen door and twenty years.

"What do you want?" the man asked.

Razor Roy was quick to respond: "I'm looking for…," but he was not so quick to respond fully, for he doubted that Magik Merlin was known in such a fashion by his neighbors, if one could even consider a person a neighbor when he lived three miles away. He tried to continue. "…a guy who I know from the internet. He goes by the name of Magik Merlin? I don't know…"

"Razor? Razor Roy?" the man asked, a smile appearing within the beard.

"Magik Merlin?" said Roy.

"Hell yeah!"

Magik Merlin led Razor Roy Edwards inside the house where he cohabitated with disorder, the clothes, newspapers, food wrappers, dust, and body odor lying about as if they had just engaged in a thorough fight where all had suffered ignominious defeat. They stepped over mounds of rotted cloth and into piles of soiled undergarments, both chatting about the fools who designed the mapping systems on the internet and the obsolescence of dot matrix printers, and thus Magik Merlin, who secretly hated the fact that his parents had named him Kenneth, showed Razor Roy around the place, pulling back the threadbare curtains to the porch and causing mild heart palpitations within Roy's chest walls when the newly revealed dogs attacked the glass, which was smeared like a slide of a microscope in an infectious disease laboratory.

The "they won't hurt you" was greeted with a tender laugh and marked their departure to the kitchen where Magik Merlin laid his meaty palms on top of the line of ants traveling from the windowsill to the dirty dishes in the sink. He wiped their mortal remnants against his stained pants leg, afterwards raising his arms (he the realtor, Roy the young couple in search of their first home, the wife pregnant, the husband awkwardly overdressed), then proceeded to walk back to the bedrooms, the first one—situated next to the bathroom that they did not enter—a storage room set up by a mental patient, the final one, a set of box springs laid out on the floor in coital communion with the mattress, two desks, each facing a wall, where two computers sat glowing, and little else.

"Well, this is it," said Magik Merlin, like a shipping mogul attempting a show of humility over his kingly manse. "You're welcome to crash here tonight."

"Um. I might take you up on that," said Roy, "but probably some other time. I gotta get the car home. Parents, you know."

"Yeah, yeah, yeah," said Magik Merlin. "You feel like eating any chow?"

"I'm good," said Roy.

They repaired to the living room, the only room containing instruments designed for sitting, and talked about the latest goings-on in the internet community as Magik Merlin ate seasoned fries from a hermetically sealed can. The conversation seemed forced. Staring uncomfortably at each other as they exchanged words, telling the other things that the other already knew, relaying jokes that each had received from the same various listservs, eyes locked on the floor during the many awkward silences. After emptying the can, a tour of the back yard was proposed, and even though Roy informed Magik Merlin of a childhood incident that had left him morbidly afraid of dogs—the paternal grandparents' house, the ripped pants leg, hydrogen peroxide, and threats of rabies shots—Magik Merlin insisted, and Roy found himself thirty minutes later back in the same worn chair, this time covered in saliva and shit mixed with a clayish dirt, his right hand sticky from the tennis ball that he had had to throw over and over again across the poorly maintained lawn for the enjoyment of the pack. It was therefore with relief that Roy accepted Magik Merlin's suggestion that they hop online and have a little fun.

FOURTEEN

The cops were not at Creighton's apartment complex. There was one off-duty policeman who Creighton felt sure lived there either for free or with reduced rates, and the noted author had oftentimes seen him drunk, harassing the bikinied women by the pool, but he did not register him as much of a threat. He therefore parked his car next to the garbage bin, away from his apartment, and hugged the walls as he made it back to *chez* Starke.

Three hours had been spent driving around the nameless town, wracking his brain for a plan for the lam, so it was now getting dark, the lights in the parking lot starting to glow. He skipped up the stairs, the blood pulsing from his heart into his head, and made it to the apartment next to his, where he knocked. After waiting several seconds, he knocked again. After several more he began to pound. After several more he gave up, pounded a few more times for good measure, then began to look around with frantic eyes. His plan, although he had not considered this before, centered around the fellow being home. The fornicator. Mister screws-all-night-on-week-nights-and-all-day-long-on-weekends. The destroyer of dreams. The ravisher of rest. It was not the sole factor, but it was certainly the primary one, and without it taking place, steps two, three, four, and five collapsed on top of one another. He stood and thought, and then he realized that he was shamefully exposed standing there, this realization sending him running back down the stairs to his car.

He would have to wait it out. There was nothing else to do. He thought once more of *Flaubert's Parrot* but knew that his brain could not take such gymnastics at present. He therefore grabbed *Lowcountry Lamentations* and sat himself underneath a light behind the dumpster, where he began to read as follows:

If I could tell you the story of my childhood
then I would tell you of days spent on the dock
crabbing, nights listening to the gnats swarm
at my bedroom window, the mornings of clam grits
and mull gravy, the days out in the boat fishing
for white tail, of the glory of the lowcountry
and my existence as a gechee girl in this land of
dreams.
But I cannot tell you of this childhood without telling you of the other. The other childhood
that I had, where the mull gravy turned to ashes
in my mouth and the crabs that I caught stood
only as portents of doom.
When my father was in the Marines fighting
overseas (he was pilot), we lived with my grandmother in Atlanta. I remember little of this
other than it was a magical time. NOt magical in
the sense of the lowcountry, but magical none the
less. We walked down the street where we lived,
Roy, Chicken John and myself, back from school
and to school, and when we were not in school we
often times walked it just the same. It was an
excellent walking street, that to me seemed magical and full of wander.

This magic, which began as white, soon turned to black magic - the kind that is evil as a hurricane hitting the lowcountry.

We were told not to talk to strangers, but we befriended an Orkin man who seemed very nice. At first. When we later learned who he was we soon realized that he was not nice at all. He was meaner than a crab in a crab pot. His name was Randolph and he worked for Orkin, a company that we children, who had seen it on the television set, felt safe in being friendly with. It was when he came to check out our house that everything turned bad.

My mother was one of the most beautiful women to have ever walked the earth. She had a beauty that would cause men to salivaeate and women to frown with jealousy. She had a fecund smell about her that was proscribed by all of those around. When she was younger she had dated a boy who later became a U.S. senator, Buford Smalls, and another that had become the chief justice of the U.S. Supreme Court, Pinckney Tradd. She had also dated a quarterback for the Washington Redskins and an olympic decatholete. It was always a sad ting for her to think back on all that she could have been when years later she found herself with my father, an alcoholic who was a fighter pilot and a shrimper.

When the Orkin man entered the house his eyes went straight to my mohter. They looked her up one end and down the other and he began to salivaeate with vigor. Even when he sprayed the chemicals to make the bugs go away, he looked at my mother, a look of lust that I shared but did not endulge.

When he was finished my mother paid him and he went away, but he did not go away for long. That night he came back. He did not knock and he did not ring the doorbell. He came through my window! Chicken John, who was fast asleep beside me, awoke first and stifled a cry. This woke me up and I stifled a cry as well when I saw that it was the Orkin man. He put his finger to his lips and told us to be quiet. Roy was watching television and did not pay him any mind.

"You git!" I finally said. "You shall not come into this house and cause harm! You shall leave this instant, or you shall learn to pay the consequences!"

"I shall not!" said the Orkin man. "I shall enter this house and I shall make love to your mother who is the most beautiful women that I have ever seen and shall ever see!"

"No you shall not!" I said. "He shan't!" said Chicken John.

My grandfather kept a collection of poisonous snakes that we had to take care of and we kept them in the room with us so that we could feed them when they got hungry. Chicken John grabbed one of them and helf it a loft.

Then my mother entered the room to see what the racket was and so did my grandfather. My grandfather was angry.

"Git!" he shouted. "Scat, Orkin man!"

"What do you want!" hollered my mother. "Why have you come here Orkin man!"

"I have come here for you. And I ain't leaving until I get you!"

"My mother nearly swooned.

"You best git!" screamed my grandfather. "If you know what's good for you! Git!"

And although we did not see it at the time, Chicken John was deeply wounded by this Orkin man. He took the snake and put it up the sleeve of his uniform. He then took another snake and put it up the Orkin man's pants. He then took another snake and put it down the Orkin man's pants where it bit him.

"Ow!" screamed the Orkin man.

"Git!" screamed my grandfather.

"The snake bit me!"

"Sweet Jesus! Them thing's is poisonous!"

"You gotta suck the poison out!" screamed the Orkin man.

"It's the only christian thing to do." said my grandfather, who was a very christian man who did not approve of the fact that we were all catholic because he was southern baptist. He prayed every night and said that the Lord spoke to him with prophecy.

"No!" shouted Chicken John. "Let him die!"

And at that moment I realized what had happened to Chicken John. And from that day on when ever a bad thing happened he would say, "Orkin man."

It really was too much to take, and he did not think that he could go on for another page. Creighton set the manuscript in his lap and breathed in the fecund musk of the garbage container, tired: tired of

58

being hunted, tired of it all. Only a few minutes had passed since he had sat down, yet the book made it seem like eons, the earth freezing over and thawing out several times, he a witness to nothing other than the boredom that man had endured since his springing from dust. He did not know what he would tell his son the next time he saw him. He did not know how he would explain the battle of fisticuffs that had been fought with Skipper. He wondered how the alcoholic did it. The many times awoken in his vomit, on the couch buffeted by hangover waves, all before the innocent eyes of his child. And then suddenly it dawned on him that he knew how the alcoholic did it: he just acted like nothing had ever happened. That he could do.

He thought to himself that he needed some way to connect with his son. Some sport to play. Some television show to discuss. And then it came to him. Yes. Yes. He could write a children's book and read it to his son. He could show him that Daddy had made it for him, and him only, and the two of them could read it together and laugh together and finally become the father and son that they should have been all along. It would need to involve dinosaurs without lasers and men with, and it would have to have some hidden message of reconciliation that his son would only get a whiff of, but that would worm its way into his little brain and stay there for the dark years to come. But what would the dinosaurs do? Would they speak? Were the men hunting them? Would it be a story of the men with lasers and the dinosaurs without and how the men hunted them and how one of the men found the dinosaur who had attacked the man's surrogate grandfather and how the dinosaur spoke to the man and convinced him that the surrogate grandfather was really just a man who, with the aid of modern pharmaceuticals, was jungle fucking his grandmother, and how the man had provoked the dinosaur so that the dinosaur did what any decent dinosaur would do and shoved the laser-shooting fake eye up the man's ass until he was dead? Something like that. Not exactly like that, but something like that.

He peered around the dumpster, spying up the door to his libidinous neighbor's apartment. There really was no reason for him to sit on the concrete, next to rotten chicken bones and diapers that had missed the mark, when his car was right next to the thing and provided a comfortable place to rest. He thought to himself that it might put the police off the scent, or that the scent from the trash might put them off in general, but no gumshoe worth his salt would fail to peek around the corner and find the author of *Finding It All in the Hole* with a copy of *Lowcountry Lamentations* nestled in his crotch.

He decided to get up, and when he did, who did he see but the resident of 7-E walking to his apartment, a backpack hanging off of his shoulders, and headphones on his head. Creighton, book in hand, made a mad sprint for the apartment, leapt over a boxwood, and hurried up the stairs.

FIFTEEN

Creighton was amazed by his bravado. Granted, it was not that much of a show of fearlessness, but still, to walk up there, knock on the door, and somehow try to get himself invited in showed some guts, and Creighton knew he had few. He knocked and waited, then heard the footsteps and the turn of the doorknob.

"What's up?" the young man asked.

"Hey, I'm Creighton, Creighton Starke, the author of *Finding It All in the Hole*? I live next door."

"You all right, man? You've got blood all down your nose."

"I'm fine. I, um, just got locked out and I was wondering if I could use your restroom for a second."

"Sure. Come on in."

Creighton walked past, a crazed smile drawn on his face, and headed for the bathroom, where he shut the door and turned on the water. The mirror revealed that the blood had dried down his nose to his chin, blood that had seeped from a cut on his brow that resembled an eyelet; it yearned for a stitch or two. He lowered his head in the sink and applied soap, afterwards wiping himself off with a towel that he threw to the floor.

"All better," he said when he came out. "Just like new."

"What did you do to yourself?" asked the young man.

61

"I had a fall. Not like Lucifer or anything—I'm an author, you know—but just a fall. Anyway, have you ever read my book?"

"What book?"

"*Finding It All in the Hole*?"

"No."

"It's really a great book. I think you'd like it… Now what did you say your name was?"

"I didn't."

"That's some funny name!" Creighton let out a hearty chuckle and noticed that the fellow let out a smile as well. It could not be described as a hearty smile, more of wincing smile, but Creighton viewed it as the first step to a wonderful relationship.

"Yeah. Um. My name's Scott." The fellow watched as Creighton found a seat on the couch, the manuscript under his arm, and grabbed the remote control for the television set.

"Scott's a great name. Great name. F. Scott Fitzgerald was called Scott. I never knew that—I guess I had never thought about it—but that was his name. You don't mind if I watch a little, do you?"

"Well…"

"Well, oh well, oh well," said Creighton with another laugh. "Come and have a seat. Some good shows are about to come on."

"I… I need to go to the bathroom myself."

"Well, I'll keep your seat warm for you."

"Okay," said Scott. He took a few steps, visibly struggling to say something, then stopped. "Hey, it's cool that you're here and everything, but…"

The smile on the face that stared at him hinted at madness, and the open sore on the forehead did nothing to remove the suspicion. He found it hard to say anything at all.

"Yes?" said Creighton.

"Well, you live next door, right?"

"Yes?" said Creighton, the smile frozen.

"Well, you're welcome to hang out for a while, but I've got a lot of studying to do tonight."

"Oh, I know how you study," said Creighton, who began thrusting his pelvis back and forth, accompanying the movement with a vocal rendition of the squeaky springs of a bed suffering the horrors of lovemaking. After he had done this for a few seconds, he gave Scott a wink, the smile still painfully decorating his face.

Scott was deeply troubled by Creighton's insinuation. His private recreations were apparently not as private as he had assumed and hoped. Was this blackmail? The wink seemed to say so. He tried to return Creighton's smile but could not, making quick flight to the bathroom, where he burst into tears.

SIXTEEN

Scott secreted himself for a good while in the bathroom, and Creighton found that the fool had either not taken the time or did not have the means to subscribe to a cable package, leaving only fuzzy views of the sitcom characters which were often interrupted by a burst of static that made one's teeth hurt. He did not like situation comedies, and really had little use for comedy as an art form in general, as he felt that art needed weight in order to have importance, but lately he had watched and secretly enjoyed several shows where people lived with each other and engaged in shenanigans such as stealing soap and forgetting to give phone messages. But the real reason why he watched, or the excuse that he used to justify the three to four hours a night that he sat in front of the television set, was to improve his own artistic powers, namely the sensation of despairing madness. The way he did this was by laughing every time the studio audience or laugh track did. If one has never done this before, the only comparison would be to try and consciously acknowledge every blink of the eyes. It is a forcing of what should be a natural response, and while there are probably no studies that have been conducted in this area, the result is to exhaust the participant to the point that he feels that every chuckle is a vampire suck of his life's blood. Three hours of this and the razor is in one hand, the bottle of Drano in the other, slowly making its way up to the mouth to empty its contents.

On the other side of the bathroom door, Scott sat on the edge of the tub, his face in his hands, the toilet tissue that he had stuffed in his ears doing little to block the constant cackle coming from the den. Hardly a handful of seconds went by without a laugh from the maniac, then there would be roughly three minutes of silence, only to be followed by more laughter. He did not know what to do. Thoughts of murder swirled in his head, but he did not know how he would get rid of the body. He had once seen a movie where someone was killed, hacked to pieces, then done away with via acid in the bathtub, but that would mean the procurement of acid, which he had no idea how to go about getting, and more importantly, the loss of his housing deposit due to the damage to the tub. Whether it was by murder or other means, what was clear was that he had to get rid of this author. And then it struck him. The fellow wrote books and writers pinched things from everyday life to put in them, so what was to stop this psychopath from using him in one of his novels?

When he finally made his exit, he found Creighton sitting in the same position, laughing away.

"You were in there for a while," said Creighton.

"Yeah, um, I had an upset stomach," said Scott with little conviction.

"Right," said Creighton, trying to keep his full attention on the television set and paying little to what Scott said.

Scott, in his fragile state, mistook this response as a sarcastic one, and when Creighton, following the lead of the television set, let out a wild guffaw immediately afterward, the misinterpretation was compounded. His eyes welled with tears; never before had he felt so helpless.

"What I do is none of your business," Scott said.

"Really," said Creighton, his conversational response mechanism on autopilot, the entirety of his brain concentrating on the program, which told him once again to laugh.

"It's no one's business," Scott said.

"Uh-huh," said Creighton. On the screen one of the characters had tripped over his roommate's science experiment. The look of befuddlement on his face drove the studio audience into hysterics. Creighton followed suit. Scott fled to his bedroom and locked the door behind him.

At this point a commercial came on and Creighton wiped his hands down his face as if to wash away his disgust. He then began saying something to Scott, who he found missing when he turned around for a response. There was no light on in the bathroom and the bedroom door was shut; that room was dark as well. He had no idea what had happened to his host, and this troubled him until the show came back on again.

SEVENTEEN

Savannah had tried to work herself into a state of trembling nerves and upset stomach, pacing the room and talking to herself as Mitzi packed a bag in her bedroom, gesticulating and whimpering as Mitzi watched television in the den, but by the time Mitzi went to her bedroom and turned off the lights, the carefully produced anxiety had run its course, which came to its end on the comfort of the couch. She saw Chicken John when she closed her eyes—an amalgam of the sandy-haired men who decorated the covers of Pat Conroy paperbacks—and imagined him walking to her from the end of a dock, the sun setting behind him, even though he was on the East Coast, shirtless, sculpted, sharing a smile that he had saved for the five-plus years since they had last seen each other. Taking the hippie beads from out of her purse, she said a prayer for him, for Jonathan and their children, for Roy, for Mitzi, for her beautiful mother, for her wretched father, then for herself. The sisters had always told her to pray for herself, although she did not have any sisters and had never received instruction from the Catholic church, and at times it felt selfish to do so, but not now. She was going to need help from God, if He existed, if she was going to make it through this journey.

EIGHTEEN

When the programs ended, Creighton was left with quite the dilemma. The apartment was apparently all his, but his own stood just next door, and although it was not an optimal living space, it still had the traces of life that made one call a place home. However, if his host had left to run an errand or go for a jog, then it was his duty to sit there and protect the abode until he returned. It was late, though, almost bedtime. He took out *Lowcountry Lamentations* and decided that a few pages would help soften the wait.

I stand in the shadows. Not of a building or a tree, but of the angry behemoth that was my childhood. No matter how far I run, no matter how fast I go, I cannot find the sun, and that is all that I want to find: the sun. Only it could help me grow, give color to my skin, make my blood flow once again.

The sun played a large part in my childhood. When we weren't crabbing, we were shrimping. And when we weren't shrimping or crabbing, we were swimming in the creek behind our house. Every time our parents had a fight, we would go out into the creek and form a circle, the three of us

paddling our feet as we held hands. The winter
months oftentimes left us with colds and newmonia.

We had a lot of things that we did every time
that someone did something. For example every
time someone mentioned the Orkin man Chicken John
cried and curled into the feetal position. When
we saw certain friends we had our little ceremonies too. My friend Nancy had once been scared
by a snake when we were in the marsh and she
jumped back so far that I nearly died with laughter. From then on any time that Nancy and I saw
each other I would jump back as far as I could
and we woudl laugh together. This got us into a
great deal of trouble at school every day but it
was great fun. It was just the southern way to do
things like that so we did them.

My father was always difficult when he returned
from his missions overseas. There he would fly
over foreign countries and kill people with his
bombs and it was like he still wanted to kill
people when he returned, but instead of him
kiling strangers he wanted to kill his family!
He had returned from a foreign country and after
a few weeks in the boat it was obvious that it
was not going to be a good shrimping season and
that made life around the house even more difficult. Chicken John needed new shoes and I needed
a new dress but Mama told us that we wouldn't
be getting either this year unless the shrimp
started biting.

We were sitting around the dinner table one
night when my father told my mother that he did
not like what he was eating.

"A dog wouldn't eat this food." he said. This made my mother mad. "Fix me something I can eat woman!"

"Father!" I said. "I like this food. This is very good food mother!"

"I like it too mother!" Chicken John said.

"You're always takin up for your mama boy!" my father screamed hitting Chicken John on the head. He then took a fork and stuck it in Chicken John's arm.

"You're hurting the child!" my mother shouted.

"Stop it!" I hollered. "He's just a boy!"

My father stopped and looked at us. "All of you is always teamin up on me! Git! Git out of my sight! I want you to og into that kitchen and fix me somethin to eat! Now!"

We had a pet lion that my father had bought from a traveling circus with our entire inheritance and we kept its food in cans so that we could feed it. My eyes grew wide when I saw my mother opening one of the cans.

"Mother!"

"Hush child! Now Chicken John you help me dice up the celery and you Savannah you help me get some parsley going."

I got the parsely going as best as I could and mother made the dish with the parsley and diced celery. When it was finished we brought it into the dining room where my father sat. He looked at it for a second and then began to eat. The lioned roared off in the distance.

Then all of the sudden a buzzing sound came out of nowhere. I did not know what it was. "What is it?" I asked. "What is that buzzing sound?"

And before we knew it the entire house was filled with locusts.

"Run!" screamed my grandfather. "Run for your lives!"

"Where!" Chicken John shouted.

"To the barn!" hollered my grandfather.

I remember running with the locusts biting at me, searching for higher ground and as I did it dawned on me that our crops would be ruined and that my father would have to go work at the gas station in order for us to keep living. But I knew that day, as I know now, that I didn't know if I wanted to go on living if life was going to be like this.

Where in the hell was Scott? Creighton thought of calling the hospitals or the police, but considering his present circumstances, he did not think that either would be a show of wisdom. The boy could be out in a ditch somewhere, however, lying with a broken leg, ebbing away into the eternal void, while Creighton sat there on the couch feeling his head ache. At that moment, down from the laughing exercise, dragged to the depths by *Lowcountry Lamentations,* he was suddenly lifted up high with an idea. It was so fresh in his mind that he considered getting in his car and driving straight to the office just to write it down. Here's what it was: a middle-aged man living a typical humdrum life of white suburbia goes for a jog one night and is hit by a car. In his ditch of agony, his leg broken, his life force slipping away, he is flooded with recollections of his previous forty-something years. These memories range from childhood to last week and the beauty of it was that he would remember it as people really remember things, not in chronological order, but just in bits and pieces flashing from age to age. These memories would be interposed with his present situation—perhaps a momentary scare on account of a rabies-ridden rat or a poisonous snake, whatever, but clearly lots of pain and despair—until it became a wonderful collage of what life is: just this and that, with a little bit of spice thrown in—yes, there would be several sex scenes with several different women (the readership! the readership!)—until he would achieve this epiphany, who knows what it would be, perhaps that his life was meaningless, perhaps that it was meaningful, until either he is saved or is found dead. Yes, yes, a touch of *The Death of Artemio Cruz* with *The Big Chill* thrown in, a few Faulknerian stream-of-consciousness passages to give it weight until he could see himself. Clearly. Standing before the students at some college in the Midwest, half-drunk and fully beloved, reading a passage here and there, throwing out pieces of wisdom, an occasional joke, until a sad, thunderous applause marked his time to go on to the next one.

This gave him great satisfaction and justified the three hours that he had watched television, allowing him to close his eyes and picture the results until they began to be driven away by his subconscious, which filled his brain with a fairly pointless situation comedy. He was looking for his toothbrush, but deep inside he knew that his faceless roommate had used it to clean his shoes.

NINETEEN

Several hours later Savannah awoke and relieved herself in Mitzi's bathroom. When finished, she flipped on the light switch in the hall, then the light switch in Mitzi's bedroom. Mitzi awoke with a hand shielding her squinting, myopic eyes, a paste of green covering her face. Savannah channeled Conroy:

"Let's move it, split-tail. Charleston is two hours away."

"What?" asked Mitzi. "What are you doing? What time is it?" She grabbed her glasses and checked the clock by her bedside.

"Be dressed and into the car in five minutes. We're breaking camp. The Japs are on the move again."

"The Japs?" asked Mitzi. "Jeez Louise, it's two o'clock in the morning."

Savannah paused for a moment, her mind racing for dialogue.

"Um. You're supposed to ask me why we have to drive at night."

"We're driving at night?"

"Yes."

"Why?"

"There you go. You make good time traveling at night. The kids can sleep, no cars on the road, it's cooler, and you don't waste a day getting there."

"What kids? Savannah, what's going on? I was dead asleep, and you come in here shouting about split-tails and Japs moving…I'm tired and I want to go to bed. Now leave me alone."

"No can do, Marine," said Savannah, with a lunatic smile. This was going far better than she had ever imagined. "Now you get your lazy split-tail out of that rack and be in the car by O-two hundred hours or you're gonna wish you'd never been born."

"Are you threatening me? Good Lord, what's gotten into you?"

"This is how it is, Mitzi. This is how it's supposed to be."

"How what's supposed to be?"

"In the books. This is how it is. Now get out of the rack, or you'll have double KP duty, sportsfans."

TWENTY

After several more minutes of cajoling and shifting in and out of character, Savannah convinced Mitzi to gather her belongings and get in the car. Mitzi, who was legally blind in the day and morbidly blind at night, conceded the driver's seat to Ms. D'Bergeolet and placed the pillow she had brought along against the doorframe where she rested her head. Savannah eased the car into gear and began to drive away.

No maps had been consulted prior to the trip and the reality of it was that Savannah had not put any thought as to how they would get there, only what they would do when they got there. She drove along the streets of the nameless town, looking for signs to Charleston, but such signs did not exist. Soon she found herself in Lexington County traveling along Knox Abbott Drive, the wind whistling through the window that she had rolled down. Mitzi had returned to sleep in the passenger's seat.

"What song should we sing?" asked Savannah, wading again into *The Great Santini* pool. "Why, sportsfans, what song do we always sing first?"

Possibly due to the noise made by the wind, but probably due to her mounting excitement, Savannah lanced the air with her words, causing Mitzi to once again bid *adieu* to the land of dreams.

"What?" Mitzi asked.

"Come on, sportsfans!" shouted Savannah.

From the halls of Montezuma to the shores of Tripoli

"Come on, sportsfans!"

We will fight our country's battles

"Sing it loud, sportsfans!"

on land, on air, on sea!

Mitzi, who was no fan of sports, shared an equal dislike for patriotic music. She emitted a groan and ignored Savannah's pleas to join in her poor rendition.

"Will you please shut up? I don't know the words and I don't like the song. Especially when it's sang at two o'clock in the morning when I'm trying to sleep."

"Okay," said Savannah, "you sing 'Dixie' and I'll sing 'The Battle Hymn of the Republic.' I'll sing a winner's song and you sing a loser's song."

"I don't want to sing any song. I don't want you to sing any song. I want you to be quiet."

Mine eyes have seen the glory of the coming of the Lord

"Come on, sportsfans!"

"Shut up! Stop it! Just shut up!"

Savannah fell quiet for a moment, and Mitzi interpreted the cessation of sound as an acknowledgment of defeat, once again setting her head against the pillow, which she squeezed and punched in order to get it in its proper shape. Her eyes could not have been closed for more than thirty seconds before Savannah began once more.

"Let me ask you a question, sentry. What are the responsibilities of a man on guard duty?"

"What?" asked Mitzi.

"What are the responsibilities of a man on guard duty?"

"How am I supposed to know?" Mitzi rose once more from her pillow and gave a look of haggard dislike to Savannah.

"Your mother always slacks up on you when I go overseas. Give me the ones you know."

"I don't know any. I don't even know what you're talking about. And what does my mother have to do with you going overseas?"

"You skipped about a hundred of 'em…"

"I think I skipped all of them."

"…You ought to know those if you're gonna be on duty. I'll give you a week to relearn 'em once we get to Charleston."

"A week? You're planning on spending a week? Turn this car around."

"Never make excuses."

"I'm not making excuses. I'm telling you to turn this car around and take me back. I can't be gone for a week."

"We're almost there," said Savannah. "Just think of the look of surprise on Chicken John's face when he sees us."

"Savannah, I can't spend a week in Charleston. I can't miss that much school. Besides, all I brought was forty dollars."

"Oh, Mitzi. First, saying that you'll have a week is just a figure of speech. You don't think Ben Meechum really had a full week to learn all of that stuff, do you? He probably had about an hour. Second, as for money, I have tons of friends in Charleston, so you shouldn't expect to pay for a meal or a place to stay once we get down there. It's the Southern way… this way… um… of not paying…for things…"

Mitzi looked deeply, blindly at Savannah, then leapt into the back of the car, stretching out on the seat. Savannah's reattempts at getting the Marine hymn going met with cold indifference.

TWENTY-ONE

Razor Roy Edwards and Magik Merlin had not entered any chat room and they had not purchased anything from a retailer. Instead, they wandered through the confines of virtual space, landing in the ripe fields of a fantasy role playing game, which was apropos, for that was where they had met several years before. Roy was a dwarf—not in real life, although he was not incredibly tall—named Ut, who carried with him a battle axe that had given the land many a drink of blood, several protective potions, a short list of spells, and a hearty love of grog, which was the drink of choice for dwarves. Magik Merlin, on the other hand, was, as is expected, a magician, who with the title of Abyssymus could calmly claim a long list of spells, the ability to shape-shift, extra health points, and a love of Gnotos weed, which he smoked in a long-stemmed pipe. They happened upon each other in an uninhabited field in the land of Mongor. Roy's screen read something like this:

```
Walk

Walk

Walk

Down a hill

Left
```

```
Abyssymus the Magician
Walk

Walk

Walk
```

From there, to steal a cliché, the rest is history. They spent the remainder of the day (night in the land of flesh and blood) walking about the Mongorian plains, occasionally seeing a tree or a bird (`Bird. Tree.`) and talking about their respective homelands, the evil of Congor that was falling over the empire, their love of grog and Gnotos weed, and other things that magicians and dwarves tend to go on about. It was after an hour that the fabrications of their parallel lives unraveled, leaving them with nothing to say. Magik Merlin first broke the taboo, and as they crossed a river (`River.`) they discussed the fact that they both lived in South Carolina, enjoyed computer role-playing games, appreciated the majesty of the musical group Rush, and in general thought that what they were doing was as exciting as space travel.

This was the icebreaker, but what turned this tentative friendship into a pact of steel was what happened two nights later in the Haunted Woods of Oberegon. Walking along (`Walk. Walk.`), they were ambushed by the Grocks of the evil Congor. Ut quickly went for his battle axe and Abyssymus, in a matter of three keystrokes, unleashed a flesh-eating pox on the Grocks that came down in the shape of a cloud. Thus, the first sally of Grocks was conquered. The next wave came as the first one had—from seemingly out of nowhere—and this time Ut cast a spell of deep fatigue over the Grocks then dispatched them with low-level swings, and Abyssymus turned into a tiger and ate his fill. This went on for quite some time, and at such a pace that the two barely had the necessary seconds to type out things like, "They're coming! They're coming!" and "Thou Grock legion, hath thou not hadst thy fill of battle axe!"

All of the above sounds very intriguing—or at least the author would hope—to the reader as it is written, but as it was lived, or perhaps as it would have been witnessed by a disinterested third party, it was not. The typing of `Walk. Walk.` can give one the idea of what was written in the battle, namely `Swing. Swing. Abyssymus has shapeshifted into a tiger. Eat. Eat.` and the like. For this was a game of creative, not visual, fantasy. There were no Grocks being thrown around. At no time did the color red in the form of a liquid or letter find its way on to the screen. Imagine somehow working yourself into a heart-palpitating set of damp hands as you, the detective, hunt down the perverse Professor Plum, who, with the candlestick, took a life in the library, then afterwards expecting accolades from the local press for your feat, and perhaps you will get the picture.

Magik Merlin faced north, and Razor Roy faced west, each eyeing his respective computer screen, each transformed into his alter ego in the town of Tribium, which is located off the coast of the Salt Sea. Tribium, as one knows from basic geography, is a town of pirates, prostitutes, and pickpockets, and very little of what is good takes place there. The night before the two had booked safe passage from Captain Silverbeard, a gentleman who worked the second shift at an automotive plant in Michigan, and although they were tossed by the waves and beaten by the winds, they found port, obtained lodging, then went to virtual sleep where they dreamt virtual dreams. `(Dream. Dream.)`

Upon re-entering the game, the two awoke and Abyssymus suggested that they find some Gnotos weed and grog, a suggestion that Ut seconded. They exited their sleeping quarters and descended the stairs to a room filled with various other members of the virtual community, all lolling around a bar, drinking, eating, and playing cards. A bartender called to them across the way, but before they could even reach their keypads, both Abyssymus and Ut were swooped down upon by prostitutes who solicited them in high-flown language with offers of low-born pleasures. Ut, whose mind centered on war and the conquering of the evil Congor, had no interest in these virtual carnalities and rebuffed the gender-confused Methodist pastor from Toronto with a showing of his battle axe and a shout to the bartender for grog. The result was not the same for Abyssymus. Unlike his friend, the adventures and pressures of the past several weeks had lain the wizard low, and he was in no mood to fight, or to continue this monk's life of discipline and denial. Certainly, he was concerned about the evil Congor, and most undoubtedly his destruction was his first and foremost goal, but Congor was going nowhere at the moment and the Iridian lass described herself in such a way that there was no doubt but that she would bring sweet balm to his tattered heart. After haggling for a moment, changing into a tiger, then sealing the financial deal, Abyssymus and Keiliae, a single mother employed as a bookkeeper at a brake factory in Ohio, walked back up the stairs and made voracious love in Ut's bed.

Thirty minutes later, Abyssymus returned to the bar, his wallet several kinars lighter and his health level several points lower. Ut, who during this time had killed two-pickpockets and cut the hands off another, was busy trying to get away from a prostitute who simply would not take no for an answer when he saw his friend. He immediately ran to his side. "We must go out and buy provisions for the long trek across the Irang desert. We must also secure guides. I have spoken to an Iridian wizard who tells me that both of these can be secured at the Shop of Despairing Souls. Let us gather our things and go."

At this point the prostitute Jerelda, a divorced labor and delivery nurse from Arkansas, refound Ut, and once again tried to entice him with her wares. "Aback and avast woman!" said Ut. "Or you will taste my battle axe!" "How much?" asked Abyssymus. Ut stood there fuming as Abyssymus agreed to swap a spell which could make water flow from rocks, one that the two of them would obviously need, or at least like to have, for a journey across a desert, in exchange for sexual intercourse wherein Jerelda would consent to allow Abyssymus to do things to her that were illegal even in Tribium. A shapeshifting into a tiger, yet another waste of resources, and the two retraced the steps that Abyssymus had just made. Ut went for more grog.

The pimp of the prostitutes Abyssymus devoured that long afternoon had never seen such business from a single customer. One can wonder why a bookkeeper, nurse, housewife, welder, and so on and so forth, would voluntarily engage in a lifestyle that in the real world is generally a result of drug addiction or dire poverty—this was their dream existence after all—but regardless of their reasons, they were all well paid, and by the end Abyssymus was near death, flat broke, and compelled to use his final spell to rid himself of the host of virtual venereal diseases that he had contracted. From the numerous tankards of grog, Ut's walk had been changed by the game masters into a stumble (`Stumble. Stumble.`), and at the moment his anger did not burn toward Congor, but towards his wizard friend.

"I see that wise Abyssymus is not so wise, squandering our resources on vile streetwalkers."

"Hold thy tongue, base dwarf, and never again speak to me in such a way. Yes, be glad that at the moment I am unable to shape-shift into a tiger, or you would feel my claws."

"Thy claws, foolish Abyssymus, will not spring forth again for some time. You have lost thy magic; you have lost thy health. You have no money with which to buy provisions. I think that life shall requireth thee to become a streetwalker thyself in order to restore thy money purse."

"Traitor!"

"I have betrayed no one, you toothless fool. It is you who have betrayed the cause. Somewhere Congor sits laughing, for the quest has been cast down on account of your base weakness."

At this insult, Abyssymus struck Ut, but the only effect of the blow was to further weaken the wizard. Ut, his mind clouded with rage and grog, did not stop to think the situation through and drew his battle axe, with which he split his companion in half.

Over to his right, Razor Roy heard a gasp erupt from the throat of someone in the room, and lost in the artificial world, he awoke to

83

the real one, suddenly remembering that Magik Merlin was there with him. He quickly sent Ut back up to his bedroom, where he put him to sleep in the damp sheets of the late Abyssymus's saturnalia.

The two men sat staring at the screens, all quiet, all still, then Magik Merlin broke into a sob, followed by a roar of rage. His hands slammed on the top of the Formica desk, and he kicked away his chair, turning to Razor Roy.

"I thought we were friends!"

"We were, but you went and ruined everything!" said Roy, his voice aquiver. "Don't worry about it. Don't worry. You can get another character."

"Another character! Oh God." And Magik Merlin broke into another sob. "All of these credit card bills. They're eating me alive. My wife just left me... and... and... I just wanted to have some fun, and...and...the Iridian wench seemed so nice...and... and... oh God...first she leaves me, then I'm going to be kicked out of my house, and now Abyssymus is dead!"

"You can revive him!" said Razor Roy. "You know that."

"Yeah, sure. For five hundred dollars I can. But how am I going to get five hundred dollars?"

There was silence.

"You, you son of a bitch. You killed me. You killed me." Magik Merlin's voice had lowered to a toneless growl, and air huffed out of his nose in porcine bursts.

Roy was unsure of what to do. He had, in fact, killed Abyssymus, a character in whose unearthly shell Magik Merlin had dwelled for the past two years night after night. In a rare moment of introspection, Roy thought of how he would feel if someone had killed Ut, thought of what he would do to the person if he got his hands on him, then he suddenly became very afraid. Magik Merlin took a step toward him, and Roy tried with all he had to channel the courage of Ut and respond.

"I can call my dad," he said. "He'll be glad to lend you five hundred bucks."

Magik Merlin stood still for a moment, his eyes burning brightly in his beard, and then he spoke: "He better."

The magician retrieved the phone from its charging cradle and handed it to the captive, whose nervous index finger shook as it tried to punch in the numbers. At the first one, a voice shocked him into terror.

"No, no, no! I'm not paying for your long-distance calls. You think I'm made out of money or something?"

"No, of course not," said Razor Roy, who hung up and began again, this time with the number zero, which really isn't a number, as Miss Sunflower had said, to which the Davinator had demurred.

The collect call was accepted by Harry Edwards, who moments before had been dead asleep.

"What? What is it?" asked Mr. Edwards.

"Dad, it's Roy."

"I know that, you idiot. Why are you calling me collect, at… at… Jesus, it's almost three o'clock in the morning."

"Um. Listen Dad, the reason I'm calling you is my friend, Magik Merlin, well, we were playing this game, and I accidentally killed his wizard, Abyssymus, and anyway, it's going to take five hundred dollars to bring him back to life, and so, anyway…"

It was at this point that Harry Edwards hung up the phone. Roy had no option but to continue speaking into the void.

"Yeah, five hundred dollars. You can? Great. No, we need it now. Yeah, I know where that is." Turning to Magik Merlin: "He can do it," and giving a thumbs up. "Yeah, I'll come right now. No, it's no problem. No problem at all. Thanks a lot, Dad. This really means a lot. Yeah, I love you, too. Bye."

Roy hit the off button and stood up.

"Well, the good news is that I've got your five hundred dollars. The bad news is that I've got to drive back home to get it."

"I'll come with you," said Magik Merlin.

"You will?" said Roy with a meager gulp. "Um. Great."

"Yeah, just let me go put some pants on."

"Cool. I tell you what. I'll go ahead and warm up the car and wait for you there."

"All right. I'll only be a minute."

The moment Magik Merlin turned his back, Roy Edwards raced towards the door. He fired the engine to a start, then threw the car in reverse. It screeched to a stop, then flew forward, leaving Magik Merlin with a pair of pants and the bitter knowing that Abyssymus would remain forever dead.

TWENTY-TWO

It was the wet-lipped kiss of fate that blessed Savannah and Mitzi with a sign that spelled out *Charleston Highway*. With an illegal u-turn, they appeared to be on their way.

"Mitzi. Wake up."

After a few moments without a response, Savannah tried again.

"What?" asked Mitzi. "What is it?"

"We're on our way to Charleston," said Savannah.

"That's great, Savannah. Wake me up when we get there."

"There's so much I want to tell you about Charleston, Mitzi. So much I want to show you." And here, Savannah again channeled Conroy. "Entering Charleston is like walking through the brilliant carbon forest of a diamond with the light dazzling you in a thousand ways, an assault of light and shadow caused by light."

"Uh-huh," said Mitzi. "Sounds great. Let me know when it's light so that I can let it dazzle me. Until then, please leave me alone and let me sleep."

"The city has a smell, a fecund musk of aristocracy, with the wine and the history of the low country aging beneath the verandahs, and sweetly decadent odors of lost causes."

"This just isn't going to happen, is it?" asked Mitzi. "This sleeping thing for me." She gave out a loud moan and crawled back over into the front seat. Once settled, she turned to Savannah. "Now what were you talking about?"

"Charleston."

"No, I know that. You said something about its fecund musk."

"Yes, I certainly did."

"Well, what were you talking about?"

"The musk of Charleston. It's very fecund."

"And what does that mean?"

"Musk?"

"No, the fact that it's fecund. I don't know what that means."

Savannah let out a laugh.

"Oh, Mitzi. There are so many things you don't know about right now, that after this journey you will. It's not something that can be explained. We Geechee girls of the low country grew up with the fecund musk in our nostrils, in our hair, in our blood, and to try to explain it, to try and describe it, especially to someone who did not grow up in the low country, is like trying to describe what an oyster tastes like, or what it's like to work on a shrimp boat. You have to live it; to be it. Words don't do it justice."

"Well, that's fine. I'm not trying to get you to describe it. I just want to know what the word *fecund* means. It sounds like it means it stinks. Like you can imagine an armpit being fecund, or a dirty pair of socks."

"Mitzi, I will not allow you to say such things!" said Savannah, turning in her seat to give Mitzi a hard stare. "Do you think I would be so excited if Charleston smelled like an armpit or a pair of dirty socks? Do you?"

"I don't know, Savannah," said Mitzi. "I wasn't trying to be offensive. I just want to know what the word means. I didn't mean anything by it."

"That reminds me of the harsh words used by the judge when he was drunk. He didn't mean anything by them either, but the people to whom they were directed felt them and were wounded by them, so that in the end it didn't matter that he meant nothing by them. His intentions were irrelevant; only the results were."

"What judge?"

"Judge McCall from *Beach Music*. The father of Jack and the others. He was a good man when he didn't drink, but not a very good one when he did. The problem was that he often drank. Yes, it ruined his marriage to his wife and caused his children to grow up damaged. Damaged each in ways that they couldn't put their finger on, but that were still clear."

"I don't want to marry a man who drinks, and I don't want to marry a man who smokes," said Mitzi. "I guess he could occasionally chew tobacco, but he couldn't do it around me. He'd have to do it while he was on the toilet or something. They say it's supposed to help you when you go, you know. Tobacco. I guess it's the nicotine, but it's supposed to help you go."

"Mitzi, how am I supposed to put this in my book? Hm? We're supposed to be talking about our parents and our high school days and the horrors that we endured and the state championships that we won and the people we knew who grew up to be governors and senators and heads of the U.N. What we're not supposed to be talking about is laxatives. I can see it now, the beginning of the fateful journey, page 89, the discussion of bowel movements. Now there is nothing wrong with calling people such things. In the books people are often called zit-face, or compared to urine samples, jockstraps, and blood blisters and such, so I guess it's okay to say that someone resembles a bowel movement, but you can't just talk about having a bowel movement."

"Well, I don't know all of the rules of your books like you do, so you start."

"I guess I should begin with my mother."

"Fine."

Conroy leapt into her brain. "My mother was as lovely a woman as I have ever seen, bred and nurtured like a gardenia, she has always seemed somehow odorless and sexless to me, yet viscerally seductive in the manner of Southern women, that taloned species who speak with restrained and self-effacing drawls, fill a room with elegance and vulnerability, move with the grace of a wind-tilted cane, and rule their families with a secret pact of steel."

"Um-hm."

"She was always too pretty to be my mother. You know, Mitzi, there is nothing more erotic on earth than a girl in love with the shape and touch of her mother. It is the most exquisite, most proscribed lust. It is also the most natural and damaging. I take my mother to bed with me every night and I cannot help it."

Mitzi did not give a quick reply.

"Um. I guess I've just never seen my mother as being erotic. I always saw her in her curlers and such, cleaning out the commodes, washing my underwear…'

"I know, you think it's a little sicko-sexual," said Savannah with a laugh. "That's what Mary Anne always said to Ben, that he was sicko-sexual when it came to his mother. But she just didn't understand how erotic a girl's mother could be to her."

"It's just…taking your mother to bed with you every night? Does that mean that you…and what does *proscribed* mean?"

"What?"

"Proscribed. What does it mean?"

"Do you want to try the Marine hymn again?" Savannah asked after a moment of silence.

TWENTY-THREE

Savannah blamed it on the fact that Mitzi would not sing the Marine hymn. A sentry had many duties, many, many duties, and although Savannah was only aware of a few, she felt sure that one of them was to keep the person you were sentrying with awake by singing songs and such. Therefore, she did not feel bad about the fact that she was getting so tired. Not her fault. Not at all.

The lines in the road had begun to blur, her neck a wilting stalk needing manure or whatever it was that kept a stalk from wilting, making her think that they needed to stop and rest for the night. Mitzi was trying to achieve sleep in the seat next to her, and all around them the night formed a hollow darkness.

It was when they reached a town known as Holly Hill that Savannah decided to pull over. To call Holly Hill a town would imply that there was a main street and shops and the like, but this was not the case. All that was visible to the eye from the highway was farmland, so this is where Savannah stopped the car and cut the engine. The relative silence caused Mitzi to raise her head.

"Why aren't we moving?" she asked.

"'Cause the car ain't moving, split-tail," said Savannah. "Now get out of your rack and let's set up camp. The Japs could be moving in any second."

"Camp?"

"Yeah, we're going to set up camp, sportsfans."

"I think I'll just stay in the car and sleep. I don't want to lay down in the dirt."

"That would be a negative, sportsfans. We're camping."

"Savannah, I don't want to camp."

"Mitzi, for goodness sakes. We can't go on some journey and sleep in the car. We're Geechee girls. We grew up camping and shrimping and boating and doing all kinds of things."

"Maybe you did, but I didn't. I quit the Brownies when they started camping."

"Well, this isn't the Brownies. And quit talking about stuff like that. No one talks about being in the Brownies in the books. Maybe someone could get kicked out of the Brownies for playing some prank on a Brownie leader—some wild Southern prank—but no self-respecting Geechee girl would ever quit, much less say she quit, because she didn't like camping."

There was little reason behind Savannah's argument, but whatever reason there was, Mitzi seemed to accept it. She opened her door and got out.

"You look for wood for the fire," said Savannah, who too had alighted from the car. "I'm going to make sure the ground's good for camping."

"It's pitch black out here, Savannah. I can't even see my hand in front of my face. There's no way I'll find any wood."

"Mitzi, again, which would be better for the book: the two of us laying in the dark, or the two of us laying by a fire?"

"Well, just put in your book that we had a fire. No one's going to know or care."

"I would care, and so would my readers. The reason these books are so good, Mitzi, is because they're so true to life. Men do support themselves by writing cookbooks in Italy and involve themselves in conspiracies with the Catholic church. Every day. Men do fall in love with women so deeply that they track them down across two states only to be eaten by tigers. People do write poetry that makes them incredibly famous, and that people actually read. You see, this is the truth, and this is how it is, so that is how my book will be. And you can't forget about the movie. How could they even shoot this scene without a campfire? Hm? You tell me that, Mitzi, and maybe we'll sleep in the dark."

Mitzi had never really thought of her life as a movie, and even if she had, she certainly would have never stopped to consider the lighting. Still, she knew that she would not find any wood unless she stumbled upon it, and she didn't feel like stumbling around in the dark. She therefore stood in place as Savannah busied herself with laying two beach towels out in the dirt. After a few minutes, Mitzi cleared her throat.

"Back already?" Savannah asked.

"Yeah," said Mitzi.

"Well, did you find the wood?"

"Um. No."

"Why not?"

"Um." The chemicals in Mitzi's brain sluiced across one another like syrup through oil, until finally she had an idea. "Um. I was out there, way out there, and I saw a light."

"A light?"

"Yes. So, I went to see what it was, and it was a bunch of men shouting things around a fire. Very bad things."

"Were they saying 'Livery of Seisin?'"

"Um. Yes. They were."

"Oh my God, Mitzi. What else?" Savannah tried to run to Mitzi and grab her by the shoulders, but she could not find her in the dark, and thus she looked like a madwoman chasing an imaginary cat.

"Um. They talked with each other, and I accidentally dropped one of the logs that I was carrying, so they stopped talking, and I was scared so I dropped the rest of the logs and came back here."

"Did they follow you?"

"No."

"Are you sure?"

"Absolutely."

"The Ten," said Savannah in a whisper.

"The what?" asked Mitzi.

"I don't want to scare you tonight, Mitzi, especially before we go to bed, but the people that you saw, if they had caught you, would have shot electrical charges into your genitals and doused you with water."

"That doesn't sound so bad."

"It would have been, especially if you had been black."

"But I'm not black."

"Be thankful. Not that you're not black—we would probably all be better off if we were, we would have a better understanding of the truer things in life, a wisdom not found in books but in the world— but just because if they had found you they would have surely shot electrical charges into your genitals."

Mitzi, who thought that electrical charges shot into her genitals could perhaps be pleasurable, silently wished that there had actually been a group of men and that she were black, but nevertheless, was sure that the thought would not keep her from sleeping as Savannah feared. She therefore walked over to the beach towels and lay down. Savannah joined her.

"Just look at the stars, Mitzi."

"It's cloudy. You can't see any stars."

"On a night like this I could navigate the Edisto River and catch a whole bushel of shrimp and mull gravy. Just by the stars."

"You can't see any stars."

"We Geechee girls can."

WEDNESDAY

TWENTY-FOUR

Savannah and Mitzi were awoken by the sunlight. It came pouring through their eyelids, red replacing black, causing a stirring that made all efforts to resituate themselves fruitless. Mitzi was the first one to say anything, and her initial words were not words, but a series of unenunciated grunts and moans, accompanied by the high whisking sounds of her fingernails scraping across her skin.

"Mitzi, do you have fleas?" Savannah asked.

"No—or at least I hope I don't." She rubbed her eyes for a moment to refocus them, then reset her glasses on her nose. "Look at this. Look at this." She pointed to the red dots that covered her skin in no apparent order, chaos brought home in the shape of welts. "We've been eaten alive."

The mosquitoes and chiggers of Holly Hill could not comprehend the reason for their good fortune—two young, blood-ripe women, who apparently did not know how to swat, laid out before them like some end-of-the-world feast—but one can imagine them having spent their entire lives raising unanswered prayers to their mosquito and chigger gods, and now rejoicing in the longed-for fulfillment of these wishes, for feast they had.

"I don't think anything has eaten me," said Savannah, "but perhaps something has eaten part of your brain. I don't know what else could possibly cause you to say something so painfully stupid."

"Not literally," said Mitzi. "I mean we've been bitten by insects."

Savannah looked at the bites, then laughed. "Oh, Mitzi, in my circles these are called low-country kisses. When we were young, we used to pretend that these were from our boyfriends."

Mitzi thought for a moment.

"My mother told me that if a boy ever gave me anything like this that we needed to get to the doctor fast and to not tell my Daddy, as he would go over and kill him, which meant that Daddy would have to spend the rest of his life in prison, and we would wind up in the poor house."

"Oh, your perfect family! How you go on about them, Mitzi. But now that you bring it up, family is a topic that I will be forced at some point to discuss at length. But not now. Oh, Mitzi, we have to break away from the past. Break away. We are shackled by history, by our grandfathers who fought with Beauregard in the Civil War and our fathers who flew jets before becoming shrimpers; we must sever the bonds that caused our mothers to be the prettiest women in the world and earn our proscribed lust. Yes, they taught us about low-country kisses, but did they ever teach us to cry? No, they didn't. They never did, and for that I can never forgive them. I think about Chicken John, and you know what, even though his loss causes me untold misery and sadness, I have never taken the time to cry over him. Never."

"You were just crying over him yesterday at my place."

"That was different. I was not crying over him—oh, how I wish I could—I wasn't really even crying. I'm not allowed to cry, but now that you say that perhaps it would have been good if I could have cried yesterday. It would have lifted me out of these dark depths where I dwell and allowed me to return to the land of the living. It's been so long. So very, very long."

"Since yesterday?"

"No, since I cried last."

"But…"

"Mitzi, I don't want to hear another word of it. The two of us being covered with low-country kisses will make a wonderful addition to the book, but what won't make a wonderful addition is you complaining about them. Act like a lady and rejoice in this plot twist. Don't sit around and mope as though you've come down with the plague."

"Fine. Fine. Whatever. I can hardly stand to be awake I itch so bad."

"Badly."

"What?"

"You itch badly."

"I think I'm doing just as good of a job as you are."

At that point, the strains of a song reached their ears, which perked a bit and caused them to drop into silence. Their heads were stilled, listening intently, and only after a few moments of this did they turn to see a black man walking through the field, coming toward them.

"Listen to that, Mitzi," said Savannah. "This is how it is in the low country. The African Americans sing African American spirituals that would make Mozart blush with envy. Listen to the pain in the man's voice. His song is of sorrow, yet at the same time, it is a song of freedom, of hope. I remember my wet nurse singing them to me as a child as I suckled her breast; they have stayed with me for eternity."

"I don't think that's a spiritual," said Mitzi. "At least it doesn't sound like one."

As to this, Mitzi could consider herself correct. Although it was an old song, it did not date back to the days of yore, and there was nothing spiritual about it, for the man approaching them was not a fan of such melodious tales of woe. He preferred a more lighthearted fare and was enjoying the tune of "Don't Sit under the Apple Tree" by The Andrews Sisters, who were as close to being African American as, well, any group of white girls from Minnesota. The words were thus:

Don't sit under the apple tree with anyone else but me
Anyone else but me, anyone else but me, no, no, no
Don't sit under the apple tree with anyone else but me
Till I come marching home.

And unlike the funereal tone that Savannah imagined, its consistency, if it could have a consistency, was that of a hardened sugared paste that breaks one's teeth. Still, given her past with such spirituals, which she did not have, Savannah was moved to silent tears. She ordered Mitzi up from the ground, and together the two of them walked over to the unexpected troubadour.

As she approached, Savannah wracked her brain for her Gullah dictionary. Although it was her belief that she had learned this language from her wet nurse, this belief had about as much validity as those held by flat-earthers, as she did not have a wet nurse in her infancy nor had she ever heard anyone speak Gullah. No, her only exposure to it was through the novels of her beloved modern Southern authors and a Gullah dictionary by Virginia Mixson Geraty that she had perused more than once. But, like always, the truth was irrelevant.

"Mitzi, I grew up speaking Gullah from the time I could make my first words." Here, she veered into Benton Frank. "Reference to the Gullah culture and its language leaves a lot of people baffled. It is one of six Creole languages still spoken in this country. My usage of it is designed only to heighten awareness of yet another distinct feature of the low country. Gullah is a language of love, taught to little white barefooted island brats like me by loving women descended from slavery."

"Um-hm," said Mitzi.

"It's crazy though. My being a Geechee girl and all. I feel sorry for people who didn't have that upbringing because it's what gives me my zip, my personality."

"Yes," said Mitzi.

"So let me do the talking," said Savannah. "We speak in a language that only those raised in the low country can decipher."

The man was now close to them, and he raised a hand and waved hello. He wore a suit and tie. His shoes were wingtips. Savannah cleared her throat to begin.

"Ebenin', suh! Cootuh good fuh mek soup. Dat clap-hat-bitch done clubbuh-claw 'e juntlemun clap 'e hat on 'e head en' gone. Ma duh aguhnize 'kase de dog nyam de aig!" At hearing these words, the man's expression resembled that given when an object is unexpectedly shoved up one's anus. Yes, he was perplexed; yes, he was disturbed, but it was not on account of his surprise at this young white woman's speaking in the Gullah dialect. The fact of the matter was that he neither spoke nor understood Gullah, but even if he did, his reaction would have been the same, for how does one respond to the following: "Good evening, sir! Cooters make good soup. That virago has mauled her husband, put on her hat, and left. Mother is fretting because the dog ate the eggs!"?

He decided that these women were either Eastern European or mentally challenged, and given that he had great sympathy for both, he gave a veneered smile and nodded his head.

"Good morning, ladies. Where did you two come from?"

"Beebuh bil' dam een de ribbuh. De hog behime de fench!"

"Yes, yes," he replied with an even deeper smile because it was true that beavers did build dams in the river, and who was he to contest the assertion that the hog was behind the fence? These poor, filthy, mentally challenged immigrants, out in the middle of nowhere. He fingered the cell phone in his pocket and pondered as to who were the proper authorities to contact in such a situation. "It's beautiful out here, huh?"

At that, Savannah laughed and said, "Uh ent able fuh credik de g'ocery. Dis de man wuh t'ief de hog."

He looked at Savannah, his smile gone, and shook his head, turning and taking out his cell phone. The police would know what to do.

"Who are you calling?" Mitzi asked.

"Ah, you speak English," said the man, snapping his phone closed and replacing it in his pocket.

"Of course, we speak English," said Savannah, with some bite. The man had not tried out the first bit of Gullah on her and she felt somewhat cheated as a result. "I also speak Gullah, the language of the low country, which I believe I can safely assume you speak as well…given that you are of African descent."

"I must say that I have great respect for your people. You have suffered much at our hands, and for that we will live in eternal shame and guilt, but let me tell you very plainly, sir, we are enlightened Southerners. We will not have you calling us 'boss man' or 'massuh so-and-so,' or even 'cap'n,' as it is beneath you, and the fact is that we are beneath you when it comes to understanding things that aren't taught in books but that are wise in a low country-wisdom kind of way."

The man, who had prepared no speech, remained speechless, looking at the two of them, one of them not so bad if given the proper light, and the other very bad even in the dark. As said, each had been the recipient of numerous bites and stings from various insects, and these were to such a degree that the man concluded that they suffered from chicken pox, causing him to take a step back, as he considered it wise to avoid any pox, even if it came from a fairly harmless fowl.

"We spent the night out in these fields of which I imagine you own a sharecropper's stake, and you must know that even though the conditions were humble, for me it could not have been better if I were sleeping in a king's castle. I think it is your connection to the earth that makes you so wise, because it does something for one's soul. If you don't mind, I'd like to show Mitzi the shack you live in."

The man cleared his throat, deeply stung by all of her insinuations and greatly disappointed that these ladies were not Eastern European.

"I hate to break it to you, young lady, but I don't live in a shack..."

"Of course, you don't. To you it is a home, just a home, and as they say, every man's home is his palace. Well then, please show us to your palace."

"I don't live here, in a palace or otherwise. This is just some land that we have."

"We? Do you live with numerous brothers and sisters and aunts and uncles and cousins who work the land together and at night get together and sing songs of marching on to Zion?"

He could not tell; he just could not tell. Was she some virulent racist out to goad him on, or simply an idiot, or was that an a redundancy, as the virulent racist is always an idiot? But does that make the idiot always a racist? He did not care what the answers were, because either way, he had had enough.

"No. I most certainly do not. I own, through my corporation, numerous farming interests throughout the country, and I'm here checking on this one because one of my employees is on vacation. As to where I live and whom I live with, I live in Atlanta with my wife and two children along with a full-time nanny and a maid."

Savannah, hearing these words, felt deep sorrow for this man. If there was one thing that her books seemed to hold without exception, black characters, wisdom-bearing though they might be, were never wealthy and didn't run corporations. She looked over at Mitzi and whispered, "He's crazy," with sufficient breath to cause it to reach the man's ears.

The man responded by grinding his teeth against one another.

"If anyone is crazy here, young lady, then it's you. I was educated at Yale, then studied at the London School of Economics. I can't imagine that you made it out of the first grade. Now, get out of here. Both of you. Get the hell off of my land and get back in that piece of shit car you have over there."

"That is no way to speak to a lady," said Savannah.

"Savannah, let's go."

"I wasn't aware that I was speaking to one. Most ladies I know don't sleep in the dirt and walk around with chicken pox in the middle of fields."

"Well, you are, and I would ask that you address me in the proper manner used when speaking to one."

"Then let me tell you this: if you don't be mindin' it too much, ma'am, I sho' would 'preciate it if you'd get the hell off'a my land."

Savannah, at first angry at these words, harkened back to her reading, and in doing so, realized that this was one of the men she had read so much about who usually spent the book trying to fight against the existing order, to no avail. This realization caused her anger to ebb away, leaving her floating in the calm waters of understanding.

"You are filled with the fires of vengeance, and that I understand. I do not judge your anger, but a word to the wise—such feelings will only end in your death."

The chase continued for approximately twenty yards, Mitzi in the lead, Savannah right behind her, the Yalie pulling up the rear. When he stopped, the others continued, feeling the dirt clods and stones striking them on their backs, a well-aimed root crashing into the back of Mitzi's skull and sending her headlong into the passenger side of their vehicle, where her glasses met with destruction.

TWENTY-FIVE

Meanwhile, back at the Edwards home, matters were in an uproar. As Roy had feared, the lack of the extra car necessitated his being driven to work by his father; as Mrs. Edwards had feared, her daughter had not returned and lay dead in a gully being eaten by wildlife; as Mr. Edwards had feared, matters were in an uproar. He calmly tied a Windsor knot to the soothing sounds of his wife's manic screeches, she still in her shapeless bedclothes, her hair a nest unfit for rats. "I wouldn't worry about it," he said. "She's a big girl," he said. "Listen, she can take care of herself," he said. All of these sentences, meant to have a soothing effect on the bearer of his two misfortunes, did nothing to calm the chemical storm brewing in the head of the woman at whom they were directed.

"You have to do something, Harry! You have to do something!"

"What do you want me to do, Helen? I have no idea where she is and we can't report her as missing because she's an adult. I don't see any option other than to wait it out. She'll contact us, probably before the day's done."

"But what if she doesn't? What if she's hurt somewhere, or lost, and she needs us desperately but can't get in touch with us? There has to be something we can do! There has to be!"

Harry Edwards gave the problem some thought; he really did. He imagined possible phone calls, the drive across the open country, his head swiveling side to side in search of his daughter, but none of it seemed remotely possible, remotely fruitful. As he had told her, there was nothing to do but wait, but reason had never had much effect on her. He had finished tying his tie but did not have the courage to turn around and discuss the matter face to face, so he lingered on it for a while, his fingers feeling the silk, flirting with the dimple.

"I think I have an idea."

Mr. Edwards turned to see his son standing in the doorway, his shirt from the video store untucked, but pressed neatly by his mother, his hair too long for someone his age, his skin too blemished for someone his age.

"Well, let's hear it," said Mr. Edwards.

"I'm not sure you want to," said Roy.

"You're not, huh?" asked Mr. Edwards.

"No," said Roy, "but I think you should."

"Then, goddammit, tell us."

"Harry," said Mrs. Edwards.

"Speak, son. Get to the point. I promise you that your mother and I have heard worse."

"Well, let's be honest with each other here. Let's, as Dad said, get to the point. No reason we should beat around the bush. Let's call it what it is without trying to paint it as something else."

"Then say what you want to say!" said Mr. Edwards.

"Harry," said Mrs. Edwards.

"All right, all right. Okay. We all agree that Erica has flipped her lid; she's crazy."

"Roy," said Mrs. Edwards.

"Mom, she is. She's changed her name to Savannah, and that's not all of it. She's changed her last name, too."

"Changed her last name?" asked Mr. Edwards. "To what?"

"D'Bergeolet," said Roy.

"Great God in heaven," said Mr. Edwards.

"She thinks she has a brother named Chicken John. She thinks she grew up in Charleston. She thinks Dad's been a shrimper and a fighter pilot and she thinks that Mom is one of the prettiest women to ever walk the earth. None of this is true."

Mr. Edwards could feel the cold stare of his wife biting into his neck, and although he didn't want to, he felt compelled to respond.

"Some of it is, son," he said as though in pain. "Your mother is one of the prettiest women to ever walk the earth."

"Yeah, whatever," said Roy. "The point is that these books that she's been reading are the worst. They make Scientology look like the Boy Scouts. They've brainwashed her and we've got to do something."

"What is it, son, that you propose?" asked Mr. Edwards.

"I think that I should take off from work, go find her, drag her back here, and then we can try and bring her back to reality."

"And how do you plan on doing this?" asked Mr. Edwards.

"Well, one thing that you don't know about me, Dad, is that I have lots of friends."

Mr. Edwards could not help but sniff in derision.

"Lots of them, all over the place. In five minutes, I can have the whole World Wide Web out there looking for her. People from Canada to Malaysia can tell their friends, who can tell their friends, who can tell their friends, and the next thing you know, Erica will be caught in my web of world wideness."

There was a pause.

"The only problem that I see with it, Roy," said Mr. Edwards, "is that the only friends that your friends have are the same friends that you have. No one makes many friends by sitting in a room all day typing to each other. They just meet people who need money for wizards."

"Oh, you're wrong about that, Dad. These guys are real players. Real players. They get loads upon loads of babes and are known throughout their communities as leaders. If anyone can find Erica, they can."

"It sounds like a stupid idea to me," said Mr. Edwards.

"I think it might work," said Mrs. Edwards.

"Good," said Roy. "So, this is what I'll need: a car, free access to the telephone line, some gas money, some spending money, and since I'll have to take unpaid vacation days I'll need you to reimburse me for my pay and the movie rentals that I'll be missing out on."

"Consider it done," said Mrs. Edwards.

"Helen!" said Mr. Edwards.

"It's the least that we can do for Erica," said Mrs. Edwards.

"I'll get right on it," said Roy with a clap of the hands. "My pal the Davinator from Manitoba will know just what to do. A crisis! A crisis! If there's anything that my buddies on the internet love, it's a crisis. Just the other day we spent twelve hours talking someone out of committing suicide. It was incredible. The guy's wife had left him or something and he was low. I mean, low. But you know what, the Davinator said some things, and I said some things, then Miss Sunflower said some things, and the next thing you know, he was right as rain. Incredible, the power of the internet. It's..."

"Get the hell out of my room, Roy," said Mr. Edwards.

"Harry," said Mrs. Edwards.

110

"I'm going to work," said Mr. Edwards.

TWENTY-SIX

Creighton Starke did not sleep well on the couch. He had given up on his back strengthening exercises, along with his stomach, chest, arm, leg, neck, and ankle strengthening exercises, and because of this he had to have a properly calibrated mattress, a pillow between his knees, and an orthopedic headrest in order to wake up and not feel like he had been in a drunk-driving accident in which he was not the drunk. As he stood in Scott's kitchen, preparing a cup of coffee and eating a croissant that he had found in the refrigerator, he decided that he needed to start hitting the gym again. He would ignore the snickers and pay no heed to the chortles, and get back in there, his singlet glistening with its newness, his arms and legs as white as the underbelly of some animal or the other that they talked about in the Bible, if he remembered correctly. Let youth mock him, he thought. They were sure to get their day, if they were not killed off before it arrived.

He was searching for the butter when he heard a noise from behind, which caused him to pull his head out of the refrigerator.

"Jesus!" said Scott with all signs of someone suffering from shock.

"Lazarus!" said Creighton. "Raised from the dead. Did you just get back?"

"From where?" Scott asked.

"From your ditch. From your jog. I don't know where. I just turned around last night, and you were gone." Creighton had decided in the end that the virile Lothario had probably gone out and torn off a piece of college tail but didn't feel like talking about it this early in the morning. Especially not before breakfast.

"Yeah, I was gone alright. I was thinking that you'd be gone too when I got up. I guess it's not going to be that easy though, huh?"

"Huh is right," said Creighton, unsure of what Scott was saying, but very sure that the croissant needed some butter. He resumed his search in the refrigerator.

"I've been thinking a lot about what took place last night," Scott said, which was true. Even in his dreamworld, his subconscious had been at work on the problem.

"Really," said Creighton. Where was that damn butter?

"Yes, really," said Scott. "I don't care what you think, and I don't care who you tell. I'm not going to let you ruin my life. There's no crime in what I'm doing. Every healthy young man does it."

"I can't believe this," said Creighton. It was nowhere to be found.

"Well, believe it," said Scott. "It's true. I've never meant anything more in my life."

"This is bullshit," said Creighton with disgust.

"It is not bullshit," said Scott. "Tell anyone you want. I don't care. I really don't."

Creighton slammed the refrigerator door shut and turned to Scott with a look of indignation. He had forgotten where he was, of his being a guest and all, the desire for butter gripping him like a painful thirst. Scott felt his resolve crumpling.

"Tell me, Mr. Humps-a-Lot, where do you keep the butter?"

There was no weapon, no word, no question, that could have destroyed the young man with such efficiency, such incalculable ease. Far be it from the author to pry into the young man's private life but suffice it to say that he ran through a pack of Land o' Lakes in a week and could empty a case in less than a fortnight. And although he had convinced himself that his behavior was nothing to be ashamed of, the details of it had not undergone similar scrutiny, and no like-convincing had been done.

"God, why are you doing this to me?" Scott cried. The tears were once again in his eyes, but he did not allow Creighton to see them for long, turning and grabbing his backpack from a chair, running out the door and into the day.

What a weird duck, Creighton thought to himself once the door slammed. You ask the fellow a question and he runs lickety-split out of the house. This caused Creighton to remember a pornographic movie that he had once seen entitled *Lickety-Split,* and the images once again came to him in soft focus, he sifting through the mental wall of gauze, trying to remember if the lead actress was a brunette or a redhead. He was leaning more toward a redhead when he took an unconscious bite of the croissant; the lack of butter once more fueled his rage.

But his rage had nowhere to go, and neither did he. There were no classes today, no visits with his son, no desire to go into the office in hopes of scratching out a few lines. How long did it take for the police to come and arrest someone? It seemed to him that it depended on the crime. Some things probably made them rush out of the head-quarters; others probably got put on someone's desk where they were forgotten until a slow day came around. His crime, if self-defense could be called a crime, would hardly qualify as something seri-ous, but that almost appealed to him less, for what was he supposed to do? Live the next week (month?) waiting for the day that they came and put him in handcuffs? It really didn't sit well with Creigh-ton. Through his work he had dealt with injustice and had been applauded for the generous treatment which he gave it; he was not about to give up the fight at this point in his life. For a warrior never gave up, as Osgood had told Belinda at the tarmac during the raining hot days of the summer solstice.

His habit of quoting from his own work had been a point of contention between his wife and him, she claiming that it was boorish and narcissistic, he claiming that she did not understand the artist and never would. And maybe that's what had really driven them apart. Not his marital infidelities, the fact that he had failed to show up for the birth of his only child, his general financial irresponsibility, his disinclination to come home at night, his forgetting of every anniversary, of every birthday including his own, nor his jumping out of the closet at her parents' house and giving her father a heart attack from which he never really recovered. Those were the marginalia, but the text concerned only her inability to coexist with a true artist. Yes, they were a mercurial lot, but the rewards did exist, few of which Creighton had ever seen. The spouse of the artist had to understand that it was a polygamous relationship. She was his wife, but so was his work, so were his admirers. And these things she could not understand and was why she had left.

His mind was swimming so. He needed to sit down. A talk show was on the television, and he watched for a while, glad that others did not work and thus gave the stations ample reason to put on something this entertaining. People had problems. This was the blood and guts of literary fiction, these problems, and if one could not see a five-hundred-page novel in each guest who had cheated, an elegiac poem in each young boy dying of cancer while visiting Disneyland, then one might as well put the pen down. It was at times like this that Creighton Starke scoffed at the entire literary establishment, with their tales of dull families with meager secrets, various rehashings of the Holocaust, or long recountings of the big nothing that is life.

The show ended, to be followed by a soap opera, and Creighton saw his options whittling down to nubs. He therefore picked up *Lowcountry Lamentations* and began to read as follows:

My mother was the prettiest woman in the town. She had been a hooker when my father met her and was low born which was something that my father's parents saw the moment that he brought her in the door to see them for th efirst time. My mother said that she had married my father because she did not know better and because she had thought that with him coming from a good family and all that he would be a good person but this was not hte case. He beauty caused great problems for me at school.

I was the only girl on the football team the year that we intergrated. I had been elected as the quarterback by the team and we had a black boy who had been elected as the running back. His name was Excalliber and at first none of us were very excited that he was on the team because we were ignorant about blacks being our equals if not our betters but when we ran the forty yard dash we found that he was a very good athelete. "Look at him go!" I said as I watched him run. "He's going to be great!" I said and everyone agreed with me.

I can remember practicing those long days on the field, running with the football and passing it and calling out plays to my teammates. It was very hot. I remember about dying from exhaustion running up and down the field and getting ready for goals that we scored. Our coach was a rough man who was not very educted but was very wise as he had been a football coach for some time.

The night of the state championship we gathered around the shrine that we had made to the virgin Mary and fighter pilots and shrimpers and

116

we were told by my mother to kneel and pary so
that me and Chicken John would play a good game
and so that none of us would get hurt because it
was a very violent game. Afterwars we got up and
got dressed in our uniforms and Roy got in his
cheerleading out fit and then we got in the car
and went to the game. It was going to be a big
game!

Before the game we got in a circle around the
coach and he said these words. "You are going to
have a tough game tonight. There is going to be
lots of violence because the other teams wants to
win and because it is a violent game. The other
team does not think much of you because you come
from a small town and because you have a black
person on your team but you should not be bothered by this. You shall go out and play as hard
as you can and if you win you win. Savannah has
been playing like no one I have ever seen play
before and Excalliber runs very fast. Chicken
John is the best player that I have ever seen in
my life and he plays with an intensity that I
have never seen before in my life. We have a good
team and I think we can win. Are you ready to
win! Are you! We roared back at him that we did.
That's what I like to hear! Now you get out there
and you win! Now everyone hit a knee and let's
say a prayer. And we prayed to Jesus to protect
us all and to maek us have a good game.

When I hit the field I felt like all the bad
that I had been living through, my father, his
alcoholism, the fact that my mother never felt
like she fit in and never got into any of the
clubs that she ever wanted to get in, my torment

at being a woman in a male dominated society, my torment in living in a racist society, wash away and that I was just a young girl out playing football and that Chicken John and I were kings! He and I ran out together and burst through the banner with Excalliber between us as if to say hey, he's alright with us and if he's alright with us then he should be alright with you. Roy was cheering on the sidelines with his megaphone and he tried to get me and Chicken John to look at him but we were too concentrated on the game.

We won the toss and we ran out onto the field and I called the play. ON the first play we ran a wishbone and I ran with the ball and at the last second threw it to Excalliber. The other side had been calling him names all night long and it was his time to shine. He caught the pass and ran with the ball all the way to the end zone to score a goal! Chicken John and I ran and grabbed him and lifted him up on our shoulders to show everybody that even though he was black he was okay with us and he was on our team and we weren't ashamed of him.

The game was very tough. It was very hot and the other team was very violent. I ended up calling time out several times just to give us a rest and the rest of us would kneel while Chicken John stood up but he was just like that. After one of our time outs I called a secret play that I had been working on because the score was very close and we needed to score if we were to win the game. We really needed a goal.

I called out the hut and took the ball and ran. I ran like I had never run before just a lowcountry geechee girl with a ball under her arm like she was running through the marsh on a hot summer day so that she could go to a crab boil. Players tried to tackle me and grab at me but I turned and spun and made many fakes that got me near the goal line. I was about there when their best player came up and was about to tackle me. He was very big and was their best player. When he tried to tackle me I knew that I was done for when I saw Chicken John coming out the corner of my eye. He hit the other player with all of his might and knocked him down and I ran into the end zone as the clock counted out the last second. We had won!

This was the biggest game in the century in high school football and their were a ton of reporters there from a lot of "big" magazines like Sports Illustrated and stuff. They were trying to interview me as I was being carried off of the field and a picture of me and Chicken John was on the front cover the next week with the title Those Amazing D''Bergeolet Twins! on its front cover! There were alos a ton of coaches from "big time" college football teams like Nortre Dame and Nebraska there and they were there to see us. I talked to them and my head was swimming!

After we were done with all of the hoopla we told Excalliber that we would meet him at the hamburger joint and went into the shower room to hit the showers. We had barely entered when we saw my father. He was very drunk.

"Well I bet y'all think y'all are all fancy now winnin the big game and all." he said.

"No father. We don't think we're fancy. We're just happy that we won the game!" I answered.

"Oh won the game. I bet you think you're something special now that you've won the game." he slurred.

"No father! We're just happy that we won the game. Can't you be happy for us?" I cried.

"You both played like a bunch a girls out there!" he screamed. "Look at Savannah. I bet she wore frilly panties out there on the football field!" he shouted.

"You git!" shouted Chicken John. Leave her alone!"

"Let me see there. Yep. You got on frilly panties!" he yelled.

My father's removing of my football pants is something that will stay with me as long as I live. I had planned to go to the hamburger joint with Excalliber and Chicken John and had worn special underclothes for that and the big game and when he pulled my pants down I was standing there ashamed with my lace frilled panties on. "Get off of me!" I holloered. "You have no right!"

"Git!" peeled Chicken John who was tyring to get my father off of me.

"Now both of you get out there on the football field and show me some hustle!" yelled my father.

We ran out there in front of everyone and they were all ashamed of him because he was so drunk and he was so mean to his children but no one said a word to him because this was not the souther way.

"Now I want you to sprint up and down that field until you puke! Now!"

We ran up and down the field until we were blue in the face. He yelled from the sidelines in front of all of hte people from Sports Illustrated and all of the "big" coaches and my mother stood on the sidelines ashamed of him and wishing that she had married the man who later became an astronaut and not him. Roy was on the sidelines too but all he did was sit there with his cheerleading uniform on drinking a Pepsi.

I finally could take no more and fell to the ground. My father started punching me and kicking me and I felt like I was going to die but even though he beat me I was glad that he was touching me because he never touched me even though I was his child! I know it's sick. I was near death when I was looking up and saw my grandfather.

"Harry D'Bergeolet you git!" he screamed. "Now!" he yelled.

"You stay out of your business!" shouted my father. "This is my young'in not yours!" he peeled.

"You git!" shouted my grandfather.

And my father walked off the field and everyone who stood by was ashamed of what he had done and I realized that I hated him and I wished that he was dead and that I would have to spend a lot of time in therapy when I got older because of him. But I thik it hurt Chicken John the worst.

Oh, the slow crawl of time! Creighton Starke eyed the clock on the VCR and saw that he had many, many hours to go before something of even minimal substance entered his life. This authorial existence was tough, if the truth be told. You put out a critically acclaimed novel—in his case *Finding It All in the Hole*—and then you sat there and waited for the next one to come and during that time, well, what was one supposed to do during that time? Like many of his heroes he had tried drinking and womanizing, but this had done little to help, and he had never really been that good at either. The only author that he seemed to emulate these days was Sylvia Plath, but he saw no honor in kneeling in front of a stove, and most of them were electric nowadays anyway. To add insult to this debilitating injury, he hated both Sylvia Plath and *The Bell Jar*. In fact, he had taken to calling it *The Piss Jar* and had even gone so far to mentally outline the story of an author who goes through some serious mental issues and has to deal with the requisite mental health authorities until he comes to the realization that he looks at life as though it were a jar filled with piss. That would be the kicker, the piss jar, because up to that point it would just be a regular boring story about craziness, but then the piss jar would come. It would be akin to Nabokov's *Despair*, with the punch line arriving long after everyone has given up hope, the lights turned on, the ashtrays dumped and cleaned, the coats in hand, and the host silently burning with anger at his wife for her long absence in the garden with the local insurance salesman.

What he needed was rest. The mind must heal. It was wounded throughout the day with sights and sounds and thoughts that caused it to stretch and tear like an athlete's muscle under stress. He cast himself back on the couch and used one of Scott's t-shirts to cover his eyes, wondering if his racing mind would allow him even a brief respite, or torture him with genius, turning the bed into one of nails. Within two minutes it resembled one made of poppies.

TWENTY-SEVEN

Charleston Highway carried them along their merry path, coursing toward the center of it all. The morning had turned out to be a pleasant one, light shimmering down through blue, the earth gingerly baking to a brown crust. Savannah, steadied behind the wheel, had a smile on her face and a swaying motion to her head.

"I didn't think that could have gone much better," she said to Mitzi, who was pushing the separated ends of her glasses against one another like some magical force would join them together if she just kept trying. "We've just had our first real experience with the low country and all that I can say is that I'm amazed by its familiarity. The lone black man in the fields, working his crops, his fiery ways. The way we communicated with him and made him understand that we were his friends, and the way that he understood this without words. It's everything that we could have hoped for, and more."

"I had hoped that he wouldn't try and kill us," said Mitzi. "Or maybe that was the more part." The front of her dress was covered in dirt and her knees were skinned, her glasses were unmistakably broken, and her nose had arrived close to that point as well. "And as for your communicating, even though you did communicate, I can't say that I liked the result."

"Oh, the results," said Savannah. "Mitzi, I've tried to make it crystal clear to you that this was not going to be a journey without tribulation. No one in the low country—the South for that matter—

ever gets anything done without tribulation. Yes, we are blessed with many things—being closely linked with numerous famous people, the beauty of the countryside, the rich culture of our surroundings, with mothers who are extremely sensual—but these things come at a price, and today we have paid such a price."

Mitzi, who previously had been holding her emotions within the walls of her meager breast, could hold them no longer, and began crying with force.

"He tried to kill us, Savannah! He tried to kill us! We should have called the police on him and… and had him thrown in jail! And… and now my glasses are ruined!"

Savannah took her eyes off of the road and placed them with disgust and indignation on the two pieces of plastic held in Mitzi's hands. The blood visibly rose into her head, coloring her face and setting her jaw to a tetanal profile.

"Mitzi, have you forgotten why we're going to Charleston? Has the name Chicken John somehow escaped the confines of your melon-shaped head? Do you want to go home? Is that it? You want to go home?"

"Yes," said Mitzi through a whimper.

"Then fine. Let's go home. Let's forget about the book I'm going to put you in and your immortality and let's just drive back home and drop you off at your apartment so that you can resume your nameless existence."

"But I want to be in the book," said Mitzi. Her sobs suddenly dwindled to series of annoying sniffles.

"Well, one thing I can assure you, Mitzi, is that if I take you back now and have to return by myself, then your name won't appear anywhere within the cover. I won't even put Mitzi Bedenbaugh in the long acknowledgment section amongst the professors, museum curators, survivors of the Holocaust, literary benefactors, and other authors who have been influential in forming my inimitable style. You'll live for a while, have two point five thankless children, then die in a home with no one by your side. Is that what you want? Do you want to be a void entering a void rather than an immortal?"

Mitzi was very aware that her existence was a nameless one, and not merely because no one could ever remember her name. She yearned for more, as does all mankind, and as life presently stood she did not see herself ever getting any of it. So, Savannah's words had their intended effect and caused her to rethink her desires to return home. Certainly, the low-country quest seemed to be one that deprived her of sleep then gave it in harsh doses, involved speaking about things that she did not understand or care to understand, and then, when all of that was done, rendered her blind with an errant root, but at times the price of immortality is high. Odysseus did not arrive at fame by sitting at home with Penelope.

"No, of course not," she said, taking her glasses and putting them on her head, where they dropped back in her maiden lap. "I didn't mean to get upset with you, Savannah, it's just that I haven't read all of those books like you have, so when you said that there'd be lots of tribulation, I thought that there'd be lots of crying and stuff about Chicken John, lots of heartbreak, not crying about skinned knees and nosebreak."

"Mitzi, you are one of the most idiotic souls to have ever walked the earth," said Savannah with a laugh. "A real dolt. A true moron. One of the clearest things in the Southern novel is that the emotional pain is often matched by the physical pain. Just think about it: Tom was raped. Jack was shot in an airport. Ben was beaten on a regular basis by his father. Will was hazed past the point of breaking. This is part of what it is to be a Southerner. We live through the rapes, gunshots, beatings, and hazings, but the thing that we learn is that these are not the wounds that… wound us. No, the emotional ones— the proscribed lust that we feel for our steel-magnolia mothers, the yearnings to be hugged by our alcoholic, steel-fisted fathers, our sorrows over our siblings' attempted suicides, and I could go on—that really wound us."

"Oh," said Mitzi. "Well, I have to say that out all of those listed, I prefer the emotional ones over the other. As I've said before, I've never felt any lust for my mother, and my father, if anything, is over-affectionate. As for brothers and sisters, I don't have any, so you can do with them what you want."

"But how about your religion?" Savannah asked. "Surely you are wounded by the teachings of your strict Pentecostal upbringing, or even better, you have grown up Catholic, as I have, and you feel that no matter what you do, you will always be an outsider because of it."

"Um. No," said Mitzi. "My parents call themselves 'free thinkers' which means, as far as I can tell, that they would rather read the paper on Sunday mornings than be bothered with church."

"Hm," said Savannah. "So, you've never been raped, never tried to commit suicide, never been ostracized because of your religious beliefs, never been shot, never been stranded out at sea with nothing to drink, never had to kill a man who raped one of your family members?"

To all questions, Mitzi shook her head in the negative.

"This is troubling," said Savannah. "Have you at least had a very dark period in your life when you grew away from your husband and forced him into the arms of another woman on account of your emotional coldness?"

"I've never been married," said Mitzi.

"But you have had dark periods of emotional turmoil?"

"No, I can't say I've ever had a dark period. I guess I was a little sad when I graduated from high school because it was kind of sad. And I had a dog that died."

"A dead dog," said Savannah, reaching deep into her encyclopedia of Southern mishaps. "No, that's not going to do. Definitely not. Mitzi, I don't know what to tell you. You have an incredible zest for life and make me do many things that I at first resist, but that I later come to enjoy and appreciate, yet at the same time, I can't fit you in anywhere in any storyline. Let me ask you this: Is there any dark secret that you're going to reveal to me at the end of this journey?"

"Like what?"

"Like—I don't know—like the reason that you've been so resistant to my search is because you and Chicken John are lovers?"

"I've never met your brother and I've never had a lover, so I don't think so."

"Hm. So that isn't it, but it must be something. Maybe in the end you and Chicken John will become lovers."

"He's handsome, isn't he?"

"Very."

"And you say that he was a soldier?"

"Yes. In the war. The Vietnam War. A Green Beret."

"Oh, then he's probably too old for me."

At that, Savannah gave out a laugh. "Too old for you? Mitzi, he's my twin brother! You and I are the same age, so he won't be too old for you."

"But the Vietnam war ended before I was born, before you were born."

"Oh, what a zit-faced moron!" Savannah said. "But I wonder. Yes. Maybe that's it." She cleared her throat, raising the level of decorum. "Mitzi, I want to be very clear with you. When you and Chicken John become lovers, it isn't going to be easy for me. It will be like when Lucy developed a relationship with Anna's father in Dorothea Benton

Frank's *Sullivan's Island*. Initially I will be very cold to you. Yes, I will be happy that my brother has found affection, and I will be happy for you as well, but still, it won't be easy. I will probably get angry at you for little things and say and think things behind your back that I don't really mean, but in the end, you'll do some of your crazy, zesty things, and I will just be happy that everyone's happy. Keep this in mind when the time comes. Can you do that for me?"

"I think I can handle it. What I won't be able to handle is being the lover of a man in his fifties. Some of them look okay, I guess, but they smell like age, you know? Something about their breath; maybe they're rotting on the inside or maybe it's their teeth. I don't know."

"No, you don't know," said Savannah. "You don't know much of anything, you blockhead."

And thus, they traveled along, with the distance from their hometown growing, just as the miles from the fair city of Charleston dwindled. In fact, if they continued along as they were presently proceeding, they would enter the brilliant carbon forest within the hour.

TWENTY-EIGHT

razorroy: lol! :)

thedavinator: No i'm lol!!!! ;)

misssunflower: lets just say we're all
lol!!!!!! :p

razorroy: that's alotta lols!!!! i need
to talk to you two about some-
thing. something serious.

thedavinator: talk on razor. we're here for
you pal

misssunflower: yeah! :p your not in trouble
are you?

razorroy: no but my sister is. we've got
a crisis on hand, and i need
your help

Razor Roy Edwards proceeded to outline the details of Savannah's departure and, needless to say, in response there was no laughing out loud, much less a smiley face with its tongue sticking out. It speaks a great deal about the writing style of the much-maligned Roy that within minutes the World Wide Web had turned from that of cob to steel. As Roy had told Mr. and Mrs. Edwards, his compatriots of mental and physical sloth had many ideas and knew many people, and given such an emergency as the missing sister, they were prepared to stay up for days, or weeks, if need be, and bring the lost sheep back to the Edwards flock.

An hour passed with surmises and suggestions that finally crystalized into a plan, which was this: Miss Sunflower would contact her friends, who would then contact their friends, who would then somehow find Savannah. Likewise, the Davinator would contact his friends, who would then contact their friends, who would then somehow find Savannah. Roy, who had taken a leadership role in the expedition, similarly swore to contact his friends, who would then contact their friends, who would then somehow find Savannah. This method provoked a long discussion about a movie with the premise that everyone is separated from each other only by a few friends and that it is only a matter of how far the separation, not the lack of a connection. An actor in the film had recently been in others, one of which was a science fiction movie, and this prompted yet another long discussion about what would happen to the world if aliens did in fact attack, the lives of the survivors, the unlikely heroes, the traitors who would attempt to appease the aliens when it was obvious that the only way to solve the problem was through their annihilation. Or so said the Davinator, much to the protests of Miss Sunflower, who felt that a dialogue was always essential and worthwhile, and that she had to believe that amongst the aliens destroying the planet there would be a group of them opposed to such martial tactics and could therefore be reasoned with. In the end, the two, with Razor Roy serving as the mediator, agreed to disagree and got back to the subject at hand, which was Roy's missing sister. The parties called a brief intermission and decided that in one hour they would return to the chat room and update each other on their progress. Roy signed off with his trademark smiley face, and found himself in front of his computer, hungry for a sandwich. His mother was downstairs. He called for her.

TWENTY-NINE

"Toodle-doo, toodle-dum. De dum, de dum."

Creighton Starke returned to the land of reality (Or was this life just a dream and his dreams reality? It was amazing how many eighteen-year-olds found this question impressively profound.), an hour having passed and his brain sufficiently regreased and able to handle the whir of activity. He sifted through the tune, raising a note by a half-step here, lowering another by a whole there, feeling the song and the joy of creation. During his period of convalescence, he had taken to writing music and the accompanying libretto, and, although it was not the same as drafting a novel, he did find a certain satisfaction in doing something to exercise that portion of his brain. His masterpiece had been one brought to life in his padded cell, his caretaker three hours late with his food, roughly four hours behind in removing his soiled undergarments, and he in heaven, nonetheless. "I'd like to see / You take that flashlight / And shove it up your ass. / It is a magnum-sized light torch / One whose beam you can see imprinted on the sky / And it would hurt / No matter how adept you are / At filthy things like that. / Won't you? / Oh, won't you? / Even for me? / I see that you are possessed. / Perhaps by a demon / Perhaps by the air-conditioner / It really doesn't matter / And I sure don't care. / You can lay down on your stomach / And show me the belt of Orion / Man, he was a great guy." The four-track recorder was his one luxury at the apartment, bought second-hand on the street, and now the keeper of his many bouts of lyrical genius. He did not play an instrument, and his attempts at drumbeats on the lamp shade were disappointing even to him, but the four-part harmony that he slurred into the microphone seemed divine, with a capital D pushing the word along.

"Toodle-doo, toodle-dum. De dum, de dum."

This was simply too good to waste. He arose from the couch, gathered his belongings together, and decided to risk an encounter with the policeman who might be waiting outside his door. But who was not. He retrieved his key from his pocket and entered, the smell of stale trash greeting his olfactory lobe with a light belch, the lamp next to the couch burning for what could only be decorative purposes, the light on the answering machine beating like the heart of haste. He stepped over the unopened mail strewn about the colorless carpet, headed toward the green blinking light that proposed a number, and punched a button. The first three were uninteresting to the common man, but to him had a note of tragedy about them, as they consisted of someone saying, "Mr. Starke? Hello? Mr. Starke?" followed by a long pause that led to the end. Behind these pleas for his attention, he could hear other voices talking, toneless and impersonal. He was considering the plotline of a would-be novel about telemarketers when number four erupted from the machine. It was his ex-wife bringing tidings of ill-will and threats of extermination; she was clearly agitated and in need of chemical assistance herself, although she had pooh-poohed every suggestion of his to this effect. Numbers five through nine produced similar messages, although their emotional volume depended on whether she was cycling high or low. What was clear was that she did not think that future visitation was a good idea and that he could expect a set of papers from her attorney ordering this thought into existence.

If he had cared about this issue at the moment, he would not have rushed over to his four-track recorder and turned it on. He checked the tape and found that he was in a good spot, and immediately hit the record button.

"Toodle-doo, toodle-dum. De dum, de dum," he sang, afterwards shutting off the machine, his idea written in the stone of magnetized plastic.

He would now, or at some point, sit down and craft lyrics to fit along with the tune, and given all that he had going on that day, he decided to do it later.

A trip to the bathroom revealed a sink and bathtub so covered in hairs that they appeared as though a series of mange-ridden dogs had been treated in them, the larger dogs in the tub, the smaller in the sink, all having black wiry hair like the kind one so often finds on the rims of public urinals, left there by nameless souls in their search for relief. He again checked the wound on his forehead and saw that it was already crusting to sepia, a corona of blue spraying out to his eye sockets. The water was immediately warm on his hands, and he worked a piece of soap into a lather, afterwards drying off on a towel of filth.

He found himself sitting on his couch, a mirror of his previous state at Scott's apartment, even to the point that the manuscript had positioned itself at his side. The idiot was such an idiot that he secretly found himself intrigued by her story, so, without his right hand knowing what his left hand was doing, he reached down, picked it up, and began to read as follows:

Tell me why adulthood has such homocidal urges towards youth? Is it jealousy? Sadness? It is my belief that they are simply part of a vicious cycle, hurt by adults as children, they must hurt children as adults.
The final days of our senior year at high school were filled with trauma. Roy had been held back a grade or two so he was graduating with us but just barely. Chicken John was graduating too

134

but just barely as well. I had made "straight As" all the way through school and Roy would call me a "suck up" and "a book worm" but that really wasn't true! In fact part of me wished that I wasn't so smart and some times I would stay up all night before tests and not study just so that I would be worn out and not know the material but I still always got an "A". Roy would go to the state college and perform with the marching band and I had offers from all of the "good" schools but I didn't know which one I wanted to attend. I thought about going to Harvard but Chicken John told me that I wouldn't like all of those poeple up in New York City and he couldn't figure out why anyone would want to live in New York City which is something he would always say when he came up and visited me there as you will see. As for Chicken John he wanted to be a shrimper like Father was and maybe join the marines as well and be a fighter pilot too although he wasn't too sure about that last part.

We were sitting on the dock next to the creek and we started talking about all of the bad stuff that had happened to us when we were growing up.

"Do you remember that time that Maw-Maw found the snake in her bedroom and we had to call Autie Hottooth to come over and perform that old geechee trick of sucking the poison out?" "Yeah." said Chicken John. "I don't remember that." said Roy.

"And do you remember that time that Father bought the convenience store down at the bottom and he got caught selling dirty magazines to all of the kids and when they caught him he tried to

say that he thought they were medical books?"
"Yeah." said Chicken John. "That Dad." Roy did
not say anything.

"I think we must be the most messed up family
in the entire world." "Why do you say that?"
asked Chicken John. "Chicken John how could you
think otherwise? Our mother is one of the most
beautiful women on the planet and she was always
trying to get in all of those clubs, and Father
was always trying out some new venture when he
wasn't out shrimping or off at war fighting in his
plane, and Grandpa was always praying and saying
crazy things about God, and Maw-Maw man was she
crazy. And look at us. We're crazy. We're just
crazy."

"I don't think that's crazy. I think it's what
I love about the south all of the characters who
live down here and do things that are different.
I bet you won't find more interesting people up
in New York when you go up there." said Chicken
John. "Oh, Chicken John you are so wrong. There
are people up there who know all about physics
and poetry and about art. They come from famous
families and a lot of them are jewish."

"I bet they don't know as many famous poeple
as we do though. With us knowing astronauts and
congressmen and movie stars and all." commented
Chicken John.

"Yes, we do know alot of famous people and I
bet one day one of us will be famous too, if not
all of us. You will be a brave marine and maybe
a professional football player and Roy might do
something. People get famous for doing different
stuff you know, like killing lots of people."

"Oh Savannah don't be be so bashful. You've already had three books of your poetry published and are seen as the brightest star of the literary establishment although I have to say that I don't understand half of them. You talk about lions and tigers and stuff living in the lowcountry and Orkin men and snakes but I just don't know what they mean." stated Chicken John.

"That is the beauty of poetry Chicken John. I can talk about things that I would never talk about otherwise and it gives me a chance to talk about them. Do you know what I've always found so funny?" I queried.

"What?" Chicken John questioned.

"Why we never cry." I said.

"A southerner doesn't cry." Chicken John replied.

"Oh Chicken John, don't you understand that it's not human not to cry. Sometimes I wish I could but I can't and I think that's part of the reason why I write poetry that is so depressing yet so amazing."

"Hey, let's get in the water and do that circle again just for one last time with everyone going off in different directions." said Chicken John.

And we got in the water in our clothes and we swam out into the middle of the creek holding hands and we formed a circle each of us looking at the other and smiling because we knew it would never be like this again although we had no wya of knowing just how much like this again it would never be.

After ten minutes of swimming in teh circle and holding hands like that Grandfather came out to the dock and said, "Hey, you children better come on in. We've just caught a batch of shrimp and mull gravy while we were out fishing and some white tail and it's going to be gettin cold pretty soon, sure nuff."

When we got back at the house we were in as good of spirits as we could have ever been. We were joking about swimming in the circle and Roy was getting picked on because he was so stupid but when we entered the house we could tell that something was wrong.

"What is it mother? What's wrong?" I queried.

"Hush Savannah. You're father's watching the television set. I just tried to speak to him and he beat me."

"Oh mother when will it all stop?"

"What?"

"All of these beatings."

"What beatings?"

"Mother you just said"

"I said nothing Savannah. There is no such thing as that that happens here."

And I knew that I had caught my mother in a lie and I wondered how long she would pretend that Father did not beat her and beat us when the truth was that he often did. I had to get away. I had to get away!

"The Republic of Vietnam just declared war on us boys. We're going to war." Father slurred as he had been drinking.

"Then I shall go!" said Chicken John.

138

"No Chicken John! You can't! You can't!" I
shouted.

"I not only should go, I must go. I shall go!"

"Roy talk to him! Talk him out of going!" I
yelled.

"I've got flat feet. Otherwise I'd go too.
I think it's a good idea that he goes." Roy
responded.

"What! What are you talking about! Has everyone gone crazy! I don't want people going to
war!" Although I was secretly glad tha tmy father
was going to war. It was one of the only times
that it was nice to live at my house. Although I
told myself that this was wrong to wish and that
I would have to say an extra rosary that night
becasue of what I had thouhgt.

"We'll both go. I can get you attached to my
unit Chicken John and you can run extra special
top secret missions with the Green Berets." said
my Father.

"I should like that very much Father." Chicken
John stated.

And I don't know what came over me but I just
ran. I ran through our yard and into the marshes
and just kept running. It was dark by the the
time I stopped and when I did I fell down and
although I wanted to cry I couldn't because I
realized that my parents had ruined me and that I
could not. I sat there and as I sat that I realized that I would spent a lot of my life running
only not real running but running from my past.

He wondered if he had ruined himself as a recording artist by
publishing that book of his. The entire crossover thing was just not

easy. If you were an actor, no one took you seriously as a writer or a painter; change the words around a bit and it likewise applied. Society craved for something new, but it had to be packaged new as well, which was what was going to cause him so much trouble. Because who would expect the author of *Finding It All in the Hole* to be equally adept at songcraft as he was at wordsmithery? Probably no one. And if that weren't enough, he had the entire ageism problem to deal with, he a professor in his mid-forties singing songs meant for urban dance floors, where most of the consumers would be uneducated and in their early teens. And the video would be difficult. Extremely difficult. He could picture himself in the back of a roofless limousine, sitting in the hot tub with various women, champagne bottles open and champagne flutes filled, his many admirers running alongside them, singing the words to the song with a certain negligent swagger. But they would want him to dance and he would have to somehow get it across to everyone involved that just because you can sing like a cherub and write songs that command people to move, it did not necessarily mean that you were a dancer. And then the touring. It would be much more difficult for a man his age and make it virtually impossible for him to see his son with his schedule and all. Yes, how the future brightened, only to have dark clouds swoop down from the mountaintops and drown us all.

God, he was depressed. He thought of erasing all of the songs on his four-track recorder, forgetting that any of it had ever happened, and throwing away his gift in hopes for a life of normalcy, because otherwise he would die with strict wishes that the tapes be burnt only to reanimate like Kafka, who too had his wishes ignored and thus gained his posthumous glory. His meds. Yes, where were his meds? Where had they been for the past two months, for that matter? A quick leap off the couch and he was in steady search of them.

THIRTY

When Savannah and Mitzi entered North Charleston there was no brilliance, and no trees with which to make a forest, but plenty of carbon mixed with an equal amount of oxygen. Savannah rolled down the windows and allowed her blonde hair to float behind her.

"Just smell it!" she said to Mitzi. "Just smell the fecund musk of the low country!"

Around them were factories and crapped out houses polluting both the air and the scenery. A man on the side of the road retched violently into a corroded garbage can as they passed by, and several feral dogs were in the process of devouring an unidentifiable animal that had been killed by a long-departed motorist. It was hot, and the humidity coated everything with a sticky patina. Mitzi, upon being told that this was what a fecund musk was, silently agreed with herself that it did, in fact, resemble that given off by a pair of dirty socks.

"I smell it," she said. "Now do you mind rolling up the windows?"

"Couldn't you just eat it, Mitzi?" asked Savannah. "Couldn't you just put it on a plate, smother it with some mull gravy, and scarf it down?"

"It would depend on how much the mull gravy killed the taste," said Mitzi. "I don't mean to be rude, Savannah, but I think the fecund musk of the low country, or at least the love of it, is an acquired taste.

It's probably like caviar. Some people'll pay hundreds of dollars to eat just a bite of it, but if you don't like it, and I don't like it, then you'd probably pay a hundred not to have to even look at it."

"But isn't it beautiful, Mitzi?"

"The smell?"

"No, around you. All that's around you."

"I…" Concrete with grass sprouting through it had never been a favorite of Mitzi's, nor had vomiting homeless people or wild dogs. As for factories, they did remind her of other factories, and she was glad that the world had factories, but she didn't like looking at them very much. "I…can't say that it is."

Conroy entered the frame and spoke through Savannah. "Yes, you can be moved profoundly by other vistas, by other oceans, by soaring mountain ranges, but you cannot be seduced. You can even forsake the low country, renounce it for other climates, but you can never completely escape the sensuous semitropical pull of Charleston and her marshes."

"I've escaped it for the first twenty years of my life and after this journey I plan on escaping it again. I'll be honest with you here, Savannah. I think you already know this, but I'm not from the South; I'm from Indiana. I just came down here because I wanted to go to school some place where it was warm. Now I know that probably isn't the best reason to choose a college, but there you have it."

"Mitzi, you've had the personality of a cup of yogurt for the last couple of weeks. What's wrong?"

Mitzi felt the sting of these words, as she had only known Savannah for a couple of weeks and therefore had had the personality of a cup of yogurt the entire time. She tried to think of the significance of the metaphor but desisted as quickly as she began.

"Well, I don't know… There… there aren't any marshes, and I don't see Charleston."

"You're in Charleston!" said Savannah. "You really are an idiot. I mean, a real mildewing jockstrap. It's all around you!"

But all that Mitzi could see around her was miserable traffic, the scenery described above, and Savannah's chuckling figure. She was attempting to find something else to look at, hoping to discover what it was that drove her friend to such a love of the place, when Savannah made a turn.

"Where are we going?" Mitzi asked.

Savannah gave a long pause, biting her lower lip and shaking her head. Mitzi asked again.

"I didn't want it to be like this, Mitzi," Savannah said. "I wanted to give you a beautiful life, one without all of this pain and horror, but we don't live inside of a book. Our lives are not made out of paper and ink, but of flesh and blood. Do you understand?"

"I think so," said Mitzi.

"But you couldn't, you couldn't understand!" said Savannah. "It's impossible to understand unless you've grown up in the low country, known her marshes, calculated the seasons by the shrimp coming and going!"

"Then I guess I don't," said Mitzi.

"Where we are going, Mitzi, is to a place that I have long tried to forget." Savannah paused for a Conroy line. "My memory often seems like a city of exiled poets afire with the astonishment of language, each believing in the integrity of his own witness, each with a separate version of culture and history in the divine essential fire that is poetry itself."

Mitzi attempted to process these words, and after a few moments it was obvious that they had become an obstruction in the bowels of her mind. She responded with an "I see." They traveled down Rivers Avenue in silence.

Where they were going was to the Citadel, the bastion of all-male white oppression that Savannah had read so much about and believed she had attended, although she had never quite worked out how she had attended since she had not. Her expectations were to find a military complex with a nearby marsh and railroad tracks, like a Hollywood set, all laid out with X's marking the spots where men had died, and other important historical accidents had taken place. But there was no marsh, nor any train tracks within sight, and the houses surrounding the grounds seemed out of place to her and a bit bedraggled.

They somehow made it to a main road and before them found the Citadel, which was, in fact, a huge set of white buildings, sitting innocently in the sun. Savannah pulled the car to a rest. It did not take long for her brain to go deeper into Conroy mode.

"Mitzi, a Southern man is incomplete without a tenure under military rule. I am not an incomplete Southern man. I am simply damaged goods, like all the rest of them."

"Oh," said Mitzi. Savannah's changing gender did nothing but further confuse her.

"You see it there, Mitzi? Do you see it?"

Mitzi raised her glasses to her face, each hand holding a side, and replied, "Yeah. So what?"

"To an unromantic eye, Mitzi, the Institute has the look of a Spanish prison or a fortress beleaguered not by an invading force, but by the more threatening anarchy of the twentieth century buzzing insensately outside the Gates of Legrand."

"It looks nice," said Mitzi.

"You say that, Mitzi, but you haven't lived within its walls. You haven't seen the hazing that takes place on Hell Night, the brutalization of African Americans by evil white men, the morbidly obese boys throwing themselves off of the towers in hopes of impressing their fathers. I wonder how many humans have died because sons wanted to prove themselves worthy of their fathers."

"I'm sure a study's been done. They seem to have done studies on everything. Just the other day I was reading one about chocolate and..."

"Stop it, Mitzi, you with your talk about chocolate. We find ourselves sitting in front of the gates of Legrand, ready to unveil the first horror of this visit, and your mind concerns itself with confections? You have to be strong, Mitzi. This is the strength I was talking about earlier."

"Are we looking for Chicken John here?" Mitzi asked.

"Not here. No, we are doing something else right now, trying to keep a poor black boy from being tortured by the Ten, the men who you saw out in the field last night. We can only hope that we're not too late."

With these words, Savannah drove forward, stopping in front of what appeared to be a guard station.

THIRTY-ONE

Savannah put the car in park and got out; Mitzi followed. In the small room stood a female cadet, and over to their left was a young man leaning against the wall with his duffle bag set glumly to his side. The female cadet quickly exited and walked over to Savannah and Mitzi.

"You can't park there," she said. "You're going to have to move your car."

Savannah was taken aback by this androgynous cadet, only to bring herself aright once she reminded herself that these were only boys—boys in the process of becoming men—and therefore one could not expect them all to have undergone puberty or to have lost their childhood fat, although this one seemed to carry all of it in his breasts.

"We will park wherever we want, cadet; we wear the ring," said Savannah.

The cadet's frown changed to a smile when she heard these words and she nodded at Savannah.

"That's great," she said. "It's always nice to see other women who've made it through the ranks."

Savannah turned her head in disgust at these words, as she felt this satyr was mocking her. A verbal poniard was about to escape from her mouth, but she decided to shove it back in its sheath and get down to business.

"No bond exists between us, cadet, except for that formed by the power of the ring, and the hell that both of us have seen. I am here to make an inquiry. There is a young man here, I believe he is of European nobility. His name is Livery of Seisin. Do you know him?"

"I don't know of a cadet Seisin, ma'am, but there are a lot of us here and I don't know everybody."

"He is stonewalling us, Mitzi," Savannah said to her friend.

"I'm not stonewalling you at all, ma'am. I really need for you to move your car. You're blocking traffic."

"Oh, traffic! The trains of Buchenwald must progress! Into the slaughterhouse they come—boys! boys!—and you know what dies in here? Boys. No, they don't die a physical death, but a spiritual one. They come out as men, but broken men, which is the same as death."

The young lady, who at first had been so impressed by a sister graduate, quickly came to the conclusion that she was not dealing with someone in full ownership of her mental faculties. No ring sat upon their fingers, and the young lady with the lunatic, given her physical appearance, wouldn't have lasted one day within the walls.

"Anyway," Savannah continued, "perhaps it's not a person that we're looking for, but a code. Are you familiar in any way with the term Livery of Seisin?"

"I'm not ma'am. Now, if you'd please move your car. If you don't, I'm afraid that I'll have to call the police."

"Then call them!" Savannah said. "Call them. I'd like an investigation done right now, because I have certain information that I'm sure that they would love to hear about the Ten!"

"I don't know what you're talking about, ma'am."

"Young man, your secrets no longer live in the shadows. Reliable sources have alerted us to the fact that a young black man—a boy, really, he's in the process of becoming a man, a broken, destitute black man—has been singled out by the Ten in order to keep the corps racially pure. We will not stand for this, and neither will society."

"I am not a man, lady," said the cadet.

"No, you are a boy as well. A boy in the process of becoming a man. A broken, destitute man."

At this point, the cadet walked away, returning to her station and picking up the phone. Mitzi informed Savannah of this, but Savannah dismissed Mitzi with a wave of the hand.

"You, young man. Why are you standing out here?"

"Um…" The boy, who was doing nothing other than minding his own business, which, as history has shown, is always a prelude to disaster, looked over with tired eyes. He wore his blonde hair cropped short and his face clean shaven. His dress was civilian—shorts, a t-shirt, a light blue friendship bracelet on his wrist that matched the color of his eyes—except for his shoes, which were black military issue, as was the duffel bag that sat at his side. "I really don't want to talk about it."

"Why is it that Southern men refuse to talk about their feelings?" Savannah asked. "I know that you are taught this from a very early age, but I can assure you from my earthly journey that I've learned that this is very dangerous. You must strive to live life, and especially to cry."

The young man did not respond.

"Are you a cadet here, and if you are, are you familiar with either a person or a code known as Livery of Seisin?"

"I was a cadet here, and no, I'm not familiar with it."

"Was?"

"Jesus. Why does everyone always have to butt in? Yes, was. I was. I was until they kicked me out."

Savannah was immediately gouged by a fishhook of delight, for this was just as the books had said. In the pertinent one, a young man had been drummed out of the Institute and only a few minutes later he committed suicide by stepping in front of a train. Savannah could not allow this to happen, or if it did happen, she had to be there to witness it, to have him look over at her with an apologetic smile the instant before the train crashed through him. It took only a moment's thought before she knew what to do.

"Mitzi, quick! Grab him. We mustn't let him get near any trains."

Mitzi looked over at Savannah, then over at the boy, then back at Savannah.

"The book, Mitzi!" said Savannah. "The book!"

Putting the two eye pieces in the pocket of her dress, Mitzi gave a nod and raced forward, enveloping the young man in a bear hug and pinning him against the wall.

"Hey!" shouted the former cadet, trying to look into the face buried in his chest. "Let go of me."

Savannah, with swift grace, ran to him and took his duffel bag, carrying it to the car and throwing it in the back seat. She left the back door open and quickly returned to the scene of the abduction.

"Keep a hold of him, Mitzi! We can't let him get near the trains! Away from the trains! Away!"

And Mitzi was not letting go. The boy had a nice smell to him, almost like that of a gardenia, and the way he struggled in her arms made her wish this moment would last forever.

"Now over here!" said Savannah. She positioned herself behind him and began pushing, Mitzi in the front, he in the middle, until

Mitzi was next to the car, the cadet still in her grip. With a violent shove, Mitzi's calves hit the bottom of the vehicle, which sent her reeling backwards, the cadet on top of her, still secured in her arms. She had initially fallen on the back seat, but they tumbled so that she was lying on top of his body, which was wedged between the front and back seats on the floorboard. Savannah, followed by the cries of the female cadet, who had witnessed the entire chain of events and was sure that a felony was being committed, slammed the back door onto the protruding legs of Mitzi and the cadet, causing further cries from inside of the car. It took only two more attempts at shutting the door in such a fashion before Mitzi and the cadet thought it wise to pull the whole of their bodies within the vehicle. Savannah found her way to the front seat, and they were off.

THIRTY-TWO

At the one-hour mark, Roy hopped back into the chat room where he found the Davinator and Miss Sunflower discussing the time they had talked a young man out of killing his wife and children while they slept.

thedavinator: And he was like, I guess you're right. Living in hell with your wife and children is a lot better than living in prison! lol! ;P

razorroy: So what have you got for me? What did your friends say?

misssunflower: I spoke with my friends but they're still talking to their friends and their friends probably haven't even gotten to their other friends. Right now I'm in a holding pattern.

razorroy: And you Davinator?

thedavinator: One of my friends knows a guy who used to have a sister who lived in Charleston but left after her divorce. She had to go to therapy and still isn't really over it. He's going to get in touch with her when she gets home from work and see what she can do. As for my other friends, they're really interested in helping you out Razor but it's going to take a little while.

razorroy: I DON'T HAVE A LITTLE WHILE!!!!!!! TIME IS RUNNING OUT!!!!! I'VE GOT TO HELP HER!!!!!

misssunflower: We're trying to help you Razor. There's no need to shout at us.

thedavinator: yeah.

razorroy: WELL WE'LL SEE HOW YOU ACT NEXT TIME YOU'RE SISTER'S IN TROUBLE!!!! I'LL BET YOU'LL BE SHOUTING TOO!!!!

thedavinator: STOP SHOUTING AT US!!!! WE'RE TRYING TO HELP!!!!

razorroy: LOOK WHOSE SHOUTING NOW!!!! YOU ARE!!! YOU'RE SHOUTING AND ALL I'M TRYING TO DO IS GET SOME HELP!!!! I'M THE ONE HURTING HERE DAVINATOR!!!!

thedavinator: WELL, I'M HURTING TOO, NOW THAT YOU'RE SHOUTING AT ME!!!! WE'RE SUPPOSED TO BE FRIENDS!!!! :-(

razorroy: WELL SOME KIND OF FRIENDS THE TWO OF YOU ARE!!!! AND YOU CAN TAKE THAT FROWNY FACE AND STUFF IT WHERE THE SUN DON'T SHINE IF THAT'S THE WAY YOU'RE GOING TO BE!!!!

misssunflower: RAZOR!!!

thedavinator: SCREW YOU MAN!!!! :-(

razorroy: THAT'S IT!!!! I'M OUT OF HERE!!! GOOD LUCK TALKING THE NEXT GUY OUT OF COMMITTING SUICIDE, BECAUSE I WON'T BE THERE TO HELP YOU!!!!

razorroy signed off at 2:36 p.m. EST

misssunflower: RAZOR!!!!!!!!!!!!!!!!!!!

THIRTY-THREE

And that quickly, after only a short series of keystrokes, Razor Roy Edwards found himself floating in the real world, his true friends cast away, with just himself to rely upon. At first, he felt sad, neglected. He had spent so many hours cultivating these relationships—listening to Miss Sunflower talk about her ex-husband and how he had taken the children from her; listening to the Davinator dissect and relive the many busted relationships that he had almost had with young women—and now they were gone. He thought of something that Miss Sunflower had once said—relationships are as fragile as April snow—and it finally made sense to him, even though it had never snowed in April in the nameless town where he had lived out the entirety of his existence. Still, the fragility part now made sense.

He walked downstairs where he found his mother in the kitchen, eating something brown out of a bowl. She dropped the spoon from her mouth and asked him what was wrong. With a dismissive wave and a turning away, he walked past her and stood in front of the kitchen window, staring out into the yard where grass grew, and trees heaved towards the sky, and birds and squirrels came and went.

"You really miss her, don't you?" asked his mother.

And Roy, his thoughts on Miss Sunflower, could not help but feel the words land like a punch on the tip of his nose. His eyes welled with tears, and he did his best to fight against their descent.

"I'll be okay," he said.

"I know you will," said his mother. "Any luck with your computer friends?"

The question brought light to her prior inquiry and his resolve cemented in a matter of moments. With a cleansing sniff, he turned to her and said, "What computer friends?"

"I don't know. The ones you talk to all of the time. The ones who are supposed to be helping you find Savannah."

"They're working on it, but you can only do so much sitting around. I've got to get out. She said she was going down to Charleston, so that's where I need to go. I'll need a car."

His mother put the bowl down, stared at it for a moment, lifted the spoon from where it sat resting on the side, licked it clean, then tried to begin a sentence, although she couldn't with her mouth filled as it was.

"You'll... you'll...we just need to call the rental car company."

"I'll probably need a van."

"Then we'll get a van."

THIRTY-FOUR

"Get off of me! Get off of me! I can't breathe!"

Mitzi heard the words but did not listen to their import. Her right hand lay trapped between her leg and the damp flesh of his upper thigh, their crotches joined, her breasts to his chest, her blind eyes staring into the open mouth from which shouted filth burst forth like real filth from a spiked sewer line.

Savannah raced through the streets, congratulating herself on saving the poor boy from death by the rails. The freeing of the black man, who was really a boy if you would only take a moment and think about it, had been cast aside and left in her dust, for she had captured something far better than the evil Livery of Seisin or the accolades for exposing the Ten: a real live cadet from the Institute who could take her to his house on the Battery and introduce her to his mother who would immediately fall in love with Savannah and lead her out to the garden, each with a mint julep in hand, where they would discuss exotic plants, the history of Charleston, the beauty of the South, and so on and so forth. When one of them would say something funny, which would be often, they would lift their heads back and emit laughter reminiscent of gold coins falling onto an antebellum table saved from the savagery of Sherman, then raise their hands to their chests to hold in their laughter-parting sighs. She knew, however, that something would come between them and that this secret would make them enemies for a time, only to reconcile on a boat while a band played African American spirituals nearby and the sun set over the sea, and she was deeply pondering what their final words would be when her thoughts were interrupted by further shouting.

"Get off of me! Now! God! You're crushing me! Get off of me!"

"Mitzi, this is no way for a character in a book to act!" Savannah shouted. "Let him up and apologize."

Mitzi had no desire to do this, as at that moment she was experiencing a feeling she imagined would be similar if electricity were applied to her genitals, but seeing as how she did not want to witness her contributions being swept away along with the dust on the editing room floor, she complied.

The cadet, a scowl on his oxygen-deprived face, arose from the floor of the car and took a seat, placing the duffle bag between himself and Mitzi. Mitzi stared at him awkwardly, her eyes squinting with eager ferocity and an imbecilic smile decorating her face. She placed her hand on top of his bag, the palm facing up, the fingers wiggling back and forth, as the boy tried to regain his breath. He inhaled and exhaled laboriously, lifted his arms up above his head, occasionally sighed, and wiped his brow more than once. No one spoke a word. Mitzi continued to stare. Savannah continued to drive. A minute passed.

"What? What is it?" asked the former cadet to Mitzi. In response, Mitzi looked down at her hand, the fingers scampering back and forth as though she were playing an invisible stringed instrument.

"What?" asked the former cadet.

"Do you want to hold hands?" she asked.

"No. God, no. Get away from me. You about squashed me like a bug." The hand returned to the virginal lap; its owner untouched by insult. "Where are the two of you taking me? You can't just kidnap people, you know. This isn't Mexico and I can assure you my parents won't pay a cent to set me free. It'll be like that O. Henry story when they kidnapped the kid and, in the end, they had to pay the father for him to take him back. Oh, what was the name of that thing? You know what I'm talking about."

"I'm afraid that I only read Southern authors," said Savannah. "As to where we're taking you, I think the better question would be why we took you."

"Well, if you want to start with the better question, then that's fine with me. I've got plenty of them and I really don't care what order you want to take them in."

"We grabbed you and put you in the car, cadet, because I knew for a fact that you were planning on running in front of a moving train and killing yourself. I have seen so much suicide and woe in my life that I knew I couldn't live with myself if I just sat idly by and let you do it."

"Suicide?" he said with a laugh. "Suicide? You're out of your skull."

"Cadet, you need to get a hold of yourself and realize that life's worth living. Sure, we endure horrors that would put most people in a mental institution, and some people do end up in mental institutions, but there is always the marsh and the sea that bring us back to the joy of life."

"Well, I really appreciate you saving me from nothing other than a ride home. That's really swell of the both of you. And I especially appreciate you about breaking my legs with the car door and then smothering me. If we were in India or someplace like that, I'd have to spend the rest of my life in your service trying to save you from having someone pick you up from school so that I could be free of my debt."

"While we appreciate the sentiment, we can assure you that we were only doing our duty. Isn't that right, Mitzi?"

Mitzi nodded her head.

"Now, cadet…"

"Please quit calling me cadet. I'm no longer a cadet and I thank God for the day that I quit being one. My name's Tradd, and with preferences being preferences and all, I would appreciate it if you would just call me that."

"Ah, Tradd. You traitorous coward. Back at games are we, especially now that Will McLean is out of the picture?"

"I don't follow you."

"Yes, and you wouldn't. I imagine we'll need to take you back to your house on the Battery where you can spend time with your mother going over floral patterns and talking about ships with Commerce."

It was at this point that Tradd realized that he was dealing with lunatics. And as this dawned on him, he also realized that he should have realized this long ago. They had cast him into the back of a car, fondled him on the floorboard, then accused him of wanting to kill himself with a train; it simply wasn't the normal way to conduct one's affairs. But now that their mouths were emitting full sentences, any doubts that he had had before, which were few once he thought about it, were dispelled.

"Yes, Commerce," he said. "He and his ships. Um. Yes. I wish my folks did have a house on the Battery. I wish they had a lot of things though. A boat. Um. A boat would be nice. The two of you aren't headed up to Spartanburg by any chance, are you?"

He received no response.

"No. I wouldn't think you would be. You see, that's where I'm from. That's where I need to go. Not that I really want to go back. I don't think my parents will be very excited that I got kicked out, but I'm positive they won't be excited about the fact that my tuition was nonrefundable. No. I still don't want to hold your hand. Please put it away. Um. So, now that I know why you rescued me, can you tell me where you're rescuing me to?"

Savannah had placed them back on the highway. The Atlantic Ocean had not made its appearance, but there was still time.

"We haven't decided that yet," said Savannah. "You see, in the book, cadet Dante Pignetti—who was affectionately known as Pig—..."

"Nice name."

"Yes. Well, he was run over by the train. If he had not gone and killed himself then I imagine he would have moved back up to New Jersey and married that girl whose photograph he worried over so much. So, I guess you should go marry your sweetheart and move on with life, although you will always carry the stigma with you that you were drummed out of the corps. You have a girlfriend, don't you?"

"Nope. Single and gay as a blade. Therein lies a greater part of the problem. You see..."

"I could be your girlfriend," said Mitzi, who again offered her hand to be held.

"Yes, I imagine you could, but..."

"Mitzi, you're promised to Chicken John," said Savannah.

"Ah, you're already sworn to another," said Tradd. "My loss is clearly his gain. I didn't know that God made such beauty until I met you. Mitzi, right?"

"I'm not really promised to him," said Mitzi.

"You most certainly are," said Savannah.

"Watch where you're going," said Tradd in a rapid crescendo as they approached the back of a logging truck.

"Savannah, he's older than my Dad," said Mitzi.

"You stupid dolt!" said Savannah. "How many times do I have to tell you that he's my twin, and therefore our age? That he's one of the most handsome men in the world? That he is the paragon of masculinity and that any woman on earth who would be lucky enough to call him hers would be a fool to turn him down or even look at anyone else?"

"And he's going out with her?" asked Tradd.

"I haven't even met him yet," said Mitzi.

"But you will," said Savannah.

"With a girl like you, and if he's like she says he is, then he could only be using you as a beard. Sorry, but that's probably the case."

"Chicken John's never had a beard!" said Savannah with a laugh. "The two of you! What am I going to do with the two of you?"

"As for her," said Tradd, "I don't care, but I would certainly like to know the answer to that question in regards to me."

THIRTY-FIVE

This too was what made him an artist. Not hard work or creativity, but this, this inability to keep from crying. It came over him every once in a while, and when it did, there was no stopping the creative process from taking place. First you were plagued with thoughts that you were worthless and that everything that you did had similar value. Your music stunk, your attempts at writing, when you used to attempt to write, were a joke, your relationship with everyone you knew was in shambles and forever would be so, your contributions to humanity lay on the debit side of the accounting chart, and the only thing that awaited you was death, the grim reaper not several states over, held up by a flat tire, but walking up your stairs at that very moment.

He huddled underneath a set of sheets encrusted with various forms of his genetic code, bawling into the pillow with deep, chest-driven gulps, trying to figure out where it all went wrong. Was it at the Iowa Writers' Workshop? It could have been. There he had arrived, freshly minted from Princeton, with a handful of short stories and a vision of staying there long enough only to return as a visiting lecturer. He found the place abysmal, as do most people when they visit that miserable state, but decided to make the best of it, although it seemed to him that he should make the best of it very quickly.

On his first day of class, he accused the professor of being a fraud. Creighton had not read any of the man's work, so he stuck to generalities—your prose is wooden, your dialogue stilted, your characters completely unbelievable—and found them to have great effect on both the person at whom they were directed and his fellow students. As for them, he savaged their stories and mocked their essays, compared the portions of their novels-in-progress to late-term literary abortions created in breakfast nooks by bored house-wives who felt that their childhood in Anywhere, U.S.A. was really something worth recounting, only to drive their husbands to divorce over the amount of money spent at the vanity press. It was not that he really thought this, but he felt that he had to strike fast and strike hard, and let these historical nothings know that they stood in the presence of an icon.

The result of this was that no one could stand to be in his presence. His offers to join a group for lunch were rebuffed with what he deemed outright hostility. His room, which he named "The Opium Den," went by night after night without a single body other than his own festooned about the pillows on the floor, the hookah never lit, the discussions on Coleridge never had. He had even gone so far as volunteering for committees and such, but the meeting notices never made it in his cubbyhole, he left to watch the goings-on of the wine-tasting party from an uncomfortable chair over in the corner.

It was during this time that he began to understand loneliness, and for him it became the cranky old lady in the house all of the neighborhood boys thought was haunted, he the fool goaded into trying to retrieve an errant ball from the second floor, only to be caught and sat down by the aged scamp whom he grew to love. Because it was loveable. The silence it gave. Its lack of demands. Its unneed for cultivation. And more than all of that, he was supposed to be a writer, and how could one write if he was always going out to lunch, sitting around talking about foolishness, and spending time deciding what color napkins should be used for the finger foods? It drove him. He had to fill it with something, and for him that something was writing.

Like many authors, his first work was deeply autobiographical. No, he had never been a soldier of fortune, he was not born in a brothel in the Philippines, he had not killed his father in a cockpit, he had not sold his sister into slavery, nor had he engaged in long discussions concerning metaphysics with Hegel or taken the man's wife for a lover. Those were difficult passages where he had to reach deep into his soul and grab what life had taught him while he was living it. But for the seventy-five pages where Osgood stared into the hole, there was no such struggle, because that was him. He had his own hole in "The Opium Den"; he had his own thoughts of nothingness. And perhaps that was the problem now. Where was Creighton Starke? Who was Creighton Starke? Where was his hole, and not the actual hole, but the metaphorical one that would move his writing hand for seventy-five pages of wonder?

But back to where it all went wrong. Was that where it all went wrong? This brought to him the question of whether there actually is one moment that defines us, for better or worse, that can be pinpointed, given a date, and rehashed and dissected as such. Creighton found that it was usually a series of mistakes or strokes of good fortune that led you to where you were, either awash in despair and performing on yourself in front of an old plutocrat who sits watching you disinterestedly from the plush divan, or awash in glory as you watch a nameless piece of flesh performing on him(her)self while you sit comfortably on your plush divan. But what if it was in fact just one thing?

Perhaps that could be the theme of his next book. The characters and the plot and the setting and all of the other bric-a-brac of storytelling would come later, but this time he could start off with just a theme. Where were the theme books? They had been all the rage decades ago, but had gone the way of the dodo, a bird that no longer existed. He would have to use lots of imagery, something that had also disappeared, with watches ticking and different colors representing certain things that would probably be biblical. Maybe a man sits in bed crying, knocked down on the street of bad luck and crushed under the wheels of ignominy, recounting the vague passages of his life until he stumbles upon the image of the girl at the dance who wore the white dress, which Creighton would accentuate with many biblical references to the color, and a ticking watch that the protagonist cannot but help keep eyeing. They hold each other in their arms all night as they waltz around the local VFW hall, promising their undying devotion, naming their children, and picking out their three-bedroom house and china pattern. Afterwards, he has violent sex with her in the flag closet and accidently knocks her out when he rams her head into the wall, and thus leaves, swearing never to see her again. As fate would have it, however, she ends up carrying his child, and only a vague recollection of how it arrived in her belly, suffering from a concussion as she was. Life goes on. And then one day he attends a watermelon festival, and he sees the child and knows that it is his, and he sees her and knows that she should have been his, but he runs away as he doesn't want to be bogged down with child-support payments that would cut into both his lifestyle and his investment in the mink farm for which he held such high hopes, but that ended so disastrously.

Yes, that was what Creighton must mine. He must turn away from the desire to have photographs and scribbled drawings in his work, from the use of different fonts to convey emphasis and wit, from four-letter words and graphic descriptions of intercourse, from placing both himself and famous figures in his work, from false dedications, fake forewords, and fallacious footnotes—all of the gilding that makes its way into modern storytelling—and get back to the ways of old. He should try his hand at an epic poem. He should attempt to write in iambic pentameter. Apples should represent youth, lemons the bitter fruits of age. His characters should have names like Mr. N_____ and Mrs. W_____.

One of the things that the Iowa Writers' Workshop had taught him was that in order to set oneself apart from the herd, one must attempt to either be talented, which few of us are, or attempt to be different. At that point in life, Creighton saw himself as both talented and different, but lately he had given up on the talent and despaired over the different. But perhaps this was the ticket. Do what no one else is doing, and no one was crafting epic poems in iambic pentameter where apples represented the youth of Mr. N_____ and lemons the decrepitude of Mrs. W_____.

He noticed that during this internal discourse his eyes had stopped leaking and his breathing had returned to normal. All of the thinking and emotional creativity had left him spent, however. Maybe some time relaxing over a comfortable read. Joyce's *Ulysses* sat on his bedside table as did some poems by George Garrett and a collection of short stories by Julio Cortázar. They were so far away, though. He tried to shift his body, his arm outstretched, but the straining wore him down even further. How he needed to put a television set in his room. A discomforting ache in his back had been bothering him for some time and when reaching back to rub it, Creighton discovered a set of papers. He looked them over, closed his eyes for a moment, then began to read as follows:

```
    I can't believe all of this is happening! Chile
you won't believe it! Mother is coming up to New
York city and she's bringing Sesame with her!
Won't she have a hoot! Sesame in New York City!
In all my days!
    I was marrying Jonathan and mother was having
a cow over that! You see Jonathan was jewish and
he was a doctor at the biggest hospital here in
New York city and had bee on the cover of a bunch
of "big" magazines but you see he wasn't catho-
lic. I told mother that waht I did didn't matter
to her and mother had a few "choice" words but
Sesame put her in her place. "Miss D'Bergeolet!
You best be leavin that chile alone! She gawn be
marry! That's the Lord's way!"
    I guess I should tell you about Sesame. You
see I had grown up on an island in South Caro-
```

lina that none of you Yankee folk would have ever heard of and Sesame had basically been my mother. She wasn't my real mother because she was black and I wasn't but other than that she was basically my mother. As I've stated before I had grown up a geechee brat and I learned things from Sesame that weren't taught in books but that were wise. She knew voodoo and you didn't want her to cast a spell on you! You sure didn't! It was from her that I had learned the Gullah language and was why I said things like "chile" and "humph".

It was going to be a whirlwind! Jonathan was always busy at the hospital and I was always busy attending my classes at Harvard and writing poetry that had won the national book award and some other awards but I had to decorate the house. Jonathan and I had been living in "sin" and this was going to be the apartment we moved into when we weren't living in "sin." But it needed so much work! I had to do something1 But I had no money! I decided I had to do something!

I went down to the local K-Mart and found a floral pattern bedsheet that they had put on a blue light special. I bought all of them for twenty-five cents, which was a steal and decided that I would use them as a very formal wall paper in the dining room. I then found another store that was going out of business and they were practically giving away furniture so I haggled with the guy and bought an entire living room set for just ten dollars! Since I grew up in the lowcountry I needed to have plants around me to remind me of the marsh so I went to a nursery but they were too expensive so I walked around for a while and saw a guy who was throwing out what he thought were weeds but were actually red turnip flowers just like we had in the lowcountry. I talked to him for a while and he said "Sure. You can have them!" So I needed something to put them in so I walked over to the "Pottery Barn" and found that an arsonist had just burnt half the place down so they were selling their pots for like nothing!

I went home with all I bought and thought of how Jonathan would be impressed with how I had decorated the place and how much money I had saved! You go girl! he would say and then we would laugh with each other and then make love which I will get to later. But the bathroom needed work! My doorman bless his soul was the nicest man who ever lived and was always happy to see me and would always kid me and Jonathan about being in love even though he was a drunk. He had a brother who specialized in bathrooms and wouldn't you know it he was out of a job and he was willing to work for practically nothing! So I got Arturo (everyone seemed to be from somewhere else in New York city which was a lot different than growing up in the lowcountry) and he mad that bathroom sparkle! We had to rip out the fern closet which a lot of "old" apartments in New York city had and extend the floor, but once that was done we were set! I hung the sheets on the wall using an "old" geechee trick and put the plants down and then loaded in the furniture. It looked like a completely different place! I couldn't wait for Jonathan to see it!

You see I had gone up to Harvard and it turned out that Jonathan was one of my teachers in a class that dealt with brain surgery that I was taking just to see how I could use this in my poetry because I had been using a lot of stuff about the brain in my poems but I really needed to know how the brain really worked and thought that by learning brain surgery that I would know it better. He was from Canada and his exotic accent nearly drove me wild when he walked into the glass room and said "Goodday mate!" He said this to the entire class but his eyes were on me and let me tell you sister chile, my eyes were on him! He started talking about the basics of brain surgery and he asked a question and said "Isn't that right Ms. D'Bergerolet!" I didn't know what to say. *You're acting the fool girl!* So I told him that I didn't know. Everyone laughed at this and I was so embarrassed! I had to think and I had to think quick. I said "Why is it so difficult to shake your head up and down and say "no" and shake your head from side to side and say "Yes"? This must have something to do with the brain." Well let me tell you everyone who was laughing before wasn't laughing then. "That's very inter-esting Ms. D'Bergeolet. What you are referring to is Quarles theorem but that is usually only discussed in our upper level clases. Come see me after class."

So I saw him after class. We went back to my apartment but I had to get ready. At that time I was living at another apartment but it looked like a littel girl lived there! I threw all of my stuffed animals under the bed and picked up my

169

dirty clothes. I then walked down to Saks Fifth
Avenue and bought a bedroom set that they had one
sale for only ten dollars! I then hauled all of
that back to my apartment and the doorman said,
"Hey, you're going to need some plants to go with
that!" And I said, "I know! But where am I going
to get them?" He took me into the apartment of an
old couple who were dying and he said that they
dindn't need their plants anymore so we took them
and put them in my apartment. He then brought me
their rug up and their fine china and I said, "Now
get out of here Jerry O'Malley I've got a man
coming! Yahn!"

When Jerry O'Malley who was Irish and spoke
with an accent left I looked at myself in the
mirror. I needed to lose some weight! I drank a
bunch of water and did an hour of cardio in the
kitchen and then I went and weighed myself and
I had lost ten pounds! I looked at myself in the
mirror and I said, "YOu better look out Jonathan Goldbaum!" I then took a shower and used
some "expensive" shampoo that I had bought at
a "fancy" store on fifth avenue and scrubbed my
sefl with a loffah that I had and then I used some
"expensive" oils and creams on my skin that made
my skin shine! I then put on some lip gloss and
then bit my lips to give them some color and old
geechee trick and then I blow dried my hair up
then down so that I wouldn't have any curls.

Jonathan ended up knocking on the door when I
was in my towel and I was frantic! I opened the
door and when I did I realized that I had forgotten to buy any food! "Hello mate he said in his
Canadian accent which made my knees wilt "you

170

look ravishing in a towel. I most undoubtedly
have never seen anything so proscribedly sublime
in my life." "You watch yourself bubba! You're
talking to a lowcountry girl! Now behave!" "That
is the least of my intetions" he said in his
canadian accent. And then our eyes locked again.
*You can't do this chile! You gwan knocked in the
haid!* But I couldn't help it. He took me in his
arms and I looked at the blonde hairs on them and
wondered how smooth they would feel. He gave me
a kiss and then we melded into each other. Our
bodies fit each other's perfectly like they had
been made for each other and before I knew it
we were in the bed making sweet love. He lay on
top of me and kissed my toes and I felt like I
had gone to heaven and met the blessed Virgin so
sweet was the love we made and so proscribedly
sublime was th eway our bodies melded into
one another's.

And now we were getting married. Since Jonathan was jewish and I was catholic we decided
that we would get married by the local justice
of the piece in New York city and get married
in our apartment. But I had cooking to do! I
diced some parseley and put some cheroot up to
a boil and then I put some cloves in garlic oil
and simmered them in a skillet with some butter
until they were a golden brown. I tasted it with
a spoon. Delicious! I then got out a bottle of
very "expensive" wine and put the duck in the
oven. I was no Julia Child but I could cook! The
duck had been basted in an orange sauce and then
stuffed with wild herbs that I had learned all
about while living in the lowcountry and then I

had flounced it in rosemary and garlic that I had diced before putting them on. I put the rolls in the oven. Perfect! I then put two tablespoons of oil and vinegar into a seasoned patte that I had heard about in a magazine and set them out on a plate with some very "expensive" crackers. Scrumptious!

The doorbell rang and I went to get it and Sesame and mother were there and so was Chicken John and Roy! I gave them all hugs and Chicken John said "You look yahn like a crow filled with dumpling sauce!" "You best be mindin yo business hoecake!" I said as we always spoke in Gullah when we saw each other. "I best be mindin nothin!" cried Chicken John and then we laughed and punched each other on the arms for five minutes! My mohter was very cold to me and immediately went into Jonathan. "Lawdy, lawdy in all my days my girl's gone and married her a jew." *Why do I put up with this?* I thought. "Mother I won't have you using that language around my family and once we're married Jonathan and I'll be family!" "You coulda done a whole lot better!" she said. I didn't know why nothing I ever did was never good enouch for my mother. She cocked her hip and pretended like she was going to swoon which was her way of flirting and reminding us that she was one of the most beautiful women in the world. And then I saw Sesame. "Lawd chile. My littl' babies gawn be married!" 'Oh Sesame. I'm so glad you could come. It means so much to me! I hope you didn't bring any of your voodoo charms!" "Lawd yes I sho been sho did! A lika get that man on the god Shedareen and make sure he good to

·mah girl!" "Oh Sesame. I love you and think that
you're ways are both fascinating and filled with
love." And then I saw Roy. "Hey you got anything
to eat? And what's that smell?" He had a Pepsi
cola in his hand and I decided not to respond to
him.

The justice of the piece arrived and so did
Senator Fritz Hollings and his wife Tinesy and
Senator Strom Thurmond and his wife Misty. After
them came several astronauts and the head of
the U.N. and two "big" time actors who we had
known from growing up in the lowcountry. My mind
was a whirl! I was busy cooking in the kitchen
and Sesame came in and said "Yahn! You best be
gettin out of here chile! Messin up my kitchen!
Where dah garlic? Yahn!" "Sesame you best not be
talkin bout my food. I can certainly take care
of it!" "I ain't havin no chile of mine cookin
on her weddin day! Praise Gawd!" Sesame although
she practiced several forms of voodoo which was
oftentimes considered a form of satanism was very
religious and you could tell this because she was
so loving and because she knew a bunch of songs.
She began to sing one.

In the cross/Sweet Jesus takin us cross the
Jordan/The sweet waters like Pharoh/Rising in
the dust/of Jesus.

I left the kitchen after telling Sesame that
I loved her very much and both of us crying and
then went and found Chicken John.

"How is the war going?" I asked. He knew that I
had been protesting it and writing lots of poems
about it.

"I guess it's going fine. I'm either flying missions over Vietnam or going on super secret missions way across enemy lines with the commandos. But I don't want to talk abou tit."

"Chicken John! Why don't men talk about their feelings? Why doens't this family ever talk about their feelings!"

"It's the southenr way." replied Chicken John. "We don't talk about these things."

I hated that war. It was an unjust war and if I could protest it then I knew that I would. Boys were dying and for what? No one knew and our president didn't even knew. He oftentimes called me or other members of my family for advice on etiquette and things and the last tiem I had talked to him I told him that I thought he should call off the war. He promised to think about it.

It was time for the wedding. We had a soprano from the Charleston singing society flown up for the wedding and she sang "Edelweis" and everyone was moved to tears. I was in the kitchen with Sesame and she gave me my bouquet and I said, "I hope I'm doing the right thing Sesame." "Lawd Chile who knows other than the Lawd whether we be doin right or ain't? It's Gawd's decision. I put some sassafrass that's been dipped in hog gravy to make Shedareen stay away and to make sure that man'a yos ain't gwine stray none." "Sesame! You didn't!" And I looked into my bouquet and saw the sassafrass dipped in hog gravy and I couldn't believe my eyes! "You wicked woman Sesame!" And she laughed and hugged me to her and I felt love like I had never felt before. "It's time chile. The Lawd say it be time." And I knew she was

rihgt. But how about all of the problems that I
was having with Jonathan? There was nothing that
I could put my finger on but something was there.
It was probably nothing, but when I said this
to myself I knew that I should have trusted my
lowcountry instict and ran away like I had that
time in the marsh. But I didn't. With my grandfather on my arm I marched down the aisle.

At the conclusion of the chapter, Creighton Starke again felt
himself overcome with despair and once more dug his face into his
pillow. An hour later he arose, wondering what Scott was up to.

THIRTY-SIX

What a mess, Roy thought to himself, sitting in the driver's seat of his rented van, the asphalt of I-26 passing underneath the tires in a solid hum. While many called it a virtual life, the computer existence clearly was not. In a span of twenty-four hours, he had had his heart ripped out by Miss Sunflower and his throat almost similarly removed by Magik Merlin, and if neither of those were real, then he didn't know what was. This was what his father and mother could not understand. To try and argue with someone, a flesh-and-blood relative at that, that a relationship with someone you had never before met, whose voice you had never before heard, could be just as strong as one with a wife of fifty years, was simply maddening. As Miss Sunflower said, didn't people fall in love with Shakespeare? Didn't Anne Frank's diary move her readers to tears? Why then was it so difficult to understand that he, Razor Roy Edwards, could similarly love Miss Sunflower or feel her pain?

As for Magik Merlin, there was no doubt but that they would meet again. Perhaps in the fields of Mongor. Maybe in the land of Iridium. It really did not matter, for what did matter was that Roy, in the form of Ut, would do all that he could to make amends, and Magik Merlin, or whatever he would be called in his second coming, would grow to understand that an attack with a battle axe, after hours of frustration and flagon upon flagon of hearty mead grog, did not constitute a true revelation of sentiment, but a statistical aberration on what was for the most part a linear path of respect and admiration across the great chart of life.

There was no telling what Erica had gotten herself into. He was her older brother, her mentor and friend, and it had been right that he should be sent to save her. He would succeed in his quest, he would do it even if he died in the process, and if he did not die, which given the light nature of the task was the most likely resolution, then he would return home, a changed man, refreshed, reenergized, with a new perspective on both life and life's relationships. And with this shedding of skin, he would reenter the chat room and make amends. A tear entered his eye, and the boldness of a lion entered the hollow of his breast.

Roy did not know how he would find his sister, but he had his mind, and that, if nothing else, would guide him toward her. They had not been separated at birth, connected by brain tissue or a shared pancreas, but there was a certain amount of intuition that each carried concerning the other. He could sense her anger when he ate all of the rolls at dinner. She could equally divine his rage when she picked up the phone late at night and disconnected him from his internet world. His blood flowed through her veins; hers through his, and given their similar upbringings and parental models, they could not help but be clairvoyants of a sort when it came to the other.

It was time for a plan. Tracking down a sister in a city of hundreds of thousands was not a feat accomplished simply by standing on a street corner, calling her name, and hoping for the best.

So here is how it would go: he would set up a home base, preferably located in a decent hotel somewhere downtown. He would try and establish an internet connection in order to see what the groping tendrils of intelligence had gathered. If a lead existed, he would follow it. If not, then he would go to the biggest tourist attractions he could find and scour them for her. Then, if still unsuccessful, he would perhaps look into posting flyers. Flyers worked for dogs and cats. He was fairly sure of that.

His thoughts took him to another time she had been lost. It was at the state fair a number of years ago when he was wasting away in the seventh grade, and she was blooming in the fourth. They had

177

become separated after riding something called The Himalaya. Foolishly, he had gone to find a corn dog after the ride and left his sister behind. Perhaps in your day and age, reader of the future, the state fair will have returned to the glory of Elysium, where freshly pressed youths wearing white bucks court hoop-skirted women in pigtails through the use of inoffensive song and dance. At that time, and at present, the state fair in this unnamed locale did not approach any state of nirvana, and white bucks were and are soon ruined by urine and dirt. Men with varying styles of facial hair and tattoos roam the midway, half or fully drunk with their half or fully drunk common-law wives and illegitimate children who curse like the bastards that they are. Gangs of teenagers agree to meet other gangs of teenagers so that they can fight with knives or guns, choosing to do so out of complete lack of concern for their own welfare or the other fairgoers. Add in the number of pedophiles working the rides and tending the concessions and one easily feels the horror that Roy felt upon realizing that they had become separated.

Knowing her as he did, he knew that she would not have the sense to simply stay put, so The Himalaya, although not useful, was helpful in the sense that he could mark it off his search itinerary. He roamed through the rides, fingering the damp tickets in his pocket, spending a few on the fun house where he appeared fat and tall and she never appeared at all. Afterwards, he strolled through the section containing impossible games and cheap prizes, all made to sound very inviting by the pederasts chomping out their glories through distorted microphones. He feasted upon another corn dog and caught a show involving an Elvis impersonator and a set of accompanying musicians who resembled the type of men he often saw hitchhiking on the side of the road.

He had no idea how much time had passed, but after the show was over, it dawned on him that Erica was truly lost and he no closer to finding her. He began running. Through the throng of adults and their small children, past the series of stinking garbage cans, from one entrance gate to another. He skipped along the lines of the waiting, examining their faces and dismissing each with computer-fast glances. He did everything but call for her, an exercise he realized would be futile given the loud music blaring from every corner.

And as all seemed lost, and the night began to wind down to its final ticks, he began to cry. He sat down on the corner of a dirty curb, buried his head in his hands, and wept like a child. It was a passing police officer who noticed him and took him to a building where he never thought anyone went because it contained no drinks, no food, no games, no rides, no bearded ladies, no transforming mirrors. It contained nothing. Nothing at all. Much to his surprise, however, within its walls were his parents and Erica. His sorrow quickly transformed to joy upon finding his lost sister but was reborn in similar haste when his father said to him, "You stupid son of a bitch. Where in the hell have you been? Huh? Answer me!" To which his mother said, "Harry, don't you dare speak to the child like that!" To which his father said, "He's lucky speaking is the only thing I'm going to do to him. Running off like a moron and leaving his ten-year-old sister to fend for herself. I should take him out and tan his hide."

But his father was wrong about what had happened, as he often was.

Roy rode I-26 into the Meeting Street exit and bore right. He then passed by the pool hall where, unbeknownst to him, Savannah was soon to make an appearance, and continued driving, finding a Night's Inn where parking did not seem a problem and service was sure to not be an issue.

THIRTY-SEVEN

They somehow made it to Meeting Street.

"Here we are!" said Savannah. "Mitzi, welcome to Charleston!"

"Your friend really likes to shout, doesn't she," said Tradd to Mitzi.

"It's how they speak in the low country," Mitzi replied. "I think it's called Gullah."

"Yes, you would," said Tradd. "So, where are the two of you from?"

"I grew up here," said Savannah, "and after attending Harvard and living in New York City where I was a very famous poet, I have come back to find my long-lost twin brother, Chicken John, who is being hunted by the federal authorities for acts that he committed against a nuclear power plant with the use of the commando tactics he learned in the fields of Vietnam."

"Indiana," said Mitzi. "I'm a Hoosier."

"Oh, I would imagine that Indiana's a great place. Probably filled with lovely women like yourself."

"It's the corn," said Mitzi. "It brings out the shine in your skin and hair."

"I'll have to try it. Now Savannah, you said that you grew up here. Where did you go to school?"

"Oh, on a little island with a group of black children. They were so afraid of swimming, these little black children, even though they lived on an island! Can you imagine?"

"Amazing," said Tradd. "Absolutely amazing."

"And I taught them all about Beethoven and Mozart and stuff. I taught them about the beauty of the world outside the fixed boundaries of their island home, while at the same time I learned that there was much beauty on the island itself and that, while these people were very ignorant in the ways of books and such, they were wise in a way that couldn't be taught in books."

"I can only imagine how they appreciated you," said Tradd. "And then you said you went to Harvard and wrote poetry. You've obviously led some kind of life." By this point, it was clear that Tradd had nothing else pressing.

"My life is filled with woe. And I say that, but at the same time it is filled with such love for Sesame and the marsh and the creeks and the tidal basins and things like that."

They had been sitting at a stop light, and when it turned green, Savannah moved them forward, only to turn into a parking space a few feet afterwards. She had brought the car to a store that read "Pool Hall" in decaying red letters above the door. Outside sat three black men on top of produce crates. They looked at the three white people in the car with mild wonder, and Tradd shared a similar stare with them, while Mitzi simply stared, and Savannah beamed.

"What are you stopping for?" Tradd asked. "And why are you stopping here?"

"This is a very exclusive club that my father used to bring me to when he wasn't drinking and beating me and my family members," said Savannah. "I thought it would be nice to drop in after all of these years and say hello to everyone. You see, although my father drank a lot and beat his family to excess, he came from one of Charleston's finest families, directly descended from General Beauregard, and that allowed us certain privileges. He was loved by everyone, my father, so it is so incredibly ironic that he didn't love us."

"Oh, I'm sure he did," said Tradd. "Maybe it was just in his special way…"

She went to Conroy: "I lived out my childhood thinking my father would one day kill me. I hate my mother and father, yet in five minutes I'll tell you that I didn't really mean to say that and I love them with all of my heart. We were born to a house of complication, drama and pain. We were typical Southerners. In every Southerner, beneath the veneer of cliché lies a much deeper motherlode of cliché. But even cliché is overlaid with enormous power when a child is involved."

"Complicated," said Tradd. "And given that, I say we skip your father's exclusive club and keep on going towards town."

"Tradd, we are here in order to confront our fears and scrape away the lies that have enveloped the truth. We aren't about to skip anything. Now, let's go inside and let me say hello to a few special people, and then we can go on."

"You go ahead," said Tradd. "I'll just stay here and keep an eye on the car."

"Me, too," said Mitzi.

"No one's staying in the car," said Savannah. "Now get out."

With much grumbling from all three sides, they stepped into the brilliant carbon forest where Savannah freshly greeted the men sitting on the crates.

"Dis de man wuh t'ief de hog!" said Savannah after the requisite hellos, directing a nod to her friends and a wink to the men, who might have been mute given their silent responses. "W'en Bubba meet de bull, 'e lick back en' gone home!" And at that she slapped her thighs, like she believed Sesame always did when she said something funny and acted as though she were wiping tears from her eyes.

Tradd had to be grabbed by the arm by Savannah and pushed from behind by Mitzi in order to get him into the exclusive establishment. And at the moment he entered he realized that it was certainly exclusive, but not in the way one would normally describe exclusivity with two white girls. He had never been in such a place in all of his limited days, and he quickly understood why he hadn't, and why he never would again, for here scattered about stood the harvest of four hundred years of slavery, one hundred years of Jim Crow, thirty more of general disenfranchisement, staring at him with bright eyes from the darkened corners of the building, with hatred, he had to presume, and murderous urges, he hoped not to be the case. In a word, it was disconcerting, and the lunatic poetess was doing nothing to assuage the adrenaline pumping through his system or the mental image of his bloated corpse floating face-down in a forgotten marsh.

"There you are!" Savannah said in her never-ending stage voice as she clasped her arms around the back of a woman drinking at the bar. The woman's response to the physical assault and spilling of her beer with the simple exclamation of "What the fuck?!" did not seem to register with Savannah, who continued on, saying, "It's me, Savannah! Savannah D'Bergeolet! You remember me, don't you?"

"Bitch, you better get your motherfuckin hands off of me!"

"Oh, I know. You remember me as the little Geechee brat who was always out crabbing and chasing roosters down by the bog. I know! I've grown!"

"I said, get your motherfuckin hands off of me!"

Although it was clear that it was not because of the demand, Savannah moved on, approaching the person on the next barstool over, a man who appeared as though he had slept in a ditch more days than he had not, and gave him a vigorous hug. Tradd felt the soft collar of his t-shirt rapidly strangling the life out of him. He turned, but saw that the door was blocked by two men, thereafter, turning to Mitzi with tears in his eyes to find that she was still staring at him with that same imbecilic smile.

183

"And you! You! Where you been, chile!" said Savannah, her head pressed deeply against his chest.

"Aw, no! Aw, hell no! I know you ain't huggin on my man, you white bitch!" The woman stood up and grabbed Savannah by the back of her hair, yanking it down with a mighty fist and raising the other to strike the winner of the National Poetry Award. "Get the fuck off'a him! Get the fuck off'a him!" The first blow glanced off of D'Bergeolet cheekbone, but the ensuing ones hit nothing but the smoke-filled air, as she was restrained by a number of people who were apparently opposed to violence.

While the woman screamed and tried to thrash off her restrainers, Savannah ran back to the much-mortified Tradd and the much-in-love Mitzi, wildly oblivious to it all. "You hear that?" she asked, referring to the yelled curses. "That's the Gullah I grew up hearing every day! Mitzi, that's what I've been talking about!"

"Huh," said Tradd. "My mother always claimed that those were French words."

"I'll kill you! You bitch! I'll kill you!"

"That's Bessie, Livvie's child. Boy-oh-boy is she spirited!"

"Yes," said Tradd. "She certainly is. Well, now that you've said your hellos, it seems to me that it's time to move on."

"Move on?" asked Savannah.

"Yes and find Chicken John. It's Chicken John, isn't it?"

Savannah did not reply, so Tradd looked over at Mitzi.

"I'm not promised to him," Mitzi said.

"Listen, you fool," said Tradd in a violent whisper, "you won't be promised to anything if we don't get out of here right now."

"We're going nowhere," said Savannah. She left the two of them and walked back to her aggressor, carrying with her an unearthly serenity, stopping a few feet away and standing there with her hands to her sides and her feet set apart. Her appearance seemed to have a calming effect on the woman Savannah knew as Bessie, as she stopped struggling and looked into the eyes of D'Bergeolet.

"What?" she asked. "What the fuck you want, bitch?"

Savannah went to Benton Frank: "Bessie, I know that Livvie's gone, but I want to let you know that she appears to me in mirrors and lets me know that everything's okay. I saw her just the other night and she was with Nelson and Mama and Father, and…and…" And here Savannah began to cry. "…they were so happy. She wanted me to tell you that she loved you. That's when I realized it. Love. It mystically transcended death. It healed hearts. It changed thoughts. And when you met it head-on, it gave you courage in return. And then I put my hand up to the mirror and she held hers to meet mine. The mirror was warm. I would have given anything to hold her hand, but the warmth was there. She faded away until she and Nelson were visible no more. Finally, I saw just my own reflection."

A hush filtered through the thick smoke of the pool hall, and the woman Savannah called Bessie stood with her mouth open and her eyes wide, silent, still. A cough came from behind the bar; someone scraped a chair on the floor. Tradd found himself holding Mitzi's shoulder with a frightened claw, as Mitzi tried to spit out a hair that she had recently found in her mouth.

And then, as though a switch had been flicked, Bessie broke into a gat-toothed smile, saying, "Bitch, I want some of the shit you got!" afterwards beginning a chain of laughter whose length would have had to have been measured in miles.

Savannah understood Bessie's statement to mean that Bessie admired her Geechee spunk and low country wisdom, whereas in reality she referred to the crack, marijuana, crystal meth, or whatever it was that she imagined had turned Savannah into a raving madwoman. It did not matter. Savannah leapt at Bessie and took her in her arms, the tears still streaming down her face, interpreting the laughter of ridicule for that of low country joy.

It would be nice to tell you here that what followed was what one can oftentimes find in Hollywood fare, with the white protagonists finding themselves in the center of the party, assimilating with the crowd, an all-friends-forever-after in a sort of I-Have-a-Dream-type of montage of smiles, soul shakes, ethnic gaffes, and the drunken white boy, with sunglasses on, singing along with the band to the approbation of the black crowd. But as much as Savannah wanted it, and as much as Tradd would have enjoyed it, this was not the case. After much laughter, Bessie turned her back once more to Savannah and reacquainted herself with her beer, and the others generally went about their business. Savannah regathered with Mitzi and Tradd, again regaling them with her love of Gullah and tales of her being a Geechee brat, but that was about it. Tradd resumed his efforts at getting them to leave, and was about to succeed, when they were approached by the two men who had previously been blocking the door.

"Y'all play pool?" one of them asked.

Tradd turned and looked at the fellow, beginning at his shoes and continuing up to his eyes, which were set approximately six feet four inches above the ground, and upon reaching them, he let out an involuntary gulp.

Savannah could not remember any of the characters in any of her books playing pool, and therefore she did not know how to respond. However, when she thought of the many Conroy men who were premium athletes and of her own gridiron glory, the response became clear to her.

"Of course," she said. "Pa bin disgus' w'en de wurrum nyam 'e crap."

The men had no idea what to make of her father's disgust over worms eating his crop but decided that her first sentence was sufficient to start a game, immediately chalking up their cues. Tradd, on the other hand, believed that she had said something to the effect of her being able to kick the crap out of them, and knowing that this was an impossibility, decided that no game should commence.

"I…I really think…" he began.

"We're playin' for money," said one.

"…um…we probably…"

"You any good?"

"Um. I…Um. I can play a little bit."

The exchange of words caused a minor blitzkrieg in Savannah's brain, for they mirrored a telling exchange in Conroy's *Beach Music*. To set the scene, Jordan was a new kid from California playing baseball with the low country boys for the first time. When asked that question, he responded just as Tradd had responded, but without the ums. Here is what the narrator had to say about Jordan's reply: "And in the secret language of athletes Jordan was letting us know that we were in the presence of a player."

"We most certainly will be playing for money!" said Savannah, a statement immediately followed by an open-eyed gasp from Tradd. "How much?"

"How much you got?"

"Mitzi, how much money do you have?"

"I told you, I only brought forty dollars."

"Well, put it down on the table. I'll add in my thirty, which puts us at seventy. How about you, Tradd? How much?"

Although flummoxed, Tradd quickly thought up a lie. "They don't allow us to carry money at the Citadel. Not a penny in these pockets."

"Seventy dollars, gentlemen," said Savannah with a bright smile. "Put up or shut up, is what I say."

The men gladly complied.

THIRTY-EIGHT

Roy found comfort in the Night's Inn. Granted, a hint of stale cigarette smoke lingered in the air, and several translucent smears stained
the comforter, but the air conditioner worked like a mighty beast and
the television set came equipped with a functional remote control,
making up for any such negatives. And to top it all off, the bed had
three pillows, whereas his at home only had one, and he began to
wonder why he did not have three or even four back in his nameless hometown, because he didn't think they could be that expensive and it certainly made one feel like a sultan or something like a
sultan when he lay around the sack surrounded by a bunch of them.

A police procedural glowed on the screen, and he watched for
a good fifteen minutes, first on top of the comforter, then partially
under it, then fully tucked in, thinking that the husband had to
have killed his wife, feeling empathy with the white policeman who
expressed this view, scorn for his Puerto Rican partner who accused
him of racism. The Davinator believed that stereotypes were valid
because they were based upon anecdotal evidence, which scientifi-
cally speaking was just as valid as any other kind, but Miss Sunflower,
who apparently had several Puerto Rican friends, found such thinking, and thinking in support of such thinking, abominable. When
in response the Davinator asked her if she were accusing him of
being a snowman, laughs out loud and smiling emoticons filled the
computer screen until Miss Sunflower had no choice but to laugh
out loud herself and tell the only racist joke that she knew: Why
wasn't Christ born in Poland? Because they couldn't find three wise

men and a virgin. And whereas she was only trying to fit in a bit and join in on the laughs out loud, it happened that the Davinator was Polish, his last name being Wlodarczyk, and he quickly shouted her down with a long list of accomplishments by people of Polish descent, none of which Razor Roy could remember at the moment, asleep as he was.

THIRTY-NINE

The money had performed a trick. Or perhaps it was the two men who had performed a trick with it. Simply hard to say. There was no sleight of hand involved, and no one in the audience was left baffled, but nevertheless, there was something magical about it. What happened was that Tradd could no more make the white ball knock in one of the colored ones than turn it into a turtledove, and Mitzi, blind without her glasses, could barely tell the white ball from the colored ones, whereas the two gentlemen could do both with amazing skill, to the extent that one would not have been surprised if they could in fact turn the cue ball into a turtledove. The seventy dollars, once the property of Savannah and Mitzi, suddenly transformed before everyone's eyes into the property of the others. Oddly enough, the entire transaction took place without so much as a *presto*.

Savannah watched the game blindly ignorant as to which way it was falling. She had never had much of an interest in billiards and therefore had little understanding of it or its rules, so all along she stood, her arms crossed, shouting out things about missing hogs and unwanted boll weevils, smiling as destruction came sailing her way. At its conclusion, she assumed that the two men took the money so that they could go to the cash register and double it and loudly congratulated her traveling companions, going on and on about getting some mull gravy to celebrate.

Mitzi, however, began to cry.

"We won't be buying any mull gravy without money," she said. "We won't be buying anything." She attempted to bury her head in Tradd's chest, but he swatted her away with a hand.

"No money?" said Savannah. "What are you talking about, you idiot? We just won seventy dollars."

"Won?" said Mitzi. "We didn't win anything. They killed us."

Savannah looked over at the bar, her face clouded with confusion. "Oh," she said.

"Why did you tell them we would bet?" Mitzi said with a wail. "We told you we couldn't play pool. And all of our money. It's gone. Gone!"

"You might as well have put a match to it," said Tradd, "or spent it on some much-needed beauty products. Anyway, we've got a car and we've got gas, and I say we use both of those to get out of here. It's only a matter of time before we're all deservedly killed."

"Don't worry, Mitzi," said Savannah, putting an arm over her friend's shoulder and leading her to the door. "That's one of the great things about being in the low country, even if you don't have money you can live off of the land and the kindness of others. We can run down to the creek and catch all of the mull shrimp and mull gravy that we want and cook it right there on the bank. And if you don't want to do that, we just need to walk up to any house on the Battery, tell them who we are, and we'll be invited in for dinner and drinks. That's just how it works, so no need to cry."

"Okay, okay," said Mitzi. "I'll stop, but I'm really not up for shrimping at the moment. Let's just find someone who'll fix us lunch. Please?"

"Consider it done," said Savannah with a laugh.

They reached the car and once more acknowledged the gentlemen on the crates, afterwards stepping in the D'Bergeolet steed and heading off.

"You're really in for a treat, Mitzi," said Savannah. "You're about to see the real Charleston. Cobblestone streets, horses and carriages, ladies dressed in finery, men dressed in livery, a certain level of decorum that is as refined as the steel magnolia that I've often compared to my mother. You are about to smell the primal amniotic smell of the sea and the ripe brimstone smell of pluff mud. We'll pass by St. Michael's Episcopal Church, and you'll see old ladies in hats standing in the middle of the street, having an animated conversation, cars will be backed up for half a mile, and nobody will blow a horn."

While the soliloquy danced its lively jig, they traveled along Meeting Street, the windows rolled down, fecund musk all around them. It was approaching noon, and the city was clogged with automobiles. The streets were not of cobblestone and the horses looked like the only things that kept them going as they carried around the masses of the visiting elderly were the whips being laid along their backs and the imminent future of the dog food factory. As to the people, they wore no finery or livery, but walked around in t-shirts and shorts, pale legs and pale arms to either pole and black fanny packs sitting on the healthy equator of their guts. One of them, sporting a Canadian maple leaf on his backpack in a fit of unwarranted national pride, was nearly run down by a motorist making a right turn. The horn erupted from under the hood, and the horns from the motorists immediately behind broke into song as though they all contained the brains of dogs. The old ladies in hats and gloves did not make an appearance but had they it was clear that they would not have done so unscathed by either horn or withering expletive. The Buick stuttered forward a few feet then stopped. And again. And again. And again. Ad infinitum.

"There's the slave market," said Savannah, pointing to her left. Tradd let out a light groan. Mitzi turned in her seat and lifted her broken glasses to her eyes.

"Did they sell slaves there?" she asked.

"Up until a few years ago," said Savannah. "My generation—say what you want to about us, but you can't say we didn't change everything and make it better—could not stand for the injustice that our parents' generation had allowed to exist. We burned our bras and protested the war. Hell, we invented rock and roll. It was a great generation, probably the greatest. Well, we marched against the slave market and made them shut it down and now, as you can see, instead of slaves it's filled with great shops and restaurants."

"A few years ago, huh?" said Tradd.

"Yeah," said Savannah.

"Like you consider over a hundred a few? Anyway, I don't think they ever even sold slaves there."

Savannah turned around in the car to look at him. He, eyes on the road, shouted as they almost crashed into the back of a car.

"You didn't grow up here, so I think it's hardly fair for you to judge us, Tradd. The South is not something that can simply be read about. It has to be lived. You have to open up that oyster and taste it and know that you're tasting your childhood."

"Whatever," said Tradd. "I stand corrected until I've eaten an oyster. But tell me this, do you actually know someone who lives on the Battery, or are we just going to go around knocking on random doors and hope for the best?"

"I would say that I know almost everyone who lives on the Battery. You see, because my family was Catholic, we were always outsiders in Charleston, but because…"

"That's enough. No need to go along any further. I get the point. So more about the two of you. I want to know more about the two of you. We're getting to know each other here, so let's open up and get it all out. Mitzi, why don't you get us started?"

Mitzi, who sat in the front seat next to Savannah, turned around and stared at him with a vague gaze.

"You want to know about me?" she asked.

Tradd was silent for a moment, pausing as though he was actually considering an answer to the question.

"You know," he finally replied, "now that I think about it, not really."

FORTY

Roy's mother had told him that people had bad breath upon awaking due to the fact that while they slept, they were eating dreams. This was during a period of her life that she held herself out as a poetess, paintress, and photographer, a period that took place for him between the ages of six and ten. He did not remember any of her poems, nor did any of her paintings or photographs hang on the walls of their home, but he did remember her artistic phase. Because that's what it was: a phase. Something that she passed through, ending up on the other side with basically no traces of it clinging to her. It was unclear what brought about its demise. Roy just remembered one day being taken away by some woman who worked for the government, his father's utter outrage in court towards both the authorities and his wife, the whispering adults discretely shuffling photographs back and forth. When he stole a glimpse at one of them, accidently left out on the table in court, he was unimpressed, as it was just some of his mother's stuff. The banal photograph of him out in the backyard, naked, urinating onto the face of a Raggedy Ann doll (or was it Andy?).

During the past hour of unconsciousness, Roy had consumed a number of dreams, and although he could not remember any of them, it was clear that he had chewed and swallowed, for the taste in his mouth was nothing short of repulsive. Out of the bed and into the bathroom, he brushed his teeth, flossed, brushed them again, then gargled with mouthwash. He then undressed and lay in the womb of hot bath. The television set talked to itself in the adjoining room, the air conditioner hummed out its mindless tune, the water splashed softly from the raised washcloth with which he cleansed his face, all joining to make the sweet sound of living alone. He, a man. Finally, after all of these years, a grown man out on his own. The nights he had spent alone he could count on one hand, and tonight he would add another finger, or perhaps a thumb, rushing toward the removal of a shoe.

When he got cold, he gave up on the bath, rising and drying himself off with a towel. He worked on his hair for a few moments, enjoying the freedom of walking nakedness, then got dressed, his shoelaces tied in double knots, a habit that he had never been able to rid himself of. And then what? He had to find Erica. Had to track down his sister in a foreign city without the help of the internet or the police.

The rough outline he had sketched on the drive over served as his only plan of attack, and as it was the initial step, he thought of all of the tourist attractions that Charleston had to offer. First, one could always see the market, which for him was only a few blocks away. Then you had the Battery. Fort Sumter. The aquarium. The new IMAX theater where the heads of actors appeared the size of gods' and nature was looked at with the same boredom as it was in actual life, except with cheap 3-D glasses. There was the Citadel, the College of Charleston. Then, really, you just had Charleston itself, which for some reason was a tourist attraction, as if tourists enjoyed heat and stores that could be found in any decent-sized American city.

He didn't understand any of it. He didn't have any money, and although one day he planned on having a great deal of it, he had no idea how or when it would come, but if he ever did, or when he did, he would not live like these people. Get the wife, and perhaps the children, leave the comfort of your home and hop in a car or on a plane and touch down in some faraway place where you checked into a hotel and worried yourself over what all you needed to see, ate until you felt sick, then walked around and around until you had seen the things that you were supposed to see and done the things you were supposed to do and taken photographs of the same things everyone else had taken photographs of, except with you placed somewhere in the vicinity of the object, and then, exhausted, bitterly angry with your spouse, swearing you'll never go on such a trip again, you head back home, where, after a few months or so, you begin to make plans for the next one. No, he would not do that. Because this is what the wife and husband could have done: never left the house, not even the bedroom, turned on the computer, traveled nowhere except on the internet, eaten pizza delivered to the door, walked nowhere, then looked at photograph after photograph, perhaps even gone on a virtual tour of the city they were interested in, maybe even put themselves in one of the photos through the use of a digital camera and some photoshop, then hit the hay, neither exhausted, both fulfilled, without a trace of anger or the thought that neither one of them would ever do that again.

That was what a modern man did. If only he had a wife. And a home. And money for pizza. And only if he married a modern woman to compliment his modern man, for while Roy liked women a great deal, and thanks to the internet had probably seen more of them naked and in compromising sexual positions than any man in history, certainly more than King Solomon, Caligula, and Hugh Hefner combined, he had never been able to find one who shared his views of modernity, except for Miss Sunflower, but she was nothing special for the eye to behold, and her photograph, given that in it she wore a polyester dress and sported feathered hair, had probably been taken several decades in the past, if he were going to be honest with himself. But it was only a matter of time before internet scientists designed a virtual woman and solved all of the problems for the modern man. The Davinator had discussed this a great deal when Miss Sunflower made her occasional visits to the local food bank. You would put on a suit or hook yourself up to some machine, and there before you would appear a beautiful woman, and she would give you the business and you would feel it just like you would in the sorry regular world, only afterwards you wouldn't cuddle or have to talk about bills or do any of the other stuff that you read about other men having to suffer through. No, you would just turn the thing off and get back to doing whatever it was you wanted to do.

He checked himself one last time in the mirror, then headed out the door.

The sun hit him like a drug cut with an industrial cleaner, causing his knees to quake and his head to spin. He lived where there was heat, heat of equal or greater value than what he was now experiencing, but he never dealt with it in the normal course of life. His home was air conditioned, the air-conditioned car stored in the cool garage, and his place of employment was blessed with arctic wind blowing through the vents as well. He did not go camping or hiking or play any sports that would cause him to go outdoors. He did not work out in the yard in order to earn his keep. When he felt heat, it was for less than ten seconds, the walk from the car to wherever he was going, which was inconvenient but acceptable. This, this flaming wok cooking him like a meal, however, was unbearable. He ran into the reception area, looking for a map, yearning for comfort.

The hotel map quickly informed him that the aquarium stood several blocks away. As he ate a complimentary bear claw left over from breakfast, he thought of traveling via van, but he knew parking would be a problem, and he didn't see any sense in paying for a garage or risking a ticket.

A gentleman, tanned to a deadly brown and with a head of gelled hair, blonde to the point of white, stood behind the check-in desk fussing with papers. He wore several earrings and had the body of an athlete trained for no particular sport. Even a child with no sexual thoughts in its head could have spotted him as being gay, but Roy was extremely naive in this area, and on the occasion that he ventured on an internet search for "big pricks" coupled with "tight asses" he viewed the collected homosexual congresses with nothing more than mild annoyance, as though on a leisurely Sunday afternoon drive he had made the turn on Green Street instead of Greene Street, and now had to retrace his steps.

Hoping to find a solution in the friendly attendant, and extremely desirous not to return to the nature-made sauna, Roy walked over to him and gave the reception bell a ring, as he had always seen this done in movies and therefore assumed that this was the proper hotel protocol when addressing an employee.

"Do y'all have any shuttles?" he asked.

The receptionist eyed the bell for a moment, then slowly looked up at him, his expression that of a man contemplating malice.

"No," he replied.

"No shuttles, huh."

"No."

"Oh," Roy hit the bell again when the receptionist began turning away from him.

"What?"

"Do you know how I can get to the aquarium?"

"Yeah. Sure. You just keep going north until you hit Calhoun Street, where you take a right. It's right there."

"Yeah. Yeah. I. Um. Know. But how about getting there?"

"Oh. You can walk or drive or take a cab."

"No shuttles, huh?"

There was a pause in the answer, during which the browned face somehow turned a light crimson.

"It's a shuttle you want?"

"Yeah."

"Oh. Why didn't you say so? One should be coming by any moment. Just stand outside there on the corner."

"Out there?"

"Yeah."

"On the corner?"

"Yeah. That's right."

"Oh. Great. Thanks, buddy."

"Asshole," whispered the receptionist, who immediately tucked the bell into a drawer.

FORTY-ONE

The shuttle service left a great deal to be desired. Roy had waited, sweating until he was blind, for at least half an hour before one stopped next to the hotel. It was colored the same dull white that all shuttles tend to display, and had red accents in the shape of letters, which Roy did not read or try to place together. It was simply too hot. He rushed over and knocked on the door, which the driver opened.

"Can I help you?" the man asked. He wore a cap with the same lettering as on the outside of the shuttle, but Roy paid the same amount of attention to both.

His damp head lowered, Roy stepped on, saying, "The aquarium."

"Yeah. But…"

Roy did not listen, as he was too busy drafting the formal complaint to the president of Night's Inn in his head. Giving a dismissive wave—the back of his hand raised, the elbow pivoting to reveal the palm, the palm dropping to his side—he walked towards the back, glum and beaten, soaked to his skin, and took a seat where he could find one.

"You…?" the driver began.

But Roy had closed his eyes and did not see that he was being spoken to, causing the driver to raise his both of his hands, as though two gave more emphasis than Roy's one, and drop them to his sides as well, thinking that he really didn't care and that no one else would either. As said, Roy had his eyes closed, so he did not see this gesture. Just as he had not seen that the vehicle he had entered was not a hotel shuttle.

FORTY-TWO

There was no place for Savannah to park along the Battery, an area located at the tip of Charleston where the homes were both extremely beautiful and expensive. It seemed as though everyone who owned a car had set it alongside the street that day, and although Savannah had images of pulling up right next to a mansion where an eccentric Charlestonian would cackle some low country witticism and offer them a mint julep, it remained only an image. They parked far, far away and trudged back, stinking of cigarette smoke from the bar and sweat from their bodies.

The first house they reached did not have anyone inside of it, nor did the second, third, or fourth. The fifth, however, was occupied by a man who answered the door.

"Whaddya want?" he asked. He wore blue socks with sandals and his hairless legs reached up into his shorts with shame. His hair was positioned in a regal comb-over and his brown eyes squinted above an ill-chosen mustache.

"Well, sir," said Savannah, "you might not remember me, but I'm Harold D'Bergeolet's daughter, Savannah, and…"

"Harold D'Bergeolet?" he asked in a grating, nasal voice. "Don't know 'im."

"Well, I'm sure you've heard of him, or at least of our family."

"Nope."

"Well, we were looking for some place to eat, and thought..."

"All kindsa places ta eat right up the street. Now go on and get out of here. I got stuff I gotta do."

"But sir!"

The door closed shut.

"This is outrageous!" said Savannah. "Absolutely outrageous!"

"Don't either of you have a credit card?" Tradd asked. "Let's just go somewhere and eat."

"Absolutely not, Tradd. No, no, and no. He was just mad because my mother was the prettiest woman in town and turned down his many offers to marry. We'll find someone who'll give us the proper Southern treatment. Never heard of the D'Bergeolet family? That's outrageous!"

It turned out that no one had heard of the D'Bergeolet family, or at least no one who answered the door, which consisted of only a few unwelcoming souls.

"Savannah," Tradd said after yet another failed attempt, two hours standing between the promised lunch and the nonexistent meal, "maybe you haven't been back here in a while, but this place has turned into a Disneyworld of Southern culture. A real live PG-13 *Song of the South* type of production where, because of all of these books you keep talking about, Yankees have taken over and bought up all of the nice houses. Half of them don't even live here, which is why all of the houses are empty, and the other half who do live here are retired Yankee assholes. They've even had to close schools because there aren't any children living here anymore. I don't know what it was like when you grew up here, and to be honest I don't know if you even grew up here, but whatever the case, it's changed."

"No, Tradd," said Savannah, "it's you who's changed. When you were a boy, you were so full of life and hope. But now, after having grown up in the house that you grew up in and having gone to the Citadel, the bitterness has worked its way into your soul."

"Yeah," said Tradd. "That's why we're walking around sweating like pigs and starving to death. Because of my bitterness."

As they began the return voyage to the car, a horse rode by hauling a carriage behind it. In the open-aired hack stood a young blonde-headed girl wearing a smile, stemming perhaps from the pride she took in sharing her meager knowledge with the completely ignorant, here represented by a family of four and two elderly couples who had retired and thus given up on participating in life in order to prepare themselves for decrepitation and death.

"Ah, Charleston," said Savannah as it passed them. The horse took the moment to drop several balls of shit out from under its tail.

"Yeah, a gem of a town," said Tradd.

"There goes that fecund musk again," said Mitzi with genuine amazement, as she had not seen the horse work its magic. "Do you smell it?"

FORTY-THREE

It took Roy several minutes before he had finally composed himself and opened his eyes. His underwear had bound itself onto his wet buttocks and his shirt stuck to his manly paunch in grotesque fashion; he could feel small streams of sweat running down into his socks where his feet baked in athletic footwear. He shifted a bit and raised his head to try and better feel the air conditioning that seemed to creep out of the vents above. A wet cry caused him to shift his attention to his shuttle neighbor. Next to him sat a young man wearing a hat with red lettering on it, his shoulders hunched, hands before him as though in prayer, but instead of a prayer book or mystic totem he held a portable computing device, this one designed especially for the use of playing video games. Although it was no internet, Roy had a deep abiding love for computer games, and its sighting caused his galloping heart to slow to a canter, and the hormones of stress to be shooed away by those of mild euphoria.

The youth had before him, within his white-fingered clutch, *Dragon's Breath*, a game wherein a pixilated knight jumped over rocks and dodged exploding spells in his quest to kill the dragon and save the princess. Roy quickly discerned that the fellow was stuck on level four, the part where the rocks came in quick succession as you strode up the hill, all while a demonic archer fired flaming arrows from up above. His boredom and fatigue—all-encompassing moments before—were replaced with foot-stamping anxiety, and it was all that he could do to not rip the thing out of the incompetent hands of his seatmate and take over. And even though he did resist this urge, he could not help but try to wheedle the machine out of those fingers and into his with verbiage.

"You're starting too close up. No, you have to let that rock get by you before you shoot. You want me to try? I can show you. No, further back. All the way back. You see where that flower is? No, not that one. You sure you don't want me to try? Yeah. There you go. Oh well, that was close. You sure you don't want me to try? I can show you how to do it. It's easy. It really is. Once you see someone else do it, you can do it easy. Really easy. Whoops. Yeah. For that rock you have to run back a little bit and then try and jump it, or you're toast."

His head inched further in. His warm body pressed up against the shoulder. His fingers squirmed about in random fashion. A rock again crushed the knight, and before Roy could say another word, the game was in his hands.

"All right. Now look and see how I do it. It's easy."

Although Roy lacked polish in many aspects of life, and in some areas even lacked the gear to which one could apply polish, in the arena of *Dragon's Breath* few existed bold enough to call themselves his equal. For the amount of time Roy had spent solving the philosophical riddles of *Dragon's Breath, Sorcerer's Lair, Alien Conquest,* and a host of others, if it had in the alternative been spent on general studies, would have rendered him a physician, attorney, and particle physicist fluent to the point of passing as native in Chinese, Russian, and all of the Romance languages.

With a run that bore no traces of effort or hesitation, he burst up the hill, jumped the rocks, killed the archer, and even had the time to grab a few bonus points by leaping into a cloud and giving it a knock. His companion of the seat clapped his hands in violent appreciation and shouted the news to the others, which caused a crowd to form, ready to witness the opening of the wonders previously unavailable to all, the glories held within the mystic gates of level five.

Level five came and went like the passing shadow of an arrow, each skip, hop, and crossbow bolt causing squeals to erupt and shouts to bounce off of the metal roof and down upon the shouters. Level six's results did not differ. Roy's sole focus was on the screen, a glass square of inches, yet the cheers of the crowd emboldened him to try for more, to squeak in the extra cloud knocks in the face of certain death. It was at the end of this screen, a lion smashed and mangled at the knight's feet, that the shuttle came to a halt. The driver opened the door.

"All right, fellows. We're here."

But none of them cared to see where here was. And how could they when the alternative promised nothing but pure ecstasy?

"Guys? Y'all come on now. We're here."

"Pause it. Hit pause."

It was Roy's seatmate, and for the first time Roy noticed that something was different about the young man. Nothing he could put his finger on, but he definitely fell outside the norm of humanity. His words disturbed the ear, and something about his face seemed to speak of oddities, problems in the womb, whispered discussions between the unwed mother and the aging doctor in the sterile maternity room. He looked up. The others rang out in the same way, a set of handbells crafted by an eccentric uncle in his basement kiln. They all wore baseball caps with the same red lettering on them, and many of them wore glasses, glasses with lenses thicker than those in a telescope. Roy hit the pause button, at a loss at what to say. What kind of hotel was this? He looked back up again. They were all smiling at him. He smiled back.

"Hey," he said. "Where can I get one of those hats?"

FORTY-FOUR

Parked in an area without shade, the car felt like a convection oven when they entered, and the modern-day Shadrach, Meshach, and Abednego further sweated, which appeared to be the only action that they were fated to accomplish. The windows were quickly rolled down once more, but this did little to aid in the dissipation of humidity or heat.

"Where to now?" Mitzi asked.

"To get something to eat, for godsakes," said Tradd. "And something to drink. I'm about to pass out from hunger and dehydration."

"You know that if you're dying of thirst, you can drink your urine," Mitzi said. "Just one time, though, I think. You can also urinate on a wound to clean it out."

"Mitzi!" said Savannah.

"Well, that's what they say," said Mitzi.

"No one I know of says anything like that, you disgusting pig," said Savannah.

"I think I'd like to find a water fountain before I drink my piss or even piss from either of you," said Tradd. "I know that's a crazy request, but I'm kind of like that. Just stop somewhere, Savannah, and let's get a cup of water."

"I'm not stopping until I've done what I need to do," said Savannah. "So you'll just have to wait for that cup of water, cadet."

"Jesus, why?" asked Tradd. "Let's just stop. Right here. Let's just stop right here." They again passed the market that Savannah and her generation had put out of business, where now restaurants abounded, and kept on going.

"Why?" asked Savannah. "I'll tell you why. In all of the great chronicles of Southern life, whether it be from a Conroy or a Benton Frank, a Rivers Siddons or even a Josephine Humphries, the only drinking done, as far as memory serves me, is of the alcoholic variety. You have drinks, but you don't go crabbing all day and then complain about being thirsty. That's the way it is in the low country, and Tradd, in case you missed it, we're in the low country."

A gas station whizzed by on the right and Tradd let out a whimper.

"As you may or may not know, I am writing a book about this trip, wherein we will have many adventures before finding Chicken John, my long-lost brother of whom I have already spoken. Someone will die—by cancer or their own hand, I can't say just yet—and things will be revealed that will cause us to rethink our relationships with our parents and with each other, but what won't be done will be the things that you and Mitzi keep talking about: drinking, defecating, urinating, and the remaining long list of unnecessaries."

"We're going to be in it," said Mitzi to Tradd.

"Well, I might be the one who dies if you aren't going to let me drink, poop, or piss," Tradd replied. "By the by," he said to Savannah, "do you think you could make me a little taller and a little bit better looking in that book of yours? I'd also like to be a bit more conflicted, if at all possible. I don't seem to have any serious conflicts, and I really think that's what's missing with me."

"Tradd, you are conflicted. Just by saying that you don't think you are I can see that you are undoubtedly so. As for your looks, you seem to me to be an Adonis with all of the Southern polish and charm that one could ever hope for."

"Good. Good," said Tradd. "I like that. The only thing that I wish is that I already had a copy of the thing, because right now you're driving us away from Charleston, and I don't see any sense in that. Unless you're taking me back to Spartanburg like I asked. You aren't, are you?"

"No," said Savannah. "There's something I must do first before we continue on. I do not know if you are aware of all that I've been through in my life." Here she paused.

"Um," said Tradd, once he realized that it was not a rhetorical question. "Given the fact that I just met you, I would say that I know... um...I don't know, maybe ninety-nine percent of it? But probably not all. I assume Mitzi might be a little more familiar with it."

Mitzi, who had again been studying how to fix her glasses, raised her head. "What?" she asked.

"I said, I assumed that you might be more familiar with it. With what Savannah's been through."

"I know that her parents haven't been too nice to her or her brother, Chicken John. She's a famous poet and she's married, but separated, and has some kids. She's writing a book about this trip we're on, and I'm going to be in it. Oh, and she and I have some classes together at school. She also graduated from the Citadel."

"Mitzi, although you have left a great deal out," said Savannah, "given your mental infirmities, I have to say that you didn't do too bad. Yes, all of that is true. However, what I have not told you was that for a period of time, when my marriage was falling apart, I was the head football coach at a high school on one of the islands right off the coast of Charleston."

"Which one?" Tradd asked.

"The name is irrelevant, Tradd," said Savannah. "What is relevant is that I was going through a very rough period. I was a coach, but then I was not. You see, I had lost my temper, which we D'Bergeolets are known to do, and beaten one of my players to the point of death. My husband was supportive of this, but my past was pulling us apart to the point that I had driven him into the arms of another woman. But that is a tale for another day. What I wanted to tell you, and the reason I told you all of the other things, was that every day I would take the bridge over to work, and like Tom Wingo, I would whisper out the name of my therapist as I drove over it, thinking of him and the love he offered me in New York, but that I turned down in hopes of reuniting with Jonathan. I have not done it in so long, and I think it would make a nice scene in this book that I'm writing. So that's where we're headed. Over the bridge."

"I hope we don't go over the bridge, although the odds of it are likely, given the way you drive," said Tradd. "Anyway, why don't you just write about it like we did it and instead we'll go get something to drink and eat."

"She doesn't do that," said Mitzi before Savannah could speak. "I wanted her to do the same thing last night so that we could sleep in the car, but she said the lighting would be all wrong."

"Jesus," said Tradd with a moan.

"Are you Christian?" asked Mitzi.

"Sure," said Tradd.

FORTY-FIVE

Hat on head, eyes squinting in the sun, Roy followed the line of them to the aquarium. From where they had parked, and from where he walked, the building stood several stories high, glass and metal and brick, posted as a sentry on the edge of the Atlantic Ocean. Its proximity made one wonder if the exhibits traveled in and out, the truly humane aquarium, where the fish were not the captives, but guests. The sun again opened the wound of heat, and Roy felt the dampness begin to return.

He had obviously made the correct choice when picking his accommodations, because the hotel paid for his ticket, and even provided a guide. And the thing about the guide was odd, for he could have been the twin brother of the hotel receptionist, down to the color of his hair and the depth of his tan. They even spoke in the same manner, causing Roy to wonder, and wonder mightily, if the same guy didn't work two jobs in order to support his wife and children. He decided not to ask, and it was unclear if the guide would have responded had he done so, because he was haranguing with excessive glee about all that they would see and how much they would enjoy it, doing it in such a way that no holes appeared for the entry of a question. Anyway, Roy did not pay attention to what he said. He was not there to actually look at the aquarium. He was there to find his sister.

At the turtle exhibit, turtles that clearly didn't have much of a say in whether they could stay or go, Roy succumbed to the pressures of the others to complete level seven. He sat down at a bench, caps with red letters poised above like umbrellas in a storm, and swung across the lava pits, timing each rope grasp with amazing precision, making the viewers wonder whether they were watching an actual game of skill or something on television. A host of cries filled the aquarium when Roy landed the knight safely on the other side. He hit the pause button and looked up into the faces of the bus driver and tour guide/receptionist, who were both staring at him.

"Come here, buddy," said the driver.

Roy arose and the shuttle driver led him over to a group of snakes situated inside of a glass case. Behind them, the tour guide/receptionist encouraged the others to follow him to the next spot, and although their lord and master of gaming was obviously not coming with them, they showed no solidarity and went along willingly. Roy fingered the video game in his pocket and stared at the driver's shoes, which were black.

"Who are you?" the driver asked. "And what are you doing here?"

Roy thought for a moment. Who he was clearly didn't matter, and it was obvious what he was doing, so there had to be an ulterior motive behind the questions. But what? The man appeared fairly normal, certainly more normal than the other people on the shuttle, but one could never be sure who was normal. Who knew what normal even was? Miss Sunflower often opined. This might be some weak attempt at stealing his identity, a little recon and his credit would be ruined, or it might be some vast conspiracy filled with vast conspirators whose purpose was known only to them. Whatever the reasons were, Roy was not eager to answer, so he did the only thing that seemed to make sense in the least harmful manner.

"23," he said.

"Huh?" asked the driver.

"My room number," said Roy.

"Room number? I don't care what room you're in. Are you trying to make me lose my job? Huh? Cause you sure don't belong here and you sure are causing a mess."

"I paid my money. What else do you want me to do?"

"I want you to get the hell out of here and leave us all alone."

Roy again repaired inside his skull and draped himself in thought. He was used to antagonism. It had been a part of growing up and, unfortunately, of being grown. The people who filled this world, your everyday man and woman, had serious mental issues. For whereas his friends on the internet saw him for who he was, and treated him accordingly, those who had yet to get plugged into the future saw him as an enemy and treated him accordingly. This bus driver had no reason to want him gone. The others clearly did not want Roy to leave, and he knew of nothing that he had done, or would do, that would cause the guy to lose his job. But whatever the reasons, Roy was not one to back down. Bullies had always been a constant presence in his life and he had never backed down to any of them; he wasn't about to start now.

"Can I at least walk around? I mean, I do have a ticket."

"I don't give a good goddamn what you do, buddy, as long as you leave us alone. You can jump in the shark tank and swim around for all I care."

"Do they let you do that?"

"Do what?"

"Swim with the sharks."

"No. Fuck no. Jesus. Maybe you do belong with this group. Just stay away from us. I never should have picked you up in the first place, and now you're here distracting everybody. And don't think they won't talk about that when they get back. They won't say a word about fish. They'll just talk about your stupid computer game."

Roy felt the sting of the computer game insult and responded accordingly.

"All right. I'll stay away. But, hey, listen. You're still going to give me a ride back, right?"

"Absolutely fucking not. You get your own ride back."

And it was at this point that Roy was ready to lay it to him. This fool with his black shoes. Black shoes. In this weather. Clunky black shoes at that. No, no moron was going to speak to him like that and get away with it.

"Okay," said Roy.

FORTY-SIX

To think that the bridge had existed for a period of decades, battered by storms, rusted by saltwater, beaten by misdriven automobiles, and so on and so forth and yet still held up its weight, much less that of the numerous cars that traveled across it every day, was nothing short of miraculous. When one saw it, it brought to mind images of Roman aqueducts, Egyptian pyramids, of engineers trained and educated at institutions for the mentally disabled at the hands of madmen. For when looking at it, one quickly realized that it was nothing short of an instrument for death and disfigurement. An ungrounded wall socket next to the swimming pool. A lawn mower missing a shield for the blade. The cars passed within inches of the side mirror, and only a few feet to the other side there lay the Cooper River some one hundred yards below. A cursory check of the lipstick or search for the much-needed carpet sample in the backseat and one was either meeting one of his fellow citizens with a crunch, or the salty gray which in the process of the fall had somehow turned into concrete.

Savannah entered the bridge without any consideration as to the danger in which she might be placing both her friends and herself. Her reasoning was not without basis: the book could not end in such a way, so it was equally impossible that anything could happen that might put an end to any of its main characters, *vis-à-vis,* her. The metal rattled underneath the wheels to the point that even a brave man would have felt his sword hand stutter, and with the windows down as they were, each passing car sounded like the noise one hears the moment before a long-dead grandparent beckons from within the pleasant haze of white light. Tradd clutched at whatever he could in the backseat, his face albino in color, his pulse in the realm of *prestissimo*. His pleas of "Jesus, please slow down!" were not directed at the Jewish Messiah, but at the strange woman in the driver's seat. The sad truth was that neither could hear them. Mitzi, thankfully for her, did not have her eye pieces raised at the moment, although it is questionable whether she had the mental faculties to realize the magnitude of the peril. Flying through the air, every second seemed the last, every moment the final, and then, without any warning to either her passengers or the motorists behind her, Savannah pushed the brake pedal to the floor.

The car fishtailed into a skid, throwing black smoke in its wake, but miraculously came to rest rightly aligned in the proper lane. All three passengers felt themselves thrown forward into their seat belts, which braced them with an unforgiving hand and knocked the breath out of their screams. And then came a moment that one often hears of in seafaring stories penned by the likes of Conrad and the host of others, who, in the days of Merry Olde England, thought that going off to sea with a group of uneducated barbarians to be used to man planks and fulfill sexual needs would somehow make them proper men of letters: the heavy silence of the moment before the crash. Here, it weighed tons. An audible howl of expectation where something in their guts told all in the D'Bergeolet automobile that unretrievable horror would at any moment make its appearance.

"Lowenstein," whispered Savannah.

"Holy fuck!" screamed Tradd.

The "fuck" portion of his exclamation, although proffered at full volume, could not be heard, for behind them came a sound resembling that given when a robot the size of a skyscraper gives birth. The robot baby scraped against the vaginal walls of steel, the robot birth canal stretched and twisted, and the robot mother revealed to the world that she had foregone the epidural. Her offspring of sextuplets, here represented by the long line of automobiles behind the

D'Bergeolet steed, exploded into the world in a mass of motor fluid and crushed fenders. Bits of shrapnel struck the back of our protagonists' vehicle, and a hubcap zinged by as though it were attached to a phantom car. Horns gave forth a mournful birth cry, only to die of slow asphyxiation. Then all fell silent.

"Lowenstein," whispered Savannah.

"Go!" shouted Tradd. "Fucking go!"

"What happened?" Mitzi asked.

"Go!" shouted Tradd. "Get us out of here! They'll lock us all up!"

"I shall never forget you, Lowenstein," said Savannah, who took her foot off of the brake and pushed them forward with a gentle coast.

It was a matter of moments before Tradd regained the wherewithal to properly express himself.

"You…you… you deranged crackpot!" he screamed. "You stark-raving lunatic! What were you doing? Huh? Trying to get us killed? Oh my God. Oh my Jesus." The initial outburst had apparently taken whatever was within him out of him, and he now displayed clear signs of hyperventilation. "I think I had a heart attack. Jesus. Stop the car. Please, please stop the car."

"I will do no such thing," said Savannah. "And watch your mouth or I'll wash it out with soap like Sesame used to do to me."

"What are the two of you screaming about?" asked Mitzi.

"I'm not screaming, he is," said Savannah. "As to why, I have no idea."

"No idea? You stopped in the middle of the bridge and caused a ten-car pile-up. You almost got us killed. Does that give you a better idea?"

"Was that what that was?" asked Mitzi.

"Don't listen to him, Mitzi," said Savannah. "I think that the Institute has done him in both mentally and emotionally."

At this point, the bridge replaced with *terra firma,* Savannah eased her way back and around so that they were headed for Charleston once again.

"No, no, and no," said Tradd. "Absolutely fucking not. No, you don't. I am *not* driving across a bridge with you again. And when I say again, I mean never again. Never. Ever. Not even for a million dollars."

Savannah did not alter her course or give him a response, and her inaction drove Tradd to drastic behavior. With a wild Etruscan yelp, he threw his torso over the front seat, so that half of him resided with Savannah and Mitzi, the other half dangling in the back. His hands groped maniacally for the steering wheel, for the gear shift, for the key; Savannah gave him a sharp elbow to his cheekbone and let out a series of startled cries. Mitzi, who did not have any clue as to what was taking place, reached over and touched his face for unknown reasons, and when a finger somehow made it into his mouth, the thwarted former cadet bit down as though it were a shell containing a delicious nut inside. The chomp drew forth a howl of deep pain and a rivulet of blood from our dear Mitzi, who began beating him about the head and neck with her good hand.

They had made it on to the bridge, the travesty of Michigan know-how piled up in disgrace to their left, when Savannah once again hit the brakes. Tradd, unsecured by seatbelt or front seat, was driven downward at an angle into the dash like a pike into the hard ground of frozen earth. Cars behind once again swerved and smashed, but this time Savannah did not mention the name of Lowenstein.

FORTY-SEVEN

Roy wandered around the maze of the aquarium, stopping to look at a few poisonous snakes and flesh-eating fish, then sat down for a while and looked at the shark tank that stood as an exhibit climax two stories high. There were sharks swimming around in the tank, as one might expect, but there were other fish swimming around in there too, which seemed to befuddle all who saw it.

Roy, during the thirty minutes that he took it all in, heard four guides answer the question that had brimmed in his head. The sharks did not eat the other fish because they were fed by the zookeepers, or whatever it is that you call someone who works at an aquarium, and therefore were not hungry. This struck him as false. He did not have any formal training in sharks, and had not done any shark research, although he had put on his internet biography that he had spent two years in South America studying sharks while working to overturn Apartheid, but he had seen a number of movies and television shows concerning sharks, and he knew them for the bloodthirsty beasts that they were. They did not, like man, rest easy once the belly was full. Limbs could still be maimed. Heads chomped. All for the fun of it. He reasoned that either they were drugged or replaced by anima-tronic sharks, the latter being the most likely solution. He wondered who controlled them. If there were some job where, with a joystick in hand and eyes on the screen, you drove the shark around all day while below the guides told the schoolchildren that the sharks had been fed and therefore were not hungry. He wondered how one could apply for the position. He wondered if he should inquire. But his shark would bite, and that would be a problem. You couldn't put a maniac like him, the hands behind Ut the dwarf, at the controls of a shark and expect it just to swim around in fantasy land.

With this thought, he passed through the exit door, the sun blinding him like lye, and walked around toward the front of the building. There he saw the shuttle driver restraining his former seatmate and trying to get him back in the bus. The young man was crying out something about having lost his game and demanding that he be let back inside to get it. Roy stopped and took a few steps back, hiding himself behind a corner of the building, his hand fingering a rectangular object in the pocket of his shorts.

FORTY-EIGHT

A message was left on the answering machine at the Edwards residence. Mr. Edwards had gone to work and Mrs. Edwards to the grocery store, so there was no one at home to answer the phone, except for the cat that they did not have.

The caller was none other than Officer Frank Jamison, a sergeant with the City of Charleston police department. The same man who, years before, had led a lost boy, way too old to be crying and sniveling as he was, to his parents where they angrily waited in a building that seemed to serve no purpose. He did not do it because he was a good Samaritan, for he was not very good at anything and his bloodline was as pure as Alp snow, and he had not acted out of moral principle. He had helped the boy out simply as part of his duties as a state fair patrolman in a city that is hardly worth mention.

FORTY-NINE

"Do you think he's all right?"

"Of course, he is. One can't die in the middle of a book. All deaths are saved to the end, and we've barely begun."

"Yeah. Well. Maybe. He's not moving, though. And it's been a while."

"He's probably in a coma, Mitzi. That happens a lot down here in the low country. Comas. I'm not sure why, but they do have their purpose. You see, while the person's in a coma, everyone else is allowed time to reflect on him or her, to sit around his or her hospital bed and cry, and this gives the reader a sense of dreaded anticipation that makes them read on to see if that person makes it or not. And they always do. Like clockwork."

"Oh. Well, since we just met him there isn't a whole lot to reflect on, and although I'm so tired and hungry I could cry, it wouldn't be over him, so it wouldn't be right, right? You would need me to cry over him, right?"

"Exactly, Mitzi. I think that you're getting the hang of it, which is extraordinary given that you are such an imbecile."

Savannah and Mitzi sat in the car which sat parked in a space they had miraculously found near the market. Tradd now rested in the backseat, probably not in a coma, but deeply unconscious, neverthe-less. Mitzi had taken off his shirt to check for wounds and caress the flesh of his torso, giving him the appearance of a concertgoer who had drunk too much in the parking lot and never made it into the show, his partially nude body covered in sweat, his figure stilled, the smell of vomit escaping with each breath.

After studying the body for a few more moments, they turned back around so that they faced the signs for several shops apparently owned by the same failed poet who could not resist a pun, no matter how bad. A Shore Thing. Wait and Sea. It was an indictment of both commerce and taste that all along the beautiful coast of the fair state decorators were cute to the point of sterile vulgarity, with a cross-stitched seagull finding its place in every million-dollar home.

"Do you want to get out and walk around or something?" Mitzi asked. "Maybe we'll find a place to eat."

"I don't see why not," said Savannah. "We are in the low country."

The temperature inside the car must have been one hundred degrees, and outside offered no solace. They ambled along the market, side by side, each silently taking it all in. They both, and particularly Savannah, felt like Southern belles strolling to cotillion, but it would be difficult to describe them in such a manner. Whatever life their hair had had prior to the trip had now wilted into death, leaving them with a look of survivors of a shipwreck, and their complexions, already poor from the bug bites, had worsened with time as the chiggers dug deeper, the mosquito bites stoked to flame by fingernail scratches. Added to this, they had not bathed or groomed in roughly twenty-four hours, leaving them less desirable to the average male than a dose of the clap, which one always hopes to avoid at cotillion.

"I wonder if they have a tape store," said Mitzi. "I really need to fix my glasses."

"A tape store!" said Savannah with a contemptuous chuckle. "Oh Mitzi, you truly are an ignoramus! Oh yes, I'm sure they have a tape store. Just like I'm sure there's a store for wooden bowls."

Savannah's laughter slumped to a dead halt as they passed by Ding and Ding, which in fact specialized in wooden bowls. Mitzi's blindness prevented her mild triumph.

"We will either find you something with which to mend your glasses or a new pair of glasses," Savannah said in a whisper. "This is too beautiful for you not to see it."

And it was beautiful. Here were the horses and carriages, the cobblestone streets. But horses do not walk upon the earth without leaving their trace, and Mitzi once again commented on the smell given off by the equine urine boiling on the cobblestones.

"Let's go over here, Mitzi," said Savannah, pointing to the market, a long funnel of open-aired building where the marketeers hocked their wares. "I'm tired of you misrepresenting the fecund musk, and the heat is becoming oppressive." Mitzi followed.

Although in such a place as a real-live Southern market one might expect to find great treasures from colonial times, relics from the Revolutionary War, moldy bullets from Vicksburg, or even a bayonet or two rusted from the blood of a regrettable Nazi, there were none of any or all of the above to be found. The market, if it ever carried such things, had long ago sold out of them, and now catered to the differing needs of a changing clientele. For instance, if one collected plastic trinkets from Hong Kong, then one had found the spot, and the only thing required to fill the lighted display case back in Ohio was legal tender. If one desired prints from failed artists moved by the muse of uninhabited houses, dead shorelines, and smiling birds with eyelashes, then one need not look further. Presiding over this hub of commerce were numerous overweight white men and women, sweating at such a rate that they appeared to be melting. Their haggard eyes followed the disappointed tourists, watching diligently for the fool willing to risk his liberty in an attempt at the bib-wearing plastic crab that held a plastic knife and fork in its plastic claws. Mitzi and Savannah glanced over a table containing silver necklaces from Mexico, then moved on to another table where one, as long as he or she did not have an exotic name, could purchase a leather bracelet specially made for him or her.

It was in this pastime of glancing and moving on that they stumbled upon six black women sitting in chairs, weaving baskets out of sweetgrass. The women were not what one would expect based upon characterizations in various forms of art that flourished like bacterial bloom in the area. No one wore a bonnet, and none of them was dressed in calico. Instead, they resembled a group of ladies fresh from a PTA meeting, not formally dressed, unquestionably not, but with the shabby wealth oftentimes found in the wives of sole-supporting husbands who have time to attend PTA meetings. Each of them had hair coiffured with great care, each with name-brand sneakers, a few in blouses, several in track suits, one or two of them wearing glasses held together by gold-plated rims. They were discussing a recent bill that had failed to pass in Congress when Savannah saw them, and the words they spoke, along with the clothes they wore, were quickly filtered in the D'Bergeolet brain until they were in fact wearing bonnets that matched their calico dresses, and out of their mouths came the sweet words of Gullah.

Savannah placed a hand on Mitzi's chest, stopping her mid-step, and blissfully eavesdropped on the debate over regressive taxation. The vowels came round and beautiful, sharp and cutting, a symphony with each voice adding a tone, a texture, bringing with them a sense of the divine. One of the ladies was suggesting getting rid of the IRS when Savannah could take it no longer. The desire gripped her—the desire to take each of them in her arms and spend a leisurely low country afternoon chewing the hog's fat with them—and she was powerless against its wants. It was time to dip into *Gullah Fuh Oonuh*: "Pa gone ch-ch een 'e shu't-sleebe! All uh we eenjy de sukkus. T'ree pastuh speak tuh de distrackit meet'n. Buh joe beat stick fuh de chillun cut de pidgin wing!"

Savannah stood in triumph after these words sped past her teeth, smiling, her eyes wet with emotion. For one of the amazing things about Savannah, as she saw it, was that while she always found a home in the most select of Charlestonian social circles and not merely as a guest, but as a guest of honor, she fit in just as easily with every other stratum of society, and especially the Gullah-speaking basket weavers.

The women stopped their weaving for a moment and looked up at her.

"Are you talking to us?"

"Of course, I am!" said Savannah. "Who else around here can speak Gullah! I'll be fit to be tied with some jessum root it I ain't talkin to you! Yahn!" She looked over at Mitzi and again slapped her thighs to accompany a wild chortle.

The fingers came to a rest, the faces slumped into blank expressions.

"I been tellin Mitzi here, a sure right cornback gal, that we was'a gonna be seein us some sweet grassin done, and I'll be doggoned taken out and had my lips peeled if I wan't tellin no truth! Yahn!" The slaps ensued. The forced chortles continued.

With a wink to the others, one of them finally spoke. "You must be from the low country. What's your name, girl?"

"Savannah D'Bergeolet."

"From the Charleston D'Bergeolets?"

"Ain't that a fact."

"Ah. I knew your great-great grandpappy when he was just a boy. Fine family, the D'Bergeolet family."

The others half-heartedly nodded their heads in agreement.

"Then you musta been a'knowin my wet nurse, Sesame," said Savannah.

"Oh, Sesame. She was one of a kind."

"That's her!" said Savannah. "You know, sometimes I see her in mirrors."

"I bet you do," said one of them, at which the others laughed.

"She comes to me in the night and lets me know everything's going to be all right."

"That's the magic of the low country," said the main instigator, a young woman wearing a blue blouse and gray slacks. "I bet she's the one who taught you Gullah."

"That's right," said Savannah.

"Where you girls from?"

"I told you, Charleston."

"Indiana," said Mitzi.

"Oh, well since y'all from these parts, I imagine you'll want to buy one of our baskets."

"We don't have any money," said Savannah. "But we would sure like to have one. Perhaps we can buy one with our love."

"Honey, I don't know that anyone would give you anything for that. I tell you what, the two of you run along and come back here around midnight tonight. If you knock twice on the old post and speak some Gullah, the Gullah fairy might bring you two baskets for free. How's that sound?"

"Great!" said Savannah.

"I didn't know that there was a Gullah fairy," said Mitzi.

"There's a lot that you don't know, Mitzi, that me and my sistren do. Of course, there's a Gullah fairy. This entire part of the world is filled with magic."

"Now y'all run along now. We've got to work."

"Midnight tonight?" asked Savannah.

"At the stroke of twelve," said the woman.

"We'll be there," said Savannah.

They turned back and continued through the market, passing by more cheap jewelry and stamped leather, stopping to catch a laugh at the plastic crab holding the plastic knife and fork in its plastic claws. It wore a bib that read "Eat mor chikin," and the two—Mitzi saw it only as a fuzzy orange ball and had to be told what was before her—wished that they had the five dollars needed to take it home. But they didn't.

"This is what the low country is all about, Mitzi," said Savannah as she fingered a rubber cutlass. "Good friends, good food, culture, and the blessings of the Gullah fairy. You have it all around you, you are immersed in it, and believe you me, you are better for it."

"I would be a lot better if I had some of that good food in my stomach rather than around me," said Mitzi. "I haven't eaten since last night, and I'm starving."

"Mitzi, like I told you, in the low country no one goes hungry. You can stop by a friend's house—and everyone is a friend in the low country—and have a meal, or if worse comes to worse, you can go out crabbing in the creek and catch your fill. I think I've mentioned to you about opening up an oyster and letting you smell it and saying to you, 'Here is my childhood,' and the more I think about it, I'd really like to do that. We just need to find an oyster somewhere."

"Savannah, I'll be happy to eat your childhood, and if your adulthood smells like a hamburger, I'll finish it and lick my fingers clean afterwards."

"My adulthood smelling like a hamburger?!!" You truly are the queen of imbeciles, Mitzi! I don't think I've ever met a bigger idiot, and that's saying a lot, considering my acquaintance with my brother

230

Roy. But I love you for it, Mitzi. Your zesty thirst for life fills me with great joy."

"Please let's find something to eat."

"After we go in here."

In the middle of the market there were a number of stores that offered clothing and home furnishings for the conformative eccentric in us all. Savannah and Mitzi graced several of them with their presence, Mitzi always an inch away from knocking over the ceramic umbrella stand shaped like an elephant's foot, and although several items whetted their interest, none were bought.

It was at this point, five such establishments behind them and only a few more to go, that they happened upon the Southern Heritage shop. Savannah, who loved all things Southern except those items forbidden by her literary heroes, felt great excitement at the discovery. She imagined Gullah dictionaries and opened oysters, sweet grass origami and Pat Conroy posters, all laid out with the solemnity required by their magnitude. For if there was one thing that made Southerners the Southerners that they were, then it was their heritage. You could live in the South, own property there, vote in every election, but if you could not trace your forebears back two centuries to the same plot of earth, then you were not a Southerner. Or at least that is what Savannah had come to believe, as it had been told to her by several authors whom she deeply admired, and therefore was not to be dismissed.

It was for the above reasons that expectations were high, and when they are situated in such a manner, as one knows from the grass walk of life, located on top of the roof of hell, the truth seldom satisfies. Immediately upon entering, Savannah's eyes were seared with the blue Xs of rebel flags that hung upon the walls. All around plastic, faceless eunuchs held up the gray uniforms of Johnny Reb. From atop shelves, Robert E. Lee and Stonewall Jackson stared at her with lifeless, bronzed eyes. Savannah found herself surrounded by the evil phantoms of the South's unfortunate past, and the power of these long-dead hobgoblins drove her to faintness. She reached down and placed her hand upon a book covered with a mildly racist dust jacket in order to steady herself, quickly pulling it back and wiping it against her dress as though the laminated paper were covered in spit.

"It can't be," she whispered. "After all that my generation went through."

"What are you talking about?" asked Mitzi.

"These... these things," said Savannah. "These things that contaminate the air with their fecund musk of treachery. They're not meant to be here. We marched. We burned our bras. We sang songs and listened to bearded men talk for hours about things like freedom and soul sisters and how we shouldn't trust anyone over forty. All so that this can exist?"

Mitzi attempted to look around her blurred world, but the vague shapes caught by her weak eyes did not provide her with sufficient clues to divine what Savannah meant. She found the shop no different than the others in that it contained four walls, a ceiling, a floor, things set upon shelves, and a number of people milling around and bumping into her, but none of these were cause for offense.

"Savannah, I don't understand..."

Savannah, however, did, and she was not about to allow it to exist any longer. With a wild groan, she upended a load of books onto the sandal-covered foot of a retiree from Michigan. The man gave out a feminine yelp and lifted his aching toes to the level of his fanny pack, the other foot sent hopping and giving syncopation to his cries. As would be expected, the next load of books did nothing to relieve his distress, and his hopping foot, now sufficiently mashed, lost its hold on the earth. He crashed into one of the Johnny Rebs, and the sound of it shattering into pieces acted on Savannah as the horn blare to charge; she raced into the enemy lines without the least touch of trepidation.

More books were thrown to the floor. Those that weren't were cast in velocity-driven anger, finding purchase on the bodies of numerous vacationers. Savannah ran around in a wild frenzy, tossing, ripping, and knocking over whatever she found in her way. At some point, Mitzi's static yell mixing together with those of the other patrons in the shop in unfortunate harmony, Savannah stumbled upon a saber, raised it high, and maniacally sliced into the rebel flags above her. Her kicks upended one rebel soldier after the next and she drove her blade deep into their heartless chests. The sword was probably what saved her. The bearded gentleman who worked behind the counter had brought himself out onto the floor, and in his eyes, one could read glorious plans to save the South with a flying tackle. But when maiming instruments came into play, he realized that while some things were worth dying for, minimum wage was not one of them.

"Aaaaah!" Mitzi cried. "What's going on? What's going on?"

Mitzi's screams did nothing to calm her, and no word came in response to her questions. The world flew about her in amorphous shapes and sharp sounds, and all that she knew was that what was going on around her was not good. She stumbled on top of the refuse bestrewn upon the floor, looking for the exit and finding the storage closet, and even that was locked. She struggled with the knob for a period that in her mind lasted hours, screaming, questioning, and eventually crying. Finally, a hand grabbed her around the wrist and before she could reach out and attack her attacker, she heard the words, "Come on, Mitzi. We've got to get out of here."

Savannah led her to the other side of the room, then back out into the heat. When the two at last reached the car, they found Tradd unmoved.

"Maybe he is dead," said Savannah as she cranked the engine to life. "I can't say that this is ideal, but perhaps it will give our story the gravitas required by all great works."

FIFTY

Mrs. Edwards received the phone message. She listened to it once, then she listened to it again. It should be noted that at neither time did she take the occasion to write down the officer's phone number.

Standing there, fingers to mouth, eyes unblinking, her mind convulsed with fearful possibilities in a way that only a mother's mind can. Her daughter was dead. Her daughter was hurt. Someone had stolen her car, and her daughter lay dying in the trunk. Probably beaten. Probably raped. Scared. Injured. Ruined. She reached down and picked up the phone. She dialed.

Harry Edwards's secretary received the call, and as it was not terribly unusual to answer the phone and have a frantic woman screaming in her ear, she calmly said, "Just one moment, Mrs. Edwards," and patched it into her boss's office. She then returned to her dictation, her thoughts on the upcoming weekend at the lake where she and her boyfriend, Donny, would hang out on the boat drinking beer, burning in the sun, and fornicating by the live well. This absence of mind caused her to type "there" instead of "their," "except" instead of "accept," and "Master Jacob's son apparently has the seminal record" instead of "Mr. Jacobson denies having a criminal record." Somewhere in the front drawer of Harry Edwards's desk waited an expectant red pen.

He accepted the call, just as he accepted his lowly fate, each with a stolid grace wherein one closes one's eyes and trudges ever onward and outward. A cacophony of misery entered his ear the second that he did. His phone apparently had a circuit breaker of some sort, for it did not take the signal in pure, clean tones, and instead howled it all together, making it appear as though Mrs. Edwards, no singer she, was attempting a tragic opera over a CB radio, all the while grinding the clutch down a gravel road. He did his best to understand: he listened intently, he asked her to repeat herself, but it was simply no use as excited as she was. His requests for her to calm down were as effective as if he had asked a mountain to move over a bit, for Harry Edwards was no Mohammed, not even a Muslim, and not really that great of an Episcopalian, if the truth be told.

However, he did somehow piece together that something had happened to his daughter and that this something involved the city of Charleston, a police officer, and, more importantly, his wife's car.

"Goddammit! Quit warbling like an idiot! Is she in jail?"

The responses came in awkward, powerful trills that brought to mind an Italian duchess bemoaning a lover lost in a duel.

"Helen! Calm down for chrissakes! I can't understand a word you're saying! What happened to the car?"

At this point the duchess reached a crescendo in terms of both volume and passion, extracted a dagger from her bodice, and plunged it deep into her bosom.

"All right! All right! I'm coming home. Jesus. I'll be there in five minutes."

He hung up the phone, grabbed his coat, and headed for the door.

"Julie, I've got to run to the house. I shouldn't be too long."

"Okay, Mr. Edwards."

She watched him walk out the door, waited an appreciable length of time to make sure the coast was clear, then took off her dictation headset and picked up the phone. The great thing about Donny's job working on a construction crew for the telephone company was that she could always reach him. That and it had great benefits. Lord knows it wasn't easy finding a man with good benefits these days. Especially with the economy being how it was and all.

FIFTY-ONE

Once again Roy lay on the bed of his hotel room, stripped down to his underwear, willing the cool air over his way from the metal box that exhaled it, the metal box into which many a drunken fool had urinated due to confusion or malice, giving the room a pale ammonia smell mingled with long-dead tobacco smoke. The walk back, along roads unmarked by trees or clouds, had been something that he would have preferred to avoid. The sun smashed into the concrete, then bounced up in angry heat, teasing him with the afflictions of hell and causing him to curse the driver of the shuttle, who would not greet the evening without a formal complaint being lodged against him.

No matter how hard he looked, he had not been able to find Erica at the aquarium. She was simply not there. Likewise, she had not been on the same streets that he had walked along, nor had she been in the reception area, where the new man-on-duty was as rude as the old one. What this proved was only that his task would not be as easy as he had hoped. He would have to try harder. He would have to think more deeply. He would have to plan with greater care. These were not difficult things to do, and he realized that his task, although arduous and just beginning, would not be met without success.

A judge sat within the television screen, listening to two women discussing how one had gotten the other fired from her job at a tanning salon. Roy listened as well, although he couldn't quite understand what goal either was trying to achieve through the court system. He changed the channel. News. Sports. More courtrooms. Policemen apprehending the guilty. Strange men and women handing out advice to even stranger men and women. He longed for the internet. For a quick chat with the Davinator or Miss Sunflower, but he was living in willful deprivation, sacrificing for his sister, which he deemed worthy, if not noble.

Someone knocked on his door and, like the person on the other side, Roy waited with anticipation to see what would happen next. He was in no state of dress to answer and unless it was housekeeping, there was no one who could need to come in. Unless it was Erica. He sat up, waiting, and then it came again. And at that point he was sure it was his sister. Throwing a towel around his half-naked waist, he crossed the room and turned the knob.

Outside stood a lady who, despite all of her attempts to appear young, did not. Her dress clung tightly to her body—the body perhaps admirable for a woman her age, the dress very inappropriate—cut down to the beginnings of her sternum where flesh spotted and worn by sun and age lay bare. Her hair had been bleached to white and makeup covered the skin of her face in a mask. She held a cigarette in one hand, the other pressed against the door frame. She was not wearing shoes. Roy asked her if he could help her.

"I wouldn't mind borrowing your towel," she said with a phlegm-stirring laugh.

"Your car must have just hit a water buffalo," said Roy.

A brief aside: Roy was not particularly funny, and he was well aware of the fact. But he had learned, from the internet and general social interaction, that one does not need to be funny in order to be humorous. It was a simple trick. All that you needed to do was watch funny movies, learn the lines, and when a moment in life occurred that was in any way similar to one in the movie, you simply said the funny line said by the funny guy in the funny movie, and if the person had seen the same funny movie as you had, they laughed. If they had not seen the funny movie, then they looked at you like you had mental issues and did not. The woman was apparently unfamiliar with Roy's film.

"A water buffalo? What you smokin' in there, buddy?" she asked, again knocking loose the phlegm that coated her lungs.

"I don't smoke, although it seems like the person who was here before me did. That stuff really lingers."

"Lingers with your fingers," said the woman.

"What?" asked Roy.

"Lingers with your fingers," said the woman. "I was just talking. I can rhyme almost anything like that. It's kind of my special talent." She coughed again. "You look like you just got out of the shower."

"No. I'm just sweaty from walking around," he said.

The woman did not seem to think much of this and she took a drag from her cigarette, giving him a look of cool appraisal.

"It's really hot outside," said Roy.

"Um-hm," said the woman. "Listen, we're havin' a few drinks over at my place and we don't have an ice bucket. I went to see that queer fellow who works up at the front desk and according to him we're shit out of luck. Anyway, I know I'm making this too long, but you usin' yours?"

"No," said Roy. He did not move.

"Well, hell. You mind if I borrow it?"

"No, no, of course not," said Roy. "I'll just need you to bring it back. I don't know what the hotel policy is on the ice buckets, but I want to make sure I don't get charged for losing one."

"I told you I just wanted to borrow it."

"Oh." Roy did not move.

"Are you gonna give it to me or not? I swear I think you're smoking something in there. You are, aren't you?"

"No, I told you I don't smoke."

Roy walked back into the room and retrieved the ice bucket from where it sat by the sink. The woman took it with a smile.

"Thanks. By the way my name's Liza. I'm right next door. Before you go out tonight, stop on by. We got drinks and stuff."

"Sounds good," said Roy.

"Smokin', smokin', smokin'," Roy heard the woman sing as he shut the door. "Smokin', tokin', jokin'. See?"

FIFTY-TWO

Savannah and Mitzi drove back through the Battery, Savannah with eyes on the mansions, hoping to catch a glimpse of someone she knew, although she did not know anyone who lived on the Battery, Mitzi purblind and still hyperventilating from the trauma of the store. And it should be remembered that Tradd lay in the back, unconscious, perhaps in a coma, perhaps dead. It was unclear to them how much time had passed, but one can safely state that all involved felt that it had to have been a great deal, for so many exhilarating, breathtaking events had taken place.

The only thing that truly told them how long they had been on their low country quest was that the sky had begun to grow faint, the blistering sun changing to more of a warming sun, shadows falling where before none fell, the ocean darkening to an even grayer color of death. Fewer and fewer people could be seen walking around the city, for tours demanded a certain amount of pain, enlightenment a certain amount of vision, and a day in the heat a certain length of time back at the hotel, watching cable television and trying to decide who should shower first. The first person missed the initial part of the television program, the second the last bit, both equally robbed.

"I've got to eat," said Mitzi. "My hands are starting to shake I'm so hungry."

"Perhaps it's the excitement, Mitzi," said Savannah. "A day in the low country, with its magic and overpowering sorrow, can oftentimes drive someone not used to it to spells of frenzy."

"I'm just hungry," said Mitzi. "Painfully hungry. My folks always eat at fixed times—lunch at noon, dinner at six, you know—and I think I've gotten in the habit. And I don't think I want to get out of it."

"Please don't talk of your wonderful parents around me, you urine specimen hanging from a mildewed jockstrap. You don't realize it, but when I hear you speak of how wonderful your father was and how kind your mother could be, it brings out the contrast in my upbringing and fills me with deep sorrow. Here. I need to stop the car. I'm so filled with deep sorrow that I can no longer drive."

Savannah thus stopped the car from its cautious roll, parking them in front of a driveway on Gibbes Street.

"Savannah, I'm sorry. I was just talking. I didn't mean anything by it."

Savannah looked at Mitzi for a moment, then began emitting loud, inarticulate sounds reminiscent of laughter delivered by an actress trying to make her comeback after being lobotomized at the suggestion of her handlers. This continued for quite some time.

"Are you alright?"

Conroy again entered: "Mitzi, I've come to realize that Chicken John and I were low country boys, strong swimmers, good fishermen, who had grown to manhood in a household of secret terrors that had marked each of us in different ways. We carried a strange darkness about us composed of mistrust and distortion. We used laughter as both a weapon and a vaccine."

"I'm not following you."

"Maybe this will help: though my whole family was bruised and tested, it had found solace in the healing unction of laughter. This dark humor had prevented us from both sanctimony and despair."

"I'm still lost."

"We laugh when the pain gets too much. We laugh when the pity of human life gets too… pitiful. We laugh when there's nothing else to do. So, when do you weep? you might ask. According to the Southern way? I would retort. After we laugh, Doctor. Always. Always after we laugh."

The changing of genders and conferring of postgraduate honors once again left Mitzi baffled, her head hurting from the cryptic tales of Savannah's childhood, from eyes squinting now for the eighth hour straight.

"What does what you just said have to do with anything?" Mitzi asked.

"The books, Mitzi," said Savannah. "You always have to return to the books."

"Speaking of which, shouldn't you be taking notes or something? How are you going to remember all of this?"

"Like the great Patrick Conroy, Mitzi, I have an indelible memory. I can remember conversations from high school and college as though they were yesterday."

"But high school was only a few months ago for you, and you're in college now."

"You truly are a mildewing jockstrap set somehow to cover a urine specimen containing a bloodblister, Mitzi. As I've told you before, I've lived life. I've been married, I've had children. I've marched with the protesters and read my poetry in front of groups of fire-breathing lesbians."

The word *lesbians* ended the act, for the stage fell dead, the lights killed, the scenery scraped across the floor with painful cries. The actors took the time to regroup, thinking of cigarettes one could smoke, pondering the initial thoughts of the reviewer on the front row. The audience sat still, perhaps asleep from boredom, awaiting the next round of inanity, hoping for the end, which was sure to come.

And when the play resumed, it happened that nothing had changed, and the two leading ladies, covered in insect bites and suffering from hunger, sat in the same spot, the minor character of the expelled Citadel cadet earning his keep by pretending to be deceased in the back seat.

"I'm hungry," said Mitzi. "I need to eat."

"Then we shall dine," said Savannah. "The moon is rising over Charleston, and its inhabitants—not of the moon, but of Charleston—are putting on their gas lights, readying their shrimp and mull gravy, listening for the silent footsteps of the Gullah fairy. And as for where we will go, Mitzi, I know just the place. It's a little bistro that, if you didn't know exactly where it was, you would just walk by and miss, which is why we Charlestonians are so fond of it. A little bistro located in a nook of this fair city, far, far away from the normal pell-mell of tourists and Yankee carpetbaggers. You will eat newly opened oysters, shrimp fresh from the nets, sip on mint juleps, and wash it all down with an apple pie that men have died for. How does that sound?"

"It sounds like heaven."

"It is. Let's go."

FIFTY-THREE

Roy had considered calling his parents. They were the ones footing the bill and therefore they deserved a certain amount of respect—respect shown by way of a status report—but his father was such an overbearing, condescending ass that he shuddered at the thought. The Magik Merlin incident had really cemented things for him. There he was, in a moment of absolute need, and what had his father done to him other than let him down? Nay, not merely let him down, but pushed him down and then stamped his foot on his neck? His mother would understand the travails he had undergone, but she did not think deeply and therefore there would never be any real connection between the two of them. So he would not call them. Not now. Once the night was through, and he had gathered some leads, perhaps then, but definitely not now.

The hours were passing by. Next door he could hear Liza's cackle and accompanying cough, both slight at first, now gathering to a force of nature. He was not a solitary type of guy. Despite the fact that he had grown up with few friends, he enjoyed the amiable banter of comradery, and without it he was left with his own thoughts, left to entertain himself, and both left him saddened and bored. Liza did not seem like a bad woman. She did not seem like a good one, there was no question as to that, but not a bad one either. She had invited him over. She had borrowed his ice bucket. He doubted that she knew anything about the internet, but sometimes the people who knew the least showed the greatest interest, almost like those who enjoyed listening to tales of treks in the jungle or up the face of unscalable mountains, but who never wished to leave the comfort of their living room. He decided to get dressed.

FIFTY-FOUR

Scott was not home. Of this there is no doubt, for no mortal could have refrained from either calling the police or dismembering the mooncalf beating on the door with both fists and shouting out one's name on sixteen separate occasions throughout the course of a day. Creighton knew that the cocksman often spent the day away from his apartment, somewhere where a backpack was necessary and women were plenty but thought that perhaps after the bonding sessions they had recently shared together Scott might trek back early and catch a few reruns at *chez* Starke. Only this did not appear to be the case.

He walked back into his apartment, leaving the door open, and sat on his sofa, staring out onto the landing with his hands between his knees and his teeth grinding in his mouth. This lasted for fifteen minutes or so, after which Creighton got up and put himself out the door, once more giving a few knocks and letting out a few shouts. He then returned to the couch.

The problem, as he could clearly see from where he sat, was that this position offered him no peripheral vision. Unless Scott walked by his door, which was unlikely given the placement of the stairway and Scott's door in relation to Creighton's, Creighton would miss him, and then who knows? Scott might go hop in the shower or put on his headphones and study, and all of that time Creighton would be trying to get in touch with him and Scott wouldn't know it, and it would just be a tragedy of errors, separating them at a time when they should be spending life together, getting to know each other better, and each learning from the other the basic tenets that friendship offers. His mind whirled at solutions, grasping at them as they raced around the centrifuge, and he was seriously considering taking a hammer and knocking a hole in the wall when he thought of the full-length mirror that he kept in his bedroom on the back of the closet door.

With a burst of energy, he shot from the couch, his momentum carrying him into the bedroom, where he wrenched open the closet door and ripped the mirror from its hold of half-inch nails. This done, he ran back to the living room and set it on the floor next to the door, angled toward the landing. It sturdied without fear, and he watched it carefully as he took slow backward steps to the couch. Only it was not exactly right. When he tried to spy around the corner, certain blind spots became apparent, causing him to arise four times to situate it perfectly. And it was done.

Now that everything was set, there remained nothing to do but sit and wait, and that is what he did. The minutes slowly oozed by; the seconds ticked off like blows from a belt. He probably needed another class to teach. There were a lot of would-be writers who could learn a great deal from someone like Creighton, and who probably had to take biology or something like that instead of creative writing because it wasn't being offered, and who knew the effects of this? A future Shakespeare could be filling his skull with seminal vesicles and bile ducts instead of couplets and unreliable narrators, and the world would be a poorer place because of it. Granted, the head of the department said that they would give this one a trial run for a semester, just to see how Creighton handled it and all, and they had only just started, but he already felt like he had proved himself and that since he was the subject in question, it should be up to him, and not some balding fool, as to when he was ready to move forward. Was Professor Hawkins his master? Was Creighton his ward? Did he need his permission to sign checks? To live where he lived?

He thought of calling the feeble buzzard up and telling him a thing or two, really clearing off the table, but after a few moments imagining how the conversation would take place, he decided that it would be better to do it in person. What he would do is search out a protégé. He had recently seen a movie that several people had recommended to him on the basis that he was a writer, and the movie concerned a writer who, like him, had written the great American novel and then vanished. Creighton was not sure how to react when these people implied that he had somehow disappeared, especially since he was standing in front of them, talking to them, eating up the same oxygen that they were, but regardless, this writer had befriended a youth who was from the streets, and the young man had rekindled the authorial spirit in the ancient.

So, Creighton watched it, thought about it, worked it over from numerous angles, and immediately deemed it terrible. Its only saving graces were moments of unintentional humor, especially the part where the aged writer prances around his book-lined apartment shouting as the youth pounds on the typewriter, "Strike the keys! Make them work for you!" or something to that effect. Because first off, no one can write a coherent sentence with someone shouting at him. Yes, allegedly T. S. Eliot had scrawled out *The Waste Land* while his hysterical wife wailed in the background, and maybe someone had drafted something while bombs pounded around him in a war, but there was something different between background noise and an actual address. Secondly, no one struck the keys. This was not a symphony or a rock and roll band. No one applauded as you jutted in a comma, and no breaths were held as you painstakingly set out the landscape in the French village where the story takes place. There were lots of reasons why this appealed to an audience of modern-day barbarians—people were becoming less and less Hebraic and living more and more in the land of the Philistines; the nation's school system lay in shambles; the culture heralded those who memorized lines and said them on a screen, and not those who had actually thought them out—but the main one was society's desire for instant gratification. One wanted the applause and wanted it without much fuss. Things that could be done over a long weekend or a few months were acceptable, but to sit down in the dark of your room, your only companion silence, and spend three hours trying to get a paragraph right was simply an unacceptable way to live. How was the written word supposed to compete with video games and free pornography? Would one rather attempt to write out something that no one would probably ever read, or while away an afternoon getting drunk watching helmeted millionaires tackle one another? The answers were simple to Creighton, but they were quickly drawn away from him, his thoughts focused on the fly that had entered the room and then quickly made its way to the dirty kitchen.

An hour passed. And then another one. During this time Creighton's frail greetings changed into hard accusations, he the wife sitting at the dinner table, the once steaming chicken condensed to congealed frost underneath her unforgiving rage. It was simply unacceptable. For their opening night had not been one of the innocent, meaningless kiss on the cheek, but the trip back to the bedroom where promises were made, and things done with the knowing that they probably should not have been. Yes, he began to fear that it had simply been some lark on Scott's part. A meaningless encounter that would vanish from his consciousness over the passing days if it had not already disappeared. The reason behind these feelings of anger and despair was that during this time Scott's purpose had transformed in Creighton's mind. By a series of illogical reasonings and fantastical interpretations, it had become apparent to him that it was Scott who would become his protégé. The young man obviously had the study habits necessary to discipline himself in the ways of prose, and he obviously had the creative energy—shown by way of libido—to craft a tale that would hold the reader captivated. Creighton had the lesson plan already scratched out in his demented skull, the reading list literally compiled by way of the set of books stacked negligently between his feet, so now the only thing missing was the willing pupil, the young lad who would start off with Shakespeare, dip into Shelley and Byron, spend some quality time with Wordsworth before sailing along into the worlds of Madame Bovary and Ishmael, only to be sucked into the vortex of hell where Burroughs and Camus dwelt. If he could, Creighton would take a hatchet, lift the lid of the cocksman's cranium, and drop the words of the masters into the pot below, where they could boil amongst the febrile gray matter.

This newfound passion inspired the famed author of *Finding It All in the Hole* to reacquaint himself with those men with whom he had spent so many waking hours, and he reached down and picked up one of the books, *Heart of Darkness* by Conrad. He was still on the river Thames when he tired of the silver-tongued Polack, setting it down and replacing it with *Lowcountry Lamentations*, where he began to read as follows:

```
    It is said that a fire that burns brightly burns
quickly, and if Ihad to compare the love shared
between Jonathan and me to a fire, that is how
I would compare it. Our lovemaking was tender,
long, and many times it felt as though we were
forcing our bodies into the others and touching
the other's soul, but after a few years and two
children it was apparent that Jonathan no longer
had any interest and with two kids and a career
in poetry and interior decorating along with a
husband to feed and a house to run who had the
time! I was always running them from one side of
New York City to the other for football practices
and singing lessons, and I was always having to
study for my classes at Harvard and always having
to write out a poem or two because of my publish-
ing contract and on top of that the president
was getting out of Vietnam (finally!) and he was
always calling me about my opinions on that and
etiquette. So it was no surprise when I found
the smell of perfume on Jonathan's shirt and the
crotch of his pants.
```

Now no lowcountry geechee brat worth her salt is going to let a man run around on her! Honey chile no! Sesame had taught me that a man was like a racoon and had to find its hole so that it could sleep but the coon hole could be a warrin' coon hole or a coon hole laid with down! I thought about the chicken's foot dipped in hog's gravy and thought that this time the geechee trick had failed, but then I said to myself just like Sesame would have said to me, "Girl, you best be gettin on gettin on!" I had let myself go. I was so depressed. And this helped out my poetry a good bit, and my Orkin Man poems sold over 500,000 copies the first week it was out, but it was still affecting my "sex" life and my relationship with my kids. I needed to "grow". And it was obvious that I wasn't "growing" at all.

I threw myself into exercise as I did lots of times when I got depressed. it reminded me of my days under the hot sun of the lowcountry when I played football at Yewakasee High. I did thirty minutes of cardio and almost a thousand crunches and then I went into the bathroom and weighed myself. I had lost ten pounds! I looked at myself in the mirror and decided that although my body looked good and my boobs still looked like a teenagers that I needed to do something about my hair. I had read lots of books on cutting hair and sometimes I cut my own. One time when I cut it I had to go to a "fancy" ball in Washington that the President was having since his wife was sick and Vidal Sassoon asked me where I got my hair cut and when I told him that I did it, chile you should have seen him 'near flip his wig! He

offered to make me president of his company but
I told him that my heart was in poetry and even
though Jonathan and I weren't making a lot of
money and could have used all of hte money that
was being offered and I could have gotten used to
all ofthe "perks" that went along with the job.
Show me a geechee girl that would't want that
job and I'll show you someone whose got the mark
of Shedareen on her! So I cut my hair like a had
seen a "big" movie star do it and then flounced it
out with some rosemary oil like Sesame taught me
and chile you shoudl have seen it shine! Jonathan
wouldn't know what hit him when he came in the
door!

I cooked a dinner of locks and bagels that he
liked and put a lowcountry touch of gyspsum seed
and crab tusks in the mix and I had bought a very
"expensive" bottle of french wine and put candles
on the table. The children were in bed asleep and
when Jonathan came in I knew that the dinner that
was supposed to be so right was all wrong.

He had lipstick on his face and he smelled of
alcohol and channel number five, which is what
his ex-wife wore. His zipper was undone. I tried
to keep my calm. "G'day mate." he greeted as
he leaned over to give me a kiss. By this point
his Canadian accent had worn out its charm and
simply was his voice. "What a nice dinner you
have prepared for me this evening!" "I prepared
it for you two hours ago!" I hollered. And then
I realized that I needed to be calm. "Jonathan
we need to talk." I whispered. He sat down atthe
table and began to eat. "What pretell shall we
talk about." he grumbled. "About us Jonathan."

I replied. "We can't go on living like this." I
stated. "It isn't good for the kids." I ended.
"Going on like what mate." he queried. "Jonathan
Israel Birnbaum don't you go sassin me! Yahn!
I know that you are making love to your exwife!
Score one for the lowcountry gal! "I really don't
want to talk about htis!" he screamed. "Jonathan we have to talk about this! This is our
marriage!"

At that time the phone rang. "Don't answer
it." Jonathan ordered. "Why areyou afraid that
it's one of your "sicko" pals!" I countered.
Bullseye! That stuck him good. I got up and went
to the phone and when I heard the voice on the
other side I felt my soul seep into my legs.

There was a cool breath coming from the
receiver, deep husky breath, and even before he
said a word, I knew who it was: Chicken John.

"Chicken John? Chicken John?" "Yeah. It's me
sis. How the shrimp runnin these days?" "Chicken
John, you know Shedareen don't llow no shrimp
up here in yahn New York City!" We always spoke
in gullah when we saw each other. It was just a
part of being from the lowcountry and it was a
bond that we had that could never be broken. "Ah
Shedareen. I sure do miss Sesame." When he said
these words I could not help but cry. I missed
Sesame too, although she sometimes appeared in
the old mirror that had been in my family since
the days of General Beauregard. "I know. Me too.
Chicken John what's wrong?" "I've got myself in
a bit a trouble out here after coming back from
the war and all. The war was just terrible. I
killed alot of children and women just because it

was a bad war and it turned people crazy. I think
I"m crazy now because of all of the killing I
did and because of the tiger cages and all. Just
crazy. Just plain crazy!" "Chicken JOhn you're
not crazy! You're still my brother! I'm the one
whose crazy! Remember all of my crazy poems and
those times that I thought about killing myself!"
"Well, I guess the old parish priest must've darn
been tootin smokin from Shadareen's pipe when he
lika took a possum down if we both bees crazy!"
And I knew that when Chicken John began speaking in Gullah that everythign would be alright.
Or did I?… "Anyway sis I got myself in deep water
this time. You know dad got drunk and decided to
sell the island to the nuclear power people and
it just ain't right. I told him he couldn't but
he got all mad and beat me with a cane pole and
hit me upside the head with a shrimp bucket and
he sold it. But I decided to stay and this place
is crawling with the federal authorities. At first
I just blew up stuff you know but then I kind of
went crazy and I blew up a train that had a bunch
of "important" people on it and I'm in a whole
heap of trouble now." I knew that this meant
trouble and I knew that there wasn't much I could
do about it. "Chicken John I'll call the president up right now and tell him you didn't mean to
do it. YOu know I give him lessons on etiquette
and he consults me about most of his major policy
decisions so he's got to listen to me. He's just
got to!" "Well do what you can do but I got a bad
feeling about this one. Like Shedareen's breathing down my back. You know." "I'll pack my things
and leave right now. I'm coming Chicken John!

I'll do my best to save you!" "I love you sis."
"I love you Chicken JOhn."

"Is Chicken John in trouble." Jonathan
inquired. "I can't talk right now." I answered.
"I've got to talk to the president. Right now!"
I called the white house on the "special" number
that I had and got the president. He told me
that he'd look into it but that he didn't knwo
tthat there was much he could do. He then told me
to make sure I said hello to my mother from him
because she always flirted with him and he always
said that he thought she was the prettiest woman
in the world and that the astronaut had really
messed up when he didn't marry her. I thanked him
and got off of the phone.

"What did the president have to say." queried
Jonathan. "I can't talk right now." I replied.
"I have to get back to the lowcountry. But first
we need to talk about us. I can't live with you
any longer Jonathan. I know that I've been very
cold lately and pushed you away and there's nothing I can put my finger on as to why. It's just
that I had such a terrible childhood that I don't
think I ever learned how to love. How can you
lov esomeone who beats you? How can you learn
love from a mother so beautiful that she loves
only herself? "But Savannah!" he cried. He began
to cry and I knew that I should take him in my
arms and take him back to the bedroom where we
woudl make sweet love like we used to do in the
old days when our bodies would meld into each
other and anneal into a band of love, but something inside of me was just so messed up that I
couldn't. "I'm leaving the children with you.

256

They'll be better off that way." I stated. "But
what am I to tell them mate!" Jonathan shouted.
"Tell them that their mother loves them but that
right now I've got to go try and save Chicken
John."

And I knew that night that I would not be
coming back for a while, but I did not know how
incredibly long a while would be. No one did.

The sun was burning its final flame of the day, sinking down below
the apartments across the way and covering the pool in shadow.
During the reading a cramp had developed in Creighton's left calf,
and he massaged it with a hand, looking out the door, listening for
the sounds of footsteps on the landing. A bat flew by, or perhaps
a bird that had lost its way, and Creighton wondered if bats had
rabies or if birds had rabies, which led to musings over how a new
screenplay concerning rabid birds would go over in Hollywood these
days, thought in such a way that if one had some special contraption
which allowed one to hear Creighton's thoughts, one would naturally
assume that the thinker had once spent some time in Hollywood,
and was comparing the old to the new, when this was unquestionably not the case.

He really needed to clip his toenails. They grew from the tips of his
toes like the thorns of a plant, developed over thousands of years due
to the vagaries of natural selection as a defense mechanism against
Lord-only-knows-what. His would only protect him from experiencing comfort in the area of footwear, and. unlike a rose, they did not
lead to greater beauty. "Ewww!" he said, shimmying his baritone up
to a eunuch's falsetto. "How gross. Why don't you cut them?" And
then he froze. This little exercise, the mimicry of a disgusted woman,
brought to him a drip of nostalgia which landed on an eyelash, then
slowly rolled down a cheek.

Perhaps every relationship has its pet names and pat sayings,
little things done over and over again until they become as much the

fabric of the connubial link as a tossed pie in a vaudeville show. This had certainly been the case in every relationship he had had with a woman, including his mother. With his ex-wife, the despicable Donna, the falsetto had been one of these hallmarks. The two of them lounging in the tub, the bubble bath foaming around their naked bodies as he scrubbed her sinless back with an actual sea sponge he had illegally harvested off the coast of some forgotten Caribbean nation, poor in riches yet rich in crime, where they had celebrated their doomed marriage by snorkeling in aquatic silence. "You're doing it too hard!" he would squeak the moment before the fins of her shoulder blades whisked back to thwart the brute who seemed to want to plane her vertebrae. "Yeah," she would say in agreement, and the two of them would laugh, or he would laugh and assume that she was as well, suddenly lost in the surrounding grout.

They had met at one of his readings. His aunt, who had never married and as cliché would have it kept innumerable cats, had always been his biggest supporter. She considered their family intriguing and thought that its history contained the roughage of fiction, which someone needed to process into a novel, and from the time he reached his teens she had goaded him on to be a writer and told him tales of uncle so-and-so, who had once met famous person so-and-so, patently thinking that this would somehow translate into a fragment he would put in chapter such-and-such. When he finally did step forth and pen *Finding It All in the Hole,* she incorrectly assumed that it was a veiled telling of the Starke family history and issued invitations to all of her friends for a reading by her authorial nephew in the hinterlands of Ohio. In cold November of that year the science-fiction tour made its rounds to Cincinnati, and given a night off, Creighton obliged the miserable spinster with his presence.

It would be fair to say that upon his arrival he gave off strong airs scented with dissatisfaction and contempt, as it would be equally just to say that secretly he basked in the rays of hope, thinking that perhaps this would be a true literary salon, containing a modern-day Gertrude Stein and her lesbian lover, who would marvel at the words as they fluttered from his mouth and champion his cause across the land of freedom. They were seated around a living room where a seemingly Egyptian cult held its secret rituals—photographs of cats, paintings of cats, tapestries of cats, sculptures of cats, everyday implements formed in the shape of cats—resting their weight upon ancient furniture and drinking tea out of mismatched cups. The crow-like chatter that had emanated from the room moments prior to his entrance fell to a whisper of quiet, and they all arose to meet the chronicler of all things Starke. He greeted the ladies with the gravity of a cabinet minister handling a necessary political function during a time of war, his lips sealed in a semi-frown, his eyes grave and reflective, his handshake firm, his carriage that of a man weighed down by the antics of an out-of-control colonel. They were all ladies, all except for a homosexual shoe salesman whom the women had adopted as one of their group, and they all contained the tragic contents of humanity that reminded one of the verity that in the end all roads lead to putrefaction. Except for one. Not road, but woman. She had a nice cut to her and pleasant eyes, and whereas the graves chomped like hungry mouths when the others walked past a cemetery, she clearly had a number of years to go before her death, unless she secretly harbored cancer inside her uterus or was fated for a high-speed rendezvous with an automobile. She caught his eye, and since everyone in the room was looking at him, he hers, and they shared a nod which seemed appropriate to both.

When the pleasantries came to their inevitable conclusion, the group took back to their seats, leaving him standing next to his aunt behind a lectern that she had borrowed for the occasion from her church.

"This, as you know, is my nephew, Creighton Starke, who has just published his first novel, *Finding It All in the Hole*." A piece of paper retrieved from a pocket signified that this was the end of the extemporaneous portion of her speech. "I remember when Creighton was a little boy. He was such a curious child." From this point on, his mind wandered, as is often the case with great artists he was to understand, flitting over to what he had eaten for lunch that day, to the chapter that he would soon read aloud, to the breasts of the daughter of a man whose novels focused solely on Martian mining accidents, to the unholy acts he would commit with this young lady who sat with her legs crossed at the knee, if circumstance were to show him favor.

A few minutes passed, then he wandered back in. He did not care for biographies. There was something absolutely disgusting about eating a person's life up in a span of three hundred pages, watching them go from birth to death over an evening or two. If there were a horror genre, then this was it. You will be born, you will do some things, few of which will be remembered and fewer yet that will matter, then you will pass on to nothingness. That sent a chill down his spine and made him want to sleep with the lights on. Stories concerning roving zombies or men who changed into wolves simply made him tired.

His aunt, who had obviously not read the book, finished her final dallyings concerning the Starke family, tried her hand at a few nonsensical French sayings that she mispronounced with *incompétence affûtée*, then handed the metaphorical mic over to her brother's genius son. Creighton, feigning extreme fatigue and ennui, stepped forward and replaced her at the lectern. He had chosen Osgood's fateful collision with a pirate ship in the salt seas west of Africa, as he felt its action and colorful descriptive passages would best suit this crowd of drawing-room women, and with careful deliberation he turned to the beginning of that chapter.

The reading mirrored every other reading in history—some of the crowd restless, some listening intently, some bored out of their skulls, some drifting off to sleep—but one can imagine that the now long-dead brains of the past, untouched by the joys of television and wide-screen movies, had had a greater tolerance for the spoken word, a simpler set of gears that allowed them to actually enjoy it. As for the present day, only shallow intellectuals and the legally insane can find pleasure in such an evening, and there were none of either in attendance that night. Creighton's aunt steamed her brains to a bubble in her quest to find fictional shades of the Starke family in Osgood's cutlass strokes, and only mildly convinced herself that Osgood's castrating of the tongueless Moor had its genesis in her incontinent grandfather who had been rendered dumb by a stroke. Someone passed gas during the elegant passage where the author compared the blood spurting from the lascar's neck to the vermillion lips of Belinda. One woman excused herself twice for trips to the powder room, both coinciding with page-long graphic descriptions of male rape. The only glint in the otherwise cloudy evening proved to be the young lady sitting with her legs crossed. She neither stirred nor shrieked, kept her eyes on Creighton, and nodded her head throughout like an unforgiving churchgoer listening to the minister condemn the long list of the damned to their just reward.

It was only after that he was able to speak to her. The others had remained seated—after having gotten up and congratulated both Creighton and his aunt, of course—and he found himself standing in the kitchen and her standing in front of him. The experience was an odd one for him. Granted, she was very pretty, but he constructed elaborate sexual fantasies concerning women much prettier, and not seldom but often. There was just something about her. His head began to ache, and his stomach felt as though he had recently swallowed half a spoon of an emetic, not sick, but not top of the tipper either. He expected ebullience, but only experienced a vague uneasiness, and his initial attempts at conversation were poor even for him.

She was a secretary at a law firm but knew little about the law or the art of secretarianism. Her father had recently retired, and she had since been spending a great deal of time with him and her mother, the woman with the weak bladder and strong prejudice against forced sodomy. She had received a college education, but from a poor school, and her interests consisted of nothing anyone would ever consider interesting. The artery of conversation continued along this course for a number of minutes, and had she not been so physically attractive Creighton would have cut it as it pulsed and ended it all then and there. However, just as he was about to excuse himself, matters took a turn for the better. Like Creighton's aunt, she picked up on things in his book that were not there, or at least were not placed there with any intent of the author. The book's alliteration, its biblical imagery, its poetic consonance, its modern dissonance, had all rung out in her ears, and she had found them divine. She carried on in this manner for several minutes, and as Creighton stood there, his chin on his sternum, the head nodding back and forth, absentmindedly toying with a hole in the sleeve of his tweed jacket with a thumb and forefinger, he realized that he was smitten. Yes, she certainly was attractive, and she obviously was fairly intelligent and cultured, but more than that, she was a fan. A fan who had never read the book, but a fan nonetheless. And to be honest, what was more important was that she was his first and only fan.

They left that night with her mother between them, walking through the snow-lined sidewalk to their cars, the streetlights reflecting against the thin sheet of ice on the black asphalt, phone numbers already having been exchanged and sexual organs already engorged from the ghostly foresight of future intercourse. He returned to Cincinnati a wreck, determined to drop out of the science-fiction tour and join her in the hinterlands, where he could write the next masterpiece with her by his side. But like all events that exist in the ordinary and not in books or on the silver screen, no great romantic, drastic steps were taken. He finished the tour. They spoke regularly on the phone. He visited her twice, she him once. He wrote her letters. She said that she enjoyed them. He obtained a teaching position at a college. She lost her job at the law firm. He visited her once more, pocketing a ring as carry-on for the plane ride. She accepted. Her mother eventually chose to come along as well, as Ohio was getting too cold and Creighton's terrifying leap from the closet had eventually made her a widow. They married. They had a son. They divorced.

It goes without saying that Creighton found no other biography as depressing as his own. The only things missing to drive him to immediate self-murder were crushing poverty, nagging syphilis, and a funereal end. He continued to look out the door, hollow and cold, wishing for something other than what he had. And to make it even worse, it was almost eight o'clock, and Scott had yet to return.

FIFTY-FIVE

There was no sign of recognition in Liza's face when Roy told her who he was and that she had invited him over. For an uncomfortable twenty seconds he stood outside the door and she stood inside of it, looking at each other, one trying to explain, the other trying to comprehend. It was only when Roy mentioned the ice bucket that her eyes came alive, her cackle returned, and Roy was ushered into the room.

Inside sat four men, two in chairs, two on the edge of the two double beds. The two in the chairs wore thick beards that swallowed their faces in bramble and briar. They did not let out a peep when Roy was introduced, nor did the man sitting on the bed closer to Roy speak words of welcome, he a tiny man, so small that his feet did not reach the floor from where he sat. One could imagine him included in a work of Dickens, where the author would describe him as having ruddy cheeks and a glint in his eye and give him a queer name like Mr. Rubberstrap and a queer job like copying typescripts. On the bed farther away, however, a shout of hello sprung from the chest of a fellow who appeared to be about Roy's age. He had brown hair and a thin frame. He wore glasses.

"Hey," said Roy.

"I'm Jeff," he said. "You want a beer? The fight's about to start up."

Roy said that he did and he followed him into the bathroom where a collection of different bottles and cans sat in the half-melted ice that filled the bathtub. Jeff let out a mild curse as he reached into the cold and drew forth a can of beer which Roy accepted with a nod.

"You from around here?" asked Jeff.

"Define 'here,'" said Roy.

"What?"

"I mean, do you mean the city or the state or the country or the planet? I don't know." This was a favorite of Miss Sunflower's, this defining of the commonplace. It gave her an air of mystery, or so thought Roy, and seeing as how she would never know that he had stolen her thunder, he saw no harm in the borrowing.

"We got a thinker on our hands," shouted Jeff out to the others. "Charleston," he then said.

"No," said Roy. "I'm not. Just visiting."

"Us too," said Jeff. "Me and Liza kind of go around from place to place, looking for the next big thing, you know. We haven't found it yet, but she says that half the fun's in the looking."

"I guess she has a point," said Roy. "Now, Liza is your…?"

"Mother," said Jeff.

"Oh," said Roy. "I didn't know."

"Yeah, a lot of people assume she's my wife. But she's not."

"No. Or at least you would hope not."

Jeff looked at him in silence.

"With her being your mother and all. Right?"

"Ah, yes," said Jeff with a laugh. "Against the law."

"Incest."

"Yeah. Hey, let's go join the others at the party. They'll think we're in here drinking all of the beer."

Jeff's description of it as a party would be argued by many to be too kind considering what awaited them in the other room. The men were for the most part silent, and not with the silence of contentment, but with that of hatred, forlornness, deep-seated morosity. The television played at high volume on a dilapidated clothes chest, and Liza walked from one man to the other, smoking cigarettes, drinking what appeared to be hard liquor in a glass, laughing with her hack, talking endlessly about topics that no one proposed, and no one commented on. When Jeff and Roy made their reentrance, she acted as though the last she had heard of them they had been off at war, and here they were, making their unexpected homecoming.

"Jeff! Roy!"

She crossed the room and took her son in her arms, placing her aged lips on his cheek and leaving her mark. She then turned her attentions to Roy.

As previously set out, Roy had enjoyed the naked talents of many a woman on the internet, but he had never sampled those of a woman in the flesh. There were no kisses under the apple tree for Roy Edwards when he was but a child, no clumsy fumblings in the backseats of cars as a teenager, no long afternoon couplings on the couch when he was a man in his early twenties. He was not merely a virgin in the twentieth-century sense, he could have well passed by the standards set in the seventeenth as well. With that said, the woman nearly deflowered him when she released her son and gave her attention to their guest and next-door neighbor. Her breasts compressed against his chest when she held him, and the horseshoe of her groin wrapped around his, digging deep into his lap, holding it there, holding it, as she gave him a kiss and then bit his earlobe.

Roy was at a loss as to how to respond. He felt, frankly, that he had been violated, but he equally felt sure that a man should not complain when violated by a woman, so he did not. He did, however, pull himself away and swipe at his kissed cheek with a hand.

"The ice bucket boy," said Liza with a hack. "Welcome to the party."

Roy looked around. The men appeared as though they were stuck in a prison cell, waiting for the guard to come and take them to their rendezvous with the firing squad. They smoked with deliberation and seemed deep in thoughts of the wasted years of the past, the future that was never to come.

"You've met everybody," said Liza.

"I just did," said Roy.

"Well, make yourself comfortable," Liza said, motioning to both of the beds. "We've only got a few minutes."

"I'm fine," said Roy. "I've been sitting all day."

The painful discomfort of silence swept into the room once this was said, all six of them staring at anything but each other. Words are unnecessary amongst friends, amongst family, but Roy did not fit into either category with any of them, and he quickly began to feel anxiety gripping him by the neck.

"Any of you know much about the internet?" he asked.

"Nope," said both Jeff and Liza.

Roy noticed the dwarf carry his gaze over to him. Their eyes locked.

"You speak of the internet," said the man.

"Yes," said Roy. "Are you into it?"

"Does it look like it?" the man asked. And at that he burst into a squall of tears and collapsed on his side on the bed. His beer spilled onto the floor and his tiny body shook on top of the mattress. Roy did not know what to say. The man had fallen away from him and now lay supine, his head in his hands, the bottom of his tiny boots revealing holes in both.

"Don't worry about Jessie," said Liza. "He's been like this all night."

"Is something wrong?" Roy asked.

"Isn't there always?" said Liza.

As Jessie continued with his crying, Roy and Jeff made a passing attempt at discussing the weather, both agreeing that it was hot and both wishing that it would cool down a bit. Roy thought of once again bring up the internet, but given the results of his last attempt, thought better of it. He also feared that he would let slip that his fantasy character was a dwarf and thus cause further insult.

Just as all seemed lost, the fight came on the television. Liza let out a whoop and the others settled themselves in their chairs, listening intently to the two announcers who spoke in earnest tones of the beating that they were about to witness. Roy had never actually seen a fight, or at least not one in the ring. He had been laid on his back by a punch or a kick on a number of occasions and had watched impotently as his one and only friend in middle school was trounced at the bus stop by a set of hooligans, but he did not care for physical violence and saw no entertainment value in it. He sipped on his beer and set his eyes on the television along with the others and waited.

The preliminaries were soon done, and the crowd hushed as a slender woman sheathed in silver walked into the middle of the ring, grabbing hold of the microphone that lowered from the heavens. The inhabitants of the room rose to their feet. With a deep breath, and a swell of background music, the woman began to sing, and along with her, to the surprise of no one but Roy, Jeff joined in.

The woman did not perform what one would call a traditional interpretation of the national anthem. She utilized trills and warblings, dips and rises, swells and falls to such an extent that the staid tune resembled an old gray sweatshirt covered in rhinestones and sparkles with lace sewn in at the neck and the cuffs. Given this, one would think that it would have been impossible to follow along, but with his head thrown back, Jeff trudged along in her wake with the tone of a castrato being burned alive at the stake.

Roy felt like laughing, because it was ridiculous, and because he had always had a ticklish spot when it came to vocal performances. As a child he had been reprimanded by his parents at several weddings during the rendering of "The Lord's Prayer" and "Ave Maria." He had suffered the revocation of recess privileges after an elementary school talent show and years later had had his nose bloodied by the boyfriend of a girl who had sung "Boogie Fever" for the talent portion of the high-school beauty pageant. All on account of inappropriate laughter. To him, singing was the soft fingernail scratch on the sole of the foot. The index finger dug into the ribs and jiggled about. But he resisted its cruel temptations, staring down at his shoes and thinking of children starving and his loved ones lying cold in their caskets. It would not go on forever, and at this point he was a man and should start acting like one, for a man did not laugh at inappropriate things, and a child was not allowed to travel down to Charleston by himself and check into a hotel.

Jeff concluded the song in double *forte* and was greeted by a round of applause from the motley crew surrounding the television set. He did not take a bow but drew forth a bashful smile and a bashful shake of the head, accepting the kiss that his mother placed on his cheek with a bashful look around the room at the other fellows.

"He's got talent," said Liza.

"He most certainly does," said Jessie.

The bearded others grumbled in assent and retook their seats.

As the ring announcer resumed his place at the helm, Jessie made it known to all that when he was in Kenya in the nineteen-seventies he had fathered a bastard child who had been named Owiti by his maternal grandfather. He informed them that he had only seen the boy on one occasion and that he was very black like his mother and had no signs of being a dwarf, although it was oftentimes difficult to tell with newborns. His one regret was that he had never been able to take the child bowling, as bowling was a passion of his and something that he would have liked to have passed down to his offspring.

"Why did you leave him?" Roy asked.

"Is that any of your business?" Jessie asked in response, face turning red, his eyes suddenly ablaze.

"You were the one talking about him," said Roy.

"I was, was I?" Jessie asked.

"Well, yeah," said Roy.

"Young man, you don't want to begin a debate with me. When I was a solicitor, I used to eat people like you for lunch. Yes, for lunch. I would mangle their words and stomp their protests, and in the end they were nothing more than my lunch. My lunch!"

"Well,…"

"Do you want to become my lunch?"

"No, of course…"

"Then stop it with the unsolicited questions. Or you will become my lunch!"

"Rowdy on down there, partner," said Liza. "Nobody's going to be eating any lunch around here anytime soon." She turned to Roy. "Ray, do you sing?"

"It's Roy," said Roy.

"So it is," she said. "So, do you sing?"

"No, at least not very well."

"Too bad. I like a man who can sing," she said, giving him a wink.

Roy was unsure of what this meant, just as he was unsure of what Jessie was getting at, but he let both go with a nod of the head and a sealing of his lips. He didn't care for beer that much and as said, he didn't like boxing, and given the conversation he began to realize that he didn't care a great deal for his present company either. With these matters in balance, he began wondering what exactly he was doing in this hotel room. Erica could very well be out there somewhere tonight, shivering underneath an overpass, and it was clear even to him that at the moment he was doing nothing to save her. He thought of asking the others if they had seen her, just to make sure that no stone was left unturned, but the fight had begun, and all were so deeply entranced by the battle of fisticuffs that he thought it better not to disturb them.

The one man hit the other man and then the other man hit the other one back. They circled each other and then charged at each other, and then circled some more. One had on black boots, the other white. One had on red trunks, the other blue. There was apparently a great deal more going on, as the sportscasters talked with great rapidity in detailing all that was occurring before their eyes, and their comments had nothing to do with the colors of the uniforms, but to Roy the simplest description was unquestionably the most objective. It was like going to a museum and listening to the eager docent go on and on about the white painting with the red dot in the middle. You had to admire the person for being able to talk to such an extent about such a barren subject, but when you came down to it, there really was nothing there.

The two men in the chairs kept their silence, but they had become a great deal more animated. Their arms moved with small jerks and their hands had balled into fists, each delivering uppercuts to the stale air of the hotel room. Jeff and Liza continued drinking and laughing and whooping, and every so often Liza would drape an arm across Roy's shoulders or try to place a hand in his back pocket. As for Jessie, he seemed to recoil with every connection of fist to flesh, and when one of the boxers received a cut above an eye, he began pacing fitfully around the room, saying, "It's all happening again. It's all happening again!" Roy watched him until it became unbearable to watch in silence any longer.

"What's happening again?" he asked.

"You have to ask? It's right in front of you, and you have to ask?" said Jessie.

Liza's attentions toward Roy did not sit well. It would have been uncomfortable for him even if they had been alone, but given the fact that the woman's son was standing a mere two feet away, it was nothing less than insufferable. Her cacklings of "you're cute" and "I could eat you like a shepherd's pie" brought mumblings of thanks from him and a delicate fending off of the hands that mirrored the meanings of the words, but his attempts at trying to get his disinterest across to her did nothing to hold her back.

It was good fortune—for Roy, for Jessie, for the man in the blue shorts and white shoes—that a punch landed squarely on the jaw of one of the boxers and sent him sprawling on the mat for a long count of ten. No psychic channels of communication relayed Jeff's and Liza's demands for him to arise from the mat, and in the end, he lay there defeated and shamed. It was only the third round.

"Well, I guess that's that," said Liza, saying it as though it conveyed the sum of the profundities she had learned throughout life.

"Yep," said one of the bearded men.

"Uh-huh," said the other.

"No, no, no," said Jessie. "Don't you see that it's just the beginning? We've just started. *They* have just started. It will all continue to swirl and swirl and swirl!"

As Jessie continued with his rant, Roy forced up a yawn from his chest and puffed it into a closed fist. Liza caught every movement.

"You're not getting tired, are you?"

"Do I bore you?" asked Jessie with anger. "Is that what you're saying? That I bore you?"

"Yes, I mean no," said Roy. "Yes, I am tired, but no, you do not bore me. It's just been a long day. A long couple of days. I just need to get some sleep."

"You're not leaving us, are you?" asked Liza. "We're just getting started."

"Just like the boxers!" shouted Jessie, a finger raised in the air.

"I think so," said Roy. "Yeah. I need to go to sleep." He put his beer down on top of the dresser and raised his arms with another fabricated yawn.

"Well, here," said Liza. "I'll walk you back. I need to get this ice bucket back to you anyway."

"No, no, no," said Roy. "It's just next door and I can carry it back myself."

"Oh, I know. I know. But I insist. Now come on," she said, picking up the bucket and putting it under her arm. "Let's go."

FIFTY-SIX

Gubba Bump Shrimp House could hardly be called a bistro, nor was it located in any nook. It stood like an unlanced boil right at the mouth of the market, catering exclusively to tourists and Yankee carpetbaggers. For Gubba Bump Shrimp House was a theme restaurant, a chain restaurant, a restaurant that served nothing fresh and that had nothing on its menu that anyone had ever died for, but probably a few had died of, although sealed financial settlements had kept the names and fates of the victims hidden from the general public. Still, it was where Savannah took Mitzi, and in her mind, it was how she described it. She gave Mitzi a knowing nod accompanied by a complicit smile when they were immediately allowed in, both actions stemming from her false belief that at an exclusive restaurant such as Gubba Bump Shrimp House one had to have a reservation, applied for months in advance and involving name-dropping and bribes and such, and here they were without one, being led to a table as though they were low country royalty, which in her mind they were. As for Mitzi, the animal part of her brain had long ago taken over her normal cognitive functions, the reason given to her by the great God in heaven to distinguish her from the other earthly beasts driven cowering into its corner, and the only thing that mattered to her, the only thing that she could process, was that cooked food steamed on plates all around her, and soon some of it would be steaming on a plate in front of her, then promptly gulped down into her aching stomach.

They had chosen to sit outside since it was such a pleasant night, or at least because Savannah declaimed it so. In truth, the ambience of Charleston was still so disgustingly hot and humid that it would have driven a permanent resident of the jungles of East Borneo away from the table without touching his food, but nothing less than such a gentleman's spear would have driven Mitzi away, and Savannah's delusions far outweighed any physical demands made by her body. The paper napkins made their way into the laps of the famished, and they sat opposite each other, waiting for the complimentary offering of peanuts that was both their right and their due.

"Oh, this place brings back memories," Savannah said. "My father brought me here after my first Catechism to celebrate my becoming a woman." She took a moment to admire the nonexistent silver etchings on the cutlery. "I remember it as a joyful day, but it was also very uncomfortable. You have no idea how weird it is to be raised a Catholic in the Deep South. I was wearing my mantilla, carrying my brand-new Catechism rosary along with me, dressed in a new calico dress that Sesame had knitted for the big occasion. Prior to the service, Father had beaten Chicken John and me black and blue and ripped out part of my mother's hair, but when we got here, when we got here, right here where we're now sitting, for the first time, we felt like a family. Roy was sick, so he couldn't be there, and mother had been able to comb her hair to cover up her bald spot, and the feeling of the Holy Ghost entering my body at communion had taken away the pain of the beating, so it seemed like everything was normal. People strode by, as they all do on Sunday afternoons in Charleston, saying hello to my father and laughing at the inappropriate things that he said, looking with envy at my sensuous mother. And as for me, they patted me on the head, and I could feel them laughing at me with my mantilla and rosary, the little Catholic D'Bergeolet girl, but you know what? That day I didn't care. For the first time I felt peace. But it wasn't meant to last…"

Any response that Mitzi might have given was choked back by the peanuts that had made their way on to the table—Mitzi the elephant, finished with her set, worn out from standing on barrels and lifting her trunk, stuffing the sweet legumes in her mouth as though they were the evidence that would send her into the hoosegow for the remainder of her unprofitable life.

"Oh, what a wonderful idea!" Savannah exclaimed, taking a handful and placing them on the table before her. "A peanut is a delicious way to begin a meal."

The waitress appeared, a young blonde-headed girl, shorts-wearing, T-shirt donning, smiling as though it counted. She placed the menus down on the table and welcomed them to Gubba Bump Shrimp House, a welcome that had already been offered and that they had already heartily accepted. But they accepted it again, as formality appeared to play a large role in this dining experience. A suggestion for an appetizer came along with a request for drink orders, and both were met with earnest attention. The waitress was then off.

"I don't know if I should be drinking neat bourbon," said Mitzi. "Growing up in Indiana, I always stuck to wine coolers."

"We drink neat bourbon or neat whiskey here in the low country, Mitzi, never wine coolers. A man of the low country can take a drink, he can swing a shrimp net, but he oftentimes can't cry. A mystery, but a fact."

The drinks came out in quick time, dropped off and left for the two ladies at table nine. Both suffered violent reactions when liquid met lips.

"This is awful," said Mitzi. "God awful."

"I think it's delicious," said Savannah, her mouth twisted and spitting. She did her best to give a smile, then attempted to take another sip, thinking that one simply had to get used to it, and failing to get used to it on the second try.

"I need a water or something," said Mitzi.

"The 'or something' is what you'll be getting Mitzi, and that 'or something' will be some more neat bourbon. The characters in the books never drink water unless they've been working in the yard or the like, seldom even then, but they always drink neat bourbon, especially when they are at fine restaurants like the one we're in now."

"But I won't be able to eat if this is all I have to drink," said Mitzi. Her peanut consumption had allowed reason to crawl back out from its penitent corner, and here it was voicing its concerns.

"You will drink. You will eat. If you don't, then that is your decision. What is my decision is what we will drink and what we will eat. This is my land, my home, and I insist on a certain amount of deference given these facts."

Mitzi again tried her bourbon, but she too found it not to have grown any more palatable with time. She eyed a glass of water at a neighboring table with great longing.

It was at this time that voices began to make themselves heard in the market. And these voices were not those of a mob or lovers caught in a public quarrel, but, as it soon became apparent, those of a young preacher and his followers. As his volume grew, his form began to take shape, a hand raised, a Bible in its palm and fingers, a group of three other men walking with him. Murmurs met their approach, and throughout history no approach greeted by murmurs has proven to be one later embraced with open arms; this one was no different. Their proclamations of Christ's love and sacrifice were countered by statements as diverse as "assholes" and "lunatics" and even by the opposing prayers such as "Jesus, why can't they just leave everybody alone?" and "God, please don't let them come over here." But the preacher's God was obviously a stronger one than that of those at Gubba Bump Shrimp House, for he stopped right in front of the hallowed gates and began to lecture the diners on fornication, abortion, contraception, and, of course, the positive attributes of his Savior, not the least of which being the superior accommodations He offered those who chose not to fornicate, abort, or contracept. Mitzi turned and watched them for a moment, then turned back, an eye on her drink, her mouth dry from peanuts, seemingly never to be rehydrated except by poison.

"These men, Mitzi," said Savannah. "I have the feeling that they have a story to tell. One of an itinerant life like that of circus personnel, childhood abuse, fights with demon alcohol, at times assuaged by their totemic faith, at times lost in bouts of drink and dalliances with prostitutes. Ask them if they'll join us."

"Savannah, no one wants them around here," Mitzi whispered, leaning across the table, eyeing the other patrons.

"No one wants them around here? I want them around here. Ask them, Mitzi. Go on. Go on and ask them."

Mitzi begrudgingly arose, wiping the dust of peanut husks off of her dress, and took a few steps over to the entrance where stood the preacher and his followers, the four in the midst of telling all who would listen that their Lord looked disfavorably on people who came from Sodom, a town with which Mitzi was unfamiliar.

"Excuse me," she said. And when she did this the other patrons again began to whisper amongst themselves, whispering with approval, again with more prayers. "Thank God someone's doing something about it," and the like. But these whispers of praise once more changed to murmurs of disapproval when the seemingly smallpox-ridden fat girl failed to complete her supposed mission, and instead invited the men to come in and dine with her and her companion.

The preacher did not look like a preacher in the Norman Rockwell tradition. His cheeks failed in the area of ruddiness, his expression failed to convey any sense of love for little children or lambs, little or big. Instead, he gave the appearance of someone who secretly beat his wife, who attacked umpires at Little League baseball games, who volunteered to lead the church youth group, only to end up in the paper via a very unflattering mug shot located above a short article chronicling his misdeeds, the names of the alleged victims withheld. His eyes contained no love; his mustache no quarter. His frame was that of the carpet installer, the man chosen by the slaughterhouse to swing the sledgehammer against the skulls of the bleating lambs.

"The food we seek is not that with which we fill our bodies," he replied, "but that with which we fill our souls. We embrace our hunger, embrace our thirst, embrace the fierce elements of this climate in order to spread the word of God."

Mitzi found herself lost at his mention of the soul-filling food, which she thought had to be soul food, something she had never seen, much less tasted, but had certainly heard about. The embracings were but knife thrusts in a corpse, perhaps meaningful to the attacker, but of no account to the dead man. They locked eyes for a moment, squint for squint, until Mitzi turned around and asked Savannah, "Do they sell soul food here? He says he wants soul food."

"No, no. I don't want soul food," said the preacher. "I don't hunger for food of the stomach, but the food of God."

"Like church food?" Mitzi asked. "Or do you mean communion wafers?"

"Neither," replied the preacher. "I am talking about the word of God. That's what I hunger for. I'm speaking in metaphor."

This made no sense to Mitzi, as her expression clearly showed.

"Then how come I understand you then?" she asked. "I got every word you said, and I've never even studied metaphor."

The patrons of Gubba Bump Shrimp House had collectively decided that Mitzi was once again a good egg, teasing the man as she was, and they laughed with a weighted laughter, the laughter given by patrons of art films and *avant-garde* theater, laughter cast at things not very funny, but used to show everyone else that they got it, even when there wasn't much of anything to get.

The differing genera of laughter were lost on the preacher, and all that he could understand was that he was being mocked. The Bible, the book that the preacher claimed to contain all that anyone needed to know, warned its adherents of the inevitability of such treatment, counseling a turn of the other cheek and the like, but here the man's faith fell short. His mustache trembled underneath his nose, his face turned red, and his eyes gave a look that even a simple lamb could tell meant his end was near. Mitzi, blindly naive and blindly blind, missed these signals, and stood there awaiting his reply, which came.

She was called so many horrible things that her flesh felt scalded after he was finished, which wasn't for some time. She was a whore, a taster of semen, a harlot, a fornicator, an adulteress, and to top it off, oddly, she thought, a tax collector. None of these things were true, of course, as Mitzi's physical appearance had kept even the most depraved of the Indiana farm boys from letting her get anywhere near their semen, and although she had been elected treasurer of her eighth-grade class, her powers of the purse were limited to collecting tickets at dances. Still, the effect of these slanderous words was to embarrass her deeply because she did not know any of these people, so they did not know her to know that she was being wrongly accused. She turned to Savannah for aid.

"I cannot help you, Mitzi," Savannah replied. "When I spoke before of wanting to know his story, I had the notion that he would somehow fit within the narrative that we are crafting. Upon second thought, however, it is clear to me that he has no place in the tale. We are to sit here and eat, drink some neat bourbon, and describe in great detail what all we are eating. During this time, you will question me as to my past, express disbelief at how awful the customs and upbringing in the South are, and then you are to ask me why I am always so sarcastic and why I never cry."

Thus, Mitzi was left on her own. The man remained standing before her, eyes of hatred protruding from his head, more biblical curses being muttered. When she returned to him, she did not know how to respond, so like Savannah, she reached into her past in order to drag out a retort.

"Sticks and stones may break my bones, but words will never hurt me," she said. "I think that's somewhere in the Bible."

"Well, you think wrong."

"-ly," said Savannah. "Wrongly."

"Well, if it isn't in there, it should be," said Mitzi.

"Who are you, who are *you* to say what should and should not be in the book of God's word?" the man cried.

"Mitzi Bedenbaugh," said Mitzi. "From Indiana. Who are you?"

The man could take it no longer. Behind him he could hear his followers discussing whether or not the "sticks and stones may break my bones" bit was or was not in the Bible, and in front of him he saw the mockery of Herodias's dinner party, everyone getting a belly-laugh at John the Baptist's hairy head. The Bible's thick spine connected with Mitzi's thin nose, knocking loose the faucet of blood contained within her skull. She turned with a scream and in a whirl of arms and crimson, launching the pail of peanuts into the neck of a precocious five-year-old sitting at a nearby table, pushing a potted plant to the side, and landing as though she were about to dine in distant lands, where dinner chairs have never been able to break in and shoes are not welcome.

The patrons of Gubba Bump Shrimp House arose in arms, glad to see the minor prophet retrieve his Bible and go, delighted in their realization that their God, who really was no big shakes except around Christmas and Easter, had won the day. Several of them offered to call the police, more simply suggested that someone else should do it, and one man, who had clearly had too much to drink and perhaps suffered from a motor-sensory disease as well, helped Mitzi get back in her chair, a process that resembled the blind leading the blind, the deaf berating the deaf, and the mute haranguing the mute.

"Have a drink, Mitzi," said Savannah, who pretended to take one herself.

"God, my nose. It's bleeding." said Mitzi.

"Pour some bourbon in there and swish it around. Bourbon always does the trick."

"I don't want any bourbon," said Mitzi, who began to cry with abandon.

At this point, the waitress came back to take their order.

"Is she all right?" she asked, a fair question given the fact that she had never before returned to a table to find a patron both bleeding and crying.

"It is to those of us who cannot cry that you should be directing that question," said Savannah. "Me, for example. I cannot cry. I wish I could, but…Ow!"

The drunken Samaritan had, in the process of making his way to the restroom, stepped directly on Savannah's unshielded toes, mashing them into the concrete with a stomp-and-twist that ripped out a nail. And it was with this that the spell was broken. Savannah D'Bergeolet, the Geechee brat born and raised on the barrier islands of South Carolina, the ill-gotten Catholic, the terrorized youth, the life-created stoic, finally began to cry. And cry she did, wailing with a bleeding toe in her lap, a paper napkin covered with peanut shells lightly applied to the unfortunate wound.

The man continued to say, "I'm terribly sorry," to the point that even if one did not believe him, and Savannah had her doubts, one would accede to the sincerity of his apology simply to shut him up. Continuing on to the bathroom, he left our two heroines weeping bitter tears as the waitress tried to calm them down, even throwing in a free appetizer in her vain attempt to do so.

FIFTY-SEVEN

An odd feeling fell upon Roy Edwards. He did not find the woman attractive in looks, personality, or spirit, but the sordidness of it all, the possibility of it, made him feel somehow disoriented. It was akin to a light drunkenness, where his legs moved only with conscious thought, his chest felt tender and tight, his head buzzed in slight confusion. She had placed an arm through the crook of his, her hand reaching down, searching for his hand, which she found stuffed in the tight pocket of his shorts. They did not say a word as they walked out the door and took the three steps to his room. It was all silence. And when they stopped, he stood there for a moment, unsure of what to do. He took his hand out of his pocket and shuffled away from her.

"Well, I guess this is it," he said, his mouth dry, his words shaking off of his tongue. "It's been a lot of fun. A lot of fun. That was some fight."

His nervousness was not assuaged by the way she stared at him. The yellowed teeth so often revealed in her laughter were now hidden behind her closed lips, and her feet were firmly planted. But it was the intensity of those eyes, the unflinching look of a determined rapist, that made him quail. He wished with all of his heart that she would just go away. In the silence of his own room, he could replay the road not taken, and hop in bed without consequence, but he did not have the fortitude to actually copulate anywhere but in his own imagination.

"Um," he said. "All right. Good night." He turned and gave her a sort of wave and began to put the plastic key in the door.

"Can I come in and talk to you for a second?" she asked.

The lock clicked and the card-key light turned green as though it were a traffic signal. He turned the knob with his quivering hand.

"Um. Sure. Just for a sec, though. I'm about to fall asleep standing here."

He went in.

She followed.

FIFTY-EIGHT

The crying finally came to its silent conclusion, blood having clotted and aches stepping in for pains, leaving Mitzi and Savannah with plates filled with shrimp frozen sometime last month and shipped over from China. Neither was incredibly hungry. New glasses of bourbon sat next to the old ones, all four largely untouched, and they both found themselves jabbing their forks into shellfish flesh, bringing the dead crustaceans slowly to their sorrow-filled mouths, where they were eaten without pleasure.

"Mitzi, surely there must be something wild and zesty that you can say to bring us out of this funk."

"I want to go home," said Mitzi.

"I am home," said Savannah. "And you are here with me, dour as a church maid. Tell me a joke or something ridiculous you've done lately. We've got to pick things up if this trip is ever going to turn into a book."

"The only ridiculous thing I've done lately is get in a car with you, ditch school, and come down here to this horrible place. I want to go home, Savannah. I want to get a new set of glasses, get in my bed, and sleep. I've had it with Southern hospitality and trips over bridges and playing pool and everything else that we've done in this place. Let's just go back to your car and drive back home. You can finish your book sometime later."

"That is no way to talk, Mitzi. Here we are, two queens of the low country, sitting in the most exclusive restaurant the city has to offer, eating a dinner fit for royalty, sipping on neat bourbon and enjoying an intriguing conversation, and all you can do is focus on the negative. I'm supposed to be the negative one here, not you. I'm supposed to respond to your comments of hope with withering sarcasm and compare things to bloodblisters and zits and such, but because you're being so glum, I'm having to play the part of the cheerleader and not the self-loathing, highly accomplished jock. You need to get your act together or you're going to find yourself heading back to that nameless city on a Greyhound bus."

Mitzi had never ridden in a Greyhound bus before. She had ridden in buses, on school field trips and the like, but never a Greyhound one. It did not seem like such a bad thing. A bus was a bus. However, its use as a warning had come to her before when she had acted up on a family trip to California years ago, and therefore she knew that it was something to be feared. But what was it about a Greyhound bus that made it so fearsome? Surely, they were safe, or they still wouldn't be in business, and she had never before heard or read of one exploding or having its wheels come off on the highway. Were criminals transported on them? She would need to look into this when she got home.

For the time being she did not know whether she should accept Savannah's offer or beg not to be sent back via Greyhound, but being cautious by nature, she decided against the bus and to prepare herself for the next time someone threatened her in such a manner so that she could respond with a full understanding of the dangers.

"I'm sorry," she said. "It's just that I think I'd be a lot better off if I could see."

"Well, if that's what it takes, let's fix that problem," said Savannah.

The waitress was called over once again, and it turned out that they had Scotch tape back in the kitchen. Within minutes, Mitzi sat with her glasses fully functional, although less than fashionable, and her mood did in fact improve. The shrimp appeared as shrimp and the glasses appeared as glasses, and the red marks on Savannah's uncovered flesh were as clear as day.

"They look great," said Savannah.

"They feel great," said Mitzi. "I really can't tell you how much of a difference they make."

"Then don't even try," said Savannah.

"I mean, I really feel like a whole new person. Like I'm ready to do something."

"Like what, you moldy jockstrap of a gal, you?"

"Like dancing," said Mitzi.

Savannah thought about this for a moment. There had been dancing in fountains in Rome. Dancing at parties celebrating new hair salons. Dancing in houses while the houses crashed into the ocean— a dangerous, forbidden dance. The books were filled with dancing, and therefore hers would be too.

"Oh, Mitzi, what a wonderful idea!" said Savannah. "I can't tell you how happy I am that I brought you along on this trip. Here I was, as down as down can be, and here you are, picking me back up and injecting me once again with the thirst for life. Yes, let's do it. Let's go dancing. You're familiar with the shag, I presume?"

"Like carpet?" asked Mitzi.

"No, you bloodblistered Kotex!" said Savannah with a laugh. "I'm talking about the official state dance. The shag. It's the dance I grew up with that was discovered in this state, and man-oh-man is it some dance. I'll show you and we'll dance the night away like the two low country gals that we are. You ready?"

"Sure," said Mitzi. "Grab the waitress and let's get out of here."

"Do you think she'll want to come?" asked Savannah.

"I don't know," said Mitzi, "but I was saying that we should get her to bring out our check so that we can pay up and leave."

"Don't worry about that, Mitzi," said Savannah. "I've already taken care of it."

"Oh," said Mitzi. "Golly. Thanks. Thanks a lot."

"Don't worry about it," said Savannah.

And arm in arm, the two left Gubba Bump Shrimp House in search of a dance hall.

It should come as no surprise that Savannah had not taken care of anything, much less the paying of the bill. Several factors figured into her decision. First, since her father had always paid at restaurants, she had never had to pay herself, and in her clouded mind, oblivious to the exchange of the credit card and the signing of the receipt, she had always assumed that it was something that just happened. Secondly, since she and her family had eaten at Gubba Bump Shrimp House on numerous occasions, which they had not, she assumed that the bill would be taken care of by the owner, who was great friends with her father and who had always secretly longed for her mother from afar. The third, and probably most important, factor was that Savannah had no money with which to pay the bill.

The waitress was beside herself, not on account of the loss of revenue to the restaurant, but because no tip was to be had, and she quickly informed the manager, who picked up the phone and called the police. Prowling the market, as was their wont, two officers showed up in a manner of minutes, took down the description of the two women, and went in search.

FIFTY-NINE

Even in the pornographic movies that Roy had seen and given that he had a fairly poor internet connection he had not seen as many as one would expect, there were always lead-ins to the love-making. The plumber would arrive at the door with his plumbing equipment and the lady of the house, draped in nothing but a towel, would show him to the bathroom where the toilet was stopped up. There they would talk about toilets and the weather and then the music would start and so would they. Liza apparently did not think much of dialogue. She preferred to get to the meat of the matter, and by the time the door closed shut, she had the meat of Roy's matter firmly in her grasp and her smoke-cured tongue shoved down his gullet. And as much as he would have liked to rid himself of his unwanted virginity, something within him screamed in protest as to the manner it was about to be lost. It was akin to a shout of "Fire!" or "Look out!" for his adrenal glands began pumping out the stuff in buckets in hopes of getting him out of harm's way.

He restrained himself at first, gently, but forcefully, pushing her away, but she seemed to have her mind set on him and held fast. When he moved his mouth out of her reach, she quickly placed a sucking on his neck that caused his carotid artery to cry out in protest. If anything, his pleas for her to release him drove her into greater wanting and within a matter of seconds, the top of her dress hung about her waist, and his belt had been undone and thrown on top of a bed.

The breasts were what did it. The flesh from which Jeff had suck-led, and numerous men had surely sucked, had long ago lost its elasticity, giving one the impression of tangerines dropped into tube socks. Veins of blue and purple snaked across skin as white as the underbelly of a mythical beast trapped for generations in a dark cavern, and together these elements proved far from appetizing and extremely close to repulsive. To touch them would be to touch a pile of dog shit onto which someone had vomited. To apply his mouth to them would be to drag his tongue along the edge of a urinal at a truck stop. The internal governor that normally restrained him from ungentlemanly behavior and would have had him treat her like a lady broke from its moorings, and suddenly she was simply an attacker and he a man ready to fight for his life. He grabbed the bottom of her dress and pulled it high above her head, fashioning the top of the garment into a rudimentary knot. With one hand he held it tight, she a wild animal caught in a sack, and with the other he reached for the door handle. He yanked the door open and then stepped back and lunged at her, driving her with his shoulder like a blocking dummy out into the parking lot, where she crashed into the hood of a car.

Between her screechings and the car alarm going off, it was quite a racket, and Roy stood there, wondering what he had done. When he saw Jeff, Jessie, and the two Neanderthals standing outside the door of the adjoining room, their mouths wide open in shock, he stood and wondered no longer.

SIXTY

Scott did in fact return. It was late and the night was black as an infidel's heart, the air almost suffocating in its stillness. The library had proved as depressing as always, and his home, once his sole refuge in a world of constant moral and mental attack, had now turned into yet another zone of persecution. When he saw the mirror angled in the open door next to his, his heart tightened in his dread-filled chest. His feet halted on the steps halfway up to the landing, and he pulled the backpack tight on his shoulders, lowering his head with thought, then looking up again with none. He crept up another stair, trying to catch a glimpse of the blood-faced maniac who had infected his life, but could only see a set of feet with a grouping of toenails like those one can only find in textbooks concerning medical abnormalities, with which Scott was more than familiar. He took another step, all of his weight to the back, which brought the hairless legs to light. It was not working. He dropped down to his belly and slid up a few more feet, inching, inching until he saw a face dead with sleep. Or perhaps just dead. One could only hope.

Arising quietly, he scaled the remainder of the stairway, placed his key into the lock, and silently shut the door behind him. And then he waited. A knock. A shout. A kick. A plea. Any one, or all of the above, was surely imminent. He stood there, his back pressed against the door, immobile as a statue, waiting. A minute passed, and across the expanse of time he felt his apprehension slowly dissipate, until when it was finally over, he found himself fairly relaxed. He stepped away from the door and threw his backpack on to the couch, where it bounced once, then fell still.

Scott had actually failed out of school the previous semester. One could not blame it on lack of preparation, a failure to execute assignments, or even a serious learning disorder that no amount of studying could overcome. He had simply failed out, a thing so odd and unexplainable that it fell close to the realm of spontaneous human combustion. Every test that he received back from his professors was decorated with an F, every paper colored with a red that signified unbounded defeat. He was too shy to approach any of the teachers for an explanation and simply bore it with the stoic woe that only the stoically woeful have.

After the walking papers made it into his hands he informed his parents, who castigated him over his shiftless ways and rejected his suggestion that he move back home until he could reapply. His father had recently retired and found life with nothing to do the best kind of existence offered and had no desire to have his golden years of bliss ruined by a son whom he had grown to hate the moment he saw him erupt from his wife's birth canal. It was therefore agreed that Scott would remain in his same apartment and continue in independent study until the spring semester rolled around.

Scott's independent studies had not taken him very far, however. He had no problems attempting to complete assignments or attending lectures, but he lacked sufficient imagination to set out his own curriculum, or at least one that would prove helpful to him or anyone else. Desperate in his search, his days were spent in the library reading over almanacs and *The World Book,* which seemed like a good place to start. The major crop of Guatemala in 1985 was brought into his head through his eyes, then sieved out a few minutes later as though his brain contained a set of rogue intestines that got rid of both the waste and the vital nutrients. On the day in question, he had focused on rainfall in the Middle East, but if one were to quiz him about it at the moment, he could not name a single fact or figure concerning rain, nor could he name any of the countries located near the birthplace of our Lord and Savior, Jesus Christ.

He walked back into the bathroom, tired and numb, and washed his hands. As he did this, he lifted his head to the mirror and looked at his face. One would have thought he had spent the day in an opium den sucking death into his lungs, given his appearance. What was he doing? Where was he going? He tried to smile, failed, tried again, and succeeded. "Happy Scott," he said. "Happy, happy Scott." This struck him as extremely ridiculous, and to add to the absurdity he began to dance about, throwing his legs to the side, raising his hands and clapping them together above his head. "Happy Scott! Happy, happy Scott!" His internal metronome sped up with each repetition, as did his dance, and it was not too long before he was laughing in a state of hysteria, which borders the states of madness and despair.

But unbeknownst to him, Creighton's bloodstained towel lay on the floor, sitting there almost as a symbol of his slovenliness and disregard for others, and with each sideways kick, Scott's right heel came closer towards it. "Happy Scott! Happy, happy Scott!" Kick to the side, kick to the side. "Happy Scott! Happy, happy Scott!"

And there it was. The foot found the towel, and the towel rebelled against the unwanted touching, sliding across the floor towards the toilet to get away.

When he had moved into the apartment his mother had come along in order to give it the requisite feminine touch. She cared little for his academic or social success, but she absolutely hated the ill-kempt dorm rooms that she had seen on dramatic television shows, where topics such as teen pregnancy and drug addiction were featured for the discerning viewer, and was determined that her son would not live in such a way. He had to have curtains on the windows and artwork in actual frames. His sheets should complement his comforter. And concerning the bathroom, it should have a good shower curtain, matching towels, and last, but not least, a sturdy metal trash can that one could be proud of.

When Scott fell, he reflexively reached out to grab ahold of something and in the process ripped the good shower curtain down on top of him. The pridely trash can, sturdy and metal, actually helped break his fall. It, and his windpipe, kept him from dropping straight to the floor.

The phrase "searing pain" has probably been used too often for it to be allowed to present itself here, but that is what it was. The ache in his throat burned, and not like that from too much sun or a cigarette nipping you on the arm as you pass by some fool waving one around in a bar, but as though a red-hot poker had been shoved down the gullet, only to get caught right underneath the tonsils. To add to this unbearable misery, his lungs felt like they had been filled with Sterno and lit. He thrashed around in the shower curtain, his mind racing with the understanding that he absolutely had to get to a telephone and dial 911. And then, in a split second, the pain began to subside, the tortures transformed into fatigue, until all that he wanted to do was fall asleep. Which he did, if one must speak in metaphor.

SIXTY-ONE

It was decided that they would go to Charleston the following morning. There were several reasons that spurred along the trip. The family car had been involved in two massive pileups on the bridges into and out of Mount Pleasant earlier that day. That same afternoon they received a call from the police informing them that a woman believed to be their daughter had destroyed several thousand dollars-worth of fake Civil War memorabilia in some shop. Another call in the evening relayed that the same person, again believed to be their daughter, had walked out on an eighty-dollar tab at a restaurant in downtown Charleston. And if this weren't bad enough, there had been no word from Roy; not even a middle-of-the-night phone call requesting five hundred dollars to save an elf or a wizard. You tried to raise your children properly. No one wanted their offspring to be law breakers or downright insane. But in his case, current events clearly proved that he had failed. Painfully. Horribly. Failed.

Although he saw no upside to the current set of circumstances, Mr. Edwards tried to place the events in a positive light. "At least we know they're alive," he kept saying in response to his wife's litany of screechings, but truth is not the greatest ally of the salesman. No, the salesman is effective only when he has convinced himself that what he's saying is the truth, whether it is or not. Harry Edwards had not done so, and his applications of elocutory balm were as effective on his wife as shoving a breathing tube down the throat of a corpse.

Fortunately for him, there wasn't a great deal going on at the office and, as he never took a vacation, he could afford to miss a day or two. But who wanted to use a vacation day to capture one's daughter in order to keep her from committing further criminal acts? To drive across the state on a workday to finish a job left in shambles by one's incompetent son? Not Harry Edwards, and as he sat at the kitchen table, watching his wife eat brown, red, green, and orange foodstuffs, bits of them spitting out of her mouth as she screamed and cried, he longed for Somerset Maugham and a glass of port, his feet on the ottoman, Mozart working his magic in the air around him. If only he could lose himself in the East Indies, find himself stuck in the rain of Pago Pago with Mr. Davidson, who in the end would throw God to the side, fall prey to the whore, then go slit his miserable throat.

"Are you listening to a word I'm saying?" his wife asked with a shrieking interrogatory.

He looked up at her. A speck of an unknown red sauce had attached itself to one of the whiskers of her face, and its presence made him feel like weeping. He had not signed up for this. He had married an attractive young woman of questionable disposition and here he was, thirty years later, married to an unattractive older one with a disposition that left no questions. If only he had suffered a neutering injury on the baseball field. He *was* a catcher, for chrissakes. The cup forgotten at home, no option but to play, the foul ball blazing off of the tip of the bat and into the warm pocket of his unprotected groin. There would have been great sadness, great periods of loneliness, perhaps a mastectomy to remove breasts formed by a lack of testosterone, but no horrid older woman in a kitchen forty years in the future, castigating him for imagined faults, demanding that he take a day off to retrieve his mentally disturbed daughter and mentally incompetent son from the evil clutches of Charleston.

"Of course, I'm listening to you. I'm sitting here, aren't I?"

"Sitting there not listening!" Mrs. Edwards replied. "I was saying, if you would only take the time to pay attention to me, that…"

She said that their daughter had been raped. That someone had fed their daughter drugs, presumably after raping her, and brain-washed her like the Hearst girl had been, and now they were out terrorizing the seaside. She said that her son was probably deep into the case. That he was gifted in ways that Mr. Edwards would never understand and that all he needed was a little help from his parents and all of this would be set aright. Harry Edwards sat and listened to her this time, taking the words one by one and allowing them to form sentences, then taking the sentences one by one and allowing them to form paragraphs, the paragraphs pages, the pages a text. As he did this, he was struck with the realization that his children were not to blame. They certainly had all of the advantages that society offered—stable financial backing, the benefits of home and hearth, and access to education and health care—but within them lurked the madness implanted inside the womb of this maniacal monologuist, the nine-month bath in hallucinogens and propsychotics. Nothing that she said made sense. Nothing was touched by the lightest passing of reason.

"Sounds like a plan to me," he said once she was finished. "We'll leave first thing in the morning and get all of this sorted out." After letting go of these words, he rose from his chair, lifted his glasses with one hand and rubbed his eyes with the other.

"Are you going somewhere?" she asked.

"Like out?" he asked.

"No. I mean, are you going somewhere? Are you leaving me here alone?"

"No, I'll just be in the study. No one's leaving you."

"But Harry, tonight of all nights can't you just be normal and not go in your study and read? Just for one night?"

"What do you want me to do?"

"I don't know. We could watch TV together. I just don't feel like being alone. Not with everything that's going on."

"Um."

"Just for one night?"

"I…"

"Please?"

"That sounds good. Um. Why …why don't we do this: I'll go read while you get settled, and then after you're settled and I've read for a while we'll get together and watch a little TV."

She met his suggestion with silence, and he purposely ignored the red-letter signals of disapproval given by her expression, turning and walking back to his study where Somerset lay sleeping, ready to be awakened several decades after his earthly demise. Somerset who had never procreated. Somerset who, he imagined, had never had to watch crap television with a needy wife. There were choices to be made in life, especially in the free society that they lived in, but it seemed that there were no options. What the difference was, he wasn't sure, but he felt the weight of it even amidst the glow of the Mozart's *Paris Symphony*.

SIXTY-TWO

Creighton awoke. It was one of his failings, his insecurities, but he never liked to admit that he had been asleep, especially when it came to the nap. Even if he were caught snoring, he would violently attack any accusation, ready with a list of implausible denials to be followed with a storming off into another part of the house. He could not really explain its cause or reasons, but whatever state his brain entered when incapacitated, it arose to the living ashamed of wherever it had been. Given that no one was around to accuse him of anything this night, he attacked nothing and stormed nowhere, but sat licking the film of rest out of his mouth, staring at his toes that sat beside the stack of books.

Shouts had awoken him, although he had not been asleep. Something next door. The books. The mirror. Yes, that's where he was, and what he had been doing. He stood up, the copy of *Lowcountry Lamentations* in hand to be used as a shining example of how even fools could cobble words together, much less someone under the tutelage of Creighton Starke, and stepped across the landing.

It was a good thing that Scott was dead, because alive he could not have borne the fists beating on the door or his name shouted out at full volume, giving the impression to all around that a gay lovers' spat was in progress.

"Scott! Scott! I know you're in there!"

Creighton did not know that anyone was in there, but hopes can oftentimes offer more sustenance than realities, and his hopes were not to be denied. He shoved a hip into the door, shouted for a good fifteen seconds more, then ripped a hand across the doorknob. With this, much to his surprise, the door inched away as though an invisible hand were slowly pulling it back after the utterance of a password. For some reason this cause and effect touched a nerve in the English professor's addled mind. He stood in silence, expecting fog to come rolling out into the night and sulfurous fumes to fill his nostrils, to find men in hooded robes sitting around a burning pentagram chanting out blasphemies in Latin. Because one could not help but sense that something strange, something wrong, had occurred, and Creighton, there by the doorway, could not help it either.

"Scott?"

He stepped into the apartment with tender foot, his eyes squinting in the darkness, his head rotating from one shoulder to the other, whispering, "Scott? Scott?" The bathroom door stood shut, pale light filtering out by the floor, water running uninterrupted somewhere inside. "Are you in here, buddy?" His touch revealed that the television set was cold, and no one had replaced the butter in the refrigerator. He had not eaten since that morning, so he treated himself to a bagel, perused a few photographs held aloft by magnets from a plumbing company, then walked over to the bathroom. "Scott? Scott?"

There was no response from inside. He was tired of all of this knocking, but in Western society the Lords of Mores believed in both closed doors and the necessity of asking permission, or at least announcing one's intentions, before opening one and stepping inside.

"You in there? I waited for you. In my apartment. You may have seen the mirror. I was using it to keep an eye out for you. Mirror, mirror, in the door. Ha. Yeah, I know. It's the writer in me. Scott? Are you in there?"

As he finished the remains of the bagel, the running faucet brought to light his thirst, taunting it, such gallons of water, wasted, off to the sewer plant, and here he was, just wanting a little. A sip. A gulp. A bellyful. Jesus, he was thirsty. "Scott!"

He pushed the door open with wild desire, oblivious to the body on the floor, his eyes, his heart, his mind, all focused on the steaming liquid jetting from out of the faucet head. The water burned his tongue, and he knocked his tooth against the metal of the spout. Cursing unknown bastards and sons of bitches for both indignities, his savage hand found the cold and killed the hot, and his savage mouth drank its fill. And then he arose. And then he saw something.

"What the...?"

He kicked the shower curtain and in doing so felt the heaviness of the object underneath it. He kicked it again. Whatever it was did not respond to kicks, nor did it respond to the numerous questions posed to it. He got down on his hands and knees and lifted up a corner, whereupon he saw an arm. His pulse boomed in his head.

"Scott?"

The shower curtain removed, Creighton stared into the open, red-lined eyes, ventured a finger into the open, blue-hued lips, then checked the throat for the hint of a beat, but it was as silent as the mind of a stillborn child. CPR! CPR! He placed his mouth against that of his pupil's and breathed onion bagel into unwashed teeth. He positioned his palms directly beneath the inert sternum and thrust his shoulders downward. He cried and begged and called out the name Scott a goodly number of times, but nothing that he did, and no god to whom he prayed, did anything to bring life back into Scott's lifeless remains.

It was minutes that passed, or groupings of minutes in tens, but it to Creighton it seemed like hours, or groupings of hours in tens. He held Scott's lifeless hand in his and forgot all that he had learned in the police procedurals that came on television late at night, where crime scenes were not to be tampered with and men sent to the gas chamber on account of dandruff being some place it shouldn't, letting his tears fall where they may, having a gas station receipt drop from his pocket, and changing the positioning of his friend and would-be pupil so that he looked more comfortable.

He tried to recite something from Tennyson's *In Memoriam* but could not bring the lines to his tongue, and nothing else appropriate or germane seemed to flow from out of his skull at the moment. Poetry simply failed him, as it always had in the end. But something needed to be done. Whatever it was inside of him had to be purged, and as he had always known, that thing was art. In this case, the flighty muse took the form of music. The desire gripped him like a bitter thirst brought by a bagel, to sing, to clap, to whistle with woe. He reached back into his treasure trove of musical compositions and chose the tune to the one concerning the flashlight, as it had a dirge-like quality, and Creighton found himself in a dirging mood. He began the first words with a mournful howl:

"I'd like to see / You wake up alive / And ask me, what's up, bro? / It is a very difficult request given the circumstances / Given that you are unmistakably dead / Oh it's so true / No matter what I say or do / To convince myself otherwise. / Won't you? / Oh, won't you? / Even for me? / Get up and walk around a bit? / Perhaps you would / Perhaps you'd just stay still and chat / It really doesn't matter / And I sure don't care. / You can lay down on your stomach / And show me the belt of Orion / Man, he was a great guy."

The song ended, and silence rushed in to fill its void. Sitting there, his head resting against the sink, his face towards the bathtub, Creighton once more found himself lost in grout. What was the poem? Something about not knowing when the end was coming but knowing with certainty that it was getting nearer and nearer. Ginsberg? Probably not. It didn't mean much to him on paper, but what an oddity it was to actually experience the nearer. He had seen both of his parents dead as doornails, and their parents before them. Waxen faces and glued-shut eyes, appearing almost (and somehow) Asian in their caskets, useless clothing covering their shame in the shame of death. All six of these had been very difficult for him, as he was an artist and thus sensitive by nature, and he remembered the difficulty he had playing baseball with his cousins after the first four, just as he had similar troubles drinking gin and watching television after the last two. Maybe this was what drove him to his writing table, bleary-eyed and sore, the clock reading two in the morning, stuck in the middle of a paragraph that never seemed to end. For if this could happen to someone as close to him as Scott, then what made him think that he would somehow escape it, or perhaps not even escape it, but die at the age of ninety in his sleep? The time was now. The iron was hot. The chickens were roosting, and the two birds were in the bush. If this was not a wake-up call, then what was? He needed to drive to his office, sit down in front of his typewriter, and will the words onto the page. The ideas would come after the first paragraph, one filled with sensuous descriptions of the landscape, for in this one the landscape would be an actual character, one that when taught in school the teacher would ask the students how many characters there were, and the students would say six, and the teacher would correct them and say seven, you cannot forget about the setting. He felt his brain on fire and the fuel that had brought Osgood to life filling the well of his bosom. He had to go. But he also had to do something about Scott. He needed to call the police. The ambulance attendants. He would have to sit around and wait on them, answer all of their questions, perhaps spend the night at the station helping them piece it all together. And as all of this happened, the fire, and the fuel, and the well of his bosom, would slowly begin to dissipate, until finally, when he got out of there, he would find himself in the same frame of mind that had cornered him for the past five years.

He cursed the authorities and his own indecision. He needed to think. To clear his mind. The copy of *Lowcountry Lamentations* lay on top of the shower curtain, which lay on top of Scott, and he reached down and picked it up, reading as follows:

I was always reminded of my childhood in the
lowcountry when I returned to the lowcountry.
There was a smell about it like a fecund musk
that comes from the creeks and bogs and tidal
basins and this smell was like an oyster that
you could open and say "Here. Take a whiff of my
childhood." I landed at the Charleston airport
and was greeted by Sesame and Mother. Mother
was dressed out in a hat and a bunch of "fancy"
clothes that she always wore in order to impress
everybody and she had white gloves on. Sesame was
wearing a dress that was calico in color and she
was wearing the brogans that my grandfather had
worn in World War Two when he had killed a number
of Germans who were fighting for Hitler.

"Sesame! Yahn! Get that girl's luggage or I'll
whip your hide till you look like a red indian!"

Mother loved Sesame but she was born in a
time when african americans were not equals and
she talked to her like she was still a slave. I
didn't like it or cotton to it one bit but you
had to understand your elders and understand what
the south had been like before my "generation"
came along and changed everything for the better.

"Mother I can get my own luggage. You don't
listen to her Sesame. She's still as mean as an
old cooter snake rapped up in jessum roots!"

"You got that right!" said Sesame and we
laughed and laughed and hugged each other and
I told Sesame how much I loved her and I looked
into her eyes and I knew that she loved me too
but african americans were not supposed to say
things like "I love you" to white people because
that was the way things were down in the south.

We got in the car and Sesame began the long
ride back to "home." But it was not "home" or
at least the "home" that I knew from growing up
since my father had sold the island for a nuclear
power plant that was going to poison all of hte
fish and kill all of the crabs until there was
nothing left in the area and it was destroyed.
Unless my brother had something to say about it…

Chicken John and I had decided not to tell
Mother why I was coming down as she was so mean
that she would probably tell the authorities
where he was and they would "get" him. I told her
that Jonathan and I were having problems which
was true and that I needed some "me time" down in
the lowcountry so that I could sort things out in
my poetry and my love life and with my kids and
with all that was happening with the end of the
Vietnam war.

Well, I'll be jack russel, but Sesame had a
lead foot on her! She drove so fast you would
have thought she was Mario Andretti! We were
flying through the lowcountry going over one
hundred miles an hour talking about the south and
culture and stuff when the next thing I knew the
police sirens were going off behind us and we had
"smokey" on our tails. Sesame pulled off to the
side of the road and the police officer got out
of his car and walked over to us. I had gotten so
used to men up in New York City and at Harvard
that I had forgotten how good a "good ole boy"
could look! He wore glasses and a police uniform
with a hat and he looked mighty fine to Savannah D'Bergeolet, let me tell you girl! "Ma'am do
you know why I pulled you over?" he asked. "Why

sir we're not rightly sure." said Mother. She had
pulled up her dress and slip so that it showed
off the top of her thighs and was looking at him
with a look that had made at least one president get out of the Vietnam war. I felt mad and
embarrassed at the same time. I had found it very
difficult to grow up with my Mother as a sexual
object and I think that it had done some thing to
me as a sexual object. I don't know why the pain
grew in me or where it came from but I knew that
it was there and that there was nothing that I
could do about it! I was just a fragile object
and I was damaged by my parents and from growing
up in the lowcountry even though I loved growing
up in the lowcountry. Oh listen to me. I had to
admit it. I was just "messed up!" "You're being
pulled over because you were goign too fast. I'm
going to have to give you a ticket." And when he
said that he leaned into the window and saw me
sitting back there and he said "Hey ain't that
Savannah D'Bergeolet!" I replied "Yes I am."
And he exlcaimed "Savannah it's me. Billy Bob
Hawkins! From school!" "Well Billy Bob I don't
likely hardly recognize you lookin' so good in
that tootin uninform." We geechee girls could
put on the gullah charm when we needed it! "Oh I
don't know about that Miss Savannah. It's just
a uniform." And I saw him blush and wag his head
like a wet dog and I knew that no one in that car
was gonna be gettin' no speein ticket! Yahn no!
"You in town!" he queried. "Likely reckon I am."
I replied. I still had it chile! And you should
have seen Mother sitting in that front seat like
a darn fool pushing her skirt down and cursing

under her breath. "Well I'm gonna let ya'll go
with a warnin. Miss Savannah if yousa gonna be
round chere I'd mighty like to call on you." he
probed. "I'd like that mighty fine!" I answered.

We drove away and Mother said "Well in all my
days I've never seen such an ungentlemanly specimen in all of my days!" "Aw you be quiet there
you ole hogs head! You be happy for Miss Savannah. She gone go courtin and Shadareen ain't
comin nowhere nears by gawd!" Sesame stated.
I told Sesame that I loved her and she did not
reply but just smiled. Billy Bob Dawkins. Billy
Bob Dawkins. He had been a "jock" in high school
and could not read very well but he certainly was
something to look at and right then I realized
that that was just what the doctor ordered!

The house was not as I remembered it because
it was a different house from the one that I
had "grown up" in. My parents lived on the ACE
Basin. For those of you who do not know about
the ACE basin, it is not really a basin but a
place that had a number of different species in
it and has lots of water and marshes and creeks
and that really is one of the most incredible
places on earth one that is not known by a lot of
people and a place that a lot of people should
know about if they don't already know about it.
With the money from the nuclear power plant sale
my parents had bought a plantation that had a
plantation house on it and it was very beau-
fiul. It had a big porch and lots of windows and
big white columns. They say that a person's IQ
is lower they more white columns they have on
their house and that is true. I found my father

sitting in the living room watching television with my brother Roy. Some football game. "Well look whose here." said my father. "Miss prissy from Harvard." my father finished. "Good to see you father. Hello Roy." I stated. Roy had inherited my father's stupidity from my father and he had never been able to hold down a job but lived at home where he watched tv. I had told them that they needed to put him in a "home" but they had told me that I needed to mind my own business and that Roy would be fine one day and that he was just a slow learner. I went upstairs and found my bedroom just as I had left it. I went into my closet and found all of the books by Faulkner and Celine and Joyce that I had read growing up. It was kind of crazy looking at those books after all of those years. There were photographs of me and Chicken JOhn from Sports Illustrated and some other "big time" newspapers and magazines hung on the wall.

When I went back downstairs my parents were fighting and I told them to stop. "We're not stopping just because someone came back here thinking they're all fancy!" my father screamed. "I do not think I'm fancy!" I peeled. "Father you have hurt us too many times and you're gonna stop that right now!" "Hurt you! I never hurt you!" he lied. "You never hurt us! You hurt us all of the time. You beat all of us and you beat mother. CAn't you see father! Don't you remember!" I queried. My father really looked like he didn't remember. "I don't remember." he stated. "Where do you think this scar came from father!" I shouted. I showed him a scar on my knee that

307

he had made with a butcher's knife when he was
in one of his drunken rages. "I don't know!"
he stated. "Oh father don't you remember when
you attacked me with a butcher's knife when you
were in one of your drunken rages!" I didn't do
that!" "Oh just forget it!" "Hey will the two of
you keep it down. I'm trying to watch a football
game." I turned to Roy and screamed, "Shut up
booger face! You have the personality of a cup of
yogurt and you're a stool sample!" I ran out the
back door and was glad to once again smell and
see the majesty of the ACE basin of Charleston.
How it could take me away. Take me away from all
of the problems in my marriage and my parents and
my poetry writing and my "sex" life. Yeah right.
Some "sex" life I had. I began to cry.

Sesame was outside watering some plants and
she saw me and she called me over. She said,
"Hey now messin round beebil in da creek quit
yo cryin." I began to speak to Sesame in gullah
and she spoke to me in gullah as we had spoken
to each other since the time that I was a child.
After a while she said "I think i'ts time now
chile. Yo got the first sight in you I can tell.
Oh yes I can tell." "What you be meanin Sesame?
Yahn?" "What I means to say and I says to mean is
that you got the voodoo eye." "Voodoo?" "Yahn."
She took me into the shack hwere my parents
allowed her to live and it was filled with roots
and parts of dead animals and in the middle there
was a cross with a chicken on it. The chicken
was wearign a crown. "Who's that Sesame?" I
queried. "That be Brogmagnar the chief spirit
of the lowcountry." "That's Brogmagnar?" "Yes."

"Allright now we gots to get you started on your first spell." She showed me how to chop up the roots and the secret gullah words to say and how to put in pinches of ground up livers and such. "But how about Jesus?" I questioned. "Jesus gots the spirit and this ain't nothin but spirit. Jesus don't mind no spirit." And I realized that what she said was true. This was not the christianity of my roman catholic upbringing but it was christianity in that it was spiritual and it used the good of the earth where Jesus lived to bring about good in the lives of the people that we loved.

When I left her shack who did I find but Billy Bob Hawkins sitting on the porch. "Hey there Sheriff Hawkins!" I said laughing. He blushed and stated "I wish you wouldn't call me that Savannah. Just Billy Bob for friends." "Are we friends?" I certainly hope so. I spect so." We went walking in the ACE basin and he showed me several different kinds of fish and birds that he knew from being in the lowcountry and he showed me a plant that you could use to put out the mosquito bites and I remembered how it was growing up with "good ole" boys and how while they were not very educated like Jonathan was and had barely even heard of Harvard they had another kind of education that someone at Harvard would never have. We passed underneath a weeping willow and he stood there and I stood there and I knew what was coming. Watch out girl! He leaned into me and I leaned into him and we kissed and I had forgotten how good a kiss could be. I was wearing a short black dress and a top that I had picked up at Saks on sale for five dollars and my stilletto heels but even though my mother had always told me to make sure that I wore clean underwear I didn't have any on! We kissed in a passoinate embrace and his hands were all over me! You watch out girl! And I thought why not! Billy Bob was handsome and he kissed good and I felt like our bodies would meld into one another's. He lay me gently in the back of a canoe and we began to make sweet love. I kissed every inch of his body and he kissed every inch of my body and it seemed like we had become one and the same body as we melded together.

I don't know how long we had been "going at it" but when we finally came up for air we realized that the canoe had gotten loose and we were floating in the middle of the ACE basin! It could only happen to me! "Holy Moses and the four fathers!" shouted Billy Bob and we laughed until we cried. We had left our clothes on the bank of the river and were now out in the middle of the river naked as jaybirds! What a mess! Billy Bob grabbed a paddle and I tried to use a boat cushion to cover myself up and we laughed and laughed until we cried. It was too funny! "I sure hope no one sees us!" I shouted. "I might lose my badge on account of this!" screamed Billy Bob and we continued to laugh and laugh. And as we moved down the river I realized that this could only happen in the lowcountry. It was a magical place where crazy things just happened! I was laughing when I looked over on the side of the creek and thought I saw someone. I let out a gasp and Billy Bob asked "What is it?" "Nothing. Noth-

ing at all." I responded. But something inside
of me told me that it was Chicken John and I was
reminded of why I had come down to the lowcountry
and even though we were laughing so hard that we
cried I realized that on the inside I was crying.

Creighton Starke found himself crying on the inside as well as the outside. This was just a mess. To think that today hope's great flame had been extinguished when so many morons, idiots, divorce lawyers, and ex-wives still sucked air into their lungs made him feel the sorrow that much more. He wiped his face with the shower curtain and spat an ounce of mucus into the trash can, watching it for a while as he tried to calm himself.

He had yet to decide who, if anybody, he was going to call. The reading had clouded, not cleared, his mind, and the emotional upheaval, growing weightier every passing second, had done nothing but add to the storm of confusion. Decision-making did not lie in the realm of his talents. To do or not to do, the eternal question.

He arose. Scott lay still. Water dripped from the faucet. The refrigerator hummed in the kitchen. Verbs continued to follow subjects and he wished for a prepositional phrase to add some color to the banal rhythm, but none came. He needed more time to think. Tomorrow, he had class to teach and oil to change and laundry to launder and a list of the other minutiae that filled life like a grotesque harlot outfitted in a child's nightie, rippling over and out from under the fabric, until it aroused no emotion other than disgust. But tomorrow would be the day. The hour would come and he would arise and he would phone the police and teach his class and do the other things that necessity cried for, and then he would sit down at his desk and face that sheet of paper and this emotion—at the moment pouring out from his eyes, coughing out from his mouth, shaking his very frame like an enraged child shaking a doll—would be transformed into creative electricity, shooting out from his fingers, activating the keys to his typewriter, whereupon it would form the written word.

He turned off the light behind him and walked through the apartment, leaving it, returning to his own. A message blinked on the answering machine, but tonight he would not answer it.

Tomorrow was the day.

SIXTY-TWO

Savannah and Mitzi moved along the hallowed streets of Charleston, looking with their eyes and listening with their ears for signs of the shag. The bars were fairly dead at this time of night, the college students still in their dorm rooms saving their money by drinking themselves into a stupor prior to arrival, and the excitement that the two brought along with them was not matched by anyone or anything around.

It was at such a point, their ebullience ebbing, hope fading into despair, that they stumbled upon Damp Dan's. The music that came from the establishment was loud and percussive, the decor gaudy and alarming. Glancing inside, they saw couples writhing on the dance floor, and it struck them that they had indeed found the shag, which they had not.

"Enter! Enter!" said Savannah, pushing Mitzi in front of her. But Mitzi needed no push, and she ran forward with her friend, ready to lose herself in senseless motion and vacant thought.

They hit the darkened dance floor with an air of ownership and began wiggling about in ways that lacked seduction or sophistication, allowing the music to move them in a manner that the composer had never imagined and surely had hoped to never see. But the composer was not there. Or it was very unlikely that he was there. In truth, the author is not sure where the composer was at the moment, nor does he know who the composer even was, be he man,

313

woman, or computer program, but none of that really matters. He could have been the curly-headed man who was grinding his pelvis against the backside of a young woman as she held onto an oddly placed chain-link fence, her expression showing her to be either very excited or very afraid, but in any case, very emotive. However, he did not know the words to the tune, so it was doubtful that he wrote it. Could the modern-day Bach have been the overweight youth who held paper towels in his hands in order to occasionally mop off his leaking forehead? Again, we will never know.

Savannah and Mitzi kept largely to themselves, their arms casting about in spasmodic whirls, their legs stamping in a rhythmless two-step, their hair swinging before their eyes, their heads twisting on necks that twisted on twisting shoulders. Occasionally they would touch hands or play a move off of the move of the other, but for the most part their style could only be described as chaos grappling with disorder as it fell into the cold abyss of swirling infinity.

The songs changed, but by the grace of the much-lauded disc jockey the rhythm never ended, one tune bleeding into the other across the capillaries of time. They took no breaks, shagging on into the night, and it seemed as though they would have never stopped had they not been approached by two gentlemen.

The lighting was very bad in the dance hall. There were lights, but they were not conducive to sight, and one could hardly imagine trying to read a book in there, unless it were a children's book where the words were few and glimpses of the pictures could guide the lector through his stumbling walk along the path of the plot. They heightened then dimmed. They came in red, then in blue, then in white, then in yellow, and then in so on and so forth. They panned to the right and the left, to the up and the down. They blinked and stuttered. Added to this, occasionally an exhalation of smoke would huff out from a machine and slowly disperse across the floor, giving one the sensation of happening upon a diseased dragon in the midst of taking a nap.

The lighting therefore served as a handicap to the two men, in that they could not easily see the meal that they desired to eat. But even such a debilitating handicap served as no excuse, or at least not a sufficient one. Fortunately, they had others. Neither of them had slept in over thirty-six hours. Both of them had consumed large quantities of alcohol in the recent past along with matching pills. Each had smoked a marijuana cigarette out in the car prior to arriving at the bar. Both needed glasses with mildly corrective lenses, but vanity and circumstance kept them from buying them. In addition to the above, their loins were heavy and burning from sexual frustration, and these two men were not just men, but true beasts with the reproductive impulses of rhesus monkeys. When the four-hundred-pound, bathing-averse woman showed up at the OB/GYN's office complaining of stomach pains and found herself eight months pregnant, they were the ones sheepishly raising the grime-covered hand when the doctor wondered aloud who could have been perverse enough to provide source material for the abomination. In short, they would mount anything that contained two X chromosomes, and Mitzi and Savannah fit that bill.

The mating rituals of the modern-day man and woman have been studied, written about, filmed, discussed, and pondered to the point that they are objectively as dull as farming rituals, but the one that took place this night provides a sufficient anomaly to warrant description. To continue with the agricultural comparison, one can imagine the surrealist farmer planting alarm clocks to show his contempt for humanity, and later humanity showing its contempt for him by letting him starve, and one gets a taste, bitter though it may be.

They approached Savannah and Mitzi, lacking a modus operandi but filled with things more powerful than forethought. Before them flailed two women with such wild abandon that in biblical times a laying on of the hands would have been necessary to expel the demons of cerebral palsy, and as both of them had been brought up in the church they each grabbed one by the shoulder, which caused

315

the shudders to cease. The women first looked at each other, then looked at the men, questioning gazes greeting whomever they saw.

"You want one of them fruity drinks?" the men asked in unison. But being as loud as it was, their questions sounded more like, "*******************?"

Mitzi was the first to respond.

"What?" she asked.

"What?" the man next to her asked.

"I can't hear you," said Mitzi.

"What?" the man asked. He cupped an ear and moved closer.

"What?" he asked.

"I can't hear you," Mitzi shouted into his offered ear, which was cauliflowered from several brutal beatings and decorated with a lightning-bolt earring. Being as loud as it was, her statement sounded more like, "########################."

While Mitzi and her fellow continued to expel white noise at each other, Savannah stood in silence, staring into the bloodshot eyes of the man with whom she had been coupled. His ears were no better than the others, and a scar on his upper lip gave an asymmetrical cut to his mustache, which he had neither trimmed nor brushed in months. His face had been sunburnt so many times that it resembled leather, and poor-quality leather at that, and a rash from housing insulation streaked across his left cheekbone. One would mark him for mid-thirties, his hair beginning to thin on top, grown out long in the back in an effort to compensate, the years having sanded him down until the grain crept out of the finish.

But in her eyes, this could have not been further from the truth. If she was not mistaken, and she was, this was the sandy-haired man on the front cover of the Conroy paperbacks. No, he was not Chicken John, no one was that good-looking except for her mother, but the resemblance was uncanny. His breath, a mixture of onion-loaded hamburger and beer mixed with liquor mixed with gastrointestinal revulsion, smelled to her of ambergris, and the hand that touched her naked arm seemed to her as soft as the belly of a turtledove, when in fact it was as rough as a cheese grater, marked with callouses and scars and missing a finger to boot. His eyes, to her, conveyed a heavenly light, providing a portal to a soul as pure as an imbecile's intentions, when in fact one could not squeeze a pin through his drug-constricted pupils, much less take a peek at what was inside. They were oily and red-streaked, a small hematoma decorating one of them due to a recent fistfight, but to her they spoke of nothing less than love.

SIXTY-THREE

Savannah and Mitzi arrived at the home of the two men, Jeb and Rex, which was located in North Charleston, next to some sort of industrial plant. All along the way, Savannah had relived the evening of shag that she and Mitzi had spent with them, mistaking paint-covered boat shoes for spit-shined Weejuns, tattered jeans for pressed khakis, heavy-metal T-shirts for buttoned-down oxfords, drug-induced hysteria for smooth, clean dance steps. Mitzi was not so sure. They seemed drunk to her, and malodorous. The one she had danced with, Jeb, had stepped on her toes and cracked his skull into hers, and the things he said had nothing to do with shrimping and seining, but a great deal to do with fornicating and drinking. The manner in which Savannah described them, the way she laid out their stellar backgrounds and raved over their exquisite manners, did not ring true with Mitzi. She understood that her friend had more experience in this area, that she had been brought up in these parts and knew practically everyone who lived in them, but something about it seemed wrong. She wished Tradd would wake up and voice his opinion, but he remained unconscious in the back seat, rolling around like a sack of dirty laundry as they drove.

"Hell yeah," said Rex as soon as Mitzi and Savannah got out of Mrs. Edwards's car. "Fuck yeah," he then said.

"My, this is lovely," Savannah said in response, her remark aimed at the house, which looked like one that Sears, Roebuck and Company had sold in its catalog back in the early twentieth century and had sat there since without update or repair. A chain-link fence squared-off the boundary line, broken and bent in several areas, and a dilapidated swing set sat over to the right. The lawn was bald in patches, overgrown in others, and a refuse of beer cans and cigarette butts was sprinkled about here and there. There were several people loitering in the street, and it did not look like they were up to much good.

Savannah, however, had somehow convinced herself that she had arrived at a plantation house that had been sitting on that spot for a matter of centuries. She saw long, rolling vistas of green grass, live oaks, and magnolias. Her nostrils were filled with the scent of newly ripened roses carried through a breeze that drifted across an ancient river. The loiterers, she assumed, were the caretakers of the property, docile, obsequious souls who were glad to see that the men of the house had returned so that they could be properly waited upon.

"Your family must have owned this place for generations," she said.

Jeb had streaked across the lawn once Savannah and Mitzi exited the vehicle, quickly squeezing Mitzi's shoulders in the vice of his arm, his other hand holding a cigarette and a beer.

"Just rentin'," said Rex. He held a six pack of beer with one finger in an empty circle of the plastic holder, hanging down by his knees. "Prices is cheap out here."

It was his modesty that most appealed to Savannah. The boys she had grown up with—the Moultries and Chisoms of the world—were quick to let you know who they were and where they came from. They wore their privilege for all to see and would take great pains to describe it to the blind. But not Rex. He acted like he was just one of the boys, even though it was clear that his blood was as blue as any Charlestonian who had ever walked down East Bay. Even going so far as to tell a little white lie, as he had just done. One did not rent a plantation home, as Savannah knew full and well.

"Let's go inside," said Jeb. "Skeeters're eatin' me alive."

Inside there wafted the unmistakable smell of poverty. Of toilets that had not been cleaned, leaking roofs and moldy ceilings, carpet living a life free of vacuum cleaners, pots and pans untouched by soap, furniture on which dirty bodies had passed out and copulated then passed out again. It was not the smell of decay, but of a sweetness soured by time and human contact. Two sofas sat in front of a television set and on the floor around them lay tattered magazines featuring unclothed women and painted automobiles. A naked bulb sat on top of an abused lamp, which sat on top of the abused carpet. Dried mud from dirty boots led like a trail of inedible breadcrumbs to the kitchen. A ceiling fan hovered above, one of its blades missing, tottering like a bicycle with a bent rim. There was not a plant in sight.

"Here it is," said Rex. "Y'all want one of these 'fore I put 'em in the fridge?" he asked, holding up the remnants of the six pack.

"We prefer neat bourbon," said Savannah.

Mitzi did not comment on this, as all of her attentions were placed on Jeb, who stood uncomfortably close to her, a hand to her mouth, a request for her to show him her teeth upon his lips.

"Bourbon?" asked Rex. "Fuck. I think we got some, but I ain't sure."

Savannah laughed at this, for to not have bourbon in a plantation home was a gross impossibility, another attempt by Rex to appear coy in the face of overwhelming obviousness. To say the least, Rex had her deeply charmed. It was like the old days, when she was in high school, where the men were men and not spineless wimps from Canada. Here she was in a plantation home with two paragons of Southern masculinity—one for her, one for her friend—being treated like royalty. She wondered if she and Rex would make love that night. Savannah had never actually had sex before and had never really thought much about the base mechanics of the animal act, but she had read a great deal about the sweet copulations that the heroines of her Southern tomes delighted in, so it seemed to her that it was something she needed to do in order to give some heat to her novel. But how would it happen? She couldn't ask for it, and neither could he, but somehow their eyes would need to meet and meld, and then they would rip off each other's clothing until they fell into each other's arms and further melded. Her thoughts were trudging through the possibilities when Rex returned, holding a bottle, saying, "How 'bout some Everclear?"

Savannah and Mitzi had as much luck with the Everclear as they had had with the bourbon. Simply the smell of it sent shivers down their respective spines, and its taste caused eyes to water and mouths to spit. Rex and Jeb handled it with greater aplomb, chasing down swigs with gulps of beer. They asked Savannah and Mitzi if they smoked and after enduring a five-minute soliloquy delivered by Savannah on how she used to when she wrote poetry but gave it up once she had children, they lit up a joint and passed it between them. They were sitting across from each other on the couches, Savannah by Rex, Mitzi by Jeb, a cable news channel delivering the only lighting to the room.

"So," began Savannah, "why don't the two of you tell us about how much you like cooking?"

"Like meth?" asked Rex.

"Yes, that and other dishes," said Savannah.

"Other dishes?" asked Rex.

"Yes, what you cook to eat, you silly."

"Fuck, I don't hardly cook nothin'," said Rex. "Usually, I'll go on Saturdays and buy a bunch of them ninety-nine-cent burritos and pop'em in the microwave all week. Other'n that, it's McDonalds or Burger King."

"Sometimes Kentucky Fried Chicken," said Jeb.

"Yep, sometimes I like to eat me some chicken."

"But Rex, my dear, you are being bashful," said Savannah. "Tell Mitzi about how you like to go shrimping in the creek and afterwards how you cook them up with some good mull gravy with a slice of onion and grits."

"Only creek round here's polluted," said Rex. "You don't wanna eat none of that. If I want shrimp, I'll go ta Captain D's. They got this five-dollar plate there that's pretty good."

Rex handed the joint to Jeb, saying, "Now, how y'all want ta do this?"

Savannah had no idea what he meant. She realized, however, that this was not fitting into the written paradigm of life and that she needed to get away to think. When she needed to do this at home, she retreated to the bathroom, and that is what she decided to do here.

"I think I would like to have a shower, if that's acceptable to everyone."

"Yeah, go on in there and get that thing clean, darlin'," said Rex. "We'll be out here waitin' for ya."

Mitzi sat shaking like a rabbit as Jeb rubbed his muzzle against her neck and growled.

SIXTY-FOUR

The bathroom smelled of mold. The bathroom smelled of urine. Both were colored by a slight hint of mouthwash and cigarette smoke. Brown rolls that once held toilet paper lay in the corner like dead roaches. Dead roaches lay in the corner dead. The shower curtain was covered with brown and green growth and the rim of the toilet was red and orange. Pubic hairs swirled along the floor like pornographic tumbleweeds. Savannah realized she had never been in a place as nice as this. In her eyes, everything was spic and span, the metal fixtures made of silver and gold, the showerhead European-exotic. She removed her dress and underclothes and turned on the water, humming a nameless tune as she did. What had she done to deserve this? While she clearly had a longing for the greater things in life, she knew that any stroke of fortune, especially this early in the plot, only meant that sorrow would soon make its inevitable appearance. But did it always have to be so? Couldn't she, just for once, have something nice happen to her and then have nice things continue to happen to her?

The bar of soap was actually a collection of bars of soap, molded together by time and force. She found it sitting in a plastic soap container, rotting in cold water caught from the showers of the past. There was no shampoo or conditioner, as Jeb and Rex could not justify the expense of either when soap was just soap, and the water came out in a lukewarm dribble. She mindlessly rubbed herself, her thoughts far away from the project at hand, on Chicken John, on her parents, on the lovemaking she would soon be enjoying with

Rex underneath an old sycamore tree where he would lay out a silk comforter and take her. Yes, he would take her. They would meld together. It would be a night that they would both remember for the rest of their lives, something that when they were old and gray they would still attempt to make sense out of, something that they would at that point—feeble and steps away from the precipice of death—give all they had to relive, even for a moment.

She was lathering up her legs when she heard the shouting outside the door. This was quickly accompanied by crashings and scufflings, all of it boiling higher and higher and shaking the lid. It dawned on her that she might very well be missing an essential part of the narrative, so she quickly turned the water off and leapt back into her clothes. And although she had missed a good part of the action, there was still enough left for her to later on draft a scene.

SIXTY-FIVE

When Tradd Jenkins finally regained consciousness, he felt far from refreshed. The only time he had ever awoken to more pain and remorse had been in the Meat Packing District of New York City on a school trip with the Summerall Guards. That night had consisted of Ecstasy, Viagra, and a self-loathing homosexual named Phil, that morning of universal hurt and disorientation. The jolt to consciousness was delivered by a coat hanger that had poked itself into his ankle. Rubbing his foot, he gazed around and found himself in the back of a car, then looked up and saw the faces of two teenagers, one of whom was trying to unlock the door through illegal means.

"Hey," he said. "What are you doing?"

The question did not constitute much of a show of force, but it was enough to scare the life out of the two youths, who turned and fled into the night.

His head ached to vomitous proportions, and his neck felt as though each of his vertebrae had been removed by a South American doctor fresh out of orphans from whom to harvest vertebrae. He sat up and felt his skull wobble on his shoulders, a faint tingling in his fingers, and a numbness in his toes. A thin line of fluid that was neither blood nor mucus dripped from out of his nose.

"Jesus. Jesus," he said, trying not to cry.

He couldn't remember much of the day. He had been drummed out of the Citadel, an occasion that consisted of no drums or fanfare, then was standing outside waiting for his friend Mike to pick him up. There were two girls. They had gone to a bar. A black bar? Had he gone to a black bar? And played pool? The entire thing was reminiscent of trying to remember a dream the day after. None of it made sense anymore, and things came in short blips of grainy film, fading with each passing second. Something had happened, though. He had been hurt. There was no mistaking that. And he needed help.

He turned his head, slowly, and saw that the car was parked in front of a house. There were no curtains in the windows, and a blue light shone inside of one of the rooms. Nothing seemed to stir inside. With cautious motion, he unlocked the door, then turned the handle, letting himself out. The night had cooled the earth, and somewhere off in the distance a million frogs and ten zillion insects croaked and squawked. His legs were weak. The tingling and numbness grew worse now that he was on his feet, and a sharp pain radiated down his right hip. He no longer tried not to cry.

SIXTY-SIX

Inside Mitzi was doing her best at preserving her maidenhood. Jeb's love play was what many women would describe as aggressive, and many others as criminal. His hands were clumsy and brutish, his legs pinning and gauche, his intentions so obvious he might as well have stated them, which he did repeatedly. Mitzi endured the never-ending task of removing hands and pushing back knees with unrelenting will, but Jeb appeared equally determined. As this took place, Rex sat across from them, watching. Savannah had only been gone for a few minutes, but to him it seemed as if she had simply vanished, leaving him lonely and jealous of Jeb and the beautiful young lady he had for the evening. Anger began to swirl within his chest, rising quickly into his head, and he was about to say something, to punch Jeb right in the teeth and take the girl away from him, when a knock echoed on the door.

A visitor at such a house in such a neighborhood at such a time of night is never a welcome one. He could be the police, a thief, or someone looking for money, but he could not be anything else. The three of them sat still for a moment, listening to the knocks, soft, pitiful knocks that sounded as though they would soon deteriorate to scraping fingernails.

"Who the fuck's there?" Rex bellowed.

"It's... I need help..."

"Well, you won't find none here. Get the fuck off of my property and stop knockin' on my door or I'll come out there and shoot your ass."

"I... I just need to use your phone. I'm hurt...I..."

"Well, if you ain't hurt, motherfucker, you're gonna be after I open this goddamned door."

"I..."

"God dammit!"

Rex sprung from the couch and slammed his feet across the carpet to the door. Jeb had also arisen from his seat. Mitzi took the opportunity to button her dress up to her neck.

"Listen. I..."

The door was ripped open.

"No, you listen, you son of a bitch."

"Tradd!" Mitzi cried. She rocketed from the couch and placed herself between Tradd and Rex. "You're alive!"

"He's alive?" said Rex. "What the fuck is goin' on here? Who the fuck is this?"

"This is my boyfriend, Tradd."

"Boyfriend?" said Rex. Every word that came out of his mouth was laced with indignation and disbelief.

"No, no, no, no," said Tradd. "No boyfriend. I just met her."

"So did I," said Rex, "and I ain't about to start sharin' her with your candy ass."

"I wouldn't expect you to..."

"You start sharin' her?" Jeb shouted. "What right you got to share somethin' you ain't got? She's with me, motherfucker."

"Like hell she is," said Rex.

"Like hell she ain't," said Jeb.

"What? You gonna fight me for her?"

"If that's what you want. I sure as hell ain't about to let you have her after I'm the one that gone out and found her."

"Well, come on then."

Tradd and Mitzi watched as the men began throwing each other around the room, taking out chunks of wall, smashing smashed furniture, delivering blows and twisting ears, biting arms and kneeing groins. The television set had crashed to the floor, bathing the room in darkness, when they heard, "What's going on here?"

"Savannah! Tradd's alive!"

"Of course he is, but where's the tiger?"

"The tiger?"

"Yes. The door was opened and a tiger ran in and began devouring the rapists."

"Savannah, there's no tiger."

"Mitzi, you don't know how these things work. There has to be a tiger. Why else would there be all of this noise?"

As this went on, Tradd's memory began to slowly return. He harkened back to the time when he had been kidnapped, to the day when he had walked from home to home in Charleston asking people for food. When the girl stepped forward and he could finally make her face out from the meager light coming from the street, he was overwhelmed by the image of that same countenance, smiling its vacant smile as its bearer caused untold misery on the bridges that hung over the Cooper River. He turned and began his way back down the stairs, going as fast as he could given his physical infirmities.

"But there's no tiger. It's just Jeb and Rex fighting over me."

The two men were on the floor, Jeb on top of Rex, grappling him in a choke hold, both silent, beaten, giving every indication that within two minutes each would be passed out cold. In the darkness they appeared as one hulk of beast, a partial Cerberus, its four glassy eyes shining from the shadows.

"Then I can't use this. I can't see anything and there's no tiger, and my story is already complicated enough without adding another subplot. Forget that they're in love with you, Mitzi. Because you're promised to Chicken John, I fear that the reader will grow to dislike you if you seem in any way unfaithful, and we don't want that. I may hate you and I may do very mean things to you, but the reader must see this more as a reflection of my own inner conflict and not as a true picture of who you really are."

"Tradd?"

As luck would have it, at that moment a train blew its whistle off in the distance, exciting the dormant neurons inside of the D'Bergeolet brain.

"Where is he?" she asked.

"I don't know. He was just standing right here."

"Then I know where he's gone. Quick, Mitzi. We have to catch him before he kills himself."

They fled from the house and ran out into the yard, calling his name at full volume, and drawing forth a number of shouts from the neighbors to shut the fuck up.

"He's not here!" said Mitzi.

"Where was that train coming from?"

"I don't know."

"Then get in the car."

Tradd had made it out onto the street. He had no idea where he was and did not know whether he was walking toward or away from Charleston, but he knew that in either case it was better than pinning his hopes on the fat girl and the lunatic. His sole desire was to have the strength to keep going until the day broke. Once that happened, he could approach someone without getting shot and get the help that he so desperately needed. If only he had been allowed to stay at the Citadel. Right now, he would have either been in bed asleep or doing pushups while someone urinated on his back, and both seemed unbearably pleasant to him at the moment. If only they had had doors on the bathroom stalls. It appeared to him such a simple thing. Such a small token of decency that inarguably formed a part of the foundations of Western civilization. But they didn't. And now he was walking along the road in the middle of nowhere, grievously injured with no hope in sight.

The car approached rapidly from behind him, casting the long shadow of his body along the road. He turned and could hear voices screaming from inside of it, noises that sounded something like, "I think it's over there! I think it's over there!" With great effort, he raised his right arm, placing a thumb in the air. And when he saw that it was coming too close, and that he was standing too far in the roadway, he did not have the ability to move in time to avoid the side-view mirror.

THURSDAY

SIXTY-SEVEN

Harry Edwards arose at four thirty in the morning. It happened every day and it was a terrible thing. His bladder woke him with its ache, he went to the bathroom to relieve it, then he returned to bed, knowing full and well that he would not fall back asleep. All of the literature on the subject said that it was simply part of growing old. The bladder weakens, just as the heart, lungs, brain, muscles, bones, will-to-live weaken, while the prostate grows, and one finds himself having to urinate with greater frequency. As for sleep, with age one needed less and less, which was fine. It gave you more time to enjoy your life. To read the books you always wanted to read. To get more exercise. To commune with loved ones. Only all he wanted to do was remain unconscious for a few more hours and leap out of bed feeling like the task of facing the world was not such an overwhelming one, not try and improve himself.

What the literature did not tell you, and what he knew, was that the reason he could no longer sleep was because he had taken part in raising two children. They had woken him up early for countless years, shouting and screaming the moment that their eyes popped open. They had kept him up innumerable nights with vomiting and fever. They had caused eyelids to spring open in the middle of deep sleep, his body drenched in sweat, wondering what destruction they were causing at the moment and how much he would have to pay in both spirit and wallet to assuage the aggrieved. They had taken away one of the few things in this world that he held dear—his sense of well-being brought on by the requisite eight hours—and seemed to have no intention of ever returning it.

He crept back in bed and eased the covers back over his frame. His wife lay still next to him, giving off a slight nasal snore, her hair in curlers and an eye shade covering her face. It had been his hope to form separate quarters with her once Roy left to spread his wings, but the boy was like a rat who had been placed in the wrong nest, and had no wings to spread, and any possibility that Erica would save him by moving on dwindled with each passing day. So now he had to stay still, not wrestle with the bedsheet, not sprawl out in search of a comfortable position. It was at these times that he imagined himself in his coffin, doomed to wear an ill-fitting tie for eternity along with uncomfortable shoes and a wool jacket with a collar that made his neck itch. He tried to remain calm. He breathed deliberately and willed his pulse to slow. However, the lid hovered inches away from his face and he felt himself suffocating. He wanted to scratch his foot. He fought the compulsion to rub his nose. He craved nothing more than to get out of the thing and move around a bit.

It was four forty-five when he crawled downstairs and turned on the coffee pot. They would leave in four or five hours. He could read all of the books he had always wanted to read, exercise, or place some early morning phone calls to family members he needed to reconnect with and scare them to death, but he would not do any of these things. He sat and waited for the machine to finish working so that he could drink his coffee. He stared out the window into the dark. He wished that he could go back to sleep.

SIXTY-EIGHT

Mrs. Edwards got up around eight and spent a half hour in the bathroom before coming down to breakfast. Mr. Edwards had already washed and dressed for the day, already eaten something, and read the paper. She shuffled about in her bathrobe and bedroom slippers, digging at the remains of a honeybun, and consuming a pastry strudel.

"What time do you want to get on the road?" he asked.

"I had hoped to talk about that last night," she said, "but you were too busy in your study."

"Well, we have plenty of time now to chat about it. When do you want to leave?"

"When I'm ready, Harry. Gosh. I just woke up and I've got all of this on my mind, and you can't be anything but mean. First thing in the morning. Our children out there, God knows what's been done to them…"

She began to cry, or not really, but simply to moan and blubber without drawing forth a single tear. He looked at his watch and waited for her to stop. She had always fancied that one day she would somehow be discovered in a shopping mall and spend the remainder of her life on the stage and screen, but no one had ever paid much attention to her at shopping malls, and it was highly unlikely that a Hollywood talent scout had ever done more than flown over their nameless hometown. She thought she had talent, however. She could fake it with the best of them, she imagined, as she was doing now, only her talent relied on the camera being miles away or the director setting her off as a dot in a corner.

"I'm going to go in my study," he said.

"You do that," she said.

He looked at his watch again and tried to brace himself for the unfortunate day that lay ahead of him. He needed a vacation. Just a week on a beach somewhere, alone, drinking the day away with a book in his lap. But only murder or accidental death would ever allow him such a pleasure.

The chair was still warm from where he had been sitting in it for the past few hours. He eased himself into it and closed his eyes. He had just fallen asleep when she came into the room and told him to hurry up and get the suitcases in the car.

SIXTY-NINE

Like his father, Roy had not had much luck in escaping to the land of dreams. The park bench had offered no give, and the night, with the wind blowing across the harbor, had been uncomfortably cold. After seeing Liza's protectors, he had run as fast as he could, cutting down Meeting Street and through the market, going on until the only way he could move farther along was to swim. There he had stood and waited for the sounds of galloping footsteps, anxiety waning and waxing within his chest as he tried to catch his breath, thinking of what his next move would be if they showed up. Each passing minute with no sight of pursuers had given him back his lungs and his relative sense of calm, and he had found a bench from where he could see if anyone was coming, unless they emerged from Charleston harbor. It had been fairly crowded at that time of night, with various people walking and resting, staring out at the water, but the people milling around had eventually headed back to their hotels. Roy had had no such option. Granted, he could have left, but that place had seemed as good as any. He had eased back on the bench and closed his eyes. He had then shivered and cursed the night away.

It was early in the morning, the sun just breaking, when he realized that it was futile. He sat back up and looked over the harbor, trying to think of what to do. He missed the counsel of his friends. He missed the safety of his home. He longed for the quick answers offered by his computer screen. As to what to do, he really didn't have much of a choice. His van and his clothes were back at the hotel room. He had his wallet, so he could survive, but it would be the

338

barest of survivals, and there was certainly no hope of ever finding Erica if he was just scraping by himself. He had to go back. His only hope was that Liza and friends would still be asleep at this ungodly hour. He arose and began to retrace his steps.

The parking lot at the Night's Inn was filled with cars and empty of people. Trash lay about the common areas, cigarettes and beer cans and candy wrappers. Roy eased himself down the walkway to his room, holding himself as close as he could to the wall for reasons that he did not understand, as it certainly wouldn't help him any if Liza or any of the others suddenly stepped out of their room.

He made it to his place and slipped in the key card, then slipped inside, throwing himself on one of the beds for a moment, wishing with an aching longing that he could stay there for a while and close his eyes. The bed had felt fine the day before, just a bed, but now, with the fresh comparison of the wooden bench on his mind and body, he realized that it was nothing less than one of the great wonders of civilization. He had never undergone much discipline when he was growing up, his father did not believe in corporal punishment and his mother favored a laissez faire attitude toward child-rearing, and he did not have much inner strength as a result. He could not make himself stay up to study for a test when he needed to. He could not hold off eating if he felt the urge. He did what his body wanted to do, and at the moment his body wanted to sleep. But he could not obey its commands this time, because if he did, his body would later regret it, preferring overwhelming fatigue over unfortunate disembowelment.

He got up, changed into a fresh pair of shorts, then threw his clothes and toiletries into the suitcase, snapping it shut and heaving it to his side. The door opened with a twist of the handle, and he stepped into the day, the area quiet, dead. He crossed the parking lot over to the van and tossed everything inside.

He then left, ready to restart his search for his lost sister.

SEVENTY

Savannah and Mitzi woke up next to a set of train tracks. They had parked off on the side of the road, underneath an outcropping of trees, and as the train rolled by at five thirty that morning, they decided that they no longer needed to sleep. It was not a volitional decision, but simply something caused by terror, the whistle blasting right outside the door, the train thundering by like the galloping steeds of the Apocalypse.

The night before they had rolled down the windows in attempt to cool off the car, and although this had worked, it had also allowed thousands of mosquitoes to fly inside and sate themselves on the blood of our heroines. If it was questionable before as to whether they suffered from some kind of skin malady, it was unquestionable now. Acne vulgaris on top of chicken pox on top of hives.

"And now he is gone," said Savannah after she stopped screaming.

"Who?" asked Mitzi, still screaming.

"Tradd. He's dead. Gone. A suicide. We did our best, Mitzi, but we couldn't stop what fate had already set in motion."

Mitzi's yell came to a stop, and she looked at Savannah, letting the words soak into her dry brain.

She soon began to cry, and Savannah reached over and took her in her arms, holding her, stroking her hair and trying out a few

Gullah phrases that she remembered Sesame whispering to her in similar situations.

"I've never had a boyfriend who died before," said Mitzi.

"I've had several," said Savannah. "Most of them were killed in the war. That damn war."

"The Gulf War?"

"No. Nam. We buried our lovers, but we can't bury our hearts. They continue to beat inside of our chests like the beating of the war toms. Pom. Pom. Pom. Just like the war toms."

Mitzi continued to cry for Tradd, and Savannah, who had greater dignity than Mitzi, held her tears back, which was not difficult given the fact that she knew no one who had ever died and had already forgotten what Tradd looked like. She wondered, however, if they should hold some sort of memorial service for him by the tracks. She did not know what would be fitting. If Mitzi had a ring that he had given her they could tie some flowers around it and set on top of a rail tie, standing there as a camera set on a crane pulled back until they were nothing but specks on the earth, a cinematic tool to show how enormous death is, how meager we are. But the truth was that she needed to go to the bathroom, and not a mere squatting tinkle. There was no time for ceremonies. They needed to get back to Charleston, the Holy City, and find a public restroom so that she could take a dump. That part, she decided, while essential, would not be catalogued in the telling of their adventures.

SEVENTY-ONE

Roy had driven about three blocks before it dawned on him that he had no idea where he was going. And not merely in the geographic sense, but in a larger one, *vis-à-vis* Erica. He was too tired to attempt to mind meld, and given his results so far, mind melding appeared to be perhaps yet another fallacy in which he had once placed his trust. The van traveled down Meeting Street, largely alone with the exception of a few dedicated joggers and some old women walking along in hopes of putting off the inevitable for a few more years. She had to be somewhere. He knew that. Her body occupied a space and that space occupied part of Charleston, and his body occupied space in Charleston, so all he really had to do was somehow make sure that his body space and her body space got close to one another where he could see her and she could see him and he could say, "Erica. I've been looking all over for you."

He drove around. Back in the residential area there were a number of streets that only went one way, and as tired as he was he disobeyed their edicts of direction and went as he pleased. The houses looked nice, but they were very skinny and very tall and he imagined that the tallness was not good for knees. He had not reached the point in life where he needed to worry about his knees, but he still did and had on more than one occasion mentioned to his parents that they should consider moving to a single-story house where it would be less likely that they fall or hurt their knees climbing stairs. On the last of such occasions, following another occasion just two minutes prior, his father had told him to shut the hell up and get out of his study.

Roy complied, but it was not without silent protest. Because what his father did not understand, and what Roy did not dare tell him, was that Roy would be the one who would bear the brunt of these two stories in the end, not him. He and Roy's mother would be old, and Roy would be taking care of them, and none of the three would have a decent pair of knees to get around in, walking up and down stairs as they had been all of these years. He imagined wheeling himself from his father's room, the overflowing bedpan situated in his lap, maneuvering through the handicapped-widened door to toss the contents into the commode. What kind of a life was that? And just to have two stories? It wasn't like they ever looked out the windows.

He pulled into the Lil' Cricket and parked the van. Inside it was already hot and the floor appeared as though they only served patrons wearing muddy boots. He grabbed a chocolate-flavored drink and some powdered sugar doughnuts and ate and drank as he waited for his correct change.

"You haven't seen my sister, have you?" he asked the woman waiting behind the counter.

"Honey, I've seen all kinds of people. What's she look like?"

"Oh, she's about yay tall and has blonde hair. She kind of looks like me, I guess, but I'm taller and my hair's brown."

"You gotta picture of her or somethin'?"

Roy left, his change in his pocket and the full roll of doughnuts in his mouth.

SEVENTY-TWO

"He walks around. His shadow walks around."

"It was not her. I was there, looking. I saw. I thought it was her, but it was not. It was not my mother. She went away when the other one laid down in her bed and drew the quilt up. She went away. 'Did she go as far as town?' 'She went further than town.' 'Did all them rabbits and possums go further than town?' God made the rabbits and possums. He made the train. Why must He make a different place for them to go if she is just like the rabbit."

It was interesting to Creighton how clearly people attempted to define themselves. Especially young people, away from home for the first time for any appreciable length, trying to find comfort in the comfortless world. The sorority girls dressed as though instructed by a manual, as did their male counterparts in the Greek universe. The budding intelligista attempted to be completely different by being just like all of the other completely different people. Of course, there were a few who simply had no fashion sense, those blessed with a void of self-awareness, who wore what their mothers had bought for them and thought no more of it. But the vast majority of them clearly had the awkwardness of an attempt behind not just the way that they dressed, but everything that they did. Even their nonchalance carried its effort.

In front of the class stood a boy in his late teens, big-headed and thick-haired, with a wide forehead and plump lips. His shoulders sat heavily atop his torso and his shoes appeared to contain a size twelve of stink. He wore a blue football jersey with the number 47 stenciled in white on both the front and back, a remnant of faded glory, short-lived but oft-reminisced, that proposed to all who saw him that he was a jock, even though he no longer was and was now simply becoming fat. He read the words concerning the woman in the bed and the rabbits and possums in a voice devoid of emotion, the pupil of a defunct school of elocution where the professor suffered from an addiction to tranquilizers.

Creighton had not had much sleep, or it had not come easy, thus causing him to sleep later than he should have, which forced him to enter the world without a shave or shower, a cup of coffee or a bowel movement. He was in no mood to listen to stories penned by idiots, nor was he in the mood to speak, walk, sit, stir, or breathe. He was simply not in the mood for living. There were no hopes of meeting a beautiful girl to spur him on, no goals of writing the next great novel to make existence worthwhile, no exotic vacation to look forward to, nothing, nothing, nothing, except to continue on as he had been, and what he had been was killing him.

"And tomorrow it will be cooked and et and she will be him and pa and Cash and Dewey Dell and there won't be anything in the box and so she can breathe. It was laying right yonder on the ground. I can get Vernon. He was there and he seen it, and with both of us it will be and then it will not be."

The boy finished with a cough into a fist, then raised his head to Creighton, looking sheepishly afraid. Surely his teacher had never read this Faulkner fellow. The act of humility appeased Creighton and he quickly reworked his critique to a milder form.

"So, Jason, what is it that your main character thinks his mother has become?" he asked.

The boy coughed again, then whispered, "A fish."

"A fish?" Creighton asked with a laugh. "Surely he thinks that she's a possum or a rabbit. You talk about that at length. Why do you think he thinks she's a fish?"

"Um. I dunno." The boy began staring at his shoes and Creighton feared that he had wounded him.

"Yes, I see," he said. "I think it's good. And I think that it's good that you don't know why he thinks she's a fish. Sometimes the author is simply along for the ride, going wherever the characters lead him. In my work, *Finding It All in the Hole*, I was continually perplexed as to why Osgood loved Belinda so much. I just couldn't understand it. But you see, it was not my reason that Osgood was using, but his. He had become such a flesh and blood character that he had his own motives and desires completely separate from mine, the very man who had created him with ink and paper. It's the mark of a genius, and I commend you, Jason, for flirting with this dangerous flame even for such a short period of time in your work. Now, were you trying to incorporate any Eastern philosophy in this piece by having the young man imagine that his mother had become reborn as a rabbit or a fish?"

"Um. Nope."

Creighton waited for more, but there was no more.

"All right. Enough of me. What does everybody else think?"

The class remained as quiet as the dead in the graveyard. One young man appeared to be asleep. The author of *Lowcountry Lamentations* had chosen not to attend this morning, and her professor was somehow relieved by this fact.

"Let's see here," said Creighton, going down the class roll. "Mr. Sanderson."

"What?" asked Mr. Sanderson, who was clearly a member of a fraternity.

"Any comments?"

346

"Um. No offense, dude," he said, looking over the ex-football player, "but I thought it was boring. It was like either the character or the author didn't have much in the way of brains. And who says 'et' anymore?"

"The provincial tongue," said Creighton. "Excellent point. Let's talk about using dialect in our stories…"

SEVENTY-THREE

That same morning, Officer Frank Jamison checked in at the station and saw that the girl in the wreck had been busy during the night. Her parents had been called again and they were coming up that morning. He looked over the rest of the complaints, and as he did, he saw something that flicked a feather across his brain. He stared at the name, then he stared at the name of the girl, and he realized that he had a family of lunatics on the loose, one causing thousands of dollars in damages, the other beating up senior citizens in the parking lot of the Night's Inn.

SEVENTY-FOUR

One always knows that he's left something when he packs to leave. There is always the toothbrush or the hat or the socks or belt or something, something that is forgotten. And this knowing, more times than not, becomes a truer knowing when one arrives at one's destination, ready to enjoy himself, only to find article X missing. So far Roy had not missed anything. He had plenty of clothes and enough toothpaste. His maps were carefully collected in the passenger seat. He had every phone number that he needed in case of an emergency. He had everything, everything except for a picture of the girl he was trying to track down.

With each step toward the van, he began to comprehend the futility of the majority of his plans. He couldn't put up posters without a picture on it and he felt sure that he couldn't draw a passing likeness of Erica. This left him with only the possibility of stumbling upon her, something he now realized was probably not likely. He sat in the van for a while, drinking the chocolate drink, sad, tired, and ready to throw in the towel.

Which he essentially did. If questioned on the point later, he would have denied it with righteous indignation, and done so with a pure heart and clean mind, but what he believed and what really happened were two different things. For at that moment, hunched over the wheel of the van, a sour smell rising from his shoes where socks and feet had lived without pause for over sixteen hours, he decided that he would go out to Fort Sumter and check it out.

Again. He had been there before. It was a school field trip many years ago that had left an impression of fuzzy images, homemaking mothers along with a few fathers trying to do the right thing acting as chaperones, an Asian classmate eating something wrapped in seaweed, a vomiting over the rail as the boat carried them across. He seemed to remember walking up stairs and playing war with his fellow rebel sympathizers, half of whom were black, the stone walls. But that was about it.

Anyone, including Roy, would know that the chances of running into his sister at Fort Sumter were slim to none. She didn't think much of war and didn't have any interest in history. She did not like boating. Roy, to the contrary, enjoyed all of these things, even war. In fact, had there been one going on at the moment, he would probably have signed up for it. Or at least thought about signing up for it a great deal.

But that was what he decided, and that was where he headed.

SEVENTY-FIVE

One of the students considered herself a poet and had given Creighton a few of her pieces to look over. She was fairly stump-like in build, and could use some work on her eyebrows, but she had a kind face and the undeniable flesh of a woman just sprung loose from the starting gate of legal consent. He asked her to come to his office at noon so that they could discuss her work, and she accepted the invitation, giving him an hour to freshen up and prepare himself.

He rushed back to his apartment, which was a ten-minute drive from school, and stepped into the shower, lathering up quickly and washing it all away. He then shaved and applied cologne, changed into clean clothes and shot back to campus. When he arrived, he had nearly twenty minutes to kill before the fated hour, so he looked at his typewriter, felt that he had nothing to give, then searched for something to read. In hopes of inviting its author for a similar conference, that morning he had carried along with him his copy of *Lowcountry Lamentations*, and finding that he had no stomach for Vargas Llosa at the moment, picked it up and began to read as follows:

```
I didn't want Roy to come along. We had never
"gotten along" and it didn't look like we would
ever "get along" but he said that he had to
come nad I didn't see how I could keep him from
"coming along". Roy had married a shedevil of
```

a woman who had three kids with him. She wasn't
a southern lady as my mother often pointed out
but just plain and simple "white trash". And my
mother made sure that she knew it! Nothing that
Betty Sue did was ever good enough for my mother.
Now I know that I've said htat nothign that I
ever did was good enough for my mother either but
it was different with Betty Sue. Because Betty
Sue tried to "fit in" and she couldn't understand it when she didn't. If my mother liked
roses and hated carnations then you could be sure
that Betty Sue woudl bring my mother carnations
instead of roses! It was just like that! It's
hard to explain but it was just like that.

Roy and her had been having some "problems"
just like me and Jonathan but to be honest Roy
deserved her. He was just as mean as her and just
as inconsiderate. Whether it was talking Chicken
John into fighting in the Vietnam war or saying
ugly things to the fire breathing lesbians that
came to all of my poetry readings he just didn't
ever do anything right. He worked at a local
video store and spent a lot of time on the internet and otherwise he didn't do much of anything
at all.

"But I don't want you to go." I exclaimed. "I
don't care what you want me to do. I'm going.
He's my brother too." He responded. "Okay, okay,
okay, okay. But you can't tell anybody Roy. It's
just got to be me and you who knows and nobody
else. If Chicken John were ever to get caught
he'd spend the rest of his life in the pen and we
can't let that happen!" I clarified. "Don't worry.
I won't. But he deserves to spend his life in the

pen after the way he's been acting. Going about
blowing up federal trains and shooting at schoolchildren. I think they should put him in the
electric chair!" he expostulated. "Roy don't you
see that he's just trying to save our land! This
is the only thing that he's ever wanted and Daddy
has ruined that by going and selling it off to
the nuclear power people!" I cried. "A man's got
to pay for what a man's done. It will be and it
shall be and forever more." he claimed. "You are
such a bloodblistered kotex!" I said.

The island had changed a great deal since we
had last been there. The nuclear power people
had bought the entire thing including the homes
and what was left was everything that we had
grown up with but it was all different. Since I am
very sensitive by nature and a poet I felt that
I could see the people who used to live there.
"Look! There's Mr. Poops, the old black man who
walked around with the whistle!" I cried. "That's
not Mr. Poops. That's just a light pole." Roy
corrected. "Oh." I said. "There's Mrs. Jabobs,
the woman who kept mama out ofthe garden club
and who kept mama from ever liking the smell of
gardenias again!" I shouted. "There's no one
here Savannah! It's just us!" Roy exclaimed. And
I realized he was right at least in the normal
sense of things. But in a lowcountry way he was
dead wrong. They were there. You just had to have
the magic in you to see it. The Gullah magic!

We found the old boat out by the old dock laid
out in a clump of seagrass and oysters shells.
I took out my pocketknife and opened up one of
the oysters and said to Roy. "Here. Eat it. This

is the taste of my childhood." I said. And he replied "I don't want to eat any smelly meat out of a shell and knocked it out of my hands. I realized hten that he had not just knocked the oyster out of my hands he had in fact knocked my childhood out of my hands. But little did I know that what he would do next would really knock my childhood into the soft pluff mud ofthe lowcoun-try...

We cast off that night and guided ourselves by the stars like we had done a million times before when we were growing up in the lowcountry. I had not told Roy where we were going even though he had asked me a million times to tell him where we were going before we went so I paddled and he sat in the front of the canoe drinking a Pepsi.

We landeded on a small island after an hour and Roy said, "I knew that you'd bring us here. Right to D'Bergeolet island." It wasn't really D'Bergeolet island but just an island but it was one that we had named D'Bergeolet island when we were children becuause it was our safe haven whenever father went on one of his drunken binges which was about every night. "You don't be sassin me boy." I stated. "Oh here we go with the Gullah again. I hate Gullah." Roy sighed. "You hate Gullah! Next thing you'll tell me is that you rootin tootin don't like you no shrimps!" I exclaimed. "Savannah please stop it with the Gullah. I don't even understand what you're saying anymore." I heard him say.

We landed the boat and made a fire. On the way to the island we had caught a bushel of sea bass, two bushels of shrimp, and it wasn't long

354

before Ihad the mull gravy going. I had taken a
fusion cooking class while I was up in New York
from so I decided to spice up the meal with some
home made cilantro, pigeon eggs and falafel. Roy
kept asking when Chicken John was coming and I
told him that I dind't know and why didn't he
just stop worrying about it for a while and eat.
He began eating and he said, "This is the best
thing I've ever put in my mouth!" I laughed and
explained, "It's what they call fusion cooking!" "Well I'm all for fusion cooking! Savannah
you really should be a world class cook! This is
amazing!" "I would love to but I've got to have
time for my poetry! It's alreay stopped one war
and I hope that it will preven the next one!"
Little did I knwo that the next one was about to
happen...

Chicken John showed up just as orion's belt
crossed across the marsh. He was just as I remembered him although you could tell that he had
been throug a lot in the vietnam war and with
his war with the federal authorities. We hugged
and cried and it wasn't before long that he was
teasing me like he always used to tease me and
we were both laughing so hard that we cried!
It wasn't long before we were doing what all
lowcountry people do when they get together:
telling stories. I told the one about the time
that Mr. Arakanak found his wife sitting in the
pew at the baptist church and Chicken John said
that he didn't remember that one. He asked me to
tell it again. And with every story that I told
he told me that he didn't remember it and I would
tell it to him. And then there were some stories

355

that he told that I didn't remember and I him tell them to me and it was amazing because we had forgotten so much of what we were. It was good to be back in the lowcountry again and reliving the tales of our childhood and it brought us together until we melded into one. "Well I guess I better be going on now!" said Chicken John.

"Is there nothing we can do Chicken John to change your mind and stop you from this! You're going to die! They're going to kill you!" I wailed. "Savannah this is my land and my country. I fought for it and held others in my arms when they died for it. I don't care what some piece of paper says about whose land it is and whose land it isn't. I just know that in my heart that it's my land and I plan on staying here."

"Not if I have anything to do with it!" screamed Roy. I had not noticed it but Roy had brought along with him a flare and a bull horn. He lit the flare and began screaming into the bull horn "He's over here! I've got him! YOu can pay me my reward now! I've got him!"

"Roy! You betrayed your brother for money! How could you do that!" I cried.

"I've got to get out of here!" "Chicken John don't! If you run away they'll kill you!" I peeled. And Chicken John stopped and looked me in the eye and our eyes melded together and he said "Savannah they killed me when they killed this land. I am already dead. Put me in one of your poems will you. I would like to be famous like you but I just don't have the brains that you do. I've got to get out of here!"

> I watched Chicken John run out into the water
> and I knew right hten and there that it would be
> the last time that I saw Chicken John.

She was late, but that was all for the better. Or at least it would be if she still came. Trying to focus on the positive and ignore the negative, an almost novel experience for him, Creighton took the time to again go over her poems, which were terrible. Manure. Crap. Unreadable shit. It really showed you how good the good ones were when you took a look at the work of someone as awful as she was. Who was the first person to decide that poems didn't have to rhyme? Who gave poems meter? Who spoke of things other than nature and love? You had to admire them because it wasn't the natural way to go. The natural way, the way of children and the mentally infirm, was to simply rhyme away about love and nature regardless of the consequences. He would bet that if you read one of these poems and then read one by a semi-talented twelve-year-old, you couldn't tell who had written what. He would have to try that some time. Only he didn't know how he would ever get his hands on adolescent poetry.

He decided to go with "Summer Squall," mostly due to the fact that it was the shortest. He read it, then tried to repeat it without looking, then read it again. It made very little sense and had even less narrative value, so it wasn't the easiest thing to piece together in his memory, but by the time she knocked on the door, he felt like he had a decent handle on it.

"Good afternoon, Jessica," he said when she entered.

Unlike him, she had not changed clothes since class, but she seemed showered, and her outfit did nothing to deflate his interest.

"Good afternoon, Dr. Starke. You said you wanted to see me?"

Creighton was by no means a doctor of anything, but he did nothing to disabuse her of her error.

"Yes. I did. Please shut the door behind you and take a seat."

Prior to her arrival he had twisted the Venetian blinds shut, leaving a small lamp that sat on his desk as the only source of light in the room. He had been in enough college professors' offices to know how to cause maximum effect, and virtual darkness was a key component. The students, poor innocent fools, actually thought that their instructors at the university level were exceptionally intelligent people who had it all together, intellectuals trapped in worlds of high thought and heavy responsibilities. They imagined an aura of mystery glowing about them, and Creighton was not going to do anything to expose the charade.

She perched herself uncomfortably on the chair across the desk from him, fixing her short skirt with a quick two-handed tug. He did not move, nor did he speak. He just sat there looking at her with the tops of his eyes, his fingertips together, forming a teepee, his jaw lowered to his sternum.

"I enjoyed your class today."

He did not respond.

"I think I'm learning a lot."

The stare continued.

"Um. So, what was it you wanted to see me about?" Her inflection did not give off the air that she was actually asking a question that she wanted answered, but rose with every syllable, like someone reluctantly speaking when she has no faith in the words leaving her mouth.

Creighton dropped his hands to the desk with a flat-palmed smack, then arose, his back to her, and walked over to the blinds. Slowly, he began to turn the rod, until the slats stood at a forty-five-degree angle. The sun charged in with cinematic effect.

"Jessica, I asked you to come see me because ever since I read your poem 'Summer Squall,' I have found myself haunted."

His back still to her, he cleared his throat and lowered his head. Then, with the most wounded voice he could conjure, he began to speak:

> There is something about a summer squall
> That fills my breast with shades of awe;
> That makes me think of maple trees
> Of newborn kittens and skinned-up knees.
> I find myself out in the rain,
> Free from worry, free from pain
> My cancer is gone, it does not exist,
> It's merely a benign ovarian cyst
> And then it is that I see your face
> And I am taken away to that special place
> Where it was that we fell in love
> As the summer squall fell from above.

Each word of the final line staggered behind the one in front of it, fading out to a death-rattle whisper. When he was through, Creighton dug the meat of his palms into his eye sockets then allowed his hands to trace the shape of his jawline. He then turned and looked at her and was delighted to find her silently crying.

"It speaks to me, Jessica, like no poem has ever spoken to me before. It's almost as if you have taken the sum of the human predicament and somehow made it fit within a twelve-line stanza. Every word is necessary, every couplet as well-crafted as a Ming vase. Someone like you comes around only once in a lifetime, if not once in a century, and I can't tell you how humbled I am to possibly think that I could somehow play a part in bringing this to the world."

By this point, Jessica's tears had been joined by bodily shakes, a runny nose, and all-out blubbering. Creighton reached into his back pocket and pulled out a handkerchief, walking to the other side of the desk and handing it to her, afterwards his hands on her bare shoulders, kneading her soft, warm flesh with his wanton fingers.

"Do… you…really… think… so?" she coughed out through the spasms of her diaphragm. "I…can't…"

"Shhh," said Creighton. "There's no need to speak. Your poetry has already spoken for you."

You did not kiss them at this point. To do so would not only be a grave breach of conduct, it would undoubtedly ruin any chance that you might ever have at actually performing a grave breach of conduct. No, you simply made contact, both in an emotional and physical sense. You rubbed their shoulders. You wiped away their tears. You tenderly touched their neck with the side of your face as you whispered calming words into their little brains. You ran a collection of fingers through their hair as you would your young son who had just hit the home run. Build trust first then destroy it later in so many wonderful, forbidden ways.

Charlotte Lennox was the name of his first victim of the Venetian Blind Twist™. He was fresh off of the questionable success of *Finding It All in the Hole,* a new professor at a semi-respectable school, and long enough into his marriage to come to the sad reality that having a woman next to you in bed every night did not mean that you got to use her womanhood as you pleased every night, or, for the fact of the matter, hardly ever. Donna's menstrual cycles came and stayed for an ungodly number of days and headaches arrived at bedtime on such a constant basis that he wondered if she wasn't allergic to the sheets and pillow covers. When she wasn't ill or menstruating, she stayed up watching television until he could no longer hold his eyes open, letting another night of opportunity pass them by. They fought daily over idiocies, and she was not one to right her wrongs through an offer of coitus. And then she became pregnant, and what was rare became extinct. In frustration he had returned to masturbation, returned to it like one who thought he had finally gotten his teeth straightened, only to have to dig his retainer out of the trash can, disgusted with himself at first, getting used to it more quickly than was healthy.

So there came the day, another dinner with his mother-in-law hovering on the near horizon, another night ending with a peck on the lips and the frustrated killing of the lights, when he could stand it no longer. Like all of his prey, Charlotte was not very attractive to her coevals. Her personality did not lead to popularity, her finances to acceptance, her looks to mutual hunger. She therefore tried to set herself apart from the herd by giving off the air that she suffered from great mental tortures beset upon her by the great questions of life. Why are we here? Why, if there is a God, do so many people suffer in the world? Is there such a thing as love? Will mankind ever evolve? She too was a poet, and not half-bad if the truth be told, but still not someone who would ever make a go in the poetry world. Her fate would be to write it in college, perhaps dabble with it in grad school, then leave it by the roadside as she hitchhiked through menial jobs and failed relationships. But the key was that she did not know this. Life stood before her unwritten, and therefore there were no limits as to what it could contain. There could be travel, adventure. She might find a handsome man who looked past her outer appearance and saw deep into the beauty inside. She might become a poet. She might become a famous television actress. Everything was possible. Or so it seemed. The truth was that she did not take several important factors into consideration: namely, Judeo-Christian dogma, capitalism, Madison Avenue, social norms, social pressures, sexism, ageism, racism, biology, fear, laziness, despair, and bad luck. They would all shape her future, shape it as though it was hemmed in on either side by granite walls twenty feet high and ten feet thick.

Charlotte had not cried as mightily as Jessica on that first day in the office, although she had cried. She held herself silent, listening to Creighton spout out his practiced speech, and when he was through, he was sure that he had failed. He waited for her to respond, retaking his seat at the desk, wondering what letters he would have to write to publishers and literary magazines in order to keep her from thinking that he had just made a pass at her. And then she spoke. She explained that her poem was her way of conveying her burning desire to explore her sexual boundaries, and for him to be able to see this, for him to be able to discern the power that she had placed into each word, made him, rather than her, the genius. Creighton demurred, then asked a number of questions about her erotic hopes and dreams, which she answered with startling frankness. After an hour she departed, leaving him alone to abuse himself mightily under the cover of his desk.

The visits continued and it was not long before they found themselves on the couch, reading poetry to each other, speaking of sexual experiences in which she had partaken, and he had only heard about and dreamed of. And then he began screwing her. First with his pants around his knees and her underthings pushed to the side, then moving on to full nakedness on the couch, on the desk, against the wall, in front of the window that looked upon the asphalt. It continued for roughly two months.

But she finally began to want more, and he finally began to tire of her. Not sexually, he could have tolerated that for the entire semester, but intellectually. He did not expect to have to talk about Rilke with her, and under no circumstances could he have helped carry on the conversation anyway, given that he had never read Rilke, but the lie he had begun, that she was an extremely talented poet, had gone to her head, and the self-destructive impulses that thrived in his mind urged him to laugh at her and tell her that she had no more hope in getting anything published than he had in becoming even remotely happy. She liked for him to read her latest works while she fellated him, and the staggeringly obvious allegory about the white lamb who wanted to be ravished by the evil wolf would turn to ashes in his mouth and make him want to dash his fists across the back of her bobbing skull. She began researching agents and decided on the few whom she would allow to represent her, at which publishing houses they would have to place her, the amount of money she would have to receive for her advance and the necessity of keeping both the foreign and film rights. She started mentioning the eventuality of his leaving his pregnant wife and moving in with her and had worked up a detailed description of what their garret in Paris would look like.

She even bought him a beret. It was red and two sizes too large for his head; he wore it anyway.

The baby came, a son, and he immediately knew that he was risking way too much for such short bursts of opiatic pleasure. He began to make excuses after class, relying on the old headache drill, refraining from claiming that he had a menstrual cycle, and after two weeks and several nasty notes, he thought that the worst was behind him. Only she found him. He arrived home late one afternoon to discover her parked in front of his house, a stack of newly written poems on the passenger seat and a clove cigarette burning between her fingers. His skin blanched and his heart spasmed in his chest, and he considered parking his car and running inside, but he knew that there was no escape, and that he might as well try and have the final stand-off with hopes that it did not spill over into his marriage.

In the cold of her car, she cried and threatened him for at least ten minutes as he sat with her poems in his lap, then for the next quarter of an hour made a rash attempt at seduction. He withstood both, tight-lipped and repentant, waiting for a possible moment of clarity from her, where he could try to lie his way out of the situation. And then it came, she had nothing more to say, and he began by telling her that he loved her, but that her love was too much for him and that he felt it burning him alive, eating him from the inside like a smoldering fire. Because of her, he had not written a word in months, nor had he been able to eat. If she wanted to kill him, he said, then they could continue, but if he were to live, then they must live apart. He would help her in any way that he could, but he was a mere mortal, a middling novelist, and not a god who could possibly coexist with someone of her brilliance.

Her tears and the doe-eyed look that she gave him let him know that everything would be all right. She understood. She knew that she had remarkable powers, but it had never entered her mind that they were killing him. This led to her proclamation that she was cursed and wished that she had never been given such talent. A hug was exchanged, more tears wept, then he went inside.

The next semester he was accosted by a colleague who wanted to discuss Charlotte Lennox with him. His blood ran cold when he heard the name, and he braced himself for his undoing. Only sex was not mentioned. The professor was simply aghast at the fact that Creighton had told her that she was one of the world's greatest living poets when the truth was that she couldn't get a job at the Hallmark Corporation. Had he really told her that? And if he had, had he lost his mind? Creighton mumbled out something about trying to inspire his students, then moved on. As for Charlotte, he had no idea what ever happened to her. A couple of years later he had tried to look her up in the alumni directory, but she was not listed.

It was with one hand on shoulder and the other in hair that he caught himself. This had never worked out before. It had always turned from sweet rose to rank manure. Not just the classroom dalliances, but relationships with every woman he had ever stumbled upon. And Scott. Yes, Scott. How could he explain himself given the fact that his best friend lay dead in an apartment bathroom at that very moment, dozens of groundbreaking novels never to be?

He eased away and took a deep breath. Jessica stopped her sobbing for a moment and looked over her shoulder at him, finding him with his eyes to the floor and his shoulders gone limp.

"Is everything all right, Dr. Starke?"

It took him a moment to respond, but when he did it came out in a torrent as if he had just been caught in some private indecency.

"Of course, of course, Jessica. Of course, it is. What could be wrong after reading "Summer Squall"? No, everything is fine and dandy. Fine and dandy. I was just thinking. Of the last lines? You know, of your poem? Anyway, I really do appreciate you coming in here today and I would ask that we keep this between the two of us. I don't want the other students to know that there is a class genius sitting among them. You know? Is that okay?"

"Of course. I won't say anything."

"There you go. Now I hate to do this, but I really need to get going. I'll see you at our next class. Try and write some more poetry before then. If you can. I know it must be hard."

Jessica stood up.

"You know, I don't find it that hard."

"Amazing. Just amazing. You've got a big future ahead of you. Big, big future."

After a few parting words she left. He sat down on his couch and cried. Cried and cried, just like a summer squall.

SEVENTY-SIX

The day moved along. Minute followed minute, hour followed hour. They had no money and were running low on gas. They were hungry. They were tired. It reached such a point that, for a period of time, even Savannah forgot that they were looking for Chicken John.

What had started off as a cool day quickly restated its intentions, and the sun shone down upon them, heating the air, causing sweat to drip down the red spots that decorated their faces. They found shade in the market, but they had lost their interest in the Gullah fairy, and it struck both of them as simply some third-rate shopping bazaar like those located in the depths of Arabia where religious zealots were sure to detonate a bomb at any moment.

They walked on, Savannah trying to remember the location of her family mansion, Mitzi slowing behind, her nose swollen from the winged Bible, her skin itching with a miserable insistence, her spirits low with thoughts of her dead boyfriend. And although they walked, it was clear that they could not go for long without taking a hearty rest and renourishing themselves with food and water.

"Let's just go home, Savannah," said Mitzi. "Let's just get in the car and go. You can write your book some other week. Let's just go home."

"Quit your whining, Mitzi. You are about to get yourself cut out of the book you refer to. I told you that there would be suffering, so you've got some nerve to complain about it now. As for the type of suffering, I agree with you that it's pretty dull and lacks any page-turning effect. I would have thought that by now we would be out in the middle of the ocean, stranded on a boat, or being tortured by members of the Ten, but this is what the story has given us, so this is what we will take."

Although Savannah said these words, the truth was that they did not reflect the despair that she felt in her heart. No book that went on for a number of pages without excitement, without zippy dialogue, would ever make it to *The New York Times* Best Seller list. She did not feel like partaking in any witty repartee, nor did she feel like telling Mitzi of the time her father did this or that and how it scarred her. The houses looked uninviting and unfamiliar, and she lacked the courage to knock and ask to come inside. She needed something fast, or the novel would be doomed to failure.

These thoughts did not exist within her head, but within her soul, which did not communicate with her brain, only clouded it. Something had to happen, something exciting, something to give the book its ending, and as they turned onto George Street, that something came into view.

SEVENTY-SEVEN

"And I assume that Roy Edwards is your son."

"Jesus. What more."

"Harry."

"What's that idiot done?"

"Harry."

"Well, it appears that he assaulted a sixty-year-old woman last night in the parking lot of his hotel, and then this morning several people reported that he was driving his van the wrong way down numerous one-way streets."

"Please tell me he didn't hit anybody."

"Well, I mentioned the woman."

"I'm talking about with the car."

"Oh. No. He didn't hit anyone with the car—a van, actually. He was just driving the wrong way down an awful lot of one-way streets."

Silence mixed with soft whimperings given off by Mrs. Edwards filled the room.

"And you have no idea where either of them is."

"Nope. But with the way they've been going, it won't be too long before we do."

"Has she been raped?" cried Mrs. Edwards.

"Jesus."

"No ma'am. Not to my knowledge. Like I said, she's just torn up a bunch of stuff in a shop, walked off without paying a bill, and caused about thirty cars to be towed off."

"Thank God."

"Thank God, nothing. Jesus." Harry Edwards ran his hands across his face and took a moment to look down at his shoes. "Is there anything else?"

"Not yet."

"Not yet. Jesus. Well, you know where we'll be. Thank you for your time, Officer Jamison. Call us if you hear anything."

After a parting shake, Harry Edwards led his wife out to the car. Insurance would only cover so much. A pro rata payment of five percent, if they were lucky. Or they would, or at least could, look to Erica for what appeared to be thousands, then there was the family purpose doctrine, negligent entrustment. He had given the car to a person whom he would have to admit he knew was insane… He let his wife in the passenger side then walked around and got in behind the wheel.

"I think this has to be some kind of awful mistake. Erica and Roy wouldn't do any of those horrible things they say they've done."

Harry Edwards was silent.

"It just has to be a mistake."

They backed out and got on the road. They were staying in Mount Pleasant, where the hotel rooms cost a great deal less.

"Where are you going?" his wife asked when he began making his way out of downtown.

Harry Edwards was silent.

SEVENTY-EIGHT

He was five foot five with hair black to the point of carrying a blue shine. His skin favored toward a light brown as did his eyes. Alonso Quijano was his name, and he hailed from Chiapas, Mexico, visiting the United States for a number of years after crossing the desert and entering the country illegally. He was currently out of work and seeking to remedy the situation, trolling through the downtown of Charleston in hopes of seeing someone who needed windows cleaned or a yard raked. He stopped when he heard the woman shout in his direction, and slowly began to walk the other way when she came running toward him. There was nothing good in people shouting at you in this country, and although they didn't look like it, those women could very well be the federal authorities seeking to deport him.

"Chicken John! Chicken John!" Savannah screamed maniacally as she rushed down the street. Alonso did not take the time to translate this to "Juan Pollo," but even if he had, he would have still gone the other way, as that was not his name.

"Chicken John! Stop! It's me! Savannah!"

Savannah had finally found him. He was just as she remembered him, although he had been changed by the war and his fight with the federal government over the nuclear power plant, and as he walked away from her it took all that she had to refrain from breaking into a dead sprint and tackling him to the imagined cobblestones. She had always hoped that he would come running toward her and that they would meet with open arms clasping around each other's shoulders, but these books were about real life, not some convenient fable, so she had to accept it for what it was. The actor in the movie should probably look over his shoulder, though. A pensive look, like he wanted to go to her just as much as she wanted to go to him, but he couldn't, given all that he had suffered.

Alonso made it halfway down the block before she caught him, and when she did, he did not know how to react. Talk was amongst his fellow illegal immigrants that you did not put up a fight because it would only make matters worse. If they arrested you then you let them take you where they wanted until they shipped you back home. After you landed, you just turned around and walked through the desert again. He had just signed a one-year lease, however, and he wasn't one to shirk his obligations. She was screaming at him, holding him, a fat girl coming along behind her, then he found her kissing him on the face and, although he wasn't sure, he suspected that this was not the way that they arrested you in the United States of America.

"Mitzi, this is Chicken John! Mitzi! We've found him!"

Mitzi was very excited about this. Now that Tradd was gone, she was back on the market, and although Savannah's brother had to be very old given the fact that he had fought in the Vietnam War, he was still advertised as being extremely handsome, which hopefully would make up for the age difference. She ran as fast as she could, squinting through her glasses which had become fogged by the humidity, and when she reached Savannah and her brother, she took them off, wiped them on the hem of her dress, then placed them back on, in doing so receiving her first glimpse of the man she would one day marry.

The contrast between Savannah and Chicken John made it clear to Mitzi that while the two might have possibly shared a mother, they certainly had not been sired by the same man. She tried to be excited, or at least to share Savannah's excitement, but it was difficult for her to do so. Savannah had joined Mitzi's hands with Chicken John's and the two kept them in this manner, looking at each other, both with wild bewilderment. To Mitzi, Chicken John looked like the Mexicans who used to work on her grandfather's farm. Mitzi had been warned about this race of people and had certainly never touched one before.

"My brother! My long-lost brother! We've found him!"

"How do you do," said Mitzi.

Chicken John did not respond, but he did finally smile.

"Come, come, Chicken John. We've got so much to talk about. I've waited years for this moment. Now you let go of Mitzi. There'll be plenty of time for the two of you to fall in love, but for now, we need to tell each other stories that we've forgotten and laugh and be sarcastic with each other. How are you, you blood blistered Kotex?"

A brief explanation is necessary to allow the reader to understand how Savannah could make such a huge blunder. In her books of Southern lore there were two classes of people: whites and blacks. To be anything else was to be a Martian or some kind of animal. The thought of a Mexican actually appearing in a Southern tome was unthinkable, so given the fact that it was unthinkable, Savannah simply made him Caucasian, which he was not. He was not black, that was certain, but the only way he would ever become sandy-haired was if he tripped and fell at the beach. (I know. I know.)

She had her arm over his shoulder, her mouth opening and shutting at a manic pace, shouting, and laughing, a skip in her step as they moved along, Mitzi acting as the caboose of their train. Alonso had not said a word, nor did he plan on speaking. His English skills were abysmal, and he communicated with the natives largely with hand gestures and nods of the head. The locals did have a firm grasp of "si" and "no" so he was not afraid to let go of those two when the situation called for it, but otherwise he kept his words to himself and let them babble along.

They had reached King Street, and turned to walk down it, the stores lazily beginning the day, the restaurants preparing for the German tourists.

"Are you sure he talks?" asked Mitzi. "At least English?"

"Of course, he talks, you idiot," said Savannah. "I grew up talking to him and he doesn't appear to have lost his tongue in the war. The Vietnam War."

"Savannah, he just doesn't look he's your brother. He looks like he's Mexican, and I didn't want to say anything about that, he might have been adopted for all I know, but he just doesn't look like he's your brother. That's all I'm saying."

Savannah stopped and turned around to face Mitzi. Alonso did the same.

"You listen here, you mildewing urine sample. Do you think I'm such an ignoramus that I wouldn't recognize my own brother?"

"I'm just…"

"You are just an idiot, is what you are, Mitzi. He has been scarred, Mitzi. He has a federal warrant for his arrest hanging over his head right now. He has fought in the war. The Vietnam War. He has just seen his sister for the first time in almost a decade. How do you expect him to act?"

"He could at least say your name. I mean, I don't think he understands a word we're saying. He just stands there smiling at us like he's been klonked over the head."

"Oh, so you want him to say my name? Is that it?"

"That would be a nice start."

Savannah turned to Chicken John.

"Savannah," she said, pointing to herself. When he did not reply, she tried again, this time using both hands to point to herself.

A light clicked on in Alonso's brain, and he let out an even larger smile.

"Sabana?" he asked…

"Did you hear that!" Savannah screamed. "Did you hear that! How do you feel about yourself now, Mitzi?"

"Sabana," he said, laughing along with his supposed sister, "como una sabana!" With these words he acted like he was tucking himself in bed, rolling his head over to a shoulder and closing his eyes.

Savannah seemed to remember that this was one of the things that they always did when they were growing up, so she too tucked herself in and closed her eyes, afterwards laughing along with Alonso.

"I don't know how I feel," said Mitzi, who found herself once again confused. Surely, as Savannah had pointed out, she knew who her brother was. That did not seem like something that one casually forgot. With that said, the man was a Mexican, and he even spoke Spanish. How he could be from another country and still be Savannah's brother was simply a mystery. A mystery that she feared she would not soon solve. "I just don't understand how your brother is a Mexican."

"He is not a Mexican," Savannah shouted.

"Mexicano. Si, Mexicano," said Alonso with grave seriousness.

Mitzi and Savannah shared a gaze.

"Mitzi, don't you realize? Don't you?"

"No."

"He's undercover. It's just like Jordan in *Beach Music*. He's pretending to be a Mexican so that they won't find him. He disguises his voice and his appearance so that he won't have to go to jail."

"Oh," said Mitzi, everything suddenly making sense, although she had no idea who Jordan was.

"Yes! Yes! That's it. He's disguising himself. Right, amigo?"

"Si, estamos amigos."

At this point, Alonso Quijano did not know what was happening to him, or at least he had the wrong impression. He had a wife back in Mexico, but he had not seen her in several years. This produced hardships on a man, and although he considered himself a staunch Catholic, his understanding of its prohibitions was limited, leaving a prostitute feast as an acceptable way of blowing off steam and keeping in shape for the marital bed. He had heard of women walking the streets in Charleston, but had never seen them in this part of downtown, and usually he stuck with the gals who hung out at the taqueria. He feared that, in this screwed up country, white women, even of this poor quality, would somehow be more expensive and he was not sure that he had enough money on him to fund an orgy. If they were even prostitutes. But they had kissed him and held his hand, and they were leading him away somewhere. Any doubts were brushed away when the skinny one did what she did next.

Savannah was hungry and she could think of no better way to spend the afternoon than going to a restaurant and talking about her past with her brother over a bourbon or two. There they would finally relive the painful events of their childhood and she would eventually cry for the first time in her life. The only better ending would be if he somehow died during the process, and given that they were in the low country, this was not as unlikely as one would expect. She therefore asked Alonso if he had any money, smiling, rubbing her fingers and thumbs together, finally reaching into his back pocket and grabbing his wallet. Alonso watched this, and when Savannah gave Mitzi the thumbs up, he knew that he was in business. He would need to buy some condoms and some sanitary wipes, as these women were obviously ridden with disease, but given his recent spate of bad luck, it was a risk that he felt worth taking.

Mitzi watched his smile grow as Savannah handed him back his wallet, and could not help but notice his awkward excitement, which he rubbed for a moment as he leered down at her backside.

SEVENTY-NINE

He had not gone to see Scott. Today had been the day, but as the day progressed it became apparent that it definitely wasn't. There was something about a certain day being the day, that something being that it never was, which pushed it off to tomorrow being the day, and he began to suspect that tomorrow wouldn't have much of the day feel to it either. It wasn't like Scott was going anywhere, if we are to be honest about the situation, and no harm lay in the possibility—or make that a probability—of someone else eventually checking out the strange smell in good old 7-E. Creighton might be questioned, he might even tell the truth, but nothing was going to change the fact that Scott was no more and Creighton had had nothing to do with it. The effect of him announcing the news or the apartment manager appearing live and in color at six o'clock was less than zero. (Pynchon?)

One o'clock became two o'clock, which rushed right into three. At this hour the habit of eating combined with the appearance of hunger to make lunch a good idea. He dragged himself off the vinyl of the couch and stumbled into the kitchen. There he noticed three dead cockroaches on the floor, all lying supine, one giving leg twitches sent by its dead cockroach brain. He had never seen a live cockroach on its back before, and he wondered how they made the flip—was it some nerve reflex given in the throes of death, or did they turn once life made its exit and their bodies shriveled to tip them over? Or perhaps, just perhaps, were they touched by art at the end, and dying on their backs was the most dramatic way? It is never good to see cockroaches in your kitchen, but he had learned from a man smelling strongly of poisonous chemicals and cigarette smoke that if you had to see them it was better to find them dead than alive. At least then you knew that your exterminator was doing his job.

He would have to include that in his next book, something people could apply to their lives. A bit of wisdom. A touch of know-how. The nonfiction market was currently burying the fiction, and the consensus was that people really didn't want to escape through books. Those left who actually read, and this number dwindled by the minute, were serious-minded guys and gals who desired to improve themselves, and not in an artistic, soul-enhancing manner, but with information that they could directly apply to their lives. They wanted to know how to lose weight and cure their cancer and teach their dogs and raise their children, and if they ever found a wild hair growing out of their asses, they dove into what Hitler was up to in June of 1943 or why Truman's haberdasher business failed so that they could have something to discuss over a business lunch other than the latest movie or television show. But if one—and in this case the one would be Creighton—could somehow combine this raving desire for esoteric facts with great prose and inner thought, then a bestseller was only a few keystrokes away. Which meant learning some facts. You couldn't read an encyclopedia to do this, however. You needed to go out and get a job as an exterminator so that you could talk about the details of the craft and have your characters say things like, "If you gotta see 'em, it's better to see 'em dead than alive. Least that aways you know your exterminator's doin' his job." The Ken Kesey method. The Hemingway method. Only this posed one major problem: you had to get a job. A real job. One that made you be there at nine and only allowed you to leave when the clock struck five. One where you sweated and lifted and strained, where you earned just above minimum wage and put yourself in harm's way, one where you had to deal with the type of people who could do no better than find jobs like this. And such a job, to be honest, was unacceptable to Creighton.

With a socked toe, he pushed the cockroaches to the side and opened the refrigerator door. The lightbulb inside had died some time ago, leaving a cool darkness that somehow reminded him of a pleasant death. On the shelves lay several testaments to his bachelorhood. Ketchup did not need to be refrigerated, but here it was, next to mustard and mayonnaise, all containers full, the fruits of his first venture to the grocery store after his release. A man needed condiments, and he had bought them, but it appeared that this man didn't need them so much. A jar half-filled with pickles lurked in the shadows. A partially eaten loaf of bread, aged beyond perfection and to the point of petrification, hid in a black corner next to a bag of potato chips. The only thing to drink was a pitcher of water. There was nothing else.

He retrieved his head from inside and shut the door. He knew that he did not have anything in the kitchen pantry and the thought of getting dressed again and driving somewhere to buy food filled him with psychic pain. The option of ordering something—pizza, Chinese—was always there, but his wallet was empty, and he had misplaced his only credit card at a comic book store last week and had yet to drop by and pick it up, notwithstanding the four phone messages asking him to do so.

Since he was a man of the mind, he decided to fast for the day, sharpen the intellect with a little denial and lose a few pounds in the process. So, he sat back down on the couch and reacquainted himself with the television. His stomach gurgled. He could think of nothing but food. He began to feel lightheaded. Still, he did not stir.

If there had been anything on television to watch, then he would have probably made it, but there wasn't. He had the full cable package, even a number of sports channels that he didn't use, but each show, brought to him with the press of a thumb, offered nothing but torture. Movies that he had seen before and disliked. Lawyers and politicians talking to other lawyers and politicians. News of famine and flood. Cartoons stolen from the Japanese. Cooking shows. Why was there even a need for entertainment? It seemed like it should be enough just to be alive. You breathed and you passed your waste and you ate and you drank, and when you felt like it, you lay down and closed your eyes for a bit. The days could go by so easily, without a thought of how badly your life was progressing in comparison to those you saw and read about, their lives filled with sexual couplings and shopping sprees, yours filled with asexual wanderings and alcoholic debris. If you never knew about these other things, and all that you learned and understood were the basic functionings of your self, then how could you feel envy, failure, longing, desire? He was beginning to think of a possible book topic concerning a hermit, when a wave of light-headedness crashed over his bow. He had to do something, or he would soon be as miserable as he ever had been. It was at this point that he thought of Scott's refrigerator idly humming next door, filled with bagels and sodas and numerous other things that he could shove down his throat and grant him the peace that was the only thing he ever wanted.

He did not knock on the door, but he did consider it, thinking that it would look suspicious if he just walked in, like he knew that Scott was dead, but then he decided that if so confronted he would tell the interrogator that he and Scott were best of friends and had a sort of mi-casa-es-su-casa type of relationship, thereby dispelling any suspicions and making him the head eulogizer at the funeral.

It became apparent when he entered that there was no need for such strategy. No one had set foot in the place since Creighton had left it. Scott remained underneath the shower curtain, over which hovered only a couple of flies; his corpse carried no smell. As Creighton suspected, and he suspected because he knew, the refrigerator was filled with food. It was not good food, the deceased apparently no epicurean, but it was food, and given Creighton's hunger, it was food good enough for him. He pulled out the remaining bagels, poured himself a Coke, and carried it all with him to the couch along with a cold jar of spaghetti sauce. It was not an obvious choice, but Creighton did not go for the obvious, as was obvious to anyone who had ever read *Finding It All in the Hole*, but a wonderful treat was to eat bread dipped in cold spaghetti sauce.

As he ate, his hunger melted away, but instead of this making him feel better, it made him feel worse. The problem with focusing on the self was that the self was unmistakably depressing. If you could only eat once in a lifetime and be done with it, then that would be one thing, but to have to do it over and over again, to have to move it through your body every single day, to have to wash it off of you in the shower, to cut the beard that it grew, to clip the nails that it sprouted, was the fate of Sisyphus. No one ever knew what Sisyphus thought about as he did the same thing each day, but they did know it was hell, and who were we if we weren't him? Granted, eating was not backbreaking work, some people even enjoyed it, but the principle was the same. Chew, chew, chew, he began saying to himself internally. Swallow. Drink. Take a bite. Chew, chew, chew. And he would have to do it again that night. And the following morning. And then every six or so hours for the rest of his days.

He placed the half-eaten bagel on the table in front of him, leaving a smear of red on its glass top. This was what art was for. You couldn't live without it. He needed to read or watch something. As it just so happened, he had carried his copy of *Lowcountry Lamentations* with him, and from it he began to read as follows:

```
My family fell apart after Roy did what he did
to Chicken John. My fatehr sided with Roy and
my mother had left my father to live with a very
rich man who had once slapped me across the face
and she said that I couldn't talk abut ti becu-
ase southern people didn't talk about things like
one brother selling out his other brother to the
federal government for a pile of money. Soutern-
ers didn't talk about things like that and my
family was southern to the core even though my
father had grown up in Chicago and thought that
```

the Battle Hymn of the Republic was better than
Dixie.

Jonathan finally filed for divorce and I began
to see a psychiatrist because Chicken John had
been to see him and he needed me to help him
understand how Chicken John could have gotten
the way that he had gotten with him being crazy
and all and blowing up trains ran by the federal
government.

He had Auburn hair and was over six feet tall
and very sexy if I say so myself! He wore glasses
but the kind of glasses that make a man look like
he's smart. He had gone to Harvard and had read a
few papers that I had written on psychiatry when
I was up at Harvard and he knew about my poetry
and had all of my poetry books in his office and I
later learned that he was my biggest fan.

I went into his office and I wanted to let him
know fast and quick that I didn't think much of
"shrikns." "You won't be getting much out of me
doctor. That's not the southern way." I scoffed
"Oh and pretell me what the southern way is?" he
queried. "Well there's a whole list of things
doctor. I could start that a southerner doesn't
cry. I could tell you that a southerner doesn't
talk about thigns like rape. I could tell you
that a southerner is always sarcastic and laughs
but that he's that way because he can't cry."
I responded. "Are you a southerner Savannah?"
he questioned. "Doctor I went through the Citadel and was hazed by the best southern boys in
the world. I was a star football palyer in high-
school. I can catch shrimp and mull gravy until
the moon sets over Orion. I will tell you that

I hate my parents and then twenty seconds later I'll tell you that I love them. I am a south-erner." I answered. "That's crazy! All of those things are just crazy! You are so different and interesting that I just don't understand you!" he exclaimed. "To understand me I would have to cut open an oyster and let you taste it and then I would say to you, here taste this. This is the taste of my childhood." I replied. "Cut open an oyster! I've never heard of anything like that before!" "That's because you're not south-ern docotr! I'm telling you I came from the most messed up family in the entire world. My motehr was the prettiest woman to ever walk the face of the earth and my father was the meanest man to ever walk the face of the earth. And w'ere Catho-lic to boot! Do you know what its like growing up catholic in the south doctor?" I asked. "No." He answered. "It's crazy." I replied.

Our sessions went on and on and sometimes we would go out and get something to eat together and I would make funny comments like pigs anus a tartare and he would think it was funny but he wouldnt't say it was funny because he didn't understand the southern way. He had a son who wanted to play football and I taught him how to play football in exchange for my "time" with the doctor. He was not very good at football but could play the "cello" like you've never seen! I told him that he better get his act together or I would rough him up on the football field and he accused me of being a fake and I knew that it was true.

While I was up in New York City I missed being
home where my family was and my southern routes
were. I missed the marsh and the swamp and the
ocean. I missed eating good collard greens and
fatback and I missed fishing. I knew that one day
I had to return and see my children again and
try to repair all of the damage that I had done
but for now I knew that I had to help out the
"doctor" with chicken John and help him understand the things that even Chicken John couldn't
understand because he was southern and "messsed
up" like the rest of us.

When it came time for me to leave I asked the
doctor if he would take me up to his cabin in
the woods and he did and while we were there the
sexual tension that had been building during our
"sessions" finally came to a boiling point and we
began to make love like our bodies melded into
one. As we annealed with our bodies we looked
into each others eyes and although I came from a
lowcountry background and he was from New York
City we understood the others soul while we made
love.

But it couldn't last because I had to get
back. Chicken John was better since I had cleared
up so many stories for the doctor and my children
needed me. I would return and anneal the bonds
that had broken between me and Jonathan and we
would learn to

Someone had knocked at the door. Creighton put the book down
and placed his feet on the floor, his body hovering over his knees,
sweat immediately forming a sheen on his brow. The knock came
again, along with the words, "Mr. Starke? Mr. Starke? You in there?"

EIGHTY

Few people can handle vacationing alone, and the few who can handle it are the same people who can go to bars, restaurants, and movies by themselves. They are not horribly unlike the rest of us, but they are unquestionably different. A bit more fearless, a bit more confident, lacking introspection perhaps, but to be envied, nonetheless. As Roy approached the ferry for Fort Sumter, he realized that he was not one of them. He did many things alone, but these were done in private, acts unavailable to the peering eye, acts committed without the merest chance of being whispered about. When it dawned on him that he would have to stand on the ferry by himself and then walk around the fort all alone, he decided that finding Erica at Fort Sumter probably wasn't the greatest idea. The best way to handle the situation, to cross it off of his list, would be to wait until the group ahead of the one waiting to go came back. When that happened he could see if Erica was in the crowd, and if she wasn't, then he could leave.

He tired of waiting after ten minutes and simply drove off. He was hungry and one did not think well on an empty stomach.

Lack of sleep had carried away many of his delusions. The attitude of certain triumph, the knowledge that he would succeed, had finally fallen into clear light and he felt himself an ant on a teeming anthill, looking for another ant, tired of all of this ant business, and waiting for the human foot to come and pulverize him into dust. Without the internet he was alone and ignorant. Without the post-

385

ers with Erica's picture on them, luck would never come his way. She had probably already called home. Or she was probably already home, the search-and-rescue mission changing its subject during the night. He should call his parents. Nothing good could come of it—either news of Erica's reappearance or insults from his father—but there was no sense in his wasting time down in Charleston when all was apparently lost.

He pulled over at a gas station and searched the van for quarters, finding a handful. The phone was located on the side of the station, next to a vagrant who immediately began harassing him for money. Usually, Roy would simply say that he had none, and he could say this without lying, but the palm filled with coins made such a statement an absurdity.

"Maybe when I get done," he said.

"Who you callin'?"

"My folks."

"Tell 'em I said hello."

"Sure."

The quarters entered the machine, and the numbers were dialed. Roy waited as it rang throughout the house in his nameless hometown and listened to the voice of his mother repeat the number that he had called with instructions for him to leave a message.

"Mom, Dad, it's Roy. I'm in Charleston. I haven't found Erica yet, but I'm looking. Um. I'm okay. I'm a little tired and it's hot. Um. I guess I'll try you later?"

He hung up the phone and both he and the vagrant looked at the remaining change in his hand.

"I'll need to call again."

"Well, go ahead. Call 'em. Tell 'em I said hello."

"Um. I probably need to call them later. No one was home."

"Oh. Well, you gonna need all that money to call 'em again, huh?"

"Probably so. I'm sorry. Um. But here's a quarter."

EIGHTY-ONE

Although Mr. Edwards had no room to do so, given the fact that he was asking them to drop the charges against his daughter in exchange for the paying of the bill, through threats and cajolery he got the owners of Gubba Bump Shrimp House to write off the cost of the bourbon drinks, as his daughter and her companion, whom everyone described as being plain and fat, had not reached the legal age to purchase alcohol. Negotiations completed, he pulled out his wallet and paid, even leaving a five-dollar tip for the jilted waitress. He noticed blood on the concrete when he left but did not think much of it other than the fact that it was there.

With his wife sitting in the running car, air conditioning pumping out in cubic feet to console her, he walked down the way and entered the market. He had no idea where the Confederate pride store was but felt sure that it would not be difficult to find. He did not want to ask anyone for directions. He feared the anger that bubbled in his chest and knew that he should only talk as much as was necessary.

The same man was there who had been working the day before. On a table in the corner lay stacked all of the items that had been destroyed by Erica and her friend. It stood about two feet high and from a metal stand hung a sign that advertised the fact that the items were damaged and thus half off.

"You shoulda seen her," said the clerk. "She was just plain crazy. Coulda killed somebody. Coulda killed me."

"And that would have been a tragedy," said Mr. Edwards. "Have you calculated how much the damage was?"

"Oh, it's a lot. This stuff ain't cheap."

"And how would you define 'a lot.'"

"A whole bunch."

"Let me be clearer with you. Exactly how much, to the penny, were the damages?"

The number was given, and Mr. Edwards shook his head in the negative.

"Maybe if you weren't still selling everything, then maybe that would be a fair price, but it wouldn't be fair for someone to pay the full price and then you go sell it off for half-price, now, would it? That way you'd be making fifty percent more than you normally would."

"Hell, you pay full price, and you can have it. Take it home with ya."

"Although I have always wanted a Johnny Reb outfit, I will have to hold back on that today. I'll pay you half. That's what you're asking for now anyway."

"Half? Well shit, sir. That don't take inta account all the cleaning up we had to do, and it certainly don't take inta consideration the mental anguish I went through sittin' here thinkin' that I was gonna be run through with a saber that's as bout a fine a replica as you can buy. And how about them other folks in here? One fella got his toes mashed and one got his head busted open when one of them statutes fell off a shelf. No sir. Half ain't gonna cut it."

"You will take half for the merchandise, and we will be done," said Mr. Edwards, his angry eyes staring into those of the clerk. "As for you and your mental anguish and the Yankees who got their toes mashed, all of you can sue my little darling for all that she's worth. Of course, she isn't worth anything, but that's beside the point."

The clerk allowed his shoulders to droop and said he would have to make a call.

With two full releases in hand, Harry Edwards walked back to the car. His wife had not brought along anything to read, and he felt sure that she had not turned on the radio, which meant that she was sitting there in silence, staring into space. For the first time in many years, he wished that she would take up the arts again, to try her hand at painting and photography, to read the poetry books and the tomes on how to get started in the publishing industry. Because although those were not good days—there had been very few good days—they were better than what he had now, which was someone who could not entertain herself. One thing he had learned in life was that stress entered in no matter what you did. It was an element of the human condition. Whether one was the president of the United States or the bag boy at a supermarket, each hit the bed after a day of work, tired from the pressures that the previous hours had brought and worried about those that the following morning would bring. A problem arose, however, when you placed the bag boy and the president in the same space and had the bag boy complain to the president for a few hours every night about how trying his job was. The president, although a kind soul born with a sympathetic ear, would politely listen to these grousings, the entire time secretly filled with contempt because a clean-up on aisle seven did not measure up to the latest threat of nuclear proliferation. While this was not a perfect analogy for what took place between Harry Edwards and his wife, there were similarities. It had placed the family in court and the children in child services, but her art had allowed him peaceful evenings and a quiet bed. And now that so many years had passed and perspective was achieved, his children in child protective services probably hadn't been that bad of an idea after all. They could hardly have done worse.

"What took you so long?" Mrs. Edwards asked.

"Nothing other than tying up two of the claims against Erica. I got releases. They can't sue her and they've agreed to drop the charges. Now we've just got to take care of all of those cars. We need to get to the hotel and call up our insurance agent and let him know what happened."

"Well, I've been sitting here waiting on you. It's hot."

"Indeed, it is."

EIGHTY-TWO

Roy drove back to Charleston. There were no clouds in the sky and the sun came down unhindered in a thunder of rays. It heated everything that was visible, melting the remnants of a candy bar on the floorboard into a chocolate paste. Roy was unsure of what his next step should be. He needed lunch, and he had grown tired of fast-food. He no longer hungered for hamburgers and fried chicken. He did not think he could eat another French fry.

Getting in shape had been a constant thought of his, and perhaps now was the time. But he was not going to merely get into shape, he would move past that point and keep on going. He thought of himself eating nothing other than organic foods and taking mouthfuls of vitamin supplements. He would arise at four o'clock every morning and go for a run, afterwards hitting the pool for countless laps. After work, at a new job where he only clocked in from nine until five, he would study kendo, judo, and karate, just to make sure that he had all of his bases covered, and then at night, when the rest of the world was counting off an hour or two before bed by watching television, he would hit the weight room. Within six months he would be a new man. Within a year he would be a new kind of man, part assassin, part nightclub bouncer. In his spare time, he would learn a foreign language or two and study exotic disciplines like poison making/detection and assault weaponry. He would gather together a full understanding of the customs of tribes and clans all across the globe and incorporate these teachings into his life. When it was all done, and he saw no reason why he shouldn't be able to accomplish this within three years, he would present himself to a special services branch in Washington, D.C., and let them assign him to missions where a man of his brawn and intellect could be of use in America's fight for freedom.

Roy felt himself sit up higher in the seat of his van and flex his grip on the wheel. He would not want to kill, but he knew that he would have to, and he also knew that while these deaths would haunt him, they would do so with the pure haunting of something that had had to be done for a greater good. His belly sat heavily on top of his belt and he sucked it in and held it there until he no longer could. It would not be long before that was gone. As to how this would affect his life, it would replace aimlessness with a purpose, fatigue with the ability to walk through brick walls. He already had the computer experience to make it in today's army, and that really was half the battle. The body could always be remade, the intellect had to have the organic foundation along with a lifetime of constant vigilance.

Back in Charleston, already imagining himself to have grown six inches in height and to have placed sixty pounds of muscle on his skeleton, Roy looked for a place to eat that would signify the sharp turn he had taken off his previous path. There were a number of restaurants in Charleston, but to him they spoke of grease and fat, not the fuel a Charles Atlas placed in his system. He drove around for a while, stopped in traffic, turning and returning, until he finally saw a shop that sold burritos. Beans and rice would do the trick.

The order came out in tinfoil, warm to the touch and as heavy as a brick. In order for the purification to begin, he had decided, this would need to be the only meal he would eat today. If he became hungry tonight, he would drink bottled water and wash down the vitamins he planned on buying once he was done with his burrito. So this needed to be enjoyed. He needed to consume every bite of it and lick up every trace of juice, for when he was in the deserts of Afghanistan, food would not be readily available, and a man would need to gird himself for the long trek with his Bedouin allies.

It was unquestionably the most intense meal Roy Edwards had ever eaten in his life. His face frowned. His shoulders stood pulled back behind his chest. His feet sat flat on the floor with calf muscles flexed. His eyes, while directed at the burrito in front of him, focused on the surrounding people, preparing himself for the day when someone would try to pick him off with a poisoned dart in a Middle Eastern bazaar. It was because of this focus that he knew that three people had just entered the restaurant, two women and a man. The man had a dark complexion, the women were white. None of them was a target and he was prepared to train his thoughts on the couple sitting to his left, when he heard the voice of one of the women. Its sound sent a shiver down his spine.

Roy swung his eyes over to the left and saw his sister. She appeared haggard and bruised. Red blotches covered her skin. Her hair was dirty as were her feet and hands. She was talking about possum fat.

His initial reaction was to get up from his stool and go to her, but as he was enacting discipline these days, he drew this back in and thought for a moment. She was delusional. He had known this for some time but had tried to counteract her insanity by forcefully pointing it out to her; this had failed. If he were to convince her, to get her out of Charleston and take her back home, then the only way to do this was to play along with her game, to become a character in the wild screenplay that scrolled throughout her head.

He stood and turned himself so that he faced her. She was trying to order a Hoppin' John burrito. The Mexican had out his wallet and was apparently going to pay for her. Roy had never seen him before, and he steeled himself for the inevitable knife fight underneath a neon sign in the dark of night. He stepped forward and cleared his throat. Erica looked up at him and stopped herself in mid-sentence. She reached out and grabbed the arm of the fat girl who stood by her, to which the girl asked what was wrong. "Roy," Erica said. All eyes turned to Roy Edwards.

"Savannah," he said, "you've got to come with me. Father's plane just went down in the swamp, and it appears that the mayor has once again forced himself upon our mother."

EIGHTY-THREE

No one grows up wanting to become a process server. But if you think about it, almost no one ends up being what they wanted to be as a child. The dreams of hauling garbage. The summer-long fantasies of putting together tax returns. So, if you have grown up wanting to be something and have actually become that something, then you should consider yourself lucky, although you have to wonder about life-planning as a child, the tender age which is so full of idiocies that one's decisions are not legally enforceable.

So being employed as a legal process server is one of those things, like losing an arm, that simply happens to you. You are out of work, looking for something to put money in your wallet and fill your empty days, and someone suggests it to you or offers it to you, and you do it because it is there. Ford Madox Ford—no relation to the author, his parents weren't even aware of the author and remain unaware of the author, as does Ford himself—had much greater dreams as a young man. The Marines was something for him, as was the police. He did not come from a family where anyone encouraged the legal or medical fields, and no one had ever suggested that he would one day become president of the United States, or even a member of county council. He thought little of desks and found reading far from joyous. He liked guns and movies that contained lots of guns. He liked driving cars and smoking cigarettes. He would not wear a tie, even to church. His goal was to get married, which he had done, have children, which he had done, and one day retire, which he had yet to do. He had never wanted to be a process server.

But he was one, and not a bad one. He could knock on doors and hand over papers with the best of them. He did not mind waiting for someone to show up at the job or come home from work. His greatest attribute, however, was how seriously he took his profession. Like most of us, he existed with many self-deceptions, and his were such that he imagined that one day he would get his own company of process servers, which would lead to private investigation work, which would lead to security for major corporations, which would lead to him as head of the Federal Bureau of Investigations. With this said, he did not simply hand out the court papers, he made himself part of the case. And it so turned out that his greatest attribute proved to be his greatest negative. The attorneys who sent him out on rote assignments had no desire to hear a thirty-minute description of what the Defendant was wearing or what was in the gentleman's trash can. They did not appreciate Ford showing up at the office with demands to be seen, only to explain in great detail the numerous steps he had taken to get the job done.

He was suspicious of everyone and saw conspiracy in the most harmless of coincidences, the most meaningless of gestures. And this was the man who stood outside the door when Creighton opened it.

"Um. Hello," said Creighton, red flecks of spaghetti sauce decorating his academic beard. "What can I do for you?"

The man on the other side of the door looked like some sort of law enforcement officer. His hair was cut short, his mustache neatly trimmed, the glasses resting on his nose mirrored and clean. His clothes were neatly pressed, and his belt held numerous items in small leather pouches that snapped. He gave off a kind of redneck strength—nothing apparent by way of muscles, but one somehow knew that he could gnaw his way out of a wire cage.

"You Creighton Starke?" asked Ford Madox Ford. "Of apartment 7-D?" With that, he looked up at the door and saw that it was in fact 7-E, and as he began to apologize for the error, he heard something that told him all was not right.

"Yes, that's me," said Creighton. "I'm Creighton Starke." Creighton stood in the doorway, sweating like a man in the hotbox, wearing his food and dressed in a filthy bathrobe with mismatched flip-flops. He was doing his best to be charming, the gracious smile, the friendly eyes, the helpful voice, but given that panic had seized him whole, the smile appeared manic, the eyes filled with lunacy, the voice quavering like a confession given from the rack. "How do you do? Well, I hope."

"Yeah, yeah, I'm good," said Ford Madox Ford. He tried to look into the apartment, shooting his glance through the open space between Creighton's head and the door, and was not surprised to see Creighton inch his skull over to block it.

"I can't tell you how glad I am to hear that. We should all be happy. Just to be alive, you know?"

Ford Madox Ford did not reply.

"You must be here for an autograph or something, huh? You've read *Finding It All in the Hole* and you've somehow hunted me down. How am I? Close?"

Ford Madox Ford stared Creighton clean in the face. "Yeah, that's partly it. You mind if I come in for a second?"

"Come in?" asked Creighton. "Here? Oh, no. Can't do that today. Place is a mess. But I'll be happy to come out and talk to you, or we can just stand here, and I can talk to you, whichever you prefer. Now about the book, what did you think of Osgood? Hm? You know, from page two hundred on he really wrote the book, not me. He was the one who told me what to say and I said it. Incredible, really. If you think about it."

Ford Madox Ford had risen to his tiptoes, stretching his neck out and looking back into the apartment. This, needless to say, made Creighton very nervous.

"Please stop doing that," he said.

"What you got in there?" Ford Madox Ford asked.

"Nothing! Jeez, nothing. I already told you, the place is a wreck. Jeez."

"Um-hm. Well, tell me this, Mr. Starke: Why are you in apartment 7-E, trying to keep me from coming in, when you live in apartment 7-D?"

Never before had the creative drought so directly affected Creighton Starke. It had ruined his marriage, destroyed his ego, made him a laughingstock, separated him from his only child, caused him innumerable sleepless nights, but this was his own undoing, his self-created ruination. He stammered, he yawed, if one can verbally yaw, he began with one line of explanation, thought better of it, moved onto another one, then back to the first one, only to think of a third that after a few sentences needed to be edited itself.

Ford Madox Ford stood still and listened until Creighton wore himself out and fell quiet. He did not know what was in there, whether the man was a pedophile or a panty sniffer or liked giving tea parties with stuffed animals as guests, but he did know that he aimed to find out. With Creighton deflated before him, his shoulders slumped and wind chugging out of his throat, Ford Madox Ford gave the author of *Finding It All in the Hole* a push to the side and walked on in.

EIGHTY-FOUR

"Oh, I knew this would happen!" shouted Savannah with a fearful cry. "We will search for him, Roy, we will go out in our boats and search for him, but word will come and the man who is driving my boat will turn to me and say, 'Son, today is the day you become a man. Your father's dead.' And as for mother, she will stay with the mayor and they will move our ancestral home after they sell our land to the nuclear power people, and one day he will slap me and tell me that I'm white trash. Oh, Chicken John! Chicken John! The glorious day of your return has been blackened by unforeseen events!"

Alonso understood none of these words, but the tone of the voice, matched with the effect the white man appeared to have on the prettier of the two prostitutes made him assume that this was their pimp and that he was not happy. He wanted to assure the man that he would pay, he was even buying them a meal, so he held out his open wallet to show Roy that he expected nothing for free.

"Oh, Savannah," said Mitzi, putting an arm over the stricken shoulder, "I'm so sorry." Mitzi, who, if nothing else, was a tender-hearted soul, began to cry with empathy. "Just take some deep breaths. It isn't your fault. The plane just went down."

"Chicken John," cried Savannah, who threw herself at the man, lost in tears.

"This is Chicken John?" Roy asked.

"Of course, it's Chicken John," said Savannah. "Don't you recognize your own brother?"

Roy looked at him for a moment. "Ah, now I do. He's just changed a lot."

"Because of the war," said Savannah.

"Yeah, the war," said Roy.

"Is everything all right here?" asked the man behind the counter. "'Cause I need you people to keep it down and move along. I'm trying to run a business."

"Her father just died, you asshole!" Mitzi shouted at him. "And she just found her brother who had been missing since the war."

"The Vietnam War," said Savannah.

The man appeared to take offense at being called an asshole, or at least one would assume so given his expression, and he moved off to the back of the restaurant all in a huff. But this was only part of it. He did not think much of Mexicans, an irony lost on him as a burrito salesman, and thought even less of homeless people, as these two girls clearly were, and he certainly wasn't going to take any grief from either sect. If they wouldn't move along peacefully, then the police would move them along with force.

"Should we sit down?" Roy asked. "Um. I'm eating a burrito."

"Burrito," said Alonso.

"Yeah, come on, Chicken John. It's so good to have my brother back again."

They found a table and the four of them sat, Mitzi and Roy on one side, Chicken John and Savannah on the other. Savannah's crying came to a quick halt, and she stared at Roy across the table, waiting for him to betray Chicken John in some shape or form, as he had done so many times before. Alonso did not know that he had previously been betrayed, or at least he had let bygones be bygones, amusing himself by eating the remainder of Roy's burrito, which was nowhere near to Mexican standards.

"So, I see you've found me," said Savannah.

"I had to, to tell you the news," said Roy. "I'm sorry to break it this way, but we've got to get back. They're burying Father this afternoon with full military honors. The entire state senate will be there. You're expected to read one of your wonderful poems."

"I will have to write one especially for the occasion in the car," said Savannah.

"Oh, good," said Mitzi. "We're going home."

"Oh, good, my father's dead! You miserable wretch!" Savannah cried. "Is this how you reward me, by celebrating in my time of grief?"

Due to Savannah and Mitzi's stink and the shoutings of all involved, a number of patrons had decided to take their burritos to go or had simply foregone eating. The owner of the shop, feeling the sting of this, shouted for Savannah to keep it down, and once again surveyed the front door, waiting for the police to arrive.

"I didn't mean that at all, Savannah. You know that. I just wasn't thinking."

"Well, that certainly wouldn't be a first for you, Mitzi."

"Mitzi, huh," said Roy. "I'm Savannah's brother, Roy."

"Don't get any ideas, Roy," said Savannah. "Mitzi's already promised to Chicken John." Savannah leaned over and kissed Alonso on his cheek. Alonso gave a sheepish smile to Roy.

"That's too bad," said Roy. "He's one lucky guy, that brother of mine."

"Thank God for that," said Savannah. "If it hadn't been for his luck he would have never made it out of Vietnam after you convinced him

402

to go there. He would have never escaped from the federal authorities after you ratted him out. He has luck, but thanks to you he's needed it just to survive. Look at him. The way he's eating that burrito it's obvious he hasn't had a morsel in days."

Roy did look at him. Alonso did not appear malnourished. If anything, he looked like he could afford to lose a few pounds. He ate the burrito in silence and without great vigor.

"So," said Roy, "about getting back. For our father's funeral."

"We mustn't cry, Roy. At the funeral, we mustn't cry. Father would have wanted it that way. He's taught us that since we were children. Whatever happens, and no matter how badly we want to, we cannot cry."

"Of course."

"Savannah says that she never cries but I've seen her cry at least twice in the past couple of days," said Mitzi. She then waggled her eyebrows and Roy could feel her fingers gently touching his naked leg. He looked at her as though he had suddenly discovered that she was criminally insane, and swatted her hand away.

"Shut up, Mitzi, you blood blistered urine sample," said Savannah. "You wouldn't know what crying is if Shadareen swooped down and stomped your haid. Yahn!"

"Keep it down over there!" shouted the owner of the burrito shop.

"No one around here understands Gullah. You don't understand it anymore, do you, Roy?"

"Um. No."

"So much has been forgotten. But now is the time that we sit around and talk about our past, and I tell you something, and then you tell me something, and then Chicken John tells us both something, and we weave it all together."

"Okay," said Roy. "I'm not sure where to begin."

"Why don't you try the beginning?" Mitzi asked.

"Shut up, Mitzi," said Savannah. "It would seem to me that I would need to start since Chicken John here is undercover and pretending to be a Mexican. I remember, Roy, how on the barrier island we named D'Bergeolet island that you betrayed Chicken John. I always wanted to ask you, what did you do with the money? Did you spend it, or like Judas, did you give it back to the government and then attempt to commit suicide?"

"Um. We really need to get going, don't you think?"

"Answer the question, Roy."

"I spent it and then attempted to commit suicide. I spent it on nice shoes."

"I see," said Savannah.

The police in Charleston, whatever their faults may have been, reacted quickly when it appeared that homeless people were overrunning burrito restaurants. The patrol car came racing toward its destination, its siren giving a whoop, and stopped in the middle of the road. The four sat and watched this take place, then Alonso, who considered himself in the middle of paying for sex and here without legal right, leapt up and began looking for he back door.

"Chicken John! Chicken John!" cried Savannah. She attempted to scoot out of the booth, but by the time she had reached the other side of the bench, Chicken John had raced the length of the restaurant and hit the door in stride. "Chicken John!"

Chicken John was once again gone. Vanished. Savannah looked over at Roy and at that moment she knew that her father was still alive and that her mother had once again fought off the advances of the mayor. There was a reason that Roy had found her, that he had waited until she had found Chicken John, and too many times she had simply allowed it to happen, mourning away while it took place, and never extracting revenge for the betrayal. She would sit idly by no more.

It is difficult to leap across the table while sitting in a booth, but somehow Savannah accomplished this. She grabbed Roy by the hair and did her best to separate follicle from scalp. With her teeth she bit deep into an ear and at that point, Roy, who was valiantly accepting the hair pulling, trying to push her off without hurting her, used restraint no longer. He punched his sister in the chest, and then connected with her chin, knocking the side of his head against her face, both of them screaming at the top of their lungs, lunging from side to side, pushing Mitzi against the wall to the point that she feared she had broken her pelvis.

It was in this fashion that Officer Frank Jamison found them. Not wanting to hurt anybody or himself, he maced all three, placed them under arrest, and hauled them out to his car. The burrito was left behind.

SEVERAL WEEKS LATER

EIGHTY-FIVE

The place smelled of cheap disinfectant splashed on top of ripe armpit. It was the kind of disinfectant that burns the eyes and throat and kills all organic matter, whether friend or foe. It was not pleasant. In fact, it was far from pleasant, so far from it that you couldn't even see it or imagine that such a state existed. A haphazard collection of furniture sat about on the floor, exhausted and dead, stuffing coming out in places, patches covering patches, covering patches. A television played from where it hung on a wall. The reception was poor and the programs it brought to life even poorer. Men mumbled to themselves. Women mumbled to themselves. Two bathrobed souls played checkers. No one carried on a conversation, there were just words, like paint on a modernist painting where you have to make your own meaning, as it is not given to you.

In such a bleak landscape, hope did not exist. A place for the condemned, for the despair-ridden, perhaps, but not for hope. Which is why it was so strange to see Creighton Starke sunk in a chair, smiling with such vigor that it appeared that any minute he would break out into a chuckle. He held a newspaper in front of him, folded to half-width and half-length, to all appearances reading it.

"Good morning, Professor Starke," came from behind him, and he placed the paper in his lap and tilted his head back, so that he looked at the speaker upside down.

"Savannah D'Bergeolet! My favorite student!"

"I can't say I'm Savannah anymore, Professor Starke. Doctor's orders. Um. These are my parents and my brother, and this is my friend, Mitzi."

Creighton literally climbed out of the chair, exiting from the back in dramatic fashion and landing on his feet before the group.

"Pleasure to meet you!" he said, taking Mr. Edwards's hand in both of his and bobbing it up and down. "The sweetest pleasure! The damnedest pleasure!" After this he took a moment or two to laugh.

"Professor Starke was my creative writing professor before all of this happened," said Erica. "He got a book published a few years ago."

"Oh," said Mrs. Edwards. "That's nice."

"A few years ago, yes, but let me tell you, that thing has legs. Legs, I tell you! Here. Look at this."

He pressed the newspaper into Mr. Edwards's chest, failing to notice that Mr. Edwards did not appreciate this.

"Read it. Seriously. Go ahead. Read it."

Mr. Edwards began reading the proffered section.

"No, out loud. Come on now, Savannah's father!" He again took a few moments to laugh.

Mr. Edwards cleared his throat. "The court ruled that Creighton Starke, a former writer-in-residence at the university and the author of *Finding It All in the Hole* has been found mentally competent to stand trial in the brutal murder of twenty-year-old Scott Freeman."

"See! You hear that! Author of *Finding It All in the Hole*! Free press! Free publicity! It's going to take off this time! You watch, Savannah! You watch! People love reading books about murderers, but they really love reading ones by murderers! I'm going to be the champ of a whole new genre!"

"That's great, Professor Starke," said Erica. "Wonderful," said Mr. Edwards. "Now let's move along, Erica. We don't want to bother the professor."

"You're not bothering me. Nothing could bother me."

The group began walking away.

"Think about it. All of this free publicity and I didn't even do it! I'm innocent! I'll be innocent and famous! What a great combo, huh?"

Mr. Edwards led his daughter by the arm to the end of the hallway. A gray door stood in front of them, and it was clear from their actions that it was a door that Erica could not go through. They stopped, all of them looking at anything but each other.

"Well," said Mr. Edwards.

"Thanks for coming by," said Erica. "I mean it. It really helps."

"Of course, darling," said Mrs. Edwards, who took her daughter in her arms and held her tightly. She began to cry, and Mr. Edwards could not help but fight back tears himself. "We'll come by whenever we can. You just get better, okay? Just get better."

"I will, Mom."

Mrs. Edwards released her, and Mr. Edwards followed in her trail, giving Erica a quick hug. "You let us know if you need anything, okay?"

"I will, Dad."

Roy did not follow up with another hug. "See ya, sis."

"Bye, Roy."

And then it was time for Mitzi. "I'm glad to see you're doing okay, Savannah, I mean Erica, and I'm sorry I believed you about Chicken John and all. And I'm sorry about messing up your book."

"Let's don't ever talk about any of that again," said Mr. Edwards.

"Yeah, Mitzi, let's just forget about that," said Erica.

"Sorry. I just… Well, you take care. Hopefully you'll be out soon."

"I know I will. I really don't know what happened to me, but I'm starting to figure it out and get back to reality."

"Good," said Mr. Edwards. "Good."

They said their remaining goodbyes and then were buzzed out by the electric lock, leaving Erica alone.

Savannah began walking back down the hall, and although none of the last thirty minutes could have been pleasant, she too had a smile on her face. She would never tell anyone, at least as long as she was there, but being locked up in a mental hospital was the best ending that she could have hoped for, aside, of course, from a death or a suicide. And the great thing about that was that there was still time for either of those to happen, because in the low country, where she no longer was, things like that were the rule, rather than the exception.

A NOTE ON THE TYPE

This book was set in Ashehoug. Designed by the Egmont Corporation by René Krolmar, the fonts are based on types first cut by Tycho Brahe (c. 1546-1601). Brahe was a pupil of Anderson Sorensen Vedel and is believed to have followed the Esbergian models, although he introduced a number of important differences, and it is to him we owe the comma we now know as "the devil's claw." He gave his letters a certain sadness and feeling of despair that won their creator an immediate reputation and the patronage of King Frederick II. Rumors abounded in Denmark throughout the 19th Century that certain of Brahe's letters, when seen in the mirror at 6:00 p.m. on the 6th of June, would cause horrific visions and lead the weak-minded to madness. While modernity has discarded this belief, scholars do universally agree that the Brahe types heralded the birth of Kim Bendix Petersen some 400 years later.